Congratulations to

Edie Meidav

Winner of the

2006 Bard Fiction Prize

Edie Meidav, author of *The Far Field*
and *Crawl Space,* joins previous winners
Nathan Englander, Emily Barton,
Monique Truong, and Paul La Farge.

The Bard Fiction Prize is awarded annually to a promising emerging writer who is an American citizen aged thirty-nine years or younger at the time of application. In addition to a monetary award of $30,000, the winner receives an appointment as writer in residence at Bard College for one semester without the expectation that he or she will teach traditional courses. The recipient will give at least one public lecture and meet informally with students.

For more information, please contact:

Bard Fiction Prize
Bard College
P.O. Box 5000
Annandale-on-Hudson, NY 12504-5000

COMING UP IN THE SPRING

Conjunctions:46
SELECTED SUBVERSIONS:
Essays on the World at Large

Edited by Rikki Ducornet, Bradford Morrow, and Robert Polito

Selected Subversions: Essays on the World at Large gathers specially commissioned creative essays on subjects as wide-ranging as rock and roll lyrics, science, movies, pornography, curiosity cabinets, jazz, contemporary art, magic, and beyond, offering rich insights into a vast spectrum of ideas.

Too often referred to as what it isn't—"nonfiction"—the essay is historically one of the most visionary and chimeric of forms. Like its literary cousins fiction and poetry, the creative essay has in recent years undergone revolutionary change in the hands of some of its most innovative practitioners. *Selected Subversions* explores not just the world, but the very words with which it's portrayed.

Among the three dozen essayists represented here are Anne Carson, Ned Rorem, David Shields, Sven Birkerts, Rick Moody, Fanny Howe, Dubravka Ugresic, Robert Harbison, John Crowley, Ben Marcus, Rosamond Purcell, Geoffrey O'Brien, Honor Moore, Joanna Scott, Ken Gross, and Michael Martone.

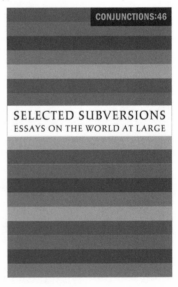

Subscriptions to *Conjunctions* are only $18 for more than eight hundred pages per year of contemporary and historical literature and art. Please send your check to *Conjunctions*, Bard College, Annandale-on-Hudson, NY 12504. Subscriptions can also be ordered by calling (845) 758-1539, or by sending an e-mail to Michael Bergstein at Conjunctions@bard.edu. For more information about current and past issues, please visit our Web site at www.Conjunctions.com.

CONJUNCTIONS

Bi-Annual Volumes of New Writing

Edited by
Bradford Morrow

Contributing Editors
Walter Abish
Chinua Achebe
John Ashbery
Martine Bellen
Mei-mei Berssenbrugge
Mary Caponegro
Elizabeth Frank
William H. Gass
Peter Gizzi
Jorie Graham
Robert Kelly
Ann Lauterbach
Norman Manea
Rick Moody
Howard Norman
Joanna Scott
Peter Straub
William Weaver
John Edgar Wideman

published by Bard College

EDITOR: Bradford Morrow
MANAGING EDITOR: Michael Bergstein
SENIOR EDITORS: Robert Antoni, Peter Constantine, Brian Evenson,
    David Shields, Pat Sims, Alan Tinkler
WEBMASTER: Brian Evenson
ASSOCIATE EDITORS: Jedediah Berry, Micaela Morrissette, Eric Olson
ART EDITOR: Norton Batkin
PUBLICITY: Mark R. Primoff
EDITORIAL ASSISTANTS: Caroline Dworin, Justine Haemmerli,
    J. W. McCormack

CONJUNCTIONS is published in the Spring and Fall of each year
by Bard College, Annandale-on-Hudson, NY 12504. This issue is
made possible in part with public funds from the New York State
Council on the Arts, a State Agency.   NYSCA

SUBSCRIPTIONS: Send subscription orders to CONJUNCTIONS, Bard
College, Annandale-on-Hudson, NY 12504. Single year (two volumes):
$18.00 for individuals; $25.00 for institutions and overseas. Two years (four
volumes): $32.00 for individuals; $45.00 for institutions and overseas. Patron
subscription (lifetime): $500.00. Overseas subscribers please make payment
by International Money Order. For information about subscriptions, back
issues, and advertising, call Michael Bergstein at (845) 758-1539 or fax (845)
758-2660.

All editorial communications should be sent to Bradford Morrow, *Conjunctions*, 21 East 10th Street, New York, NY 10003. Unsolicited manuscripts
cannot be returned unless accompanied by a stamped, self-addressed enve-
lope. Electronic and simultaneous submissions will not be considered.

Conjunctions is listed and indexed in the American Humanities Index.

Visit the *Conjunctions* Web site at www.conjunctions.com.

Printers: Edwards Brothers

Typesetter: Bill White, Typeworks

ISSN 0278-2324
ISBN 0-941964-61-2

Manufactured in the United States of America.

TABLE OF CONTENTS

SECRET LIVES OF CHILDREN

EDITOR'S NOTE 7

Shelley Jackson, ⌐⌐ 8

Robert Clark, *Life with Father* 13

Melissa Pritchard, *The Hauser Variations (As Sung by Male Voices, A Capriccio)*. 37

Paul La Farge, *Adventure*. 58

Rikki Ducornet, *A Secret Life*. 73

David Shields, *Three Essays* 80

Karen Russell, From *Children's Reminiscences of the Westward Migration* 89

Elizabeth Robinson, *Boy*. 109

Joshua Furst, *Close to Home*. 113

Donald Revell, *Three Poems*. 124

Emily Barton, *The Distillery* 127

Howard Norman, *Two Incidents* from *Exist to Kiss You* 147

Micaela Morrissette, *Ten O'Clock* 163

Gahan Wilson, *Nuts*. 174

Gilbert Sorrentino, *Mikky Waze*. 177

Yan Lianke, *Nizi Goes to Market* (translated from Chinese by Karen Gernant and Chen Zeping) 182

Ben Lerner, *Fourteen Prose Poems*. 196

Diane Williams, *Four Stories* 200

Lois-Ann Yamanaka, *The Big Betty Stories* 203

Peter Gizzi, *Fretless* 211

Mary Caponegro, *Girls in White Dresses* 217

Scott Geiger, *Two Stories*...............................225

Brian Evenson, *Younger* 242

Ilona Karmel, *Life Drawing* (translated from Polish
  by Fanny Howe and Arie A. Galles) 251

Kim Chinquee, *Five Stories*...............................258

David Marshall Chan, *Memoirs of a Boy Detective* 265

Danielle Pafunda, *Five Poems*...........................276

Julia Elliott, *Digging to the Devil*.........................279

Lucy Corin, *Walking Hand in Hand with Dinah,
  A Book without Pictures or Conversations* 291

Elaine Equi, *Conversations with Fountains*.................297

S. G. Miller, *Latona Street*...............................302

Malinda Markham, *Three Poems* 319

Mark Poirier, *Thunderbird* 323

Can Xue, *Two Stories* (translated from Chinese
  by Karen Gernant and Chen Zeping) 337

Stéphane Mallarmé, From *Nursery Rhymes* (translated from
  French with a preface by John Ashbery) 370

Robert Creeley, *Caves* 382

NOTES ON CONTRIBUTORS...............................388

Online *Secret Lives of Children* supplement
  available at *Web Conjunctions* (www.conjunctions.com):

Sandra Leong, *Birth of a Brother*

Catherine Imbriglio, *Two Poems*

Lesley Yalen, *Levittown*

Daniel Coudriet, *Three Poems*

EDITOR'S NOTE

THE COMMONALITY OF IT, for those who manage to make the passage into adulthood, in no way lessens the vast jumble of experience that childhood visits upon us. Wonderment and delight are obvious players in this early phase of life, but also at work are trauma, mystery, terror. It is a time of vulnerability, animation, ignorance, growth, obsession, wit, frustration, dread, callousness, curiosity, anger, learning, duplicity, joy, pain—a trial by fire whose mixed reward is most often more of the same when we grow older. While assembling this collection, our definition of childhood was necessarily somewhat open, though the children conjured here would, for the most part, consider themselves just that: children. Some infants and teenagers have made their way into *Secret Lives of Children,* so the edges of adolescence are occasionally blurred. At the heart of most of these works is an impulse to observe childhood as a dark challenge, a tough tour through the unknown, rather than some blissful, sentimental voyage. And yet, in these stories, poems, novel excerpts, memoirs, and essays, darkness often mingles with laughter. Not merely the laughter of innocence but that of freshly earned knowledge.

—Bradford Morrow
New York City
October 2005

Shelley Jackson

THE GALLOWS IS THE highest thing for miles. I empire in the sky. It's gray as brains, puzzled by breezes.

Below, it's gray too, but simpler. The field is monotonous with thistles. A throng of schoolchildren in uniforms trample them, socks mud starred. Their heads are thrown back, mouths open. It looks like they want me to feed them, sounds like crying. Really it is speech, a reduced language consisting of the names of letters. These are long, difficult words. Pronouncing them correctly takes a child's full strength, though they sound only two notes, sometimes rising, sometimes falling, like the names of lost dogs. These calls have no answers. This is good speech for solitude.

A name like a smoke ring floats up: O. After it is all over, one thick-waisted girl hunches over, bubbling wetness from her nose. O sounds the way my head feels, like a hole the day deflates through. I have no face, only some edges for what I'm on the outside of. I am hollow and round, like a mouth, a mouth making that disappointed sound, O.

I would like to say there is no hangman, that this is between me and the children. But there is always a hangman. In a hood, what else, with the requisite trinity of slits forming a sly QED, balanced on its fulcrum. He has an answer for everything. "No," the hangman says.

The thick-waisted girl wipes her nose, her face blank.

In front of the gallows, where a thin shadow ticks and tocks, there's a hole in the ground the size and shape of a door. Inside, under a layer of loose clods, I can easily make out the forms of head, torso, arms, and legs. Breasts, too, if I'm not mistaken—splayed mounds. Already I'm sure she's beautiful. Even the kids feel it.

Wrong once already, though, they are uneasy. They look up and to the side as if hoping to crib answers written there. Their feet treadle, moiling the mud. Finally, a long girl with thick, trembling knees pushes her hair behind her ears, clears her throat, and grins out a reedy E. Her chin turns pink and dimpled. She jabs it upward to give her guess a final push, then sinks back. Her oblong cheeks go spotty. She blushes birthmarks, then hurls herself out of the crowd to retch.

But she's right. The hangman descends the stairs with the iambic pace of a bride, one two, one two, settling both feet together on each riser before venturing the next step. There is a noticeable pause to aim before the final launch into the thistles. The hangman's long despondency is rolled up the calves and secured with red rubber bands, a practical measure against mud and thistles. The bare ankles are thick and yellowish. A thorn has signed the recto in blood.

Groaning delicately, the hangman stoops over the grave, unhooking from its holster a small whisk broom. The hangman is, I decide, a woman. Some ease in the hips upon bending establishes this for me.

Only the first row of children can see into the grave. But I, aloft, have a clear view. As the hangman frisks the straws back and forth, she gradually bares a pair of muddy young breasts, surcurves red, undercurves pale. Their nipples have been harried to hardness by the bristles. When every clod has been chased to one side, the hangman stands up, hooking the broom onto the belt again, and stumps back up the stairs.

The children surge forward all together, to the very edge of the grave. The front row brace their legs and link arms, though they, too, are craning their necks. Two breasts look up from the dirt.

Earlier, I breakfasted with the kids in the communal eatery, and we tucked into some buckwheat pancakes. The hangman moved among the tables, already hooded, whisking her skirts around her more vivaciously than seemed fitting for the occasion. She had her favorites among the children, stooping over these maternally and seeming to whisper, though when I too felt her long sleeves brush against my back, she merely nudged and pointed, nodding vigorously, at the pancakes. I nodded. The children nodded. Nods all round. Sixty-some shoes knocked on wood. It was convivial until I passed the syrup, remarking, "*Syrup*, unusual vowel patterns. Tricky." After that the children ate in silence, barely cracking their jaws to admit the buttery forkfuls. *Please*, they seemed to say. *We can handle this.*

Earlier, I said, but that must be a lie. With what mouth would I eat pancakes? With what stomach digest them? I'm just a zero on a rope. I empire in the sky? It empires in me. The light, if there's light, passes right through me.

9

A breeze comes up and the rope smacks the riser. It snags on a long splinter.

"I," someone shouts, like a volunteer. A bony boy's eyes widen. He looks surprised to be speaking. "I?" he asks. "I," he answers, putting all of himself into it. His lips peel back. His teeth air-dry, his gums go white. The other kids fall silent. His solo, a siren, is thin as my body: a naked spine, or a plumb line showing which way down is.

The hangman jerks the rope smartly, freeing it from the snag. "No," she says, but I don't need her to tell me that. It's all there in the letter I, the word that starts as a sigh and ends as a scream.

A flurry of rain dots the muddy breasts with pink.

Here's what I think: she's buried treasure, tricky with glyphs and gold. She's salt of the earth, sugar and spice; she's a brick outhouse, with curtains; she's a long stretch of unmarked beach where something great has washed up. She's ridged like a palate, and her wet parts are tongue colored, but she's not just a rubbery friend for the mouth. Name your pleasure: gobs of honeyed poppyseed, form-flattering swimwear, aviaries, a radiant plastic bag flouncing in a tree, rumps being cornholed, sardines: that's her. You have no idea how big she is. Even naked she never unfurls all the way, though you curry her till she purrs.

But the name escapes me. I look for clues. Sometimes I study the gallows itself: its simple lines off true, its thin splintered beams, of some cheap untreated wood, never meant to last, though it has obviously been standing a long time already, since the wood, maybe pine, has gone a bluish gray from exposure and is probably rotten at the core, just pulp; I can in fact see it bend when I swing, and can't help hoping it will crack, though I know it won't.

My attention moves on to the rope: an appendage, or the riddle itself? The knot: *the* knot?

The hangman: her large dry hands, her somewhat scaly ankles are familiar. I might have thought I knew her from somewhere, if I had ever been anywhere but here, on this rope. Together, we face the children, and there is almost a companionable feeling up here on the gallows. I wonder if she could possibly be an ally, but then she slaps the rope against the upright and bellows, "Come on, kids, take another stab at 'er!"

The children resume coughing their guesses against the alphabet. A girl sinks to her knees, and stays there, as if in prayer. I acquire an arm, slant as the side of an A, the scapegoat word that singles one out of a crowd, but not by name. The rope tightens. A big boy with a

10

varnished coif sits down with his back to the crowd, sloped shoulders shaking.

She acquires an arm. If she gains a second, it means I do not. If I do, she doesn't. Ordinate and abscissa, we are each other's complement. Everything she isn't, I am.

The kneeling girl tilts. I acquire an arm.

The kneeling girl falls.

To figure out her name, it would suffice to figure out mine. But we don't have that much time.

The children are wary again. Raindrops blister their foreheads. Slowly, they begin to ready themselves for another round, hawking and spitting. Finally, a girl with curvy, accomplished hair rises to her toes, stretches her pink throat from her Peter Pan collar, thrusts her neat ribcage, tenses her curved arms like a flamenco dancer. She poses so long like this that the children nearby bundle their ties into their mouths and look to her. "J," she lilts, jaunty and facetious. Her voice is almost inaudible, but the lull buoys it up like rising water. A little blood pearls in the setting of her nostril, then melts down her upper lip. Her tongue comes out and takes it carefully as if she needs it. It is a strange and risky guess, but she seems calm. When the hangman shakes her head, she smiles.

J is a barbed letter. Teeth come into it. It can be perpetrated through clenched jaws and a dental smile, the one she wears like a badge as I shake a leg that's hooked at the end like a J.

With a leg, I find, I can swing, or rather twist, and this movement gradually intensifies until I am rotating from side to side a full 180 degrees. I see that the plain is forested with gibbets, each with its partial scapegoat and moaning crowd, that the muddy ground is gaping with graves. Here and there a school bus idles on a paved roundabout.

In the next grave over, a beautiful girl hears her name and sits up. She brushes dirt off her lashes, shakes her hair, reaches up a small hand to the disappointed but courteous hangman, and rises out of the dirt, naked and clean as a crocus. Look, her ribs flare, her diaphragm flutters. Her small hairs rise with the wind. She lives.

I envy her? Yes. I would like to staple something. Dice a hard green apple. Ants: do they taste nice? I'd like to familiarize myself with the way things get smaller as they go farther away, so they fit inside smaller, closer things, like the chinks between fingers or the slits in an executioner's hood. But there are only two possible endings to this game. 1. She leaves me hanging. 2. We both die.

Now, at the next grave over, one of the children is stepping forward,

11

shouldering gamely out of his too small navy blue school jacket, unbuttoning his white shirt, baring his cotton vest, but wait, he has forgotten his tie, garroting him now; we all see his fingers slow on the knot; he is thinking, I am sure, of the noose, so much tighter than the tie that is already unpleasantly constricting his windpipe; his blood beats in his temples, a headache flares up behind his right eye, his ears redden; his fingers pluck and figure, they yank the stiff tie flap through; triumphant, he beams; his thin shoulders are revealed, his narrow chest, the ribs trembling; he unfastens his belt and his trousers slide down in one movement; with a magician's smoothness, he unties his shoes, kicks them off, steps out of the sideways 8 of the pants, pulls the white briefs down his hard, skinny flanks; he has pubic hair, a little; his penis is retracted from the cold; he plucks at it surreptitiously, to coax it into proudness; it responds, sufficiently; he walks to the edge of the grave.

He takes off his socks, drops them behind him.

He waves away the hangman's extended hand, jumps in.

These are also words: hangman, gallows. Grave is a word. Death is. But that does not make them any less mortal, though mortal is also a word.

A patch of light races toward us from far away. In an instant we are in it and everything slows and is golden and outlined in light. The gibbet and its incomplete burden is inked on the ground below. The shadow of the hangman in her hooded robe is the shape of a tongue. It moves back and forth as if trying to find something to say.

The children cry out. If one of them says my name, perhaps entirely by accident, does that mean I am forgiven?

The hangman's shadow grows, as if it ate guesses. It stretches across the grave. It laps at the children's feet.

Life with Father
Robert Clark

BOB WAS ONE of my mother's boyfriends. He was not my favorite but he was the one she married. There was, for example, Joe, who always brought an ice cream roll for me and my sister; Irving, whose house had a pond we could skate on in winter; and Henry, who was a photographer and had a kind of glamour on that account. By contrast, Bob did not make much of an impression on me until I was five years old, when he and my mother announced they were going to marry.

What my mother's boyfriends all had in common was that they were gay. In the case of Joe, Irving, and Henry, at some point it became "common knowledge." As for Bob, he told me himself. That, of course, was later. So in most of what follows, the facts—what I knew when I was five and what I knew when I was, say, twenty-five, and what I've discovered in the last few years—occur on parallel levels that don't fully overlap until just now.

They're all true, these facts: the revelation of one doesn't falsify another, or even necessarily color it or call for its reevaluation. If this were a drama, we might see ironies unfolding, but as it stands I see only varieties of innocence, of taking things at face value as they change and weather with time. They changed me—they are still changing me, I suppose—though scarcely in ways anyone might have imagined. And of course everything might have been otherwise.

Bob's family owned a large and well-thought-of chain of flower stores and greenhouses, and Bob, who had a degree in horticulture, oversaw several of these. In addition to arranging flowers, he liked interior design and figure skating. He loved society gossip and had a high, tittering, screeching laugh. At some point in their courtship he advised my mother that he was "well hung," which, as she pointed out many years later, was, however well meant, perhaps not the most romantic thing to say to a girl.

Now perhaps you, the reader, are already asking how my mother could possibly *not* know what sort of man she was involved with. Were this a novel, you would be having trouble finding the characters "believable."

Let me try again in terms a fictionalist might use. What did these characters believe? What was at stake for them? What did they *want?* Bob surely wanted position and status, and there simply wasn't much of either attached to the role of "confirmed bachelor" for the son of second-generation Swedish immigrants, no matter how successful. As for "coming out," the concept didn't even exist: not in Minnesota, not in 1957.

Bob's first wife—he'd tried before, he was persistent, not to say ambitious—was the heiress to a brewing fortune. At the greenhouse, the employees called her "the duchess." The marriage was childless and broke up after perhaps two years, eighteen months or so before Bob set his sights on my mother. Socially, she wasn't in the duchess's league: she wasn't rich, and while she was from a pedigreed "old St. Paul" family, they were no longer in the top tier.

But she would do. For one thing, she was fun. She liked to go out and socialize and drink. She knew people—the kind of people Bob wanted to meet—and she had, by St. Paul standards, a sense of style. He'd seen the gray den, the blond furniture, and her chic short Italian haircut. He liked what he saw—the surfaces—and so he liked her, after his fashion. Bob was, as my mother would later say, "deeply superficial."

She liked him in the same way. He was lively. He liked to work around the house and in the garden. He was eager, almost hungry, to attach himself to her family, to her whole milieu. More seriously for her, the position of single mother was no more tenable at that time and place than was "confirmed bachelor." It was expected—it went without saying—that she would remarry. The most compelling imperative of all was to provide a father for her children and in particular "masculine influence" for her son—for me.

According to the parenting experts of the time, the need for "masculine influence" was no mere matter of what we now call "role models." Psychology was at the apex of its prestige as a science, and the literature, the scientific laws, stated that a boy needed a father for the obvious reasons—the inculcation of masculine culture and pursuits like sports, hunting, and camping—but more crucially as a necessary counterbalance to his mother. Mothers were essential to their sons in their own way, but left to their own subconscious devices, absent a countervailing man within the family drama, they were as pernicious as communist sleeper agents. Simply put, single mothers (especially ones with domineering, strong, or flamboyant personalities) caused homosexual pathology in their sons.

I can't say exactly how much this weighed on my mother or if it was on her mind when she accepted Bob's proposal. It didn't need to be: it was in the water like fluoride, in the air like fallout. My mother had majored in psychology in college. She knew the science. On the other hand, I can't recall my mother ever in her life saying a derogatory word about a gay or lesbian person or about homosexuality in general. For her, that too went without saying. But you didn't toy with pathology. You didn't put your son in its path.

So Bob and my mother—absurdly, wrongly, if for apparently right reasons—needed each other. They married in a small ceremony conducted by a Unitarian minister in my grandparents' living room. One didn't make a display of second marriages. While the rite transpired I was minded by a babysitter in an adjacent room for fear that in a burst of rambunction I might disrupt the solemnities. I resented this, but I also can't say that I might not have been tempted to burst into, say, "The Oldest Established Permanent Floating Crap Game in New York" from *Guys and Dolls* during the blessing or the vows.

And what did I want? Transcendence, I think, although this was not a word I would learn until ten years later, under the tutelage of another masculine influence. Of course I wanted and needed what every child does: security, affection, and the freedom to grow in accord with my own inner inclinations. But I also sought some deeper, closer embodiment of the way music, images, and stories made me *feel*; a tactile sense of their origin—their creator or, perhaps, father—whose presence it seemed to me must somehow be attained and apprehended.

I didn't know the word for it, but I knew what I was after. I sought it by means of beauty, love, and faith. I didn't understand those things as concepts either, but whenever I happened on them I knew them and slipped into them as easily as a pair of my black high-top sneakers. Nor did I have any notion of transcendent qualities, of the eternal or infinite. But I suppose as a child I was ahead of the game: when I was happy and unafraid, the days ahead of me seemed numberless, the spaces I might inhabit illimitable. I had faith by default and I existed leaning into what seemed the headwind of eternity. I was forever in midleap—in the gap between being poised to jump and landing—throwing myself into the world. It did not occur to me to know as adults do that the only guaranteed encounter with eternity we have is in death. I rode around—as parents then used to allow children to do—standing heedlessly on the front seat of the car, taking it all in as though I were king.

After the honeymoon—Bob and my mother went to the Virgin Islands while my sister and I stayed with that same babysitter—we moved to a new house Bob had bought in another Minnesota city. It was capacious compared to our old mock Tudor and had a large yard and was near the school where I would begin kindergarten. I quickly saw that my new life could be congenial. I made friends in the neighborhood, built a succession of forts and hideouts in the alleys and parks nearby, and learned to ride a two-wheeler. This last took some doing: on the slope outside our house, I kept crashing headlong into trees and parked cars. My nose flared blood; my knees were abraded to the consistency of hamburger.

But while I was warming to some of these masculine (or at least boyish) pursuits, some of my other interests became cause for concern. In kindergarten I conceived a fascination for washing machines, detergents, and dryers. I collected empty miniature boxes of soap from a local launderette and haunted our basement laundry room, paying obeisance to the Maytags. At some point I discovered (perhaps through an ad on Saturday morning TV) the existence of a child-scaled toy washing machine and I announced that for my next birthday this was my heart's desire.

I was an acquisitive and fanciful kid, full of wishes and requests, and in the normal course of things these were granted, refused, or shrugged off without much ceremony by one parent or the other. But this occasion prompted a full-scale family Summit Meeting (held, or so I want to remember it, in my very sanctum sanctorum, the laundry room) with both my mother and Bob. They stood together and tried to persuade me that I didn't really want *this* particular toy, and when I proved unmovable, explained that although I might think I wanted it, this was not a boy's toy, but a toy for a girl. Surely I didn't want a girl's toy?

But I did. I didn't care. But I should care, Bob and my mother said more darkly. It was *odd* for a boy to own such a toy. People would think I was odd. Other boys would think I was odd. I don't know why this didn't persuade me. I must have been impassioned or obsessed. I might have replied that I was only going to use the washing machine in the privacy of our basement; that no one would know.

Here the mood—and it is the mood rather than the words spoken that I recall so precisely—became grave. I was given to understand that having the toy washer was not merely silly or socially awkward but dangerous: that having it could harm me; that I could catch something from it that would make me less of a boy, a sick boy.

I knew about being a sissy. I wasn't one—not yet. But this unspecified infection was worse than that. Bob and my mother didn't give it a name or describe the symptoms. They merely impressed upon me that it was very, very serious. I knew the etiology—toy washing machines—and the disease's progress—sissification leading to debilitation and misery—but no more. How much simpler if Bob had simply said, "It will make you into someone like *me*. And despite appearances, I am ashamed and unhappy."

But by that time I liked Bob. We had worked together in the backyard. He had taught me to ride my bike. He had given me a silly nickname. I liked him and I wouldn't have minded being like him one bit. And we were happy, all of us, and no one was ashamed of anything.

As it turned out, I got the toy washing machine. It was my first

17

guilty pleasure. It sat in the basement next to the big, grown-up Maytags, and I lost interest in it after perhaps a month. Of course, a month is a very long time when you are five-going-on-six, but that was the end of my interest in gender-inappropriate toys. That's not to say I didn't remain a little "odd." I continued to have a fascination with basements, boxes, and containers, and underground passages and chambers: with caves and snow forts and hollow trees. They made a kind of underground world and perhaps, in that, I knew Bob better than I might have imagined.

Bob, meanwhile, was beginning to immerse me in "masculine influence" and I was glorying in it. He bought a motorboat and I got a sailor hat and played the first mate. We went hunting, tramping through gelid corn fields, searching for pheasant. And we not only went camping, but went camping with a whole Boy Scout troop of which Bob was the scoutmaster. (Don't laugh. Or wince. *Of course* he was a scoutmaster, just as he was a florist and a member of the Jaycees and drove a Ford Country Squire station wagon.) It was like having the ultimate dad and a dozen big brothers.

We went on fabulous vacations to San Francisco, Disneyland, and Aspen. At home, Bob built us a new house closer to the countryside and bought a jazzy new black Oldsmobile convertible with red upholstery. Best of all, Bob had a dog—a cocker spaniel—and it became my dog. We tramped all over the woods and fields around our new house. We found, if not a cave, at least a hollow lined with rock, a sort of tiny black-walled canyon in which the dog and I could hide.

That's not to say I was a loner. I had three or four close friends. We built forts and tree houses and they knew my secret places. We had cap guns and rifles and canteens and cowboy boots. My friends came over to our house on Saturday mornings to watch TV with me. The day maid Bob had hired made us all pancakes and we'd eat them in front of *Sky King* and *Yogi Bear*.

My mother and Bob had more friends than I, many more. In addition to tracking down and attaching themselves to the city's leading Episcopalians and Harvard graduates, Bob and my mother were almost lousy with doctors, heart surgeons, and celebrity specialists. The city was the home of a famous clinic, and perhaps Bob's most prized social connection was to the younger generation of the clinic's founders, the Mayos, together with access to their estate, Mayowood.

Bob owed that social success to my mother, and he was frank about it: my mother was gracious and charming and fun. She seemed indifferent to people's position, and I think she largely was. Bob, on the other hand, perhaps less frankly, wanted to drop their names, drink, and gossip in their swell homes and country clubs, and acquire them as customers. They weren't in any sense strictly my mother's friends, but in the siege of Mayowood it was my mother who'd conquered.

There was another couple, however, whom Bob had discovered himself, and they were perhaps my mother and Bob's most frequent companions. Their names were Bud and Gloria and what I chiefly recall about them is that they were young (younger than Bob, who was several years younger than my mother) and attractive. Bud was as fit and handsome as an astronaut and Gloria was pretty and blonde in Scandinavian/Californian mode, which at that time was the gold standard of American beauty.

I don't know—I'm sure I never knew—much more about them. Whatever Bud did—he wasn't a doctor—it was not consequential enough to bear mentioning, nor were the forebears or provenance of either him or Gloria. But they had an impact on us. Bob began hunting when they came along, and the four of them shot skeet from our backyard. I can recall any number of trudges through the cornfields in late autumn with Bob and Bud in the vanguard with their shotguns, myself just behind in a state of high excitement, and my mother and Gloria resignedly and dutifully bringing up the rear.

I know that neither Gloria nor my mother liked the hunting or most of Bob and Bud's other masculine pastimes, but they didn't commiserate, and it seemed clear to me that was because they didn't like each other either. My mother's customary graciousness gave way to something close to snobbery on the subject of Gloria. What Gloria made of my mother, I don't know, but there were no warm feelings. They both knew, I suppose, what was up.

I can recall my mother complaining and rolling her eyes about having to socialize with Bud and Gloria, and I know I heard her and Bob fight about having to see them again. She'd rather have gone to Mayowood. I don't know the impetus or context of these conflicts. In any case, they would soon be fighting about many things.

Later, when I was a teenager, my mother was frank in saying that she assumed Bob and Bud had been having an affair. Two decades later, I was able to ask Bob about it. He was uncharacteristically cagey. You might think he was reluctant to confess he had cheated on my mother, but today I'm more inclined to think he had gotten nowhere with Bud despite all his eager, almost fawning efforts. Bud, I think, had rejected him; had broken his heart—such a heart as he had.

I make the qualification knowing that, however much I liked him, Bob was accustomed to and practiced in cruelty. His parents were nasty and cold, and there was mutual contempt between him and his only sibling, an older brother named Skip. When matters began to escalate between Bob and my mother—the staggering and cursing and wailing that woke me and my sister from our sleep at one in the morning—the rancor was both bitter and gleeful. I recall a night when my mother took a hammer and pounded for five minutes on the master bedroom door behind which Bob had locked himself. When the door finally sprang open, Bob was nowhere to be found. He'd lowered himself out a window and let himself back into the lower level of the house where I discovered him lying on the upper mattress of my bunk bed, smirking.

By this time I was eight years old, going into the third grade. I had, if not sophistication, a certain satiric take on the world and its deceptions and pretensions; about status seeking, political and corporate disingenuousness, and the idiocy of television and what *Mad* magazine, my bible, called "Madison Avenue ads."

So perhaps I was ready to adopt a cool, sidelong glance at what was to come; to be unsurprised at the tawdry and awful idiocy of grown-ups. One night that winter, Bob and my mother came home very late and very drunk from Mayowood. Bob or my mother—it was never clear who had been behind the wheel of the beautiful black convertible—drove into the garage and lowered the door with the automatic opener. Bob exited the car and went into the house through the connecting door, closing it after him. The engine was still running.

My mother was in the car, dozing or perhaps passed out from the night's drinking, her head on the dashboard. At some point she came to in the sealed garage, now clouded with fumes. Either she made her own way into the house—it's not clear from anything she and Bob ever said—or Bob returned and pulled her from the car.

The first I knew of any of this was the next morning when I came upstairs and discovered a puppy, a basset hound, in the house. Bob had gone out at dawn, found a kennel, and brought him home. The rationale for this—the shards of what had transpired the previous night—came out slowly and disjointedly, but the crux was that my mother had survived but our cocker spaniel, bedded down in his basket in the garage for the night, had not.

I have to give Bob credit—it's no mean trick to gauge the precisely needful thing a disastrous situation requires—and I gave it to him then. I fell in love with the new dog, and I named it Theodore. I don't think I gave the cocker another thought. Perhaps I had learned a little about callousness from Bob, or perhaps I was merely becoming inured to the middling tragedy that visited itself upon families like ours.

In retrospect, I see that Theodore was as much my mother's dog as mine. He was a decorator dog, a whimsical, baroque creature designed to accent indoor space rather than patrol the woods with an eight-year-old. But that was OK: I was a little baroque myself. And I also see that Bob was at that time "trying" with my mother in the manner of couples at the marital precipice. We took one of our trips to Chicago and did dinner and the show at the Palmer House, where Joey Bishop came over to our table and interviewed me and my sister as part of his act. My mother, too, was "trying," but I am sure Bob wasn't having any fun.

We took our Chris-Craft out one weekend and camped on the deck. Theodore went overboard, got lost, and drowned. Bob replaced him with an identical basset named Theodore, who by temperament and sex was even more meant to be my mother's dog. It did no good. In April, Bob moved out, and in June he and my mother sat me and my sister down and announced they were divorcing.

I received the news somberly, with no great surprise or horror. This is how it goes, I thought to myself. There was a conference with the judge, a formality about which I'd been coached. He asked me if I wanted to stay with my mother or Bob. I said I wanted to stay with my mother, knowing full well I'd been having the time of my life for the previous four years with Bob. I exhaled, and my sense of the boundless, my faith in my run of infinite happiness, emptied out. But the masculine influence had taken: I'd acquired a sense of resignation in the face of duty; that, and the hardened heart.

My mother, my sister, and I moved back up to St. Paul that summer. Two months later, Bob persuaded my mother to let me ride shotgun in one of the flower store's delivery trucks and come down to visit him for a day. I stood leaning forward on the floor in front of the passenger seat of the flat-fronted van, nose pressed against the glass of the windshield, as the highway ripped by just beneath my feet, as though the world were an aquarium. The truck dropped me at the flower store, and then Bob and I drove out to our old home. He'd already redecorated much of the house, reupholstering the den furniture in a masculine red plaid.

But the showpiece was the living room. Under joint administration with my mother, the walls had been painted a bland powder blue with couches and chairs to match, accented by pieces of Colonial-style furniture in oak and walnut. In the space of a few months, however, Bob had recovered the walls in yellow felt and brought in a pair of sumptuous divan sofas done up in yellow, white, and gold fabric with welting and cylindrical Roman-style pillows. I thought it looked swell. I wondered where Bud was.

I think I sensed Bob's audacity in this. I know now that Bob had done no more or less than import a taste of High Fag style to a medium-sized city in Minnesota. Within a year, he left for Los Angeles, where that and much of the rest of his life was not so strange and alien. In his wake, I later learned, there followed a fleet of collectors, bailiffs, IRS agents, as well as his father, his brother, and my mother in pursuit of her alimony payments. Our wonderful life—the house, the vacations, the boat and the convertible, the pedigreed dogs and the maid—had been conjured by Bob with funds embezzled from the flower business, unpaid debt, and tax dodges.

I didn't see him again for fourteen years. In the immediate wake of the divorce, however, there was a new home, a new school, and new classmates to adjust to. It did not go well. I was high-strung, attention seeking, and failing school. Within a year, I was in treatment with Dr. Wiener, a child analyst (the significance of whose name—as phallic as it was Viennese—gave me endless mirth).

Dr. Wiener gave me tests and showed me Rorschachs and illustrations of adults glowering at one another. He asked me to make up stories about them and I obliged. But Dr. Wiener couldn't get anywhere with me. At last, he prescribed "masculine influence."

I was sent to an Episcopal Church boarding school in the south of the state, not too far from our old home with Bob. It was run on military lines and with the exception of a housemother and a few day teachers, the faculty was entirely male. With the exception of two—an ex-collegiate boxer who ran the dorm and a crew-cut ex-Marine who coached sports and ran the military drills—they were all bachelors.

Looking back, it seems clear that a majority of them were probably homosexual. The headmaster, for example, was stunningly nelly in bearing. He walked on his toes and the balls of his feet, licked his wispy lips as he scanned the room for mischief, and carried his tiny hands before him as though they were pinned to his chest, palms splayed, fingers dangling, in the manner of one of the smaller carnivorous dinosaurs.

For all that, he was terrifying. His voice was high, even mincing, but it had the distilled authority of generations of no-nonsense headmistresses and formidable schoolmarms. For that reason, he was deferred to by both faculty and students and perhaps that is why conventional Minnesota parents entrusted their sons to his care. They, and especially the fathers among them, had been humbled, pinched, made to write sentences on the board, and given the switch on their backsides by the likes of this person. They would obey.

I suspect, in fact, that he ran a tight ship. In my time, I remember hearing of only two incidents of the staff touching the boys. (I recall at least as many teachers let go for excessive drinking.) Of course, by the second of my three years there, in the seventh grade, we were busy touching ourselves and even each other. Mutual masturbation was endemic, and fellatio—often coerced by older boys on younger— not uncommon.

I was in the middle of these things and I took them in stride. I had become a good student in my classes, competent at military drill, and outside of these my erotic education was proceeding apace, as was my religious formation. These seem to me today linked in some way, and I think I understood them as such at the time. I arrived at the school knowing nothing of either.

I hasten to add that the priests, deacons, and other ministers I dealt with never touched a boy that I knew of. And as eager participant in Bible classes, acolyte duties, and every liturgy made available to us at the school, I might have known; or even—as a fatherless, sensitive, and somewhat "artistic" boy—become the object of someone's pederastic intentions. That simply never happened. On the other hand, there was scarcely a room in and around the school chapel that my friends and I had not used for mutual self-display and circle-jerking. Sexual release was all the more exciting for taking place in the chapel, in the ambience of the sacred. I suppose there was a baser reckless thrill in the risk of being caught—in the frisson of lowering your pants in the sacristy, of unbuttoning your cassock on the bell-tower landing to display your erection—but that was the least of it. We weren't transgressing: we were bringing ourselves, naked, that much closer to the holy; we were making the ecstatic leap.

25

So, if anything, I brought eros with me into the church and despite all the obvious contradictions and proscriptions to the contrary, I couldn't help feeling it belonged there. Because in my pursuit of eros I was being driven by beauty in the form of the exquisite; or at least that is how the sensations my body was producing felt to me. Both their origin and their aim seemed mightily powerful, greater than anything I had ever encountered intimately, at least since we'd left Bob.

That it was private and self-contained, yet scented with the transcendent—so internal and specific to me and yet so immense—made it seem a kind of answer to my prayers for connection and intimacy, for awe, and for the presences and the things in the world that would compensate for the losses of my first eleven years of life. I wanted— I prayed for—love and beauty and I found them in my body and the bodies of others, and I found them in the body of Christ, in the church and its liturgy—in its rendering of desire and praise into an act of beauty—and in the God who made me and all those other bodies and presences.

This, you might say, is the thinking of a very confused young man, and I suppose you would be right. There's no visible morality or responsibility attached to it—no sense of sin or of the need to not only admire but emulate Christ—and yet, while I had no especially strong sense of shame, I felt what I was doing was good or at least had the capacity to make me good. I had been, I understood, a bad student and a trial to my mother, but now my grades and conduct were exemplary and that was as far as my conception of goodness went at the time. I was a bit priggish and overweening about my religiosity, but I never imagined I was storing up points in heaven. Rather, it became simply what I liked to do—what gave me comfort and pleasure—as did my sexuality.

Of course I'd understood that sex was a secret pleasure, that it was dirty or naughty, but, once discovered, it also seemed to me a birthright, and with that I shrugged off whatever shame I might have felt. It was later, perhaps in the seventh and eighth grades, that I came to think it was wrong; or, rather, that male-male sex was wrong. My appreciation of this was social and psychological rather than moral: it wasn't so much evil as odd. It made you a "pansy" or a "fairy" or a "queer" or a "homo." Now that I had the words and the contempt that colored them before me, on my lips, I finally grasped what my mother and Bob had tried to express to me eight years earlier.

For all the mockery, fear, and hatred those words contained, I understood that kids our age were granted a free pass to experiment provided we didn't penetrate each other (known among us as "corn-holing") and gave up our mutual experimentation in favor of girls once we were in high school.

I more or less followed that prescription—minus a few small slips—after I returned home to live with my mother and begin the ninth grade. My religiosity, too, seemed to fade along with the hot-house boy-with-boy eros of my early adolescence. My interest in the church ebbed increment by increment until it was entirely below the surface of my life by age sixteen. I never stopped believing, but for a long time I surely forgot that I believed. Perhaps I believed but without faith, without any sense of the presence of what I be-lieved *in*. In the same way, sex—the categorization, the obsessing, and all the bullshit and lore that adolescents trade in—took over from eros.

I had, of course, no experience, but I did have increasingly sophis-ticated opinions. For example, as against the prevailing hysteria and name calling, I and my friends began to acquire a more sophisticated and thoughtful view of homosexuality. It was a psychopathology, but I also believed that in some sense practically everyone and every family was afflicted by neurosis or even psychosis; that, in fact, the whole of American society was "fucked up." That being the case, while you would never want to be a homosexual yourself, you might be prepared to tolerate or at least understand it in others. You might even joke about the biddies and anal retentives who worried so much about it.

There was a piece in *Mad* magazine—it was still more my bible than the Bible itself—featuring witty ripostes to common pieces of graffiti. For example, somebody was supposed to have desperately scrawled "My mother made me a homosexual" on a bathroom wall. Beneath it someone else responded, "Great! Would she make one for me too?"

It was a typical piece of midsixties satire, both hip to and ulti-mately dismissive of the antique Freudianism that underlaid the fear of homosexual pathology and just on the verge of being prepared to dismiss the whole notion of pathology itself. It was a joke I loved and one I repeated with no sense of irony. But I may have been protest-ing too much.

Since I'd come home for the ninth grade I'd been unavoidably con-scious of my mother's social life. Our apartment was, by St. Paul standards, a sort of salon, its visitors much preoccupied with politics and the arts. "Boyfriends" of the kind my mother had always favored were part of it, but increasingly so were women friends (divorced, widowed, or never married), often interested in golf and tennis but also of a bohemian and independent cast of mind, introducing me to Billie Holiday, Lenny Bruce, and Judy Garland's *Live at Carnegie Hall* album. They were for the most part funny, appreciative of my interests and take on the world, and kind and understanding as I passed through several adolescent crises. I liked several of them as much as I have ever liked any human being.

Of course, while I'd been away, mother had changed. Or rather she'd simply settled into a new life with new friends. I don't know to what extent she would have identified herself as bisexual or lesbian but that was, I realize now, the milieu in which she was most comfortable. Still less would I want to speculate on whether she had loves or who they were. But she was, I think, having the time of her life, much as I had been having under Bob's masculine influence; much as I suppose Bob was simultaneously having in the Hollywood Hills.

I, meanwhile, was lost in the way adolescents are usually lost but perhaps in a way special to that time, to the late 1960s when personal "realization" and "liberation" seemed so imperative. I felt I was no one in particular. I wasn't a protohomo or an Episcopalian anymore, but I wasn't anything else either. At the same time it seemed to me that in other places, on campuses and on the coasts, an entirely new religion and way of life was being formed, although I could only watch it from a distance. At school, I was merely serving time; I was studiously unmotivated and unprepared. At some point in my sophomore year, I simply stopped doing the work.

When I failed half my final exams that June, the school administrators had the same advice they'd offered five years earlier: boarding school and, it went without saying, masculine influence. In the fall I found myself in rural Colorado at a school whose curriculum extended to ranching chores, mountaineering, and white-water kayaking. I lasted scarcely two months before I ran away, hitchhiking to Denver, then flying to Chicago on my TWA Youth Fare card. I read Hesse's *Siddhartha* on the plane and I wondered if the plane would crash. I gave some desultory thought at O'Hare to trying for New York, Cambridge, San Francisco, or Berkeley, but took the last of my money and bought a ticket home to St. Paul. I was, even by my own estimation, unfit to serve in the youth revolution.

During the few days that I'd been missing, my mother's contact in Colorado was the school's dean of students, and after I turned up she continued to talk to him about what ought to be done with me next. I categorically refused to go back to school, and my mother responded by offering me the alternative of enlisting in the service branch of my choice. That meant Vietnam, a field of battle I felt even less suited to. I compromised by saying that I would find some way of continuing my education informally for the rest of the school year with a view to reenrolling somewhere, someplace, in the fall.

My mother ran this scheme past her adviser, the dean in Colorado, who made a surprising counterproposal. Between his teaching and administrative duties, he was overburdened and had just recently been diagnosed with a heart condition. Living alone, unmarried, and without family nearby, he could hardly manage his household chores and errands without help. Would I consider becoming his assistant and valet in exchange for room, board, and private instruction in the subjects I needed to keep up with for the remainder of the school year?

I returned to Colorado in a matter of weeks. The dean had never been my teacher during my few months at the school. But I knew about him, and perhaps he had noticed me. He taught French, Spanish, literature, and philosophy. He spoke three additional languages, had graduated from Columbia summa cum laude in the 1930s, and had brought old teachers and classmates like Jacques

Barzun and Paul Goodman to the school. He was one of a generation of sons of Jewish immigrants who aspired to and attained academic excellence, were deeply conscious of what they'd been given, and intended to repay their debt by inculcating high culture and the classical virtues. He was warm and stern, acute and sentimental, exacting and forgiving. By my lights he might have been Socrates.

Because I was ambitious and because I was genuinely intellectually curious, within days of arriving I grabbed *Being and Nothingness* from his bookshelves and announced I was going to read it. He didn't laugh. More usefully, I cooked spaghetti, did yard work, and made trips to the grocery store and the post office. He began to teach me French and to read Martin Buber, Thomas Mann, and Camus. At the end of the day, I sat with him in front of the fire. We read (I gave up on Sartre after ten or so pages) and on the phonograph the dean worked his way through Bach and then Mozart on my behalf.

Of course we talked, often until late, and it must have been then that I heard about transcendence; of how it preoccupied Sartre and Buber and manifested itself in Mozart and Bach. Of course the talk came around to sex, among other worldly matters, and much at my behest. I am sure I strove to display my tolerance and insouciance, and he in turn told me some impressive stories of his own: how he'd run with a crowd in New York that included Aaron Copland, Leonard Bernstein, and other sexually indefinite geniuses and artists; how he'd been offered a pubescent boy as a gift by a family in Morocco he'd befriended; and how it was his view that bisexuality was the natural and rational state of human affairs. I would have agreed, although I would have stated that, on balance, I preferred girls.

I could say that he put these things forward in an intentionally provocative and suggestive manner, that he was seducing me. But I know how precocious I was, and how anxious to prove that I was as sophisticated and self-possessed as any adult. I know, for example, that one late evening I masturbated in front of him. I could not say it was my idea, but I also know he did not encourage me. I was trying, beyond any idea or plan, to make an impression. The daring of it, the recklessness, made it sexy, of course, but also rendered it sincere, authentic, even transcendent in some way. The dean merely sat across the room with an amused smile on his face as I showed him my youthful vigor. He neither approved nor disapproved. I suppose Socrates did much the same.

During the next few weeks that may have happened once or twice more, but I suspect I had proved my point. We were preoccupied with other things: I with my identity, with the need to weave my desires into a tolerable self; he with his faltering heart. I think in our late-night discussions he had told me that its fragility put sex out of bounds for him. But later he came to me with a simple request, based, he told me, on the latest advice from his cardiologist.

It was, the dean explained, dangerous for him to have an orgasm, either during intercourse or even masturbation. The strain was too great. On the other hand, surely I understood that every man needed an occasional release of tension, a discharge of pent-up semen and sexual energies. Would I, therefore, be willing for him to come into my bed from time to time? I wouldn't have to do anything nor would he do anything beyond lying next to me. It was a matter of his health; even, I might have imagined, one of life and death.

I assented, not eagerly but dutifully. The whole business sounded reasonable but somehow odd; intimate yet sterile. The dean didn't appear in my room for several nights, and I think I almost forgot about it. But then he came, one night after I'd already fallen asleep (it was his habit to stay up very late, reading, writing letters, and listening to Mozart) and climbed into bed behind me. I felt his erection grinding against me and then a spot of damp that he daubed away with a tuft of Kleenex. A moment later, without a word, he was gone.

This happened perhaps every two weeks over a course of several months, perhaps four or five times in all. We didn't speak about it, although he did thank me several times for my being so understanding. I didn't like these night visits, although never to such an extent that I contemplated objecting. I disliked them the way I might have disliked having my temperature taken rectally (although he never attempted to penetrate me) or getting a shot or a blood test: unpleasant but medically necessary.

I think what bothered me more was that it had been the dean's idea rather than mine; that he'd trumped the erotic powers I'd displayed to him with his own more serious needs. I may also have worried that he was making a homo out of me, although since our contact was both passive on my part and consciously undesired by me, I wasn't overly troubled. And on the other hand, I felt there was something a little noble in my subjecting myself to his medical needs, a sense of Christian sacrifice, of yielding at my own expense, and so what I lost in psychopathological terms I gained in spiritual ones.

Still, I left Colorado earlier than I'd planned, but on perfectly friendly terms. I went east to investigate schools I might attend the next year near my relatives in Massachusetts. The dean and I kept up a steady correspondence and talked on the phone occasionally as I entered my senior year of high school. He seemed genuinely interested in my future and hoped I would do something worthwhile with my intellectual gifts. He hoped I would remember what he'd tried to teach me about culture and the virtues.

Throughout high school I'd dated, attended dances, and done some making out with girls, but I'd never gotten much past deep kissing, writhing and grinding, and several breasts cupped through a layer of mohair. But in senior year, I became aggressively—what would later be called performatively—heterosexual: I would swim into the deeper water of heavy petting and beyond, or drown trying.

I made some progress. I saw my first bare breast in the woods of a summer camp where I worked that summer. And then I saw another. Later, in the winter, I felt around inside a girl's jeans, and I was chagrined to hear from a mutual friend that she had been disappointed I hadn't tried to go "further." But I never succeeded in arranging a return engagement with her or in moving toward "further" with other girls. Neither, of course, did most of my friends and acquaintances. Sexual frustration is the daily bread of male adolescence, but in my mouth it tasted of ashes.

I feared that what had happened with the dean—or perhaps even back in junior high—had become a kind of destiny; that if I wasn't a homosexual by pathology, I'd become one by default. My mother hadn't needed to make me a homosexual: I'd done it myself.

In the spring I wrote the dean a letter. The term "abuse" wasn't in wide use yet, certainly not tied to the word "sexual," nor were many "victims" in evidence, never mind "survivors." But that wasn't what I wanted to say. I simply needed to declare that what we—and especially he, with me—had done was wrong: not in general, of course, but wrong for *me*. It was not who I was and I wanted him to know and understand that.

I know my tone must have been strident and self-important to a fault. I didn't hear back from the dean for perhaps six weeks—he was ordinarily a prompt, even fastidious, correspondent. Finally a letter arrived: he'd been traveling and then had undergone some incidents regarding his health about which he would fill me in later.

Then he turned to the matter of my last letter. He called it "brave" and "forthright" and "mature." But he concluded, "I think you still misunderstand the sexual aspects of your stay here and why I permitted you to do some of the things that were done." He closed by wishing me a happy high school graduation and offering his hope that the pride he took in me would be justified.

I was not happy with this response. It seemed to put matters exactly upside down and to condescend to me in the process. He had focused, I supposed, completely on my self-exhibition and forgotten about his own nocturnal visits to my bed. Or did it mean that those, too, were things he had "permitted [me] to do"; that I'd somehow *meant* to happen?

I was perplexed and angry and I needed to straighten this out with him: my identity—the case I was making for myself being one thing and not another—was at stake. But the dean had the last word. Before I had the chance to write back, he died of a massive heart attack. But he was, after all, called the dean by dint of being wiser than any of his students, and perhaps most of all me. He left me a puzzle that I had to figure out on my own, not the least of which was the question of what happened to faith, love, and beauty in the face of this new acquaintance, this eternal being called death.

I attempted that over many years, among bodies and hearts, of my own desires and boundaries of others, in the places where these matters are rightly worked out. For all the hurt and confusion that occurred, I am glad I did it during that time rather than more recently. I'm glad I did not cast the dean in the role of my abuser and myself as the innocent survivor of his evil. For I was not remotely innocent. I knew that myself, back from the time I began to go to chapel in the sixth grade. I knew I was lonely, broken, and full of want. I needed saving.

It would have been better, of course, if the dean had stayed out of my bed; if he had not insulted his own considerable intelligence by concocting the lame story of his need to ejaculate on my sixteen-year-old buttocks for the sake of his heart. But perhaps the matter was, after all, his heart. Perhaps he loved me as Bob loved Bud: blindly, deceitfully, and unwisely.

My mother put me in his path: his and Bob's and the boarding school in the sixth grade; those, and then her own friends, who were the inverse, the photographic negative, of all those gay men. But then she also put me in the way of art—art understood as a kind of intimacy with the created and the tragic—and, through that, of faith: faith, too, on account of doubt, on account of a life so lacking in sureties that the doubt it engendered had no choice but intermittently to effloresce into faith, however quickly it might flame out. And I loved them all, the men and the boys and the women and the whole world that came with them. That was my choice.

My mother might have thought she could make me a homosexual, and if the authoritative, homophobic science of her time had been correct, she might by her folly have succeeded. Of course the science was wrong, and her worst sin was not to know her own mind or to mistake her own heart's desire, which is no sin at all. It was the same fault that afflicted us all: her, Bob, the dean, and me, too. That, and wanting what we believed we loved, which is no more than our nature.

As it turned out, I am heterosexual. It might have been otherwise, in this matter as in any other; with me or with any of us. Suppose my mother had loved men a little more, or loved a different sort of man; or Bob had loved her rather than Bud; and I had not been so willful and sad a child, or had liked Bob and his dogs a little less; or the dean hadn't died, and I had loved him, and was just now—when he was very old—putting him in his grave? But it is like this, not that.

The dean was the first adult in my life whom I knew as something like an adult who died. When I began to pray again—in a derisory way—not many years ago, I included him in my prayers. It was without regard for what had happened between us, for what he may have intended toward me or how I felt about it. It's no real sacrifice; much less than that involved in his permitting me to do the things that were done. I know he was important to me, and it is the only way I know how to keep his presence in my life, to insist on his existence.

I pray, too, for my mother and Bob. They are both dead now: my mother of natural causes; Bob, of ones rather less so, or perhaps especially natural to him. When I was in college in California, I looked up Bob in the phone book and there he was. It was surprisingly easy. We still liked each other. He was openly gay and I was openly straight. I held my wedding reception at his house in Benedict Canyon. He met my mother for the first time in almost twenty years there.

Later, because we had become very frank with one another, he confessed that he was surprised by how much her looks and dress sense had declined. "She had style," he said, almost wistfully. "She had pizzazz."

For my part, I wondered why she didn't remarry. My sister and I both felt she shouldn't spend her old age alone. Of course, the nature of her true sexual preferences—of what, perhaps, *her* mother had made her—didn't even occur to me. In that, I was an innocent. One day with Bob, thinking aloud, I wondered why she had never gotten together with Henry Smith, for whom she had apparently carried a torch since high school.

"My dear," Bob hooted, "Henry Smith brought me *out* when I was sixteen."

Soon thereafter, Bob and I went into business together fixing up and reselling derelict houses. Initially, we used his capital, but then, when I received a bequest from my grandfather's will, we went in on a house fifty/fifty. A few days after we'd gutted it, Bob left a bar, much the worse for wear, in order to follow someone he'd met there home to his apartment in his car. Not seeing a red light, he struck another car head-on. Its occupants walked away unscathed, but Bob's body—he wasn't belted in—leapt from the seat. The top of his skull was thrown through the windshield.

I sat next to him for some weeks in a neurology intensive care unit. Unconscious, in a coma, he looked like the Tin Man in *The Wizard of Oz*, his head shaved with a drainage tube coming out the top through a funnel-shaped shunt. I wondered if the duty nurses who dealt with his catheter had commented to each other on his penis. I'd seen it once and, about that, he hadn't lied to my mother.

After a time, when the neurologists said he was past hope, I helped the brother who hated him move Bob to a shabby welfare-recipient nursing home. He hadn't had any money to speak of in his accounts, a fraction of what he'd led me to believe when I agreed to go in on the latest house project. I had to finish that with my own funds. Moreover, since I'd co-signed a loan document with Bob that contained something called a cross-collateral clause, it turned out I was responsible for other debts of his I didn't even know existed. So went my grandfather's legacy and much more.

The last time I saw Bob, who had never regained consciousness, he was in that state nursing home, perhaps a year or two before he finally died. He was on his side, curling up upon himself, not just his trunk and his legs, but his head and his neck; his hands had become frail and delicate talons. I could not feel angry about the spot he'd left me in. He was a known quantity and I should have known better. I couldn't hate him. Anyway, now, since the accident, he'd paid and paid and paid. What a waste.

It might have been otherwise. I suppose he had met someone beautiful that night, someone as handsome as Bud. He might have thought he'd seen God in that stranger's eyes, in the composure of

Robert Clark

the limbs and torso, and he'd lost his balance, driving when he ought
to have known better. He launched himself at this new body, at the
chance to love it, and intent on the stranger's taillights, mistaking
the way, fell shrieking into Beauty's—his Maker's—embrace.

The Hauser Variations
(As Sung by Male Voices, A Capriccio)
Melissa Pritchard

TIERMENSCH

FERAL CHILD

Variation 1
In a quiet, narrative tone, not too fast.

> *I want to describe it for myself, how hard it was*
> *for me.*
>
> —Fragment from Kaspar Hauser's
> Second Autobiography*
> November 1828, Nuremberg, Germany

Cribbed in dirt, toed down in stone—cradle, nursery, grave all one, one education, one schooling. A narrow space, scarcely four feet by seven. Not once did he think to stand, for he knew neither how to think nor how to stand. Over his head, rough-grained planks. On the ground he sat and slept sitting up, legs thrust before him, back ever against the same wall, upon a thrifty mouse nest of straw, reeking and silvered with mold. Two windows, each no larger than the span of two starved hands set alongside one another, were set so high that not even shadows, flitting suggestions from another world, mocked him. A single low wooden door, locked from the outside. An oven of whitened plaster, beehive shaped, threw its meager, bullying heat at him. In the packed earth, a hole had been neatly dug for him to relieve himself. He wore short leather pants, black suspenders, a rough shirt. Since he knew neither how to dress nor undress himself,

---

*In May 1828, fifteen-year-old Kaspar Hauser, rumored to be the Lost Prince of Baden, became, upon his mysterious liberation from the earthen dungeon in which he had been imprisoned twelve years, a sensation, a source of philosophical wonderment and physical experiment, known as Child of Europe and Tiermensch. Some months after his release, he became obsessed with writing his autobiography. Who exactly was he? Fragments from three autobiographies still exist. Others are presumed lost, destroyed, perhaps by Kaspar Hauser himself, grown discouraged by the demented incapacity, the mangled idiocy of language, to ever reveal his true identity or experience.

Melissa Pritchard

a square had been cut from the back of his pants in order that, without difficulty, he could relieve himself. So life went. Inside such a place, he slept, a thick, leviathan sleep, costive, without dream. In such a place, cradle, nursery, grave, Kaspar Hauser grew.

Variation 2
Tender and in a quiet tone.

> *I had twe pley horse, and such redd ribbons where I horse decorate did.*

—Fragment from Kaspar Hauser's
First Autobiography
November 1828, Nuremberg

Rosy worm, dank grub, cabbage vermin, white, hairless, altricial slug. It scarcely flourished in its cradle plot, its solitary necropolis, neither living nor dead, its budded tongue a fleshy club, its legs fwumped and futile. Making only the shallowest of motions in its musky ditch, eyes open or shut, lungs chuffing jaundiced, pernicious air, watered and fed by He Who Had Always Been With Him, an upright creature it never saw. The Unknown One would lace its water with opiates, then while it snored, insensate, he would trim its fingernails, toenails, hair, freshen the sad bed of straw, empty the hole of its raw, stinking slop. The windows gazed down, indifferent citizens with square, lidless eyes, somber and impenetrable. Who has endured such Non-Being? A self minus itself, queerish slug-a-bub, ignorant of distinction between air and skin, skin the same as dirt, dirt no different from sweated flesh, salted skin, calcific stem of bone. Straw the same as cloth, all parts uncovered, exposed, interred, an austere rot, a nothing/everything—what nonsense of Being!— what distinction between It and Other, where did it leave off and things begin? Permeable, invaded, skinless, no resistance, every particle of air, dirt, straw, wood, shit, water, bread, urine interchangeable, rendered into one original universe. Two rigid black bands, suspenders, on its smooth chest, two filthy red ribbons snugged across the implacable white necks of its horses, the dearest, most darling things, breaking bread, play-stuffing their tight Trojan bellies with that which nourished, star seed of cumin, insects of anise, pale, pitted larvae of coriander, plunging stiff snouts into water poured into its own starved palm, making them snuffle from that roseate, hungry pool, nudging their carved, lipless muzzles, bidding them

38

Take, Eat, from that most holy and budded cave of bread, chewed, curdled, sweetened with viscous saliva. Slug-a-bub, denied temperament or climate, was all inside a Great Egg of nothing, hueless, huckshouldered, sicklebacked, nothing had less specificity, less definition, less temperature, less calculability, than it did. A worm gyring, sepulchral revolution, an inconstant severity of air seeping from its bellowed, albescent lungs. It existed in lustless, dull stasis; waking it did not sleep, sleeping it did not dream. Devoid of the slightest qualities, thingish, possessed of no lusts no raptures no aversions no joys, not even the puerility of riddles, no solace of hymns, no scalded teat of nursery rhyme.

Variation 3
In a quiet, relating mood.

> *I will write the story of Kaspar Hauser myself! . . .*
> *I will tell you what I always did, and what I*
> *always had to eat, and how I spent the long period,*
> *and what I did . . .*
>
> —From Kaspar Hauser's
> Third Autobiography
> November 1828, Nuremberg

When and why was it that young Kaspar Hauser, pudding soft, quaggy limbed, a honied larva, was rudely exhumed to live a second, even more piteous life? Dug up and roused from his underground classroom, punished for making a bit too much noise as he fell backward upon his little horses, uttering a cry—inrushed the Unknown Man, thrashing at Kaspar's bare legs with a long green stick, shut up shut up shut up. And later, when U.M. brought in the usual black bread and water he carried also a board of wood, some thin pieces of white, and an odd little stick to make shapes of gray against the white . . . sitting down, his fat legs pinching mine, he laid the board across my legs, grabbed one of my hands in his, jabbed the short stick between two of my fingers and pressed, shoving gray lines over the whiteness. Letters, he said. . . . Gripping my fingers in his large hand, pressing, shaving down shape, shape, shape. . . . Each bread and water time he repeated this, until once, when he pushed the stick between my fingers, held his hand over mine for the opening letter, K, then took away his hand and made me finish. Thus did I learn my name and how to write it. More bread and water times passed, before

Melissa Pritchard

He Who Had Always Been With Me rushed in loud with clothing in his arms and a letter he had written himself. He dressed me in this noisy, flapping garb, crushed the letter, along with other items, into my pockets. Then heaving me, like a lean sack of drowned cats, over his thick, mole-heavened shoulders, the Unknown Man carted me down high and low roads to the Big Village.

*List of clothing and various articles found upon the person of Kaspar Hauser, noted this second day of Pentecost, May 26, 1828, being a young man of approximately fifteen bodily years, found wandering in confusion near Vestner Gate, Unschlitt Square. (As noted by one Andreas Hiltel, aged fifty-one years, jailer.)

1 felt hat, round in shape, with yellow silk lining and red leather stitching
1 pair of half boots with high heels, their toes ripped, the soles hammered with horseshoe nails
1 black silk neck scarf
1 janks, or gray cloth jacket
1 coarse shirt
1 linen vest, much washed
1 long pants, gray cloth
1 red-and-white-checkered handkerchief

Miscellany: pocket rags of blue and white sprigged material, a brass key, rosary beads of horn, prayer pamphlets, religious tracts, a letter.

CA! CA! GESCHMAUSET
Cling! Clang! Drink Roundly!

Cling! Clang! Drink roundly!
We are no feather-headed fools,
Would you live soundly?
Live by our rules!

Drink today, feast today,
While we're in clover!
Swiftly the years away,
Drinking is over!

—Deutsche Volkslied
German folk song

Melissa Pritchard

WUNDERMENSCH
WONDER CHILD

Variation 4
Bright, lively, with humor.

(*Two brothers, shoemakers named* OTTO *and* KLAUS, *or more wittily,* HEEL *and* TOE, *discover* KASPAR HAUSER *wandering dazedly near Vestner Gate, Unschlitt Square, Nuremberg, on March 26, 1828, the second day of Pentecost, between four and five in the afternoon.*)

HEEL. Look! What is it?

TOE. A drunkard, obviously. Look how he staggers.

HEEL. He is dressed like a beggar, yet lacks a beggar's beard.

TOE. Those boots! What a disgrace! Better they'd stayed on the hide they came off of.

HEEL. Saint's entrails! He's taken a fall. Let us go to him.

TOE. Let us step over him. (*To audience.*) I'd rather.

HEEL. No. It is a holy day of Pentecost, and our Christian duty to help him. Look. A mere child.

TOE. A youth with an overslung jaw and a letter in its hand. (*Schemingly, to audience.*) Perhaps a bit of money, too. (*Humming.*) My horse needs feeding and the dog's grown thin. . . .

HEEL. (*Ignoring his brother's greed.*) Indeed, it is a letter and addressed, too. (*He reads.*) To the Well-Born Captain of the Fourth Squadron of the Sixth Regiment of Light Horses in the city of Nuremberg . . . well, that would be Captain von W., who lives steps from here, I repaired his parade boots just last week. Look here, what else is upon this small person . . . religious pamphlets? (*Holds them up, reading titles, one by one.*) *Spiritual Sentry, Spiritual Forget-me-not, Prayer to the Holy Blood*, and this last—*The Art of Replacing Lost Time and Years Badly Spent.* Oh now, brother Klaus, there's one for you to ponder. The boy is not drunk, he is a Catholic!

41

(*The two shoemakers, squatting down on either side of the small figure, contemplate him and arrive at reversed conclusions.*)

HEEL. Likely he is a saint in beggar's disguise. One of God's Angels, sent to test us.

TOE. He's a moron, and so are you to think anything else. Why must everything be a religious quiz for you? It drives me wild.

HEEL. Because I've kept the faith I was born with while you lost yours in a series of hayricks with goose-eyed girls, ending with the worst, that spitfire wife of yours. Look, he's waking up. How are you, boy? Do you have a Christian name? Can you hear me? Where are you from? He's not answering.

TOE. How can he, with you yammering away at him? Clamp your jaw and let's wait.

(*The two brothers sit, expectant, watching the figure on the ground between them.*)

TOE. You see? I told you. An idiot. An empty pate.

HEEL. Not at all. It's only true that we've frightened him. I'll ask again, soft this time. (*He whispers in a wheedling tone until the boy breaks forth in a torrent of sobs and wet, slurred sounds . . .* rossbubenrossbubenrossbuben*. . . .*)

TOE. (*Jumping up.*) That does it. A simpleton. Let's leave him and go home to our suppers. My wife has a fine blood sausage cooking.

HEEL. I couldn't agree less with you and your blood sausage, your big-mouth stomach. How can you fail to see? It's Pentecost, the town deserted, everyone off to the countryside for a holiday, and here in this empty square, we've come upon a holy wonder, a Christian miracle, an angel dropped down from heaven, speaking in tongues of fire. (*As if to prove* HEEL's *point, the boy bursts out sobbing afresh . . .* rossbubenrossbubenrossbuben*. . . .*) It is God's test of our faith, Klaus, and you, my brother, have failed.

TOE. I have failed nothing, Otto. It is you who, as usual, have failed to keep the common sense you were born with.

---

*Buben: boy, ross: horse.

Melissa Pritchard

(*Lugging young* KASPAR, *weeping* rossbubenrossbubenross, *between them, the two shoemakers argue until they reach the door of* CAPTAIN VON W.'s *house,* HEEL *insisting they have met with a celestial being preaching God's word,* TOE *shouting back that the witless oaf, bastard son of Gypsies, should be taken off to Lugensland Tower, the proper place for vagrants, vagabonds, and debtors.* TOE *has faith, but* HEEL *prevails. There is a short pointless debate with* CAPTAIN VON W., *who, displeased at having his supper, a halfway decent plate of pickled cod and boiled potato, interrupted, scarcely looks at the boy's letter, addressed to him, tearing it to shreds, muttering, Rubbish, rubbish, rubbish, a button of cold potato fixed to his loose, indignant lower lip, ordering this floundersome pest be carted off by stablehands to Lugensland Tower. Thus* KASPAR HAUSER *ascended not into any Christian heaven or even up the steps of the nearby cathedral to be proclaimed a pentecostal Messenger, but instead, found himself hauled off to debtors' prison, given a sack of hard straw and a granite-hewn corner of the high guarded tower in which to sleep.*)

VILLAGE MONKEY or: MAJESTATSVERBRECHEN*

Variation 5
Lively, weary, not too fast.

From an unpublished account of Andreas Hiltel, baritone, aged fifty-one, jailer, Lugensland Tower, Nuremberg

I fasten my good eye, the right, against an orb in the wood door, fashioned for the secret observation of prisoners, a hole seldom used, if I may be frank about it, until now. I see no one, and for a moment, fear the creature has escaped. Then I hear him, out of my right eye's sight but within my left ear's hearing, making piteous gibberish, slight departure from the words he repeated over and over when first brought to me from Captain von W.'s house. *"Reuta, wahn, wie mie Votta wahn is."*** Like some disconsolate, shorn-feathered parrot, he repeated himself endlessly.

*A crime against royalty.
**"I want to be one such as my father was."

43

Melissa Pritchard

Eight weeks later:

If God himself were to name my charge a fraud, as many in Nuremberg have recently accused the boy of being, I would have to contradict him. Contradict God. The child is innocent. He is a chick without feathers, a monkey without a hide, that is his only crime. He is, in my opinion (unlikely to be listened to), a victim of *Majestatsverbrechen*. The boy, no more than fifteen, with the mind of a child of three or four, is rumored to be the son of the adopted daughter of Napoleon, Stephanie de Beauharnais. It is even believed by some, who claim proof, that he was switched at birth and in his place was put the sickly infant of the royal gardener, a ninth child, sure to perish. This same gardener, they say, was promoted after the child's "birth," and now lives in conditions of unheard-of prosperity. I say no more. But the boy has a gentle nature and sits on the floor beneath the wooden table, drawing pencil likenesses of toy horses, gifts from visitors. When he finishes one sketch, he sticks it to the stone wall with his spittle, strangely thick and viscous as boilt glue. Dozens of such drawings flutter whenever he gets up or moves about. His visitors arrive at all hours. It is said a visit to Nuremberg is not complete without stopping to climb the circular staircase of Lugensland Tower to see the mysterious Child of Europe. The women gawk and titter behind painted fans and silk parasols, the children roll their eyes, pull faces, and the bolder, meaner boys jab and poke at him. Worse than these children are the grown men, scientists, philosophers, doctors, and dignitaries, who cluster in somber frock coats, squint through shining pince-nez, give sober examination with cold instruments of inquiry. From Mayor Binder, pompous with his city's sudden fame, to the royal forensic examiner, Dr. Preu, to Herr von Feuerbach, the city's chief judge who has, it seems, taken it upon himself to solve the mystery of Kaspar Hauser, this crime of "soul murder," I have seen grown men, with science their excuse, run at him with a drawn saber, to see if he will flinch, then hold a candle flame nearer and nearer his face, until they provoke a response. He might as well be an ape in a royal menagerie, a caged hyena. No, it is not only Kaspar Hauser I press my eye and ear to the spyhole for; I wish to overhear their speculations as to the child's true identity as I watch, often with boredom (for science, man-made pursuit of truth, can be monotonous), their various tests upon him. This past Sunday, one physician, a colleague of Dr. Preu's, from Brussels, went so far as to fire his pistol straight into the air, without warning, to test the child's response. Someone else threw a lit candle at the boy's head. Both acts succeeded in terrifying Kaspar into fits of convulsion ending in a lapse of consciousness. My authority is nil; I am helpless to stop these monkey tricks. Just yesterday a philosopher from Paris came to gawk, returning early this morning with his pet monkey. He bade the monkey do tricks, delighting Kaspar initially. But as the monkey carried on, tirelessly repeating the same tricks, all at once Kaspar cried out in despair . . . seeing himself too much in the monkey's piteous, repetitive antics. Never have I known a kinder, gentler, more sensitive soul than Kaspar Hauser. I sometimes muse that were we all to be locked away in dungeons, suspended in our separate dreams, would our world not be the kinder for it? These are the idiot, half-mad musings of a man paid to confine other men. Oh long march of pokers-at-the-soul, keen to further their own prestige, fatten their own purses, sharpen their own reputations on the miserable story of this young man, it would not surprise me if one day I catch old Dr. Preu here yet again, scurrying off with a cold coil of the boy's stool to prise apart with metal tongs and wonder over, in the profane sanctity of his laboratory. Sinful examinations! He suffers and grows weak. He eats less, I fear he will not survive such brutal, sentimental curiosity. I will speak to Judge von Feuerbach when he arrives to visit, as he does each Sunday after church, with his wife and children. I will beg him to put a stop to this monkey show. I care for this boy and wish him no more harm.

He has been removed to Professor Daumer's house. Daumer shows rare kindness and restraint, so I am sure the change will be good for the boy. I leave his drawings upon the walls, where they faintly rustle, like pale, wintry leaves. Kaspar Hauser was the mirror of innocence. He had nothing false in him. He caused me, old fool, to take notice of things. Helped me to feel pity again.

Melissa Pritchard

Variation 6
Sustained and with warm expression.

> Ich weiss nicht, was soll es bedeuten,
> Dass ich so traurig bin;
> Ein Marchen aus alten Zeiten,
> Das kommt mir nicht aus dem Sinn.
>
> *I know not why I am so sad; I cannot get out of
> my head a fairy-tale of olden times.*
>
> —Heinrich Heine
> Dei Lorelei
> 1797–1856

La, it is I, George Friedrich Daumer, aged twenty-eight, poet, philosopher, misanthrope, abject and subject to black fits and outcroppings, morbid excrescences of melancholy. Former tutor to Hegel's children—imagine!—and Hegel's sometimes scribe. Herr Hegel himself, grand author of *Geist,* once my very sun and celestial fixing point, begins, of late, to depress me. Here the most recent tone of the man in a letter that I, with my failing eyesight, was made to scratch and piddle down: "*—this descent—into dark regions where nothing reveals itself to be fixed, definite, and certain, where glimmerings of light flash everywhere, but flanked by abysses, are rather darkened in their brightness and led astray by the environment, casting false reflections far more than illumination.*"* Such talk of darkness and false reflection—think!

To counteract this recent lowering effect upon me of Herr Hegel's own depression and driven as well by a desire to cure myself of doggish melancholy, I have developed a surpassing interest in Dr. Christian Samuel Hahnemann's astounding doctrines of medicine, his new system of Physic, Homeopathy, with its basis in philosophy, for which he has been both celebrated and reviled. One way of thinking of Hahnemann's doctrine is to consider this: two loud sounds may be made to produce silence, and two strong lights may be said to produce darkness. *Brilliant.* Having cultivated no thought system of my own, I am doomed to paddle in the footsteps of great men, even in the smaller, fleeter footsteps of great men's children, never to be great myself. (Though Thomas Mann himself—and by the

---

*From Hegel's letter to K. J. H. Windischmann (1775–1839), Catholic doctor turned philosopher.

governance of time I am not supposed to know this—will call one of my passing stabs at poetry the greatest poem in the language, and a composer, whose name escapes me, will set a body of my poems to music—so, as it turns out, I will not be entirely forgotten nor barred entrance to the thousand side-branching, tributary halls of greatness.)

I console myself with the notion that great men require an audience of nimble yet modest minds. They require men of slight genius to act as mental sycophants, cerebral slaves, theoretical devotees. I am that slave, sycophant, and devotee, mongrel croucher to Schelling, Hegel, Hahnemann (comet of controversy, double-headed pedagogue!). And now, new hope underlies this chronic gloom of mine. I have been asked by my friend Anselm von Feuerbach, a distinguished judge in this city, to house the feral boy, Kaspar Hauser, found wandering our fair city and now held in Lugensland Tower, an object of crude curiosity, a specimen exposed to merciless scrutiny. Anselm believes the youth will die of fever of the nerves or lapse into idiocy or worse, insanity, so constantly is he held up as a freak of nature. La, the trust placed in me by such a request—consider! Staggering! My poor mind a flea, ajump with notions of how to instruct this untainted, Rousseauian creature. I drop to my knees (theoretically), grateful for the long chance at distinguishing myself, acquiring luster in the world's eyes. And—heaven have it!—that low black cur, that beast of melancholy, has, I note, slunk off.

HERR DAUMER'S INITIAL ACCOUNT (WRIT LARGE),
AS REGARDS DR. HAHNEMANN:

I have been in correspondence with Dr. H. himself—marvelous!—the famous doctor is much intrigued with my K. Hauser and asks that I begin my record as a physician, beginning with the exact order of questions Dr. H. himself begins each of his patient interviews with.
1. *How is it with the motions?*
2. *How is it with the urinary discharge?*
3. *How with the sleep, by day, by night?*
4. *In what state are his disposition, his humor, his intellectual faculties?*
5. *How is it with the thirst?*

6. *What sort of taste has he in his mouth?*
7. *What aliments and drinks does he most affect?*
8. *What are most repugnant to him?*
9. *Has each its full natural taste or some other unusual taste?*
10. *How does he feel after eating or drinking?*
11. *Is there anything else to be told about the head, the limbs, or the abdomen?*

ADDITIONAL ACCOUNT OF KASPAR HAUSER BEGINNING
WITH HIS ARRIVAL AT THE DAUMER HOUSEHOLD, 18 JULY, 1828,
CONCLUDING WITH HIS DEPARTURE, 15 DECEMBER, 1829

1. Exhibition of Strange Faculties and Hypersensitivities
   a. ability to distinguish shapes of letters and complete words in utter darkness
   b. ability to "feel" someone pointing to him from behind
   c. an exquisite, mostly painful sensory apparatus: loud noises occasion convulsions, bright light is agony to his eyes, the merest drop of alcohol or mort of meat, mixed in with other substances, creates violent sickness, difficult bowel movements, copious vomiting (thus confirming Dr. Hahnemann's belief as well as my own that a vegetarian diet and calm compassionate nature are linked)
   d. speaks aloud to all creatures, all animals, cats, dogs, birds, and the like, as if they were human, like himself
   e. the scent of a rose revolts him; the color red pleases him to hysterics; black disgusts him; animals, a chicken or horse or cat, for example, terrify him if they are black in color
   f. music enraptures him; I have fashioned a sort of drum upon which he will beat out a tune, over and over, for long hours

2. General Progress
   a. begins to distinguish between the organic and inorganic, the vital and the lifeless
   b. begins to know the difference between a joke and a serious topic
   c. begins to write his life story, makes numerous attempts, appears frustrated

3. Physical Progress
   a. less prone to daily sickness

b. exclusive diet of black bread and water increased by a healthful cup of hot chocolate most mornings

c. whereas his face had lacked expression in repose and his lower jaw protruded slightly, and the gaze held an animal-like lethargy, his facial deformity has corrected itself, the eyes have gained human luster and the fingers that formerly were held stiffly and straight out, fingers far apart, now flex and move with a greater naturalness. The walk, once a halting gait, a kind of lurch and stumble, is such that he is now able to accompany me on short, daily perambulations outside the house.

4. Sorrows

a. The caging of small animals upsets him greatly. He cannot understand why people want to cage and harm, kill, roast, and then eat an animal of any sort when he himself would not harm so much as an insect. Surely, he pleads with me, all creatures wish to live free and unharmed. Just yesterday, until I freed a grouse intended by our cook for roasting, he was enraged with me. This animal has harmed no one, he wept in anger. Why not eat bread and water, as I do?

5. Of Meats and Metals

a. As it is well known that people are inordinately affected by substances around them or fed to them, I tested the effects of various metals and foods upon him. Forcing him to eat small bits of different animal meats (boiled beef in particular revolted him) brought him to such a prolonged agony of sickness I promised never to inflict such suffering upon an innocent creature again*, and wrote to Dr. H. to say my conscience would no longer permit me to tamper with the purity of my young charge's nature, even for a cause so noble as Science. I deeply regret my subjection of this foundling to such long and arduous experiments in metal and the eating of animal flesh. I can scarcely forgive myself. I note that the keenness of his senses has diminished as a result. I note that even language, both spoken and written, has muted his original sensitivity. The former blank slate of his soul is marred, muddied, befouled by the arrogance of man's inquisitiveness. I now believe it a Sin, man's lack of restraint in the quest of knowledge. Had I known how brief an hour Kaspar Hauser had to draw breath, I should have left off my experiments and encouraged him, instead, in his Raptures.

---

*I will later appoint myself founder of the Society of Prevention of Cruelty to Animals.

THE THREE RAPTURES OF KASPAR HAUSER

I. FEATHER BED   Upon giving him a proper bed of goose feathers, rather than straw, the boy is in a confoundment of joyful pleasure. It was upon this feather bed, in our home, that he first began to dream, though he could not, at first, distinguish between waking and dreaming.

II. STARS   In August 1829, on a warm, windless summer's night, as we walked, I bade Kaspar gaze upward at the constellations. Amazed, he could not stop looking, exclaiming over and again at the bright beauty of the night sky. How was it, he wondered, he had never seen this before, why had someone wished to keep him beneath the earth, deprived of such a staggering sky? This question affected him, as much as the stars, upon which he continued to gaze with woeful awe.

III. HORSES   He has received, as gifts, a great many toy wooden horses of all sizes. He never tires of playing with them, spending long hours alone, playing and talking with them, decorating them with bits of ribbon, feathers, sequins, and the like. They are like living creatures he dotes upon.

6. An Unwelcome English Visitor
One year to the day after the thwarted attempt upon Kaspar's life in our outhouse in the courtyard, the fourth Earl of Stanhope stopped unexpectedly at our home. My wife, her sister, and I welcomed him. He curtly dismissed our hospitality, asking instead for Kaspar Hauser, who was upstairs painting with the watercolors I had recently given him. Lord Stanhope further inquired if he might take Kaspar out for a ride in his carriage as the October afternoon had only a mild wind with intermittent bursts of sunshine. Without asking Lord Stanhope's approval, I went along and was dismayed when, after only moments, the Englishman had Kaspar on his lap, caressing and even kissing him in a manner I found unseemly if not repugnant. Kaspar seemed unaware of anything being done *to* him, though I grew horribly disturbed. Was this, I fumed indignantly, the way of English lords, to dandle boys upon their knees and to kiss them in a most intimate manner? When I summoned him to sit beside me for the remainder of the ride, Kaspar obeyed, seeming most cheerful. Outside my home, after handing Kaspar down to my waiting wife, I

coldly thanked Lord Stanhope, truly loathing the man. In a haughty manner, flicking his yellow skin gloves arrogantly, he informed me I would hear from him shortly, as soon as he had spoken with Herr von Feuerbach. He wished, he said, to adopt the boy and take him to his estate in England. He only required von Feuerbach's legal consent in order to do so. Going inside, I found Kaspar in his room, calmly resuming his watercolors. Butterflies, he was painting clouds of ethereal butterflies in fragile colors. How illusory his safety! How illusory my guardianship. I vowed I would not let him out of my sight, would plead, in a letter to Anselm, to not give Kaspar into the privileged, repulsive hands of Lord Stanhope.

7. Kaspar Taken!

My letter, suspiciously, never reached Anselm; he granted Lord Stanhope full guardianship of Kaspar. On December 15, several weeks after that carriage ride, two lawyers showed up with official documents, sealed and signatured, authorizing them to take Kaspar to Ansbach, some fifty miles distant, to stay with a village schoolteacher by the name of Johann Meyer until such time as the fourth Earl of Stanhope could arrange for Kaspar to live permanently in England. With heavy hearts, my wife and I helped Kaspar pack his few things, and with the three of us crying inconsolably, the lawyers standing drily by, we bade one another good-bye, my wife and I promising Kaspar we would come to see him in Ansbach. Perhaps he will be safer elsewhere, my wife and I tried to persuade ourselves. After all, someone had tried to take his life in our home and certainly after that dreadful day none of us ever felt truly safe again. Yet how wrong we were to hope for Kaspar's greater safety away from us! Within one year, our young friend would be dead at the hand of an assassin. The sorrow assailing me made my former melancholia, by comparison, seem a very benediction.

DOCTOR EISENBART
Doctor Irongray

My name is Doctor Irongray,
Valleralleri, hurrah!
To cure the folks I know the way,
Valleralleri, hurrah!
'Tis I that make the dumb to walk,
Valleralleri, hurrah, hurrah!

51

Melissa Pritchard

And I can make the lame to talk!
Valleralleri, hurrah!

—Deutsch Volkslied
German folk song

HASENFUSS
SISSY!

Variation 7
Vigorous, unaffected, impatient.

From the small Catechism of Johann Meyer:
I assigned a man of God to the boy after telling him fear was to be his first lesson and God his Fearsome Headmaster. I never knew a boy not to fare better on discipline and calculated privation than on laxity and excessive praise. And this particular boy would require a sterner measure, a harsher dose, than most. *Herr Hasenfuss* arrived in my home pliant and pale as dough, weak as blood pudding, loose and uncooked. He had been coddled, proclaimed pure, sinless, innocent, a *"wundermensch,"* darling lamb of Nuremberg and so forth, every whim doted on—bah!—puerile whining, all of it! All his silly games of what he could and could not do, eat and not eat, what he could and could not wear, tolerate or not tolerate—pure folly! He soon caught on to my pedagogy, which was to rub his nose hard in whatever he said he could not stand, until he could stand it and stand it and stand it. To beat a boy is wise insurance against future mischief. Daily thrashing, ice cold water baths, praying on cold stone with bare knees, fasting Sundays, these are a few of the cures prescribed by myself, his newest master. No frivolous music, no painting of butterflies, no feather beds, cocoa drinks, or lazy walks, meanderings leading nowhere. These had made of him a girlish, silly creature, spoilt, puling, pandered to, and I began at once by making no allowance, none, for his so-called tragic history. This fanciful talk of a lost prince, a life in a dungeon (had anyone visibly seen this dungeon?) were false stories. Lies. Gypsies roam everywhere, and it is well known they send their most comely brats into villages bearing fantastic and well-rehearsed tales devised to excite pity and loosen the purse strings of foolish sentimentalists of which every village has more than one. How am I to believe he is not the wily sport of Gypsy folk? Perhaps even now he plots to murder and then rob me of what little I possess—this happened just last month in a village nearby.

52

Hasenfuss. Little liar. Each morning I set out to catch my stuttering, stammering H. in his latest nest of lies. This morning, for instance, when he complained to me of being sick in the night, saying he had gone into the bathroom to vomit, I said that could not possibly be true. If his sense of smell is so keen, as he says it is, he would not have gone into the bathroom, he would have used the sink in his room. I said to him: either it is not true you have a sensitive nose or it is not true you vomited in the bathroom or anywhere else for that matter. Choose. Either way you lie.

I am head of this boy's family now, responsible for his godly education, which I render in plainest form. It is I who must convince him of the truth that all good is rewarded and all evil punished.

Why does he not believe me?

> *Do you pray? I asked.*
> *Every night, he answered.*
> *Tell me your prayers.*
> *I don't know them by heart.*
> *You are lying, I said.*
> *Thus Hasenfuss earned another day's thrashing.*

Variation 8
In a slow and solemn manner.

1. Do you believe that you are a sinner?
   Yes, I believe it. I am a sinner.

2. How did you obtain your knowledge thereof?
   From the holy decalogue or commandments; these I have
   not kept.

3. Do you feel sorrow on account of your sins?
   Yes, I feel sorrow for having sinned against God.

4. What have you deserved of God on account of your sins?
   His wrath and displeasure, temporal death and eternal
   damnation.

5. But do you still hope to be saved?
   Yes, such is my hope.

Melissa Pritchard

MORDER!!
AND THE OLD FIDDLER'S SONG

Variation 9
Agitated and with great passion.

On a wintry twilit evening, December 14, 1832, not five years after he had first appeared near Vestner's Gate in Unschlitt Plaza, discovered by two brothers, Otto and Klaus, Kaspar Hauser received a written message from a stranger saying news of his mother awaited him at a particular location at a certain hour. So Kaspar snuck out of Johann Meyer's icy, unheated house and hurried through a bluish drizzle of snow to the Court Gardens in the Orangerie, where he was to look for a man standing directly in front of the statue of the poet Uz, beside a little-used bridle path. Distracting Kaspar with the supposed contents of a woman's green silk purse, saying there was a note from his mother in it, the man, with skilled aim, stabbed Kaspar Hauser in the heart, then fled. Managing to stumble back to the house where he had lived for one miserable year, Kaspar climbed the stairs to Meyer's bedroom, where he found the schoolteacher in bed reading by candlelight, a black woolen nightcap upon his head. He was reading what he continually and obsessively read, Luther's Augsberg Confession. Kaspar, managing to gasp that he had been stabbed, showed Herr Meyer the wound. Coolly, Meyer asked that Kaspar take him to the exact spot where he had been attacked. . . . (*I told him to quit making such a fuss, that at any rate he deserved a good thrashing for telling such a tale when it was clear his wound was slight and no doubt self-inflicted. I did not believe a word of his story and made him take me to the place of the supposed attack, which he did. When we returned home, I told him to go upstairs to his bed, that there would be no supper for disobedient boys who snuck out of houses at night. I admit, when I climbed the stairs to his room the next morning, I was astonished to find him not whining or fussing or twitching with all his usual complaints. Hasenfuss lay silent, scarcely making a sound, and when I asked if it hurt, he answered only once, in a monosyllable. This time I lectured him—then you have played a most stupid prank for which God will not forgive you. He looked up toward the heavens, past me, and cried out—in the name of God, God knows I tell the truth!*)

It took three days for him to die. Johann Meyer was slow to call the doctor and when it became clear, even to him, that the boy was dying, he continued to insist the wound was self-inflicted. Kaspar Hauser was heard to whisper once and to no one in particular, for there was no one to hear him other than the doctor and the pastor, that *"many cats are the death of the mouse."* His last words, before he lay down on his right side and died, were, *"Tired, very tired, still have to take a long trip."*

By those inclined to believe in higher powers, it did not go unnoticed that on the day Kaspar Hauser's small coffin was carried to the cemetery, the sun was setting in the west at the exact moment the moon was rising, keeping perfect time with the sun, in the east.

Es Wohnet ein Fiedler
There Lived an Old Fiddler

Thou crooked old fiddler,
now fiddle to me,
I pay thee with pleasure
a generous fee;
Play a frolicsome dance
the time not too fast,
the time not too fast,
Walpurgis night
has come at last.

HOHERER RUCKSICHT
SPIRITUAL MATTERS

Variation 10
Agitated and secretly.

Confession of the Unknown Man:
Death turns men honest. *Aller guten Dinge sind drei* (all good things are three). Three times I murdered you. I extinguished your spirit in a dungeon for twelve years—I cannot say who paid me. I attempted your death in Nuremberg, as you squatted in the outhouse; yes, my voice you heard beneath the black hood, my knife jumping back, failing to open your puppy's moist throat. The third

time, I hid in a grove of trees, coward and spying, as one hired, drove the dagger deep. Tending you, I was richly paid. Thanks to you, my own nine children flourished. Uneasy sin, agilely done! The rarest plant, savaged. With small hope, I taught you to scribble your name, put you in pilgrim's clothes, took and pushed you through one of the city's many gates—rid of you for a time. A gardener tends life, does not murder. Your blood is on me. I am past saving.

Variation 11
Gently agitated and with spirit.

Daumer's Lament:
How could I have saved you? What more could I have done? I was born a man of ideals who lacked conviction, a man of poetic dreams and no courage. I handed you over to sadists and murderers. How could I have known? I am a healthy man who no longer sees. A blind man who cannot forgive himself. A poet who writes only of you, a philosopher asking one question: why on this man-muddled earth was Innocence itself harmed?

QUODLIBET
WHAT PLEASES

Otto and Klaus, two brothers known to all in Nuremberg as Heel and Toe, sing a popular folk song as they repair and stitch, make strong for daily use, the shoes of the common man.

> *It's so long I haven't been with you,*
> *Cabbages and turnips have driven me away!*
> *Cabbages and turnips, yes, have driven me away!*
> — Deutsche Volkslied

FINALE

> *Reuta, wahn, wie mie Votta wahn is.*
> I want to be a rider like my father. . . .

Strange, to lie underground a second time! From a dungeon with straw, lifted to a high tower, then lowered into a series of ordinary rooms (one with the bliss of a feather bed!), interred again in dirt, once more on straw, a withered, blood-drained root, unlikely to sprout or be resurrected in the same manner again. In death, as in sleep, I am all things. Like any true mystery, I am a mirror, a reflection of the self, gazing back upon itself. Buried, resurrected, shown a host of stars including the solitary sun, buried once more. And though my grave is but a small space, wondrous little, yes, a narrow patch, there is, I assure you, no end to its heights.

On a white wooden horse, I fly upward, outrace the first sorrowing fields of stars. And whether or not my life is Eternal, I cannot or will not say, but I know this, dear ones: it is you who allow pain into the world, and you, poor friends, who look away from human suffering, and in that bright, lively way of yours, break faster and faster, inching toward death, into Song.

Adventure
Paul La Farge

1.

MRS. REGENZEIT WAS TALKING on the telephone when I came in, but she motioned for me to sit down, and, as she talked, opened the refrigerator, took out a bowl of twilight purple vegetables, and set it on the table. "I don't give one sheet about that," she said, opened a drawer, and handed me a fork. "He should know better than to listen to such stupid things." I tasted the vegetable, I think it was eggplant, soaking in sour, spicy fluid. "Well, I am not sorry," Mrs. Regenzeit said. "You tell him, not one beet." I bent my head and ate until my tongue buzzed. "Yes, good-bye." Mrs. Regenzeit hung up the phone and sat down with me. I had never seen her sitting before. "So," she said, "you like that?" "Mm." "Better for you than candy," Mrs. Regenzeit said. "You are getting a little beet fat." I put the fork down. "Tell me, how is school?" I didn't know why Mrs. Regenzeit was asking me about my life beyond Thebes, but I told her that it was all right. "You are a good student, yes? You make good grades? Go on, eat, it's only vegetables." I ate and answered her questions as best I could. I was well, my mothers were well, New York City was all right, I guessed. "Listen," Mrs. Regenzeit said and poked at me with her finger. "I need your help." Kerem was in trouble, she told me. Soccer had made him popular and popularity had turned him into a hoodlum. He used to have good friends, Mrs. Regenzeit said, people like me who made good marks in school and read books, good, quiet people, but now his friends were strange children who put safety pins in their pants and one of them had shaved part of his head, *not his whole head,* and now Kerem was talking about doing that, too. She did not know what would be next, whether it would be drugs or crime or what people did when they had hair like that. "We try to talk to him," she said, "but in his head there is only the terrible music he listens to." "Do you want me to talk to him?" I asked. "No," Mrs. Regenzeit said, "what could you tell him that we did not say? No." She stabbed the air. "I want you to work with him on the computer." This, Mrs. Regenzeit explained, was their latest and maybe their last hope for Kerem, a computer they had ordered from a catalog, which might get him interested in science and mathematics. The computer came in a kit, the whole family had labored long to assemble it, Mr. Regenzeit had given up many hours of work, and finally they'd hired an engineering student from Rensselaer Polytechnic to finish the job. Now it was working, Mrs. Regenzeit said, but would it work? She touched the back of my hand. "You're a good boy," she said. "Help him to take an interest in this computer."

Kerem came downstairs just then, rubbing his eyes and scowling. In the last nine months he had become skinny and pointed and his curly black hair stood on end with the support of some glistening goo. He looked like Anthony Squamuglia, a social pariah in my class at Phlogiston who was renowned for his frequent and disruptive midclass nosebleeds, only tougher. Anthony was a comic nuisance; Kerem looked capable of doing harm. "Good morning, Kerem," Mrs. Regenzeit said sweetly. "Would you like some breakfast?" "No thanks, Mum," Kerem said. He squinted at me as though I might be something from a dream. "You back?" "I just got here today." "C'mon," he said, "let's go to town." I followed him out and as we left Mrs. Regenzeit stabbed at me with her finger and mouthed the word *computer*. We walked down the hill to town. I wanted to ask Kerem a thousand questions, but I was afraid he would remember that for the last two summers we hadn't been friends. Finally, timidly, I asked if he was going to soccer camp again this summer? "Football," Kerem said. "You play football?" "The name of it is football. It's only Americans who call it soccer." Kerem shrugged. "I guess you couldn't know that, since you don't know Billy." Unbidden, he explained to me that last August he'd met a real Englishman named Billy, an assistant coach, who had demonstrated to him the superiority of all things English, and, incidentally, turned him on to punk rock. "He got me started on the Pistols, right?" "Right," I said. "No," Kerem said, "that wasn't a real question. You just say right, at the end of a sentence. Right?" I didn't say anything. "Right," Kerem said. "You're going to be fine." We stopped outside the public library and I met his friends, a boy named Eric with a shock of red hair, his natural color, and protruding ears, and a girl named Shelley who had made her skirt by cutting up a sweatshirt and sewing it back together. Kerem introduced me as his mate from New York City, and Shelley and Eric drew long hollow breaths. "I really want to go there," Shelley said. "I've just got to check out the scene in New York." "Lower East Side," Eric said, "that's where it is, right?" I knew better than to answer. "CBGBs," said Eric, but I didn't understand him; I thought he meant the Seabees, the navy engineers, whom I knew about from my grandfather's encyclopedia of American wars. I wondered if there was a naval training center in lower Manhattan. "When we come to New York," Shelley said, "can we stay with you?" "I can ask," I said, "but my apartment is pretty small." After this unpromising beginning we walked to the Texaco station and stood by the pumps, watching people go in and out of the convenience store. Now and then one of the group would point to a customer and murmur to the others: "Known fag." "Definite fag." "Total fag." Once Shelley approached a couple of men in a low-slung Camaro and persuaded them to buy her cigarettes. She offered me one; I said no but this didn't change Shelley's mistaken idea of my status. "I shouldn't be smoking either," she said. "My mom's really on me to quit." Kerem was talking to Eric about what would happen if you put a lit M40 in the gas tank of a car. "You just drop it in and run, and the car explodes," said Kerem. "No way," Eric said. "The fuse would ignite the gas fumes. You'd seriously die." This was what they taught you in the Seabees, I surmised. At sunset we dispersed, and I walked home with Kerem. Mrs. Regenzeit was cooking; Kerem tugged my arm and muttered, "Got to show you something." He brought me up to his room and shot the bolt on the door. England had invaded Kerem's bedroom and brought with it disorder and the smell of feet. A big Union Jack hung over his bed and opposite it a poster of Sid Vicious, who also looked like Anthony Squamuglia, and who was, according to the poster, dead. Then full-color photographs of soccer players, or *footballers,* as I was supposed to call them now, razor cut from imported magazines, ruddy men who seemed to be all tendon, caught in midleap, grimacing as though they were keeping themselves aloft by force of will. The bed was covered with clothes and the remnants of more than one meal. I asked him if that was where he slept. "Naw." Kerem pointed to a sleeping bag that lay unrolled by the window. "I'm squatting." He steered me to the desk.

Computers still belonged, at this point, more to my imaginary world than to the world I shared with other people. Computers were *2001* and *Forbidden Planet;* they were big, blinking cabinets, sinister friends who did what you wanted to but couldn't, like causing the New York subway to trap your enemies in perpetual darkness, or could but didn't want to, like pre-algebra homework. Computers joined me in my daydreams; sometimes they came in the form of robots, and sometimes as voices, whispering directions in my ear so that I would never walk down a bad block in Manhattan by accident, or think of a good insult hours too late. They looked nothing like the Acorn Micro on Kerem's desk, a gray box the size of a record player, almost entirely devoid of lights and switches, an appliance that was no more exciting in appearance than my grandmother's microwave oven, and considerably less exciting than her electric toothbrush, which, with its rocket-ship styling and brightly colored interchangeable heads, its three speeds and warm rechargeable battery, seemed truly to announce the beginning of a new era. "Check it out," Kerem said. He switched the machine on, and on a gray television screen set up on a milk crate, underneath a pennant for Manchester United, green words appeared and vanished, leaving only a prompt,

>

the beginning of the beginning. The Acorn Micro was intended more for hobbyists than for recreational users, and came with no software other than a BASIC interpreter and a game, intended to demonstrate the computer's capabilities, where letters and numbers appeared near the top of the screen and fell slowly downward; you had to type each one on the keyboard before it reached the bottom or you lost. Kerem played a game, then I played. It was too easy at first, then, as the letters sped up, it became too hard; only a machine could have kept up after the third or fourth round. "It's stupid," Kerem admitted. "But look at this." He typed,

```
>10 PRINT "FUCK YOU!"
>20 GOTO 10
>RUN
```

and an unstoppable column of insult flickered up the screen. This was power. It didn't matter that it was a tiny, ineffectual kind of power that would strike no fear into the hearts of my enemies or save me from getting into trouble in the street; all that mattered was that the gray box was in our camp now. It was better than a baby brother; it did what we wanted without questioning; our power was, in the first instance, power over it. We taught the box new obscenities, and had it shout them over and over at the top of its lungs, until Kerem's mother called him down to dinner.

2.

I wanted more, and by the end of that first day Kerem and I reached an understanding that seemed brilliant to us at the time, although it ended up costing me my integrity, my future at the Phlogiston School for Boys, and my hope, already slim, of becoming an ordinary human being. I would make the computer work, and Kerem would take the credit. I went to his house in the morning; Mrs. Regenzeit greeted me with a glass of sticky-sweet tea and whispered, "On the computer, it is going well?" "Yes," I said. "Kerem is teaching me a lot." "He is very good with the computer?" "I don't know how he does it," I said deviously. "He just seems to know everything." "Good!" Mrs. Regenzeit whispered, delighted. "You go up and learn!" She patted my back as I went upstairs, sticky sweetness on my lips, and in my stomach, a flutter of fear at the lies I was telling. I slipped into Kerem's room. He was asleep, half in and half out of his sleeping bag, a worn, torn T-shirt twisted across his chest. I wondered what he did at night, that he could sleep until noon, one o'clock every day. I wondered if he was really asleep. Sometimes he'd say something, "No, no," or "Give me *that*," or, once, intriguingly, "I love," and then a mumble, a name no one would hear, if Kerem even knew it himself, all without opening his eyes. I turned on the Acorn Micro and got to work.

It came with no software, but the manufacturer, Acorn Systems of Akron, Ohio, which was, perhaps for this reason, never a big player in the personal-computer market, included a book of programs with the Acorn Micro kit. A book, a paper book, with programs you could type in, to play games, perform calculations, or sort a list of names in alphabetical order. Even the shortest program was many dozens of lines long, and stayed in the computer only until you switched the power off. If you wanted to run it again after that, you had to retype the whole thing. The work was excruciating, endless, monastic, exalting. If I typed a line wrong, the only way to correct my mistake was to type the entire line again; if I didn't catch it right away, the Acorn would bide its time, then ambush me with a syntax error when I tried to run the program. The screen was only tall enough to display twenty lines at a time, which meant that I had to check my work in tiny increments, looking for a typographical error that was sometimes to be found in the book itself. After a couple of hours Kerem woke up. He looked around the room and sighed, as though the people who were supposed to take care of the decor had once again let him down. "I fucking hate this place," he said. I pretended to work while he got himself out of the sleeping bag and stood at the window, hand thrust down the front of his underpants, scratching his balls. He was shameless and at ease; I, hunched over the keyboard, was embarrassed for him. He stalked to the bathroom and I heard him piss, then the water in the sink. When he came out, his hair was all on end; he pulled on the jeans he'd worn the night before and together we went downstairs. "Morning, Mum," Kerem said, forgetting that he was supposed to have been awake for hours. "You have a good lesson?" Mrs. Regenzeit asked. "Really good," I said. Kerem agreed that I was making progress. He jogged down the hill, kicking at rocks, dodging the invisible members of the opposing team; I went home and read one of the books I'd brought up from New York. I had discovered the classics of science fiction earlier that year, and my suitcase was full of novels by Robert A. Heinlein, Arthur C. Clarke, E. E. "Doc" Smith, A. E. van Vogt, and even, somewhat precociously, Samuel R. Delany, men whose stories etched themselves as indelibly on my mind as did their middle initials. I had a space suit; I could travel; I met Rama; I fought the Boskonians; I traveled in time and spoke with robots and cracked alien codes, none of which were as interesting to me now as the human code that came with the Acorn Micro. At dinner I listened impatiently as my grandfather read us the news from the morning's *Catskill Eagle*. Eastern Gas was laying a new main in Ashland. Police had chased a group of suspicious youths out of the cemetery. A collarless dog was loitering behind the Italian deli; the library was selling unwanted books to raise money for its new reading room. I helped my grandmother clear the table and wash up, then I went to the Regenzeits'. Kerem was listening to a tape he'd made off the radio, *The Monster Mash* from WARK, *The Saturday Night Stomp* from WRPU. He paced around his room, looking for something—a sock, a leather wristband. "Where are you going?" I asked. "None of your business," said Kerem. "Did you ever go to the graveyard?" Kerem glared at me. "Mate," he muttered, "stick to the box." He found what he was looking for and climbed out the window; the rubber cleats of his football shoes shushed down the garage roof. I worked at the computer until my eyes hurt; then I lay down on Kerem's sleeping bag and breathed in his reek, while green phosphenes swam across the orange land on the inside of my eyelids.

I was afraid that Mrs. Regenzeit would discover our trick, but she never did. She must have wanted badly to believe that the computer was working, that Kerem was working. How she believed! Sometimes, when I came over in the morning, I'd hear her talking on the phone about her son, the *whiz kid*. All the signs she'd read formerly as meaning that her son was in trouble now seemed to mean that he was a genius. He had messy hair, he wore the same clothes day after day, he didn't speak much, but on the computer he was something! I think Mrs. Regenzeit believed he was the equal of the young Bobby Fischer, or the boy in Florida who could solve any Rubik's Cube in a minute flat. I didn't mind that Kerem's genius was all my doing. I got to lie on his sleeping bag, I listened to his tapes, I shared his secret. What was better, what was even better, Kerem passed on to me a portion of the adoration he was getting from his parents. He was the *whiz kid*, but I was the wiz. One night he took me with him, down to the steps of the public library, which were broad, deep, and secluded. Eric had a battery-powered boom box and a collection of tapes he'd swiped from his older brother; we listened to Minor Threat and Murphy's Law, the Dead Kennedys and Big Black, and a live Sex Pistols recording Kerem had got from Billy, which had been copied and recopied until Johnny Rotten's call to the faithless was practically lost under the hiss of tape. Eric stopped the music each time we heard an engine, for fear that it would be one of Thebes's two patrol cars. I had my first swallow of beer, from a six-pack that Shelley had sweet-talked some college students into buying. I didn't like the taste and gave it back to Shelley, who told me that she hadn't liked it either, not until she really started smoking. We talked about what we would do if the world ended. "Like, if there was a nuclear war," Eric said, "but all the people up in the mountains were OK." "We'd still have democracy," Shelley said. "You can bet the people up here would keep it going." "Not bloody likely," said Kerem. "You wouldn't have television, so there couldn't be democracy. You can't have democracy without television." "You could still vote on stuff, though." "Television and the central bank," said Kerem, who had ordered some tracts from an ad in the back of one of his football magazines. "Without that, you have anarchy." "Anarchy!" My friends knocked their cans together. "What I think is, we would still be together," Shelley said. "No matter what other people were doing, you know?" We agreed that we would be anarchists together. Shelley would make our clothes, and Eric would provide our food, because his family had a farm farther up the valley, with cows and shit. Kerem would be the leader, because he knew the most about how anarchy was supposed to go. And I, "You'd be, like, my adviser,"

Kerem said. "You'd help me plan our takeover." Because we wouldn't be content to be isolated anarchists. We'd get other people to join; we'd spread anarchy all up and down the valley, and on the far side of the mountains. The apocalypse held no more fear for me that night. I leaned back against a brick column and closed my eyes, warm with the knowledge that I wouldn't ever have to be alone. "My adviser is falling asleep," Kerem said. "I better take him home." I wasn't falling asleep, though. I was thinking about a problem I'd encountered in the code.

3.

My magnum opus that summer was a game called, simply, Adventure. It was at the back of the book of programs that came with the computer, and I avoided it for weeks because it was much, much longer than any of the other programs, a thousand lines or more, an epic of code. It was written more densely than the other programs also, so that it was hard to figure out what the game was supposed to do. I read it over, and tried to make sense of the long DATA statements, the multidimensional arrays, the variables marked with unfamiliar signs, the complex string functions, the subroutines, all of which left me with the impression that the program was itself a kind of labyrinth. I started it only when I'd finished the list-sorting program and the program that was supposed to turn the keyboard into a piano, and in fact made it sound like a canary being tortured. For a long time, Adventure did nothing at all. With each line I fixed, a new error manifested itself, more cunning than the last one had been, better at hiding its true nature or appearing to be in one part of the program while in fact it was in an entirely different part. I was haunted by the thought that someone would turn the computer off before I was finished, or that there would be an accident, Kerem would trip over the power cord, a storm would blow down the lines that led to his house, a generator would fail, Russian missiles would arc over the horizon, civilization would collapse with Adventure still unfinished. I had stomach pains, dark circles under my eyes, and the beginnings of an irreversible stoop. My grandparents worried about me. "What's that Turk teaching you now?" my grandfather asked. He was tutoring me in science, I said, so that I could pass the entrance exam to Stuyvesant, a public school for talented children in New York City. "You want to go to public school?" All my friends were going, I said, and they were really, really smart. My grandfather knew I wasn't telling the truth, but thought I was covering for the Celestes, who had decided to send me to public school for perverse reasons of their own. My grandmother's questions were gentler and more astute. "So Kerem's good at science?" Oh, yes, I said. He's a whiz kid. "I'm glad to hear it," my grandmother said. "I heard he was in trouble." She let the subject drop, but—and this was my grandmother's usual strategy—she returned to it days and even weeks later, hoping to catch me off guard. "You'd know," she said, looking up from the Sunday newspaper. "How does oxygen become ozone?" Or, as she trimmed bushes in the backyard, "Maybe you can tell me. Are these little critters going to turn into butterflies?" But I had learned something from Kerem. "Ung," I said, studying the green squiggles that scurried across the underside of a leaf. I discovered, as he must have a few years before, that adults didn't expect me to make sense. "Go eat something," my grandmother said. "You're as gray as a pencil sketch." I slouched off. Days and nights passed, and strange things happened, marvelous things, that would have filled me with wonder if I had been able to pay attention to them, although really, if I had been able to pay attention to them, they probably wouldn't have happened at all. Here I was, tiptoeing out of my grandparents' house, crossing the lawn in socks because I was afraid my grandmother would hear my shoes crushing the grass. Here, here, here I am, in Kerem's room, almost cross-eyed, when Kerem and Shelley come in. Kerem puts his finger to his lips. He whispers something in Shelley's ear. She stands behind me, she leans forward and rests her chin on my shoulder. "What is that?" she asks. "Game," I say. Shelley digs her thumbs into the base of my neck and I almost scream. "Wow, tight shoulders." Shelley rubs my back until Kerem tugs her away. They murmur behind me, they rustle. I hear the high swish of the sleeping bag. Shelley giggles, tickled, and Kerem hisses, "Ssh!" And here I am, in my own bed, in the little room, laughing because I'm wearing all my clothes and one of Kerem's sweatshirts, it's eleven o'clock in the morning, and I have no idea why.

Then it was finished. Something gave, something moved, something opened. Run, I could say, and it would run. Nothing flashed across the screen, no dancing letters, no space invaders, no canary cries or ping-pong pings. Only words.

Entrance to Cave.
You are standing outside a dark and gloomy cave.
There is a gold key here.

66

>

I had made a world. Not a large world, not even, from any reasonable point of view, an interesting world, but a world nonetheless. Compared to the work of getting the program to run, the adventure of Adventure was absurdly simple. You typed,

>take key

and took the key; you went into the gloomy cave and crossed the subterranean river at the ford, you found the sword, surprised the troll, and navigated the maze where all the rooms looked exactly alike. You entered the castle, you read the note, you opened the secret door and found the locked treasure chest. Did you have the gold key? You did, you did! The castle, the maze, the troll, the river, and the cave were the whole of my kingdom, but they were, to my mind, like a kaleidoscope, like one of the holograms pressed into a tiny button or pin, where, as you turn it in your hands, a three-dimensional pattern seems to repeat itself in infinite space. I saw not what was there but what could be there, if only I had written it, a world of rooms where I would be free to wander as I pleased. It was as though the gray box had been working in secret to fulfill my oldest dream about its powers, although, like many dreams, the coming true bore only a metaphorical or tangential relation to the dream itself. Yes, I could know all, do all, create and destroy at my whim, I could make subways and strand my enemies within them, yes, everything, yes, only I would have to do it in the gray box. It was enough. It was too much to take in; after I had unlocked the treasure chest and won the game twice, I needed to tell someone what I had done. I found Kerem with Shelley and Eric, at the gas station, talking to some older teenagers in a rust-bottomed Ford pickup. "Hey, Kerem!" He waved me away. I sat by the air pump and waited for him to come back, and he came, hands clasped in the pocket of his sweatshirt, smiling wolfishly. I told him that I'd done it, Adventure was working. "Oh?" Kerem frowned at me, as though he'd expected me to say something completely different. "That's so cool," Shelley said. "Can I play?" She asked me and not Kerem. I said it was just a little game; she might not think it was that fun. "But you made it. That's what's cool." I mumbled something about having only typed the program in from a book. "Yeah, OK," Kerem said, shaking his head as though he had just figured out that we were talking to him, which we weren't. "Yeah, that's great. We're all going to play." Before the power goes out, I said. "Right. You, wow." Shelley put her head very close to mine and whispered, "We're a little stoned." She squeezed my arm. I knew almost nothing about drugs, only that the Celestes had smoked marijuana at some point when I was very little, and that one of Older Celeste's fellow teachers, a painter named Larry who looked as though he were made out of wax, had a problem with cocaine, although what this problem was, and how it manifested itself, I couldn't begin to guess. I nodded gravely, as though Shelley had told me that the three of them had contracted a life-threatening disease. Their lives had become more serious, suddenly, and also more exciting. They would probably die. But secretly, if their being stoned meant that I got to have Shelley's breath in my ear, I was all for it. Eric was hopping in tiny circles around the air pump. "Are you going to tell him?" Shelley asked Kerem. "Shelley's brother is having a party," Kerem said. "We're all going to go, OK?" "We're going to have a great time," Shelley said. She still hadn't let go of my arm. I said, "OK." Consequences were whirling around me in a cloud of great seriousness. If, and if, else if, else. Then. Then. Then.

4.

You are standing at the entrance to a dark and gloomy cave. Ahead of you, in the darkness, there is music. "You're OK?" Kerem asks. "Just be cool, and if anything happens that you don't like, come find me. OK?" Say OK. "Let's go-oo," Shelley moans. You follow Kerem and Shelley and Eric into the cave. You're in Shelley's brother's apartment, on the second floor of an apartment complex at the far end of Thebes, the bad end, by the storage facility and the graveyard. There are many people here, and you don't know any of them, although some of their faces are familiar from town. There's the guy who works at the dismal grocery store, and there's one of the guys from the ski shop. You associate them so closely with those places that seeing them here is like being in a dream, where heads are pasted on new bodies and one city borrows the name of another. What's more, everyone in the room is twice your size. Shelley has gone off to talk to her brother, and Eric is talking to the grocery-store guy. Only Kerem stays with you, and only because he doesn't know anyone here, any more than you do. "Let's get some beers," he says. Follow Kerem. You follow him into the kitchen, which is, if anything, even more crowded than the living room. You are pressed by waists, hips. Girls in tall vinyl boots are laughing. Men are looking at you; they want to know what you are doing here. Kerem opens the refrigerator and gets a can of beer for himself and one for you. It tastes as awful as the last time, but you hope that if you are seen drinking, people may mistake you for a midget or a late-blooming fifteen-year-old. Kerem says something to you, but everyone is talking at once and you can't understand him. He waves, he is leaving you, he is gone. You are alone in the forest of giants. "Hi," says a girl with vast blonde hair. "What's your name?" Say your name. "How old are you?" Lie. "Do you live in Thebes?" In New York, you say. "Oh, wow, that's really great." You tell the tall girl about New York. She screams, "Mike!" and one of the giants turns around. "I want you to meet my new friend." "Hey." Mike tips his beer toward you. "Hey," you say, and tip your beer toward Mike. "He's from New York," the tall girl says. This is good, Mike no longer looks at you as if you were a pituitary oddity. For all he knows, everyone in New York looks like this. It might be something in the drinking water. Keep people small to make the housing more efficient. "The big city," Mike says. "I love it. Wish I got there more often." "It's not very far away," you say, emboldened. "There's a bus. It's like two and a half hours, and it goes right to the Port Authority." Mike grimaces. You didn't need to tell him about the bus. You turn to the tall girl, hoping for reassurance. "Do you, uh, ever go to the city?" She shrugs as though now she doesn't know what city you're talking about. "Or do you mostly stay up here in Thebes?" You have come to a dead end. Find Kerem. You look for him in the living room, but there are too many big people; if you go into that crowd you may never come back out. You end up perched on the back of a sofa next to a kid with stripes shaved in his hair, who is willing to talk to you about the Dead Kennedys. "I kind of like the lyrics," you say. "Like, you know, too drunk to fuck? That's funny." The kid looks at you. "Have you ever fucked?" "No," you admit. There is a lull in your conversation. "Have you?" The kid shrugs. "I think so." Much later, you'll understand that this is what Mrs. Regenzeit meant by *not his whole head*, and you will laugh and wish you could tell her that there is nothing to fear from the partially shaved. You excuse yourself, you have to pee. You wait on line for the bathroom. Shelley is here. "Oh my God," she says, "it's you!" She takes your hand. "I am so happy to see you." Her eyes are red. "I just don't feel like I ever got a chance to know you," she says, "and I think you're probably a really great person." She tells you how few great people there are in the world, and how her ambition is to own a big farmhouse somewhere in the mountains and to get them all together, the great people, in a big sleeping loft in the barn and, like, talk. The bathroom door opens. "Don't go away," Shelley says. She goes in, she comes out, you go in. You have never peed so quickly in your life. But she's gone when you come out, and you can't find her again. You go back into the kitchen. Three boys are sitting at the table, taking turns throwing a quarter into a glass of beer. If the quarter goes in, they drink; if it doesn't go in, they drink. One of them is dangerously overweight and appears to have been dipped in oil. He takes the quarter out of the glass and licks it on both sides. "You want to play?" he asks. This is a game with no victory conditions. The rooms lead only to other rooms, and there is no treasure in any of them and no way out of the cave once you have gone in. You can't remember ever having been as sad as you are now. Leave the world. You can't leave that. Go. Where do you want to go? The kitchen is full of smoke, and there's no place for you to sit, and you suspect that people are looking at you again, thinking midget thoughts. You find a door that leads out to a balcony. From here you can see the graveyard, the upslope of the ski hill, the stars. A few people Mike's size are leaning on the railing and talking. They pay no attention to you. You sit on the ground with your back to the wall. You are suddenly very tired. You fall asleep.

Time passes. . . . Lightning wakes you up. A storm has crossed into the valley, the wind hisses through the trees across the road. Beyond the roof's overhang, rain falls in sheets. The big people have gone inside, sensibly. The thunder breaks over you, then the lightning, then the thunder again. You would be happy to stay here all night, watching the weather. Then Shelley finds you. "Thank God," she says. "I thought you might have left." She sits next to you and takes your hand. "I'm so glad Kerem brought you. He's sweet." You agree. "Do you think he likes me?" Shelley asks. "Definitely." Shelley rests her head on your shoulder. "It's just so hard, you know?" Shelley complains that Kerem has been avoiding her; she's afraid that he drinks too much and smokes too much pot. You aren't sure you should hear these things, but the storm has cooled the air and it's good to be sitting next to someone warm. "You know what I think the problem is really?" says Shelley. "Thebes is so small. There's only, like, four or five places to go. And then, if you want to do something else . . . " "You have to write new code," you say. Shelley looks at you solemnly. "You're very interesting," she says.

"I want to know more about you." You wish there was something you could tell her, but when you think of yourself, only stupid things come to mind. "I'm pretty much a book person," you say. Shelley laughs. "You're so grown up." Lightning. "Wait," Shelley says. She gets up and sits down facing you. "Kiss me," Shelley says. You would like to, but you don't know how. Shelley presses her hands to your cheeks, immobilizing your head. Suddenly her tongue is in your mouth. Her eyes are closed; you stare at the smudges where her eye shadow used to be. "Mmm," Shelley says and lets go of your head. "You're a good kisser." Compared to what, you wonder, like, robots? "Don't tell Kerem." Shelley goes inside. After a minute, you follow her. The shiny boy is still in the kitchen, resting his chins on his hands, staring at a half-full glass of beer. "Your turn," he says. The living room is ruined; human beings will never live here again. Shelley and Kerem are here, and they don't look happy. "Where were you?" Kerem asks. "He was on the balcony," says Shelley. "Jesus!" Kerem says. "I've been looking for you all night." "I fell asleep," you say, truthfully enough. "How come you didn't tell me he was on the balcony?" Kerem says to Shelley. "I didn't know where you were," Shelley says. What is this? The storm seems to have followed you in; the air is prickly, electric, charged with potential consequences. What if Kerem guesses that you and Shelley kissed? What if Shelley tells him? You don't like this logic. "He could have gotten hurt," Kerem says. "Mike's friends are creeps." Shelley shrugs. "He's fine, OK?" "I'm responsible for him," Kerem says, though he doesn't look responsible. His face is greenish and his hair has fallen back into its old curls. Visibly, he needs help. Help Kerem. But how do you do that? You're just a child, a clever child, but still a child, and so you shout, "I'm going home!" and you open the door. It will be a very long time before you understand how tricky this adventure is and know that the door you left by that night was not the same door you came in. Years will pass before you see it, and then you'll wish that you could retrace your steps, but your map is no good and there are too many rooms and even if you could come back to this door, which you open effortlessly now, there is no guarantee that it would be the door you are looking for, or that you would undo anything by going through it. Now, however, there is only the wind. It pushes you up the street like a downed leaf. You run, and when you look back, you see that Kerem is running after you. "Stop!" he shouts, but you don't stop. You run up the hill as fast as you can, the wind very strong at your back, so that it seems as though you're flying. Of course Kerem catches you. When you're almost home, doubled over and out of breath, he grabs your shoulder and presses you against a soaking tree. "Promise me you won't tell anyone what you did tonight," he says. You promise, you never will. The next morning you learn that the storm knocked down a power line, and Adventure is gone. It doesn't matter. You have already won. Did you kiss Shelley? You did, you did!

A Secret Life
Rikki Ducornet

GRETEL'S FATHER WAS VIENNESE, as was his father, and his father's father before him. They looked alike, and Gretel took after them. Gretel's favorite pastime was to ponder their portraits in the family album. She appreciated the fact that they all lived well into their nineties, and were—as was Gretel—shaped like pears. When among her peers she lagged behind on her bike, or proved unable to scale a tree, Gretel recalled the sturdy paternal line and was assured that, if her life was unexceptional, it would last a long time. For this reason her appetite was good, even exemplary. She appreciated the *wurstels* and *schlagobers* her mother, an American, had taken pains to master. She slept without dreaming, was well behaved, punctual, without ambition, tidy. She liked doing things for her papa, such as fetching his rolled paper from the front stoop and, on wash days, folding his socks. When he trimmed his moustache, she watched and saw to it that no hair fell on the soap.

Her father had come to America as a boy, but had never left Vienna in his mind. He extolled her qualities whenever he could: the café counters piled high with cake, the many preparations for cabbage, the incessant, merry ringing of tram bells. He told of how he had often been beaten with bundles of switches, and that an infamous Viennese Jew named Freud had been born with a mane of coal black hair.

Gretel liked it when her father told her she was a *model Viennese;* she liked it when he chucked her playfully beneath her rounded chin or pinched a dimpled cheek. A *model Viennese,* she did her papa's bidding gladly. Should she disgrace herself, she'd turn her back to him, lift her skirt, and, without a whimper, wait for the smack. When over the evening bratwurst it was announced that they would be setting off for Vienna as soon as school was out, Gretel became so pink her mother feared a fever and gave her a tall glass of iced licorice water to sip slowly. A few days later her father presented her with a pocket diary in which to inscribe her thoughts each day. Because the pages were illustrated with things Viennese—a *dudelsack* (or Austrian bagpipe), the Austro-American Institute, the university chemical laboratory—there was room for only a very brief thought.

That night, buttoned up in her flannel pajamas, and this despite the mildness of the weather, Gretel took up a stub of pencil and wrote, with letters so round and pale they might have been inscribed in bubble bath:

WE SHALL GO TO VIENNA WHERE
PAPA WAS BORN AND WHERE HIS
PAPA WAS BORN. TONIGHT WE
ATE BRATWURST.

From the first instant, Vienna delighted Gretel. She took to the equestrian statuary, the bronze river gods spouting water, the beer gardens where her father surprised her by drinking a great deal of beer. Their hotel, der Dudelsack, on the corner of Angstneurose-strasse and der Minderwertiggasse, provided liberal boxes of ham sandwiches and salami, and these they trotted about on their daily excursions. Gretel saw with satisfaction that the Viennese ladies whom her father acknowledged with approving glances were all plump. She admired der Dudelsack's restaurant, its beams as black as her father's tortoiseshell glasses, and above all, its napkins that lay weightily on one's lap and knees. The napkins were rolled and folded into irresistible shapes: crowns and roses, dunce caps and boats, palm trees and flutes.

They ate

NOODLES WITH MELTED BUTTER
AND NUTMEG. BREADED VEAL.

They ate plenty of breaded veal in Vienna and pastries bloated with *schlagobers*. They ate pigs' knuckles and at the opera cracked their hard-boiled eggs on the chair backs of the persons in front of them. Her mother assured her that the shells would be swept up later; indeed, she had seen a young girl in an apron standing in the shadows with her broom. In the meantime, Gretel could enjoy *The Magic*

BUSINESS REPLY MAIL

FIRST CLASS MAIL PERMIT NO. 1 ANNANDALE-ON-HUDSON, NY

POSTAGE WILL BE PAID BY ADDRESSEE

CONJUNCTIONS

Bard College
Annandale-on-Hudson
P.O. Box 9911
Red Hook, NY 12571-9911

CONJUNCTIONS Give a subscription to yourself and a friend!

Your subscription:	Gift subscription (with a gift card from you enclosed):
Name	Name
Address	Address
City	City
State Zip	State Zip

☐ One year (2 issues) **$18**	☐ One year (2 issues) **$18**
☐ Two years (4 issues) **$32**	☐ Two years (4 issues) **$32**
☐ Renewal ☐ New order	☐ Renewal ☐ New order

All foreign and institutional orders $25 per year, payable in U.S. funds.

☐ Payment enclosed   ☐ Bill me   Charge my: ☐ Mastercard   ☐ Visa

Account number _____   Expiration date _____

Signature _____

Flute, smartly crack her egg, and hold it, clean and cool, in her palm against her cheek, before taking a nice big bite.

After the opera, they each had a slice of layer cake, spread with raspberry jam and glazed with bittersweet chocolate. Noodles, breaded veal, boiled eggs, chocolate cake—it was altogether too much. Until very late, Gretel was agitated.

Although Vienna is in the throes of an early summer, Gretel is up to her neck in flannels and a feather comforter. Beneath her foams a feather bed. An hour passes, then another. She is thinking of der Dudelsack's lovely linen tablecloths and those elusive napkins—so artfully pleated and tucked, with creases so deep that when she dips her fingers into them, they vanish. And she wonders: Who spends her days in the pantry folding napkins? Who trained her? Is there an academy in Vienna where girls are taught the art of napkin folding? And now:

Gretel imagines them. Row after row of model Viennese girls in their pinafores at their little desks, each one with her iron in hand and a snowy napkin. They have been at it so long the tips of their fingers, the knobs of their knuckles, are sore, and their bottoms, too. And should a girl cause an unintentional crease, she is scolded by the Mistress of Napkin Folding Herself, told to lift her skirts, and, utterly exposed, is smartly smacked.

Sandwiched between her feather bed and comforter, Gretel's world is heating up so fast she thinks she is very like a fat dumpling, round and white and steaming hot. Rolled in sugar, she ignites.

In her fever dream she presses napkins with astounding dexterity—or so she thinks, her little desk piled high. Ah! But no! The Mistress of Napkin Folding, as thin and black as a poker, has seized her by an ear. Within the instant, Gretel is tossed over her bony knee and smacked.

"I told you to make the 'Javanese Temple!'" the Mistress of Napkin Folding booms as the other girls titter (although some, recalling past humiliations, are quietly weeping). "Not the 'Pig in the Poke!' Take this! And that! And this! And that! From this day on, naughty Gretel, you will never forget the Mistress of Napkin Folding!"

Morning comes. Gretel is roused by her papa, who must violently shake her. "The flannels," he scolds her mother, "are far too hot for summer! See what a state our Gretel is in!" Sentenced to silence for the rest of the morning, her mother bows her head.

Gretel is made to take a cooling bath. Dressed in a crisp Viennese pinafore and apron—an outfit that, should she wear it to school in the fall, will elicit hoots of laughter—she cautiously descends the waxed stairs that twist and turn downward into der Dudelsack's dining room. She breakfasts on cheese and tongue and fruit and sweet rolls and cucumbers—the whole washed down with bowls of chicory. Unlike the ones at dinner, the breakfast napkins are neatly pressed into triangles. Their folds are deep, and Gretel slides her fingers inside and out of them. Is there a waiter? A waitress? In later years she will have no memory of them, but only of her papa waiting for her to finish her breakfast, his hands wedged beneath his buttocks. She hates to see him sitting thus. An odd habit. Sometimes her papa's behavior is incomprehensible. For example, he has bought himself a pipe. He alone smokes it, yet Gretel's mother keeps the pipe cleaners and tobacco in her purse.

Gretel's father is eager to visit der Allgemeines Krankenhaus, to see for himself if it is, indeed, the largest hospital on the continent. It is fortunate for both Gretel and her mother that an irritable bureaucrat will not allow them access to the Krankenhaus's forty acres. Off they fly instead to a manufactory of barometers, where they are left to journey an immense room in which barometers, thousands of them, are set out on tables as far as the eye can see. Barometers are also suspended from the ceiling and walls. Some look like birdhouses with porches; others like the castles one encounters in fish tanks.

Depending on the inscrutable workings of the weather, either a little lady—dressed as Gretel is dressed—or a little man will appear all alone on a porch or a castle balcony. Or it is a priest or a devil, Adam or Eve, Saint George or the dragon, Jesus in the cradle or crucified, a plate of sausage or a plate of fish. As her parents are unable to decide, they are directed to a manufactory of cuckoo clocks just down the street, where Gretel is at once impressed by a minute circle of Viennese schoolgirls who, at the sound of chimes ringing the hour, slide out from a tiny garden gate and circumvent the clock's face and inner workings—cleverly hidden from view. After a brief discussion, her parents buy a clock of the classic sort, sporting a cuckoo with, or so Gretel thinks, an unforgivably stupid expression on its face.

They have just enough time to return to the barometers before supper, where they purchase a dour little couple condemned to a lifetime of simultaneous isolation and proximity for, Gretel realizes with a shudder, they can never be in the same place at the same time.

Although the rigors of the day have thoroughly exhausted Gretel, still she polishes off her cutlet and, before falling asleep, the Mistress of Napkin Folding exacts a full measure of punishment.

The next day Gretel and her parents visit a nearby castle in which are displayed saltcellars dating from the eighteenth century. One of these takes its inspiration from the sea; its three fused cups sit on a bed of coral, and the shell at its crown serves as a handle. The arrangement evokes a particularly fanciful folded napkin; its shells and cups clamor to be touched. When next day they come upon rows of finger bowls, Gretel nearly swoons.

"Hand washing," her mother speaks with evident nostalgia and for the first time that day, "was once a sort of ceremony."

The impact of the word "ceremony" on Gretel's imagination is phenomenal; it quickens her.

"Only the fingertips," her mother murmurs, lost in a dream of her own, "should touch the water."

An extensive collection of snuffboxes, some made to look like figs with hinges, precipitate a new set of private associations. Gretel's precocious interest in antiquities causes her parents to nod at one another with satisfaction.

Before leaving the castle, they climb its tower to admire the view of the Danube and surrounding hills and planes from the Alps to the Carpathians. As her papa sputters with nostalgia the world shivers in its haze beneath them. In later years Gretel will recall the immense silence of the moment although, in fact, birds are rioting in the trees, and on the tower stairs, tourists, and in her father's pockets, coins. The afternoon ends at a haberdasher's, where, as Gretel furtively fingers a pleated dickey, her father buys himself a hat ornamented with a miniature whisk.

That evening, bathed in the eternal twilight of der Dudelsack's opaline ceiling lamps, Gretel does not notice her father's voice rolling around the room like a great suet pudding. She does not notice the voices of the other diners, nor the music that is being played at the far end of the room. She does not covet the edelweiss stuck in its little flute of glass. Yet a disapproving glance suffices to keep her from toying with her napkin and, again, from prodding her delicately folded sweetbread turnover with the little golden spoon intended for the after-dinner demitasse. And when the dessert omelet overtakes the table as though a cumulus cloud had chosen to squat there, she gasps with surprise.

The academy is now the size of a castle. Blazing like ice beneath the moon, it sits smack on a black needle of stone. A place of blizzards, high winds, tumultuous weather. Impossible to reach; impossible to escape. A castle, yes, sitting high in the sky and yet the sun never seems to reach it. Below, far below in the summer meadows, the sun shines, but not here. An ancient place, its clocks are hexed. Time moves back and forth in two directions only. *Dawn!* the cuckoo cries once and then, within the instant: *dusk!*

The castle is grand, yet has no central heating, no elevator or baths. Only spare faucets of scalding water for which the girls scramble in the dark before being confronted by a breakfast that they are forbidden to touch. Indeed, the castle is mined with explosive temptations that, despite the dangers, are impossible to resist. Hungry and improperly washed, the girls stand in their thin pinafores and buttoned boots to weather the day's instructions.

The castle's interior unfolds onto marble halls and deep stairwells. There are sooty kitchens where maidens in spotless aprons are threatened with undisclosed vicissitudes. Here: a door opens to reveal a perpetual theater where instructive tableaux are staged. There: chastened maidens sweep between spankings. Across the hall, the library's heavy ledgers record each infraction in thick black ink. And on every floor are rooms where lessons are taught: The correct use of starch. Pipe cleaners. Spoons. (It does not occur to Gretel to consider the castle cellars, its dungeons, and crypts. The upper castle alone suffices.)

It is rumored that beyond the moat and thickets a park lies hidden. An obelisk and a grotto are cradled in the hedges. Should Gretel manage to escape the castle and reach the park, she will discover a small garden gate overgrown with briars. A gentle push, the briars fall away, and she is released from the castle's inexorable cogs and gears. Gretel descends a nearly perpendicular path and, looking down, sees the twinkling lights of the city.

That night when Gretel's papa steals a look at his daughter's diary, he is perplexed by an emblematic yet somehow expressive series of associations:

BEE ROSE IRIS LILY FLUTE CRAB
PALMTREE TAPER BOAT JAVANESE
TEMPLE OBELISK GROTTO

—and a line (does he recognize Horace?) taken from a clock or a barometer, perhaps, or possibly, a snuffbox:

Here find a hid recess where
Life's revolving day
In sweet delusion softly
Steals away . . .

Three Essays
David Shields

OUR BIRTH IS NOTHING BUT OUR DEATH BEGUN

HUMAN BEINGS HAVE EXISTED for 250,000 years; during that time, ninety billion individuals have lived and died. You're one of 6.5 billion people now on the planet, and 99.9 percent of your genes are the same as everyone else's. The difference is in the remaining 0.1 percent—one nucleotide base in every thousand.

You're born with 350 bones (long, short, flat, and irregular); as you grow, the bones fuse together: an adult's body has 206 bones. Approximately seventy percent of your body weight is water—which is about the same percentage of the earth's surface that is water.

A newborn baby, whose average heart rate is 120 beats per minute, makes the transition from a comfortable, fluid-filled environment to a cold, air-filled one by creating a suction fifty times stronger than the average adult breath. I was a breech birth, the danger of which is that the head—in this case, my head—comes out last, which dramatically increases the possibility that the umbilical cord will get wrapped around the neck—in this case, my neck. I entered the world feet first, then remained in the hospital an extra week to get a little R&R in a warm incubator that my father guarded like a goalie whenever anyone came within striking distance. If I laid still for more than a few minutes, my father reportedly pounded on the glass dome. I wasn't dead. I was only sleeping. All my life I've told myself I sought a cold, air-filled environment (danger), but really what I'm drawn to is that comfortable, fluid-filled environment (safety).

A baby is, objectively, no beauty. The fat pads that will fill out the cheeks are missing. The jaws are unsupported by teeth. Hair, if there is any, is often so fine as to make the baby appear bald. Cheesy material—called vernix caseosa—covers the body, providing a protective material for the skin, which is reddened, moist, and deeply creased. Swelling formed by pressure during the passage through the birth canal may have temporarily deformed the nose, caused one or both eyes to swell up, or elongated the head into a strange shape. The skull is incompletely formed; in some places, the bones haven't fully joined together, leaving the brain covered by only soft tissue. External genitalia in both sexes are disproportionately large due to stimulation by the mother's hormones. For the same reason, the baby's breasts may be somewhat enlarged and secrete a watery discharge called "witch's milk." The irises are pale blue; true eye color develops later. The head is very large in proportion to the body, and the neck can't support it, while the buttocks are tiny.

The average baby weighs 7¼ pounds and is twenty-one inches long. Newborns lose five to eight percent of their birth weight in the first few days of life—mainly due to water loss. They can hear little during the first twenty-four hours until air enters the eustachian tubes. They miss the womb and resent any stimulation. They will suck anything placed in or near their mouth. Their eyes wander and cross. Their body temperature is erratic and their breathing is often irregular.

At one month, a baby can wobble its head and practice flexing its arms and legs. At two months, it can face straight ahead while lying on its back. On its stomach, it can lift its head about forty-five degrees. At three months, a baby's neck muscles are strong enough to support its head for a second or two.

Babies are born with brains twenty-five percent of adult size, because the mechanics of walking upright impose a constraint on the size of the mother's pelvis. The channel through which the baby is born can't get any bigger. The baby's brain quickly makes up for that initial constraint: by age one, the brain is seventy-five percent of adult size.

Infants have accurate hearing up to forty thousand cycles per second and may wince at a dog whistle that adults, who can't register sounds above twenty thousand cycles per second, don't even notice. Your ear contains sensory hair cells, which turn mechanical fluid energy inside the cochlea into electrical signals that can be picked up by nerve cells; these electrical signals are delivered to the brain and allow you to hear. Beginning at puberty, these hair cells begin to disappear, decreasing your ability to hear specific frequencies; higher tones are the first to go.

A newborn's hands tend to be held closed, but if the area between the thumb and forefinger is stroked, the hand clenches and holds on with sufficient strength to support the baby's weight if both hands are grasping. This innate "grasp reflex" serves no purpose in the human infant but was crucial in the last prehuman phase of evolution when the infant had to cling to its mother's hair.

David Shields

According to Midrash, the ever-evolving commentary upon the Hebrew scriptures, when you arrive in the world as a baby, your hands are clenched as though to say, "Everything is mine. I will inherit it all." When you depart from the world, your hands are open, as though to say, "I have acquired nothing from the world."

Similarly, if a baby is dropped, an immediate change from the usual curled posture occurs, as all four extremities are flung out in extension. The "startle reflex," or "embrace reflex," probably once served to help a simian mother catch a falling infant by causing it to spread out as fully as possible.

When my daughter, Natalie, was born, I cried, and my wife, Laurie, didn't—too busy. One minute, we were in the hospital room, holding hands and reading magazines, and the next, Laurie looked at me, with a commanding seriousness I'd never seen in her before, and said, "Put down the magazine." Natalie emerged, smacking her lips, and I asked the nurse to reassure me that this didn't indicate diabetes (I'd been reading too many parent-to-be manuals). I vowed I would never again think a trivial or stupid or selfish thought; this exalted state didn't last, but still.

The Kogi Indians believe that when an infant begins life, it knows only three things: mother, night, and water.

Francis Thompson wrote, "For we are born in other's pain, / And perish in our own." Edward Young wrote, "Our birth is nothing but our death begun." The first sentence of Vladimir Nabokov's *Speak, Memory* is: "The cradle rocks above an abyss, and common sense tells us that our existence is but a brief crack of light between two eternities of darkness."

Much mentioned but rarely discussed: the tissue-thin separation between existence and non-: in 1919, at age nine, my father and his friends were crossing train tracks in Brooklyn when my father, last in line, stepped directly on the third rail, which transformed him from a happy vertical child into a horizontal conductor of electric current. The train came rattling down the tracks toward Miltie Schildkraut, who, lying flat on his back, was powerless to prevent his own, self-induced electrocution. I wouldn't be here today, typing this sentence, if someone named Big Abe, a seventeen-year-old wrestler who wore black shirts and a purple hat, hadn't slid a long piece of dry wood between galvanized little Miltie and the third rail, flipping him high into the air only seconds before the train passed. My father was bruised about the elbows and knees and, later in summer, was a near corpse as flesh turned red, turned pink, turned black, and peeled away to lean white bone. Toenails and fingernails crumbled and what little hair he had on his body was shed until Miltie himself had nearly vanished. His father sued Long Island Rail Road for one hundred dollars, which paid—no more, no less—for the doctor's visits once a week to check for infection.

Lady Astor, the first woman member of British Parliament, surrounded by her entire family on her deathbed, said, "Am I dying, or is this my birthday?"

PARADISE, SOON LOST

Natalie is celebrating her ninth birthday with twelve of her closest friends at Skate King, a rollerblading rink in Bellevue, a suburb fifteen minutes from Seattle. The lights are low. The mirror ball glitters. The music crescendos every thirty seconds. The bathrooms are labeled *Kings* and *Queens.* Teenage girls, wearing rollerblades, look as if they're on high heels. Wearing high heels forces women to throw back their shoulders and arch their backs, making their breasts look bigger, their stomachs flatter, and their buttocks more rounded and thrust out; their legs appear more toned and elongated—the shape of a leg tensed by arousal.

Several of Natalie's friends buy Best Friends split necklaces: one girl wears one half while her best friend wears the other. There's quite a competition for certain girls. Natalie's best friend, Amanda, asks the DJ to play a Michelle Branch song, and when it comes on, Amanda beams.

Seeing the lights go off, all the younger girls rush onto the rink. They like the dark setting, which makes them feel less noticeable, and yet Natalie and several of her friends are wearing orange glow sticks. So they don't want their bodies to be noticed, but they do want their bodies to be noticed. This, I want to say, is the crux of the matter.

The girls skate backward. Then they skate in the regular direction. After a while they do the limbo. The DJ plays the standards: "I Will Survive," "Gloria," "YMCA," "Stayin' Alive"; Madonna, 'N Sync, Backstreet Boys, Usher. Some of Natalie's friends buy plastic roses for themselves. Two teenaged kids are feverishly making out in a far corner. Duly noted by management and quickly remedied.

David Shields

As the father of a daughter who loves Skate King, I find the place utterly terrifying. It's all about amplifying kids' sense of themselves as magical creatures and converting that feeling into sexual yearning—a group march toward future prospects. In the dark, Natalie holds Amanda's hand and, as she calls it, "lip-sings" to Aaron Carter. For Natalie and her friends, still, just barely, the purpose of Skate King is to dream about the opposite sex without having to take these romantic feelings seriously, let alone act on them.

The last song of the afternoon is "The Hokey Pokey," which, the DJ explains to me, "adults don't care for." Of course adults don't care for it. You wind up having to put your whole body in. What—Natalie and her friends are wondering—could that possibly consist of?

Girls develop breast buds between eight and ten years old, and full breasts between ages twelve and eighteen. Girls get their first pubic hair, armpit hair, and leg hair between ages nine and ten, and they develop adult patterns of this hair between ages thirteen and fourteen. I once heard statutory rape defended by the phrase "If there's grass on the field, play ball." In 1830, girls typically got their first period when they were seventeen. Due to improvements in nutrition, general health, and living conditions, the average age is now twelve.

The average menstrual period is a little over twenty-nine days. The moon's cycle of phases is 29.53 days. According to Darwin, menstruation is linked to the moon's influence on tidal rhythms, a legacy of our origin in the sea. For lemurs, estrus and sex tend to occur when there's a full moon.

At age nine or ten, a boy's scrotum and testicles enlarge and his penis lengthens; at age seventeen, his penis has adult size and shape. Boys' pubic hair, armpit hair, leg hair, chest hair, and facial hair start at age twelve, with adult patterns of the hair emerging at fifteen. First ejaculation usually occurs at age twelve or thirteen; at fourteen, most boys have a wet dream once every two weeks. I've forgotten the names of nearly everyone I went to junior high school with, but I'll never forget Pam Glinden or Joanne Liebes—best friends, bad girls, reputed "drug addicts"—to whose yearbook photos I masturbated throughout eighth grade. At the time, this activity seemed magical, private, perverse, unique, all-important; it wasn't; it was blood flowing through me that, at some point in the not entirely unforeseeable future (eighteen thousand days, say, at the outside), will no longer flow. "The difference between sex and death," explains Woody Allen, "is that with death you can do it alone and no one's going to make fun of you."

Boys are heavier and taller than girls because they have a longer growth period. The growth spurt in boys occurs between thirteen and sixteen; a gain of four inches can be expected in the peak year. For girls, the growth spurt begins at eleven, may reach three inches in the peak year, and is almost completed by fourteen. At eighteen, three-fourths of an inch of growth remains for boys and slightly less for girls, for whom growth is ninety-nine percent complete. Between ages fifteen and eighteen I grew from five feet four inches to six feet one inch; I still visualize myself being small.

When Natalie was two, Laurie and I were putting on Natalie's clothes to take her to day care. She cried crazily, complaining that the clothes were the wrong clothes—this was the wrong color, that was too tight. She kept saying, "Mine, mine, mine." Afterward, I asked Laurie what she thought Natalie was trying to tell us, and Laurie said, "She meant, 'These limbs, these legs, these arms: they're mine. Don't do this to my body. It's my body.'"

RATTLESNAKE LAKE

Testosterone initiates the growth spurt; increases larynx size, deepening the voice; increases red blood cell mass, muscle mass, libido; stimulates development of the penis, scrotum, and prostate; stimulates growth of pubic, facial, leg, and armpit hair; stimulates sebaceous gland secretions of oil. Throughout high school, my acne was so severe as to constitute a second skin; oil leaked from my pores; I kissed no one until I was seventeen.

Acne flourished on my chin, forehead, cheeks, temples, and scalp, and behind my ears. It burned my neck, appeared sporadically on my penis, visited my stomach, and wrapped around my back and buttocks. It was like an unwilling, monotonous tattoo. There were whiteheads on the nose, blackheads on toes, dense purple collections that finally burst with blood, white circles that vanished in a squeeze, dilating welts that never went away, infected wounds that cut to the bone, surface scars that looked hideous, wartlike protuberances at the side of the head. I endured collagen injections, punch grafts, and chemical peels.

I washed with oval brown bars and transparent green squares, soft baby soaps that sudsed, and rough soaps that burned. I applied special gels, clear white liquids, mud creams. I took tablets once, twice, thrice a day; before, after, and during meals. I went on milk diets and no-milk diets, absorbed no sun and too much sun. I took erythromycin, tretinoin, Cleocin, PanOxyl, Benoxyl, isopropyl myristate, polyoxyl 40 stearate, buylated hydroxytoluene, hydroxy-propyl methylcellulose. I saw doctors and doctors and doctors.

My father would ask me, please, to stop picking at myself. Some-times he'd get impatient and slap my face (as if he were both repri-manding me for squeezing scabs at the dinner table and expressing compassion by striking the source of all the distress), but he was certainly justified in whatever frustration he felt. My hands were always crawling across my skin, always probing and plucking, then flicking away the root canker. The inflammatory disease bred a weird narcissism in which I craved the mirror but averted any accu-rate reflection. I became expert at predicting which kinds of mirrors would soften the effect, and which—it hardly seemed possible— would make things worse.

My sophomore year of high school my zit problem reached such catastrophic proportions that once a month I drove an hour each way to receive liquid nitrogen treatments from a dermatologist in South San Francisco. His office was catty-corner to a shopping center that housed a Longs drugstore, where I would always first give my pre-scription for that month's miracle drug to the pharmacist. Then, while I was waiting for the prescription to be filled, I'd go buy a giant bag of Switzer's red licorice. I'd tear open the bag, and even if (espe-cially if) my face was still bleeding slightly from all the violence that had just been done to it, I'd start gobbling the licorice while standing in line for the cashier. This may sound a little gooey, but, looking back, I'm hard-pressed now to see the licorice as anything other than some sort of Communion wafer, as if by swallowing the licorice, my juicy red pimples might become sweet and tasty. I'd absorb them; I'd be absolved. The purity of the contradiction I remember as a kind of ecstasy. My senior yearbook photo was so airbrushed that people asked me, literally, who it was.

In "Is Acne Really a Disease?" Dale F. Bloom argues that, "far from being a disease, adolescent acne is a normal physiological process that functions to ward off potential mates until the afflicted individual is some years past the age of reproductive maturity, and thus emotionally, intellectually, and physically fit to be a parent." Dale F. Bloom's thesis seems to me unassailable.

In one study of teenage boys with the highest testosterone levels, sixty-nine percent said they'd had intercourse; of boys with the lowest levels, sixteen percent said they'd had intercourse. The testosterone level in boys is eight times that of girls. Testosterone is responsible for increasing boys' muscle mass and initiating the growth spurt, which peaks at age fourteen. From ages eleven to sixteen, boys' testosterone levels increase twentyfold.

Hair grows about half an inch a month; it grows fastest in young adults, and fastest of all in girls between ages sixteen and twenty-four. Brain scans of people processing a romantic gaze, new mothers listening to infant cries, and subjects under the influence of cocaine bear a striking resemblance to one another. According to Daniel McNeill, "Our pupils reach peak size in adolescence, almost certainly as a lure in love, then slowly contract till age sixty." As Natalie would say—as she actually did say—"That's awesome."

She asks me why people write graffiti, and I try to explain how teenage boys need to ruin what's there in order to become who they are. I talk about boys at the swimming pool who simply won't obey the pleasant female lifeguard asking them to leave the pool at closing time; they leave only when asked gruffly by the male African-American lifeguard, and then they leave immediately.

According to Boyd McCandless, "A youngster *is* his body and his body is *he*."

Tolstoy said, "I have read somewhere that children from twelve to fourteen years of age—that is, in the transition stage from childhood to adolescence—are singularly inclined to arson and even murder. As I look back upon my boyhood, I can quite appreciate the possibility of the most frightful crime being committed without object or intent to injure but *just because*—out of curiosity, or to satisfy an unconscious craving for action."

Woody Allen, that eternal adolescent: "We are adrift, alone in the cosmos, wreaking monstrous violence on one another out of frustration and pain." No punch line.

A dozen or so teenage boys stand atop a jagged rock in the middle of Rattlesnake Lake, four miles southeast of North Bend, an hour out of Seattle. Several teenage girls do the same. The boys wear cutoffs and, nearly without exception, boast chiseled chests. The girls wear cutoffs and bikini tops, and they seem slightly less statuesque. (During the pubescent growth spurt, girls' hips widen in relation to shoulder girth. Boys' shoulders widen in relation to hip width. Eighteen-year-old girls have twenty percent less bone mass in relation to body weight than do boys of the same age.)

The rock is perhaps one story high. The boys choose to dive from the higher parts of the rock into the lake; most of the girls dive, too, but less spectacularly, less dangerously. One girl who doesn't dive keeps being pestered by her friend: "I can't believe you're seventeen and you won't dive. If you don't, I'm never going to speak to you again."

The boys at Rattlesnake Lake keep asking one another about their own dives, "How was that one? How did that look?"

It looks like this: the average penis of a man is three to four inches when flaccid and five to seven inches when erect. The range for an erect penis is 3.75 inches to 9.6 inches. In the 1930s, mannequins imported from Europe came in three sizes according to the size of the genitalia: small, medium, and American (compared to other cultures, Americans are obsessed with the size of sexual organs: penises, breasts). LBJ frequently urinated in front of his secretary, routinely forced staff members to meet with him in the bathroom while he defecated, and liked to show off his penis—which he nicknamed "Jumbo"—to Senate colleagues. Pallocrypts, sheaths that cover a New Guinean man's penis, run to two feet in length. The length of my penis when erect is six inches (boringly, frustratingly average); I've measured it several times.

From Children's Reminiscences of the Westward Migration

Karen Russell

> *In the winter of 18 and 46 our neighbor got hold of Fremont's* History of California *and began talking of moving to the New Country & brought the book to my husband to read, & he was carried away with the idea too. I said O let us not go.*
>
> —Mary A. Jones
> *Women's Diaries of the Westward Journey,* Lillian Schlissel

MY FATHER, A MINOTAUR, is more obdurate than any man. Sure, it was his decision to sell the farm and hitch himself to a four thousand–pound prairie schooner and head out west. But our road forked a long time ago, months before we ever yoked Dad to the wagon. If my father was the apple biter, my mother was his temptress Eve. It was Ma who showed him the book:

Freeman's Almanac of Uninhabited Lands!

Miss Tourtillott, one of the fusty old biddies in her sewing circle, had lent it to her as a curiosity. It contained eighteen true-life accounts of emigrants on the Overland Trail, coupons for quinine and barleycorn, and speculative maps of the Western Territories. The first page was a watercolor of the New Country, a paradise of clover and golden stubble fields. The sky was dusky pink, daubed with fat little doves. In the central oval, right where you would expect to find a human settlement, there was nothing but a green vacuity.

Unflattened Pasture! the caption read. Free for the takers!

"Can you imagine, Asterion?" My mother smiled like a girl, letting her finger drowse over the page. "All that land, and no people."

You could tell that even my mother, in spite of her sallow practicality, was charmed by the idea. Easy winters, canyon springs. No one to tell the old stories about her husband, or to poke fun at his graying, woolly bull head. She let her finger settle on the word "free," the deed to an invisible life. She traced the spiky outline of the mountains, a fence that no church lady could peer over.

"Look at that, son," my father grinned. "More grass than I could eat in a lifetime. All that space for your ball plays. Now, wouldn't you want to live there?"

I frowned. Whenever my folks promised me something, it always turned out to be both more and less than what I had expected. My sisters, for instance. I'd spent nine months carving a fraternal whimmerdoodle, and then Ma had given birth to Maisy and Dotes, twin girls. The New Country looked nice enough, but I bet there was a catch.

Besides, we had plenty of grass already. My father had retired from his wild rodeo life. We leased a small farm, raising mostly flowers and geese, where my father had negotiated a very reasonable price on rent. The lunatic asylum was a block away, and the intervening lot was vacant. It bothered my father that we didn't own the land outright, and my mother kept a pistol in the watering can, in case one of our gibbering neighbors ever paid us a visit. But that intervening lot was great for ball plays.

"Don't be silly, Asterion," my mother snorted, a habit she'd picked up from Dad. "Every member of my family lives in this town. Why, if we went west, I would never see them again in this world! My sisters, my mother . . ."

"Now wouldn't that be a tragedy?"

A charged looked passed between them.

Since retiring, my father has gotten to be on the largish side for a Minotaur, not fat so much as robust, and now he gathered his bulk to an impressive eighteen hands high. He pawed at the earthen floor. (Ma liked to complain about this, Dad's cloven trenches in our kitchen. "Go do your gouging out-of-doors, like a respectable animal!")

"Asterion," my mother said, slamming the book shut. "Stop this nonsense at once." Ma is a plain woman, with a petite human skull that calls no attention to itself, but she can be just as hot-blooded as my father. "We have a life here."

Outside, the sun was setting, spilling through our curtains. My father's horns throbbed softly in the checkered light. His ears, teardrop white, lay flat against the base of his skull. His expression was unrecognizable. Who was this, I wondered, this pupilless new creature? I had never seen someone so literally carried away by a desire before. All the reason ebbed out of his eyes, replaced by a glazed, animal ecstasy. If he hadn't been wearing his polka-dot suspenders, you would have mistaken him for a regular old bull.

"And are you happy, Velina, with our life here? Have you stopped hoping for anything better?" This last bit got drowned out by the five o'clock scream from the asylum, which set our blood curdling like clockwork. My mother winced, and I could tell that Dad had a wedge in the door.

"Why not make a fresh start of it? Six hundred acres, and all we have to do is claim it. You will be the wife of a very rich husband. Think of the children! All those unwed miners—your daughters will never want for a dancing partner. Young Jacob will have a farm of his own before his twentieth birthday."

"Asterion." My mother sighed. She gestured around her, palms up. "Be reasonable. You're no frontiersman. Where would we get the money for a single yoke of oxen?"

"Woman!" Dad boomed. He pushed out his flabby barrel chest. "You married a Minotaur. I'll pull our wagon."

"Oh, please!" Ma rolled her eyes. "You get winded during the daisy harvest!"

I was still rocking in the willow chair, slurping up milk.

"Your husband is stronger than a dozen oxen!" he roared. Dad patted his ornamental muscles, the product of flower picking and goose plucking. "Or have you forgotten our rodeo days?"

He tusked his horns at her with a brute playfulness that I had never seen between them. Then he charged at her, herding her toward the bedroom door. And my mother giggled, suddenly shy and childlike, letting herself go limp against him. I coughed and slurped my milk a little louder, but by this time they had forgotten me completely. "We have each other," he bellowed. "And everything else, we will learn on the trail. . . ."

I was startled by this, the speed with which one apocryphal water-color was transforming our future. A minute ago, there had been an opened book, a crazy notion—we could go or we could stay—and now, not five minutes later, the book was shut. We were going. Simple as that.

We have been on the trail for over a month now. Last night, we camped on Soap Creek Bottom. Down here, it's all soft green mud and yellow bubbles of light. No potable water for our stock and barely enough for us. The weeds we suck on for moisture taste bitter and waxy. Ma's been complaining of bad headaches, and the twins have been doing most of our cooking. Basically, this means they wake up early enough to beg boiled coffee and quail eggs from the other wagons. Dotes lumps some salt into the yolk and calls it an omelet. Apparently, my sisters still haven't mastered the pot and the spatula, that fiery alchemy whereby "raw" becomes "food." So help me, if I have to eat another stewed apple, I am defecting to the Grouses' wagon.

We have joined the Grouses' company, at my mother's insistence. Ours is a modest wagon train, twelve families, among them the Quigleys, the Howells, the Gustafsons, the Pratts, a party of eight lumberwomen, and a sweet, silly spinster, Olive Oatman, who is determined to be a schoolteacher. Olive trails the wagons on a tooth-less mule, each step like a glue drip. "Hurry up, Olive!" the men yell, and the women worry in overloud voices that she'll get lost or fall victim to Indian depredations. But nobody invites Olive to join their family's wagon.

In the beginning, everybody was gushing about the idylls of the open road—look at Hebadiah's children, sitting high on the wagon! Listen to Gus, warbling on that mouth organ! Let's sleep outside! Let's close our eyes and drink in the cool violet dune glow with our skin!

But now, we spend most of our time scowling, sunk in our private nostalgia for well water and beds. It is cold and cloudy, with the wind still east. We are on a very large prairie. The few trees are stout and pinky gray, like swine, and the scrub catches at our wheel axles, as if it wants to hitch a ride with us to somewhere greener. Dad's back is carved solid with red welts. His skin is coming off in patches. Flies twist to slow deaths in the furry coves of his nostrils. Dad shakes his head more violently with every mile, a learned tic, to keep the buzzards from landing on his curved horns.

We keep passing these queer, freshly dug humps of soil. Ma told Maisy and Dotes that they are just rain swells and the domes of prairie dog houses, but I know better. They are graves. Nobody leaves markers here, Pete says, because there's no point, no chance that you will ever come back to visit the site. We have decided to count them, these tombless losses. It seems like somebody should be keeping score:

Made twenty-two miles . . . passed seven graves.

Everybody is coming to the grim conclusion that we have overloaded our wagons. Our necessities, the things we couldn't have lived without just two weeks ago, are now burdensome luxuries. The whole trail is littered with cherished detritus: heirloom mirrors, weaving looms, broken, loved-up dolls. Maisy and Dotes got Dad's permission to pitch Grandma's empress china set at the trees. Our mother ducked the antique pestle and cried a little bit.

At dusk, we entered a tall shadowy belt of timber. Pete spotted an orange polecat sinking into the mud, nibbling at the little hand of a giant clock face. Brass kettles glowered in the shadows. Empty cradles lined the sides of the road, rocking soundlessly in the wind.

During the day, my mother sits on the high chair, shouting instructions to my father. Maisy and Dotes sit inside, shelling peas. Both of my parents continue to implore me to ride in our wagon, but I refuse to. If my dad is sensitive to the weight of a china plate, I don't want to add one bone to his load.

Instead, I walk in the back with the lumberwomen. I love the lumberwomen. They are widowed and ribald and sweat through their tongues, like dogs. Sometimes they let me roll inside the deep tin wells of their hunger barrels. They ask lots of cheerful, impolite questions about Dad, which are far easier to endure than the frank horror of other emigrant children or the veiled pity of their mothers.

"Your pa," they holler, "he the one with the . . . ?" Then they scoop at the air above their temples and whistle. "Whoo-ee! What a piece of luck, that, you children taking after your mother!"

It doesn't feel so lucky. Most times, I wish that I had been born with a colossal bull's head, the bigger the better. People on the trail act as if it's just as strange, and even more suspicious, my seeming normalcy. We are freckled and ordinary, and it makes every mother but our own uneasy. I could be Pete's brother; my sisters look just as peachy clean as their own daughters. This seems to alarm them. They wrinkle their noses slightly in our presence, as if we are the infected carriers of some hideous past.

My father is doing the heavy labor, sweating through the traces, plunging into the freezing water, into rivers so deep that sometimes only the shaggy tips of his horns are visible. But he is happier than I have ever seen him. People need my father out here. In town, there was always a distinct chill in the air whenever he took Ma to birthday parties or pumpkin tumbles, barbecues especially. But on the trail, these same women regard him with a friendly terror. Their husbands solicit him with peace pipes and obsequious requests:

"Mr. Minotaur, could you kindly open this jar of love apples for us? Mr. Minotaur, when you have a moment, would you mind goring these wolves?"

And I am so proud of my father, the strongest teamster, the least mortal, the most generous.

Ma is, too, even if she won't admit it to him. She told Louvina Pratt that he looks like the Minotaur she married, before he was a father. It's hard for me to imagine, staring at my Dad's gray belly hair and blunted horns, but I guess he was a legend once. At the early rodeos—my mother keeps all of his blue vellum posters, hidden inside her Bible—he bucked every gangly cowboy on the circuit. The Pawnee gave him top billing:

The bronco with a human torso, a chipped left horn, and a questionable pedigree!

Back home, people told so many stories about my father. Especially those people who had never seen him perform. That he was a sham man, or a phony bull; that his divinity has been diluted by years of crossbreeding with wild heifers and painted ladies. My own cousins called him a monster. I always wished that they could see my dad just being my dad, covered in goose dander or pulling a wheelbarrow of poppies. Here on the trail, people are finally getting to know all the parts of him.

As for my mother: well, things could be better. She spends most of her time gathering twigs and buffalo excrement and saying terrified prayers with the other women. Her face is brown and wizened, like apple skin left in the sun. She looks shrunken, stooped beneath the absence of small pleasures: fresh lettuces, the seasonal melodies of geese, the anchored bed she used to share with my father. I think she even misses the asylum, its predictable madness.

Ostensibly, the women meet behind the wagons to beat laundry with rocks or plait straw grass into ugly hats. But mostly, they just make implications.

"Velina, you must be so proud of your husband, pulling your wagon," Louvina smiles. "My Harold would *never* consent to walk in the traces."

"Yes, Velina," the Quigley sisters chorus. "Why, he's just as good as any oxen!"

"Our husbands are going to kill themselves out there," my mother snaps. All of her wrinkles point downward, like tiny pouting mouths. "It makes no difference if they are pulling or driving. We are going to forfeit every happiness we had, for a bunch of empty scrub."

"Don't pay her any mind," my dad laughed later. We were sitting on the outskirts of the campfire, watching the other men dance around its pale flames. Dad was working ancient alluvial pebbles out of his hooves and handing them to me for my collection. They are a translucent yellow, pocked like honeycomb. Children toddled toward our log, playing slow games of tag. The stars were impossibly bright.

"Velina can't see the West the way I can."

Dad claims that human women are congenitally nervous and shortsighted. "Like moles, son. If your mother is hungry for green corn, or if her bloomers get wet from the dew, she forgets all about the future. Believe me, when we crest those mountains and she sees the New Country . . . listen, everything will be different when we get there, Jacob. I promise."

That much, at least, I believe. . . .

We have lived a string of dull, thirsty weeks. Everybody is irritable and looking for someone to blame. Our wagons bump along, a pod of wooden leviathans, eaten away from the inside by mold and wood-boring mites. Our road is full of tiny perils, holes and vipers, festering wounds. Today would have been indistinguishable from the twenty before it, except that Pete and I finally got a good ball play going.

As soon as we got done striking camp and picketing the horses, we went exploring. Just north of the campsite, a quarter mile down-stream, we found a clearing in a shallow stand of pines. In the center, a shrunken lake, an unlikely blue, was fringed with radish reeds.

Behind us, you could see the white swell of the wagon sails, foaming over the trees. And the sky! The sky was the color that we'd been waiting for, our whole lives, it felt like. An otherworldly alloy of orange and violet, the one that meant a thunderstorm at sundown, and night rain for our stills.

"Look!" I pointed to the rising storm, a spider tide of dust and light. Future rain, cocooned in red filaments of cloud. "Pete! See that? My dad says that in the old days . . ."

"Jacob," Pete rolled his eyes. "Just play the ball, OK?"

Ma had insisted that I take Maisy and Dotes, so that they could get some fresh air, which I found infuriating, since they are girls and should be doing girl things, playing mumbly-beans or wearing yellow ribbons somewhere unobtrusive. Pete and I propped them up against some nearby boulders and used them as markers.

"Ready, Jacob?"

I swung wide, sending the ball to a delirious altitude, high above the blazing aspens. I rounded Maisy and Dotes, who clapped politely, while Pete ran off to retrieve the ball. A second later, we heard a terrible roar from behind the trees. The aspens started quaking, and I scurried to join him. We peered through the golden leaves.

"Hey," Pete said. "Isn't that your dad?"

My father was shedding his summer hide. His work shirt was hanging from a green sapling. Black fur caught like bits of cloud on the low branches. And there was my dad, rubbing his head right into a bifurcated stump, his horns sparking against the wood. "Uhhhh," he groaned, scratching harder, his back spasming with pleasure.

"No," I lied.

He snapped up when he heard my voice. "Boys!" he stamped. I felt traitorous and embarrassed for everybody; Dad preferred to take care of his animal functions in private. "What are you doing out here?"

"Hi, Jacob's dad," Pete squeaked. "We were just having a ball play with the twins."

We all turned. The girls had wandered down by the lake to attend to their own functions. Maisy had unfolded the gingham curtain of modesty and was holding it up for Dotes. When she looked over and saw us watching, she squealed and let go. The curtain of modesty went flapping off in the wind, revealing a horrified Dotes, bare legged and squatting in the purple brush.

"Eeee!"

Dotes dove behind a rock.

"Good Christ," my father grumbled, looking away. "Get your bloomers on, Dotes."

On the trail, propriety is a tough virtue to keep to, even if your curtain of modesty is made of the heaviest fabric, buffalo flannel, or boiled wool.

My father snatched his own thick shirt from the tree and started buttoning up. He plucked at the pink, scabby spots around his ears and neck—they startled me, these hairless patches, they looked so much like my own raw skin. He avoided our eyes.

"Who told you to take the girls out here, Jacob?" he bellowed. "Who gave you permission to leave the company?"

"Ma did."

"Oh. I *see*. Well." He glanced at Pete, scowling through a nimbus of bull fluff. "I say they go back." Then Dad trotted down to the creek, to where Maisy was wringing out the sodden curtain, and swept the girls up in his arms. He took long, regal strides back toward the camp, poised and paranoid, the way he walks when he suspects that he is being watched.

Afterward we couldn't find our ball. We both sat on a log, sulking, staring into the coming storm, and waiting to be called for dinner. Our bellies grumbled at the same time. A cloud of pollen floated past.

"Hey," Pete demanded, "how come you don't look like your dad?" It was spoken as a challenge, sudden and accusatory, as if we had been fighting all this while.

"What? But I do!" I pulled at my nostrils and blew, a nasally mimicry of my father's anger. "I do! How come *you* don't look like *your* Dad?" I tried another wild snort, but it came out sounding like a sneeze.

Pete just smiled at me, aping his own parents' expression, a doughy swell of pity and smug piety. He patted my back. "Poor Jacob. Bless you."

That did it. I charged him with my invisible horns, and suddenly we were fighting in the dirt like animals, dunced into a feral incomprehension. Kicking and scratching and biting, full of a screaming joy, hot and ugly. We kept at it until the dinner bell returned us to our selves, and suddenly, as if by magic, we were back at the camp, gorging on buttered oats and quail cakes, full bellied and friends again.

That night, I found my father at the edge of the campfire. The company was having a barbecue, and this always makes my Dad uncomfortable. The teamsters tore into the antelope meat like savages. The men wore linen work shirts during the day, but at night they stripped to their bare chests. Then they rushed at each other, half in jest, tipping their bottles back with a taut fatigue. In the center of the corral, Olive had hiked her skirts up, drunk and merry. She was sitting on Gus's lap, slapping a tambourine against her bare knees. The wives sucked air through their teeth. They were flushed with scandal, and clapping along all the while.

"Dad? Will you cut my hair?"

"Sure, son." This was our favorite ritual. He put on his reading spectacles and removed a tiny pair of scissors from his belt. Then he started cutting at my curly mop of hair. He cut with a tender precision, squinting furiously, his thick tongue lolling out of the side of his mouth.

When he finished, he held the cold, flat edge of the scissors against my scalp. "Can you feel your horns, son? There?" And I smiled happily, because I *could* feel them, throbbing at my temples, my skulled, secret horns. Ingrown, but every bit as sharp. And I knew that no matter what Ma or Pete or anybody said, I was my father's son.

We had our first true storm last night. Acres of lightning! A smokeless heat, and the choking smell of ash and sage. The wide, roiling prairie announced itself in liquid glimpses, apocalyptic and familiar. We had been sleeping in tents outside, and now we all ran for cover. Blue discs of hail blew into our wagons. The soaked canvas shuddered, and this became indistinguishable from the tremors within our own divided bodies, the hollow vibrato in our spines and human skulls and bellies, during the thunder.

"Mother," I said, to say something.

I had been eagerly awaiting just such a disaster. Storms, wolves, snakebite, floods—these are the occasions to find out how your father sees you, how strong and necessary he thinks you are. As it turns out, I am still just a buff-colored calf to Dad. I watched the older sons and brothers leaping off the wagon tongues all around me, a shoeless stampede. There went Pete, in a peppery cloud of dust. There went Obadiah, eager to assist.

But none of the fathers called me out of the wagon, least of all my own. I huddled with my mother, nuzzling into her neck, while the men shouted commands to one another, weighting the wagon boxes so that they wouldn't leak or capsize. Our family was in good shape. Months before we set out on the trail, Mr. Gustafson had come over and treated our cover with linseed oil, until the canvas shone like opal. Now we could actually see the accumulation of each raindrop, held in an oily suspension above our heads. It was freezing inside our wagon. I peered through the cloth portal, searching for my father, lost in a haze of swung lanterns and the wind. The wagon train blurred and shifted around us, like a serpent uncoiling.

The twins kept on crying in fright, and all around us the treasures we had sewn into the pockets of our wagon cover were shaking loose, pewter spoons and wooden toys, a grainy mess of stone meal, my father's musket. It's a wonder it didn't go off and kill someone. My mother, cold and comfortless, was cursing "our luck," by which she meant the gods, my father, all fathers. I thought about my hard bed and the many things I used to hate about our old life—keeping the Sabbath, harvesting the roses, all the honking, stupefying demands of our geese—and wished and wished that we had never left.

We think the wolves got Olive. When the rain cleared, she had disappeared. The grown-ups all screwed their faces into identical grimaces. They tried to make their sorrow sound as genuine as their surprise. "Poor Olive!"

Jebadiah Hatfield found her mule in a ravine eight miles to the west of us, grazing on a circle of brush, its grizzled snout stained red from the berries. Torn yellow ribbon hung from the low branches. There were bits of a woman's skirt clinging to the currant bushes. My dad volunteered to lead the search party.

"Are you mad?" Mr. Gustafson shook his bushy head. "We could lose a whole day if we send a search party. At this rate, we'll never make it to the New Country."

My dad looked from face to face, incredulous. "What is wrong with you people?" His horns were shaking involuntarily, no longer a mere tic but an obvious compulsion. His voice sounded small and human. "What about the contract?"

Before we left, we had had Reverend Hidalgo officiate our wagon union. Every family had to sign the contract: many wheels, a single destination, all for one until the trail's end.

Somebody snickered, a thin, hysterical sound. "The contract, Mr.

Minotaur?" And I flushed, seeing my father the way the other men did: his puzzled hairy face, his dumb cow eyes.

Our company took a group conscience, and most everybody agreed to be hopeless. My father and half-blind Clyde were the only ones who voted in favor of sending a search party, and Clyde later insisted that he had just been stretching.

"Think about it, Mr. Minotaur," Mr. Grouse said with a dark twinkle in his eye, fingering the ribbon. His cheeks were flushed, as if he were telling a naughty joke. "What solution could there be to this mystery? Who wants to waste half a day, burying the answers?"

"Velina!" We all turned. Mrs. Grouse was squatting a few yards away, waving frantically at my mother. She reached into a rain-soaked satchel and held up one of Olive's lacy, begrimed shirts. "Velina, do you want this? I think it's your size."

Yesterday, my father was the last wagon but one to cross the Great Snake River. We rafted across in the boxes, jowl to elbow, crammed in with albino cats and babies and buckets of bear grease. The men swam alongside their oxen. Pete and I banked first and sat watching our fathers from the opposite shore. I didn't want to tell Pete, but I was very scared. The cows had churned up a crimson froth of silt and mud, water rising to their necks, and I lost sight of my father in the lowing melee, his ruby eyes, his chipped left horn. For a horrifying instant, I couldn't tell him apart from the regular cattle. I worried that the other men, preoccupied with their own stock, wouldn't know to help him if he started to go under.

"Do you ever worry that your pa won't make it?" Pete asked carefully. His own father was struggling below us, his gum boot caught in the rapids. "I mean, to the end of the trail?"

I shook my head. "Nope. Of course he'll make it. My father is a legend."

All my life, I have believed only the best parts of my father's myth. But as it turned out, this belief makes little practical difference on the trail. Dad still got the chills and had to stop and catch his breath on a small rock island. I got a fire going, and my mother knelt in the sand, wringing the water out of the furry knots of hair around his neck. She murmured something into his wet, mud-rubbed ears. I don't think it was a soothing something. Even now they are fighting inside our wagon:

"Who do you think you're fooling out there, acting like you're immortal? I should have listened to my mother! I should never have married a Minotaur!"

Ma likes to talk as if she could have done better than my father. All of my aunts married postmasters and prim, mustachioed mayors.

"Your mother," my father snorted, between a laugh and a sneer, "you women, you're all alike. . . ."

"It's not too late, you know. It's never too late, to turn the wagon around. . . ."

"Listen, Velina," my father is saying. "I'm telling you, it's too late. We can only go forward. Our geese have been eaten. There are strangers living in our house. . . ."

There is some wooden clattering that sounds angry and deliberate and an iron shudder. Then silence on my mother's end.

For the first time, I feel just as sorry for my ma as for my dad. Everybody wants to go home, and no one can agree on where that is anymore.

Today, we nooned in a purple grove, along the dry riverbed of Snail Creek. It was cool and pleasant. After biscuits, I found a dead snake and skinned it, and made a toy out of its rattler to give to my sisters. They are both quarantined in the wagon, sick with ague. Their heads are swollen and bluish, like tin balloons. Maisy coughs less than Dotes, but Dotes is better at keeping boiled peas down. My parents haven't spoken to one another for three days.

"Hey, Pete?" I asked him. "What does your father talk about with your mother? You know, in your wagon?"

"Huh," Pete frowned. "Your folks talk to one another?" He shrugged. "My mother mostly bangs pans around or folds the blankets real loudly. Sometimes they pray together."

Without anybody taking verbal notice, in imperceptible increments, we have slipped to the back of the company. After the third time Dad fainted, Mom quietly stepped down from the high seat and slid into the canopied box. Now Ma refuses to drive our wagon. She curls up with the girls on a feather ticking and sleeps during the day. It has fallen to me now to drive my father.

101

Karen Russell

Every morning, I wake up at dawn. The sky is still prickled with stars, and it will be a full hour before the first blue ribbon of smoke gasps up from the first campfire. I shake my father awake and help him into the traces. It's a special single yoke, made to order. My father drinks a tiny glass of flame-colored liquid, his breakfast, while I clasp the collar slip around his neck and secure the nails in his crescent shoes. Then I take the reins. I'm OK once we get rolling, but I'm still uncertain, a herky-jerky greenhorn, when it comes to the commands for stopping and starting:

"Gee? Oh! I mean . . . haw! Sorry, Dad!"

Even when I close my eyes now, I see the outline of my father's back, swaying in front of me: the bent, pebbled steppe of his vertebrae, bruise purple from sun and toil, the shock of his bull's mane tumbling out of his hat, bleached to the color of old milk.

Gus traded his mouth organ for a sock and a sack of millet, so now we travel in silence. I miss the camaraderie of that first prairie, everybody traveling with a single aim, to the same place, and music even on the worst days. The lighter our wagons get, the quieter our daily sojourn becomes, and the more determined we are to get there and be rid of one another. The lumberwomen are mute and sour, except for the hollow growl of their hunger barrels. At night, after we make camp, they break long bouts of wordlessness to ask for whisky and matches and soda crackers, and various other trail alms.

"Don't you give them anything, Jacob," my mother hisses. "Remember, if you give those women so much as a single cracker, you are taking it from your sisters' mouths."

Lately, my parents can't seem to agree on the value of things. Last night, well after eleven o'clock, my father trotted back to our wagon, bashful and out of breath, fresh from a barter with the local Indians.

"Velina! Open your mouth, close your eyes, I have for you a great surprise. . . ."

Then he put a raw kernel of corn on her tongue and waited, beaming, for her reaction.

My mother smiled beautifully, rolling the kernel in her mouth. "Oh, Asterion! Where did you get this?"

"I sold our whiffletree," Dad said proudly. He pulled an ear of green corn out of his back pocket and, with a magician's flourish, stroked her cheek with the silky husk.

"You what?" My mother's eyes flew open. She spit corn in his face. "You did what?" Then she took hold of his horns and drew him toward her slowly, half laughing and half crying, pressing her face against the white diamond at the bridge of his nose. "You did WHAT?"

Dad's nostrils flared; he lowered his head and pawed at the caked dirt. I dove into the wagon and slid beneath the blankets with my sisters. The candles had guttered out but moonlight seeped through the rips in our wagon bonnet.

"Girls?"

Maisy opened one brown eye and held a finger to her lips. Dotes had her fist in her mouth, stifling a cough. I felt proud and sad that my sisters knew enough to pretend to be asleep. Outside, our parents were still arguing:

"Is that what we're worth to you," my mother was yelling, "five dollars and an ear of green corn?"

". . . besides, YOU were the one who said you wanted corn. . . ."

"Do you even have any idea how to repair a whiffletree, Asterion? Well, I hope that is some consolation to you, when the wolves are gnawing on your daughters' bones. . . ."

"C'mon," I said, loosening the cinched portal and sneaking my sisters out the back. I carried them over to the Grouses', two wagons down.

"Hey, Pete," I said. "Can we sleep in your wagon tonight?"

"No," Pete said sadly. "No, my ma says that we're only allowed to be friends in church now. They think your dad gave me lice." He brightened. "You can sleep under the wagon." We all peered beneath the hickory box. The undercarriage of the wagon was white and wormy. Light leaked through the planks, a palsied glow, sopped up by a dark mosaic of soil. In the dead center, the darkness pooled and shifted. Dotes gasped. It was a clotted mass of dogs, spotted dogs, yellow dogs, swimming dogs, all huddled together for warmth.

"You first," Maisy said.

Today I was poking at the fringes of the campfire, gathering stones for my collection, when I overheard some of the other men talking about my father.

"That Minotaur is spreading sucking lice to the children!" Mr. Grouse said, shaking and red, with a rage out of all proportion to his insect allegation. "He is titillating the milk cows and curdling our children's milk!" I flattened myself against the ground and inched forward. The other emigrants were all frowning and nodding. Watching them, I could see the way that Mr. Grouse's anger spread from man to man, the hot, viral coil of it, a warmth the men breathed in like a welcome fever.

It's enough to make you hate people.

I ran off to find Pete. He was out back, catching lizards behind the corral.

"Howdy, howdy, Jacob . . . ow!"

I butted him in the ribs sharply, wishing fervently that I had inherited my father's might. I butted him once, twice, and then stomped on his buckskin shoes.

"What was that for?"

"If you don't know, I am not going to tell you." I ran off into the sunset, crying hot, frustrated tears, cursing the Grouses at the top of my lungs. Then I lost sight of the wagons and got scared and ran back. I hoped Pete wasn't watching.

When everybody was ladling soup at the bean cauldrons, I snuck into Pete's wagon. I stole his sisters' dolls, the ones the Grouse girls have been making out of corn husks since Fort Charity, and ate them. In my vengeful fury, I forgot to remove the button eyes. My stomach is still cramping.

I hope the West is big enough for us to really spread out. It's a terrible thought, one of my worst fears, that we are going to get there, and these people are still going to be our neighbors.

Three nights ago, I was sleeping under my own family wagon, my bare arms and face covered in a fine cedar dust from the box and dreaming of the most ordinary things—chalk and pillows and ceiling boards, pitchers of lemonade and gooseberry pies—when I woke to a hand—not my own—pinching at my cheek.

"Wake up, Jacob."

I rolled over, eye level with the tip of my mother's caulked boot. I slid out from under the wagon. Ma had Maisy in one arm and Dotes in the other. Their eyes looked shiny and protuberant, their throats bulged with the echo of swallowed coughs. I felt the danger, too, sensed it with an animal intuitiveness, and froze.

"Come out of there, Jacob." My mother spoke in a low, careful tone. "Come gather your things."

"Why?" I was surprised at how alert I sounded, wide awake, without a trace of grogginess.

"Circumstances have obliged us," she glanced nervously over her shoulder, "to part ways with your father."

I gaped up at my mother and let her words sink in. I'd known for some time that a change was coming; I welcomed the idea of it, I wanted it, almost, or tried to want it, like my ambivalent prayers for rain in open country. But *parting ways!* This was a lunatic move, as ghastly and extreme as digging up coffins because we needed some wood.

"Jacob," she pleaded. "Now."

We stared at each other for a long moment. I drew my blanket up around my chin, flat with panic, and wedged myself under the carriage.

"No."

Ma bit her lip miserably. She squatted in the dust, inches from my face. I could see my name, two puffs, in the chilly air.

"Ja-cob!"

I linked my arm around a wheel axle and glared at her, daring her to try to grab me. The spokes shifted, ever so slightly, sending up a pearly exhumation of sand and flint. A light came on in our wagon.

"Velina? Is that you?"

With a soft cry, my mother rose to her feet. She glanced down at me a final time, pressing her hand to her cheek. Then she stumbled back toward my father's voice, the amber penumbra of our wagon.

The trail is full of surprises. The following morning, Mr. Grouse announced that two wagons had deserted our party, the Quigleys and the Howells, heading back east. My mother was seated by the camp-fires, boiling water for porridge, and she received this news without so much as a *huh*, an anesthetized murmur. I waited for her to look up at me but she just sat there, staring blankly at the bubbles.

And then, just when I was at my most muddled, besieged by all sorts of flickering, waxy fears, another surprise. Through the eyelid transparency of our wagon tarp, I saw my parents' silhouettes, blurring together into a single, monstrous shadow. I held my eye up to a hole in the cover. Dad's head was in my mother's lap. His great eyes were shut. My mother had an iron bucket and a thin, dirty kerchief. She was daubing a whitish solution of borax, sugar, and alum onto the sores beneath his fur. My dad was running his long, rough tongue over her boots, licking up the lichens and the toxic-colored spoors. His horns scraped against the floorboards. "I love you," my mother kept muttering, over and over, pushing the rag into his wounds. "I love you," as if she was trying to torture the true meaning out of the words. My father groaned his response.

So much of what passes between my parents on the trail is illegible to me. It's as if they speak a private language, some animal cuneiform, pawing messages to one another in the red dirt. During the day, my father continues to pull our wagon forward. My mother hasn't spoken of that evening since. . . .

Mr. Grouse's oxen died in their traces today. They were a team, his beloved blue-ribbon leaders, Quick and Nimble. It took three men to cut them loose. All I could focus on was the coiled rope, slack and slick with blood, and the thought that Pete would probably not be interested in ball plays for awhile. All the mothers shielded our eyes and scooted us toward the wagons. They said that the oxen had "failed in the traces," their euphemism to protect the youngest children, which seemed a little silly to me, since everybody had to step over a big dead ox.

"Ma," Dotes asked, making a paper daisy chain in the wagon, "if I die, promise you'll dig a grave deep enough so the wolves can't get at me?"

My mother looked up from her knitting with a bleary horror. "Oh, sweetheart"—she poked her head out the wagon—"are you hearing this, Asterion?"

We all looked outside, to where Dad was standing in high, dun-colored grass with the other men. They directed, while he used his hooves to tamp down some perfunctory dirt over Nimble. Lately, the men's requests have grown a lot less obsequious. Just the other day, Vilner Fitfield persuaded my father to wear a silver cowbell, so that the company will know when he's coming. ("You have a tendency to sneak up on a man, Mr. Minotaur," Vilner shrugged, with an aw-shucks sort of malice. "And to tell you the truth, it spooks our women.")

At the sound of my mother's voice, our father looked up and waved. His horns and hide have darkened to a dull yellow-gray; the skin hangs loosely from his arms.

"Ma," Maisy asked, sucking on the fizzled wick of an old flare. "Is Dad going to fail in the traces?"

There was a time when my mother would have said no and reassured us with shock or laughter. These days, she leaves our hair unwashed and our questions unanswered. "How should I know, Maisy? What can I know? You go and ask your father. You go and tell your father," Ma said, her eyes glinting like nail heads, "what you are afraid of."

*

Finally, we have reached the bluffs. From up here, we can see the midway point, the alkali desert of the Great Sink. It's a tough landmark to celebrate. The Great Sink is a weird, treeless terrain. Even the clouds look flat and waterless. A wide, dry canal cuts through the desert, a conglomerate rut, winnowed out by a thousand wagons. It looks as if someone has dug out the spine of the desert. The Great Sink reminds me of home, an Olympian version of the trenches that Dad used to paw in our kitchen. When I mentioned this to Ma, she laughed for the first time in many days.

This patch of our journey feels like a glum, perpetual noon. The lumberwomen are in low spirits; there is no wood for them to hack at. Suddenly, their curses sound hoarse and sincere. Wolves skulk around our wagons by day, just beyond rifle shot. Pete and I scare them off by singing hymns and patriotic ditties. Above us, the pale sky is greased with birds.

Inside our wagon, Dotes shivers beneath three horsehide blankets. Maisy sleeps and sleeps.

Ma wanted us to stop days ago, but my father was afraid of losing the company. At night they stepped outside again, to take a spousal conscience. Ma made me hold up the curtain of modesty, now soiled and tissue thin, as a courtesy for our neighbors.

"Do you see any doctors around here?" Dad asked, making a big show of looking under a rock. He squeezes the rock in his fist, crushing it to powder. "Any medicine? Be brave, Velina. We have to press on now, we are over halfway there—"

He broke off abruptly. I had lowered the curtain. My arms were tired, and I had to scratch my nose. Our eyes met, and my father saw something in my expression that made him trot over.

"Jacob." His teeth were shining. He wobbled a little, eyes burning, his hair on end, full of radiant, precarious cheer, like our town drunk. He touched the nick in his horn to my cheek.

"Don't pay her any mind, son. We'll get there. Have a little faith in your father."

Then he picked me up and waltzed me through the ashes of our campfire. "Hold on, son!" He charged around and around the corral, making his shoulder muscles buckle and snap like oilcloth, an impromptu rodeo. "Gee!" I pleaded, giggling in spite of myself. "Haw!"

"Don't let go!" I yelped, even though I was the one holding onto his horns.

Then Dad spun me away from my mother, beyond the edge of our camp. We waltzed straight to the edge of the bluff.

"Look at that, Jacob," he whistled. "Look how far we've come."

Viewed from my father's shoulders, the desert stretched for eons, flat and markerless. It was an empty vista, each dune echoing itself for miles of glowing sand. A silent windless night, where any horizon could be west. The heat made me mistrustful of my own vision: I couldn't be certain if the blue smudges I saw in the distance were mountains or mirages. The wagon trains camped below us were no help. With their snubbed, segmented ends, they looked like white grubs, curling into themselves, each head and tail identical. Tiny fires spangled the dark.

"Do you see now?"

I peered into the desert.

I had no idea what my father saw out there or what he wanted me to see. Still holding onto his horns, I pivoted, slow and halting, in a direction that I desperately hoped was west.

"Oh! Yes!"

Dad grinned. The firelight limned the absent places in his hide, the burn marks in his skin. Some of his bull's hair had come off in my fist. He lowered me to the ground and then whispered directly into my ear, as if this was a secret between men:

"They say the clover grows wild all over the West, Jacob. So *green*, so lush and dense! So high, son, that when you wade through it, it covers your face. . . ."

Boy
Elizabeth Robinson

On the shelf
that was my self
rings nothing but
implements of
exit

On the ledge that
was my self, I hasten
my   bone   horizon
frustrated with
or not with

On my measure
such to get set
remnants of hair
growth symbol
sheared
away

Some magic word
despises the child
that was   Who sports   This way
he ceases to be
Most eloquent dissection
        parts with force

I was a boy and now
am not a self Horrendous
says self of self
with glee
Part from particle
Abridge   or
or   flee

This genteel cry
of pain   takes away
the victim does he   he
does mature I do ugly
progress from this life to
the next

He knew the forms of
surgery from both ends
there for
his elegance
Above and below
as types of innocence

all to be treated with knife
and suture   The divine
perspective is torture
or extraction   Lovely oh
lovely shelf now forsaken
of its burden

As each soul is
and only is
a boy   I am
As each artist
would force his way
into the boy

That is, the idea of
the boy to be climbed
into   Shucking off
the artist   joy   us   horrible
To prove the idea of boy
as and only

as fit   The hand
in the exemplary glove
is a fraud We memorialize
him on his shelf surfeit as a garment
outstretched or stretched out
The self shivered

in its ugly dress Grown
out or outgrown He
might escape   I might
be a child no longer though
he gets away He might claim
this ledge as a blade

Elizabeth Robinson

I see   that hastens or deletes his fall
Figurative fall   I was my own
perverse boy and the world
stank   I was the artist that
drew the gown   all complete   on selfhood
I saw it cheat

The victim is forbidden despair   In
that air he makes himself   an   I
who am puppeting him so that
on this day the cloak I call suspension
will be cut   Lasting string hard   shard
on impact

No despair can fashion
itself to this   In turn   he
will fall to   this self
The failure of weight on an empty
shelf   The garment of the soul   hissing
would rape my insides until
what will grow   up   outgrown

112

Close to Home
Joshua Furst

I.

I WAS MAYBE THREE, I don't know, very young.

I knelt on the floor in front of the refrigerator, playing with bright plastic magnetic letters. I must have asked a question because she was responding, looming over me, exasperated. *Give me one second,* she said. *Give me just one second.* She was annoyed with me. She kept repeating herself. *Give me just one second,* she said, until the words began to slur into each other. They became indistinct, an unceasing loop of syllables. I could no longer tell when one word ended and the next began; they all had the same emphasis suddenly and the rhythm of her voice had a texture, a reverb, a wha-wha. Her voice was the sound of a thumb rubbing circles on corduroy, the sound of friction, of wales catching wales, smudging and squeaking and echoing, a topographical wailing. Or the sound of an electric sander overextending its engine as it furrowed into hard wood. Sound, an abrasive crescendo. Fortissimo. The rumble of reprimand, under which fluttered the minor harmonics of her despair—a simultaneous staccato and legato. It overtook and it shook the room and I dropped the magnets and curled on the chipping linoleum. I was subsumed in the sound of her voice, my face turned away from her. I didn't look at her. I didn't see her.

This is my only early memory of her.

I was taken to the Seattle Institute of Something Something Ecumenical Something. A convention center of some sort. A convergence center. Massive, off white, modern. The concrete exterior molded and manicured until it looked too precious for human use, though cheaply precious: gilt instead of gold, chrome instead of silver. It was a bauble of a building. People left their lives behind to live there. I don't remember how I arrived and I don't remember how long I stayed—a long time, maybe months, maybe over a year. I don't know who brought me to the institute, she hadn't, but I hadn't come of my own volition either. I was just suddenly there.

People at the institute walked the same patterns each day: wake up at six for the communal breakfast, confer in small groups until noon, then break for lunch—the rest of the day was given over to isolation, contemplation, dinner was consumed alone in silence, and then, in the evening, everyone gathered in the chapel to sing. I don't know why I'm so sure this is true, but I am. Each day was empty of event in exactly the same way each previous day had been empty of event and when one went to sleep, one knew that tomorrow would be empty, too. Time stagnated and loneliness bred like bacteria within it.

I shared a room with a man with a patch over his right eye. He was supposed to be my protector, but he was strange and frightening and I didn't know his name. He loomed over me as I crouched at the milk crate in which my clothes were stored. He watched me rummage for something to wear as if I were a biological specimen. I don't think I ever heard him speak.

A faux-marble staircase curved along the back wall of the massive lobby. A potted plastic orange tree blocked the nook of dead space under this staircase from the rest of the room. It was my secret place. I would crawl in and hide there all day. The shadow of the staircase conspired with the tree to stop other people from seeing me. A strip of blue carpet muffled the footsteps above me. No one knew where I was. No one was looking for me. If I sat still and quiet enough, I could periodically forget how desolate life at the institute was.

She was no longer with me. What I remember most is that she had disappeared. I was at the institute and she was not, and then later, I was no longer at the institute, but I was still not with her.

Could I have been four? I was four at the most.

II.

I woke from my afternoon nap convinced that I hadn't been sleeping, or rather that the moment at which I awoke was actually the moment at which I had fallen asleep—in other words, that I had been awake during my nap, but now I was sleeping and whatever I thought I was now experiencing was actually the dream. I couldn't remember falling asleep earlier in the day. I couldn't remember anyone telling me, *I know you want to go out and play, but it's nap time, so close your eyes. You don't have to sleep, but you have to lie like that for at least half an hour.* Which is what people were supposed to say to me at nap time.

I had an acute lack of trust in the room I had awoken into: the venetian blinds caked in dust, the browns and tans of the furniture, the coffee table shoved against one wall with a small television—its antenna a mangled coat hanger wrapped in tinfoil—propped upon it. A blanket was draped over my legs and my head was in a woman's lap. Her fingers twirled in my hair when they weren't turning the pages of her magazine. I recognized the woman, but I knew she wasn't my mother—she was the woman who asked me to call her Mom even though I had no reason to.

The room and everything in it seemed two-dimensional, like if I poked it hard enough, it would tear and behind it would be something else, something that would wake me up, something that would be real. To test this theory, I turned my face to the woman's leg— she was wearing shorts—and I bit into her thigh. She yelped. She knocked my head with the base of her palm and I let go. I looked at her skin where my teeth had been and watched the blood bead in a dotted oval.

I remember thinking that if I closed my eyes and went back to sleep, I would return to my real life, but I couldn't because the woman had my chin in her hand, she was talking at me, saying, *Look at me now. Look me dead in the eye. Why did you do that? When did you get to be such a nasty child?*

For years after that, I wondered, as I went to sleep, whether I would wake up somewhere else—back in the place I had come from—in the morning.

Sometimes I still do.

My third foster mother was upset that I wanted everyone to call me Dorothy. She refused to humor me—she called me Sammy. Each time she said this name, I would hop in place, my tiny fingernails piercing the palms of my hands. My face would turn red as I howled, *I'm not Sammy. Don't call me that. I'm Dorothy.* She would plead with me, *Sammy, how would you like to go to the playground? Get out that excess energy? You'd like that, wouldn't you? Would you? I'll let you swing on the big-boy swings? You could play on the teeter-totter? It's got a carousel.* But I didn't want to go to the playground and I wasn't Sammy. I was Dorothy. Maybe if she had asked Dorothy to go to the playground, I would have gone, but then, if she had been willing to call me Dorothy, she wouldn't have needed to bribe me with trips to the playground. If she had been my mother—my real mother—I could have been Sammy. Then she and Sammy could have gone to the playground and she and Sammy could have played on the swings and the teeter-totter and she could have gotten Sammy to smile and show off his missing tooth for the camera. But she wasn't my mother and I was Dorothy.

I had a speech impediment. I wasn't even Dorothy. For almost a year, I was Dorpy.

Sometimes, she gave me no choice. *Turn off that TV and get some fresh air now. I mean it, you've had enough brain rot for today. Out,* she would say. I walked in circles around and around the block, pretending I was going somewhere while counting the time before I could return to the house. I would ball my fists in the pockets of my windbreaker and fix my posture, feeling the space between each vertebra expand as my spinal column stretched toward a straight line, noting the changing angle of my shoulder blades—as they rose in the wind I felt as if sails were unfurling behind me, billowing, arching with air that until then had been shut out; secret rooms opened inside me. I was light and porous. I imagined being lifted and carried off by the wind, but as if in direct relation to the expansion happening inside my body, the air around me seemed to compress, to thicken, congeal into strands, like hair, that would get in my mouth and catch in my throat and whip and cling to my arms as I swiped at them. I had a vague notion that I could push the air apart as if it were a curtain of beads, and stepping through it, I'd be somewhere else—that reaching somewhere else was as easy as that—but beyond the air was merely more air. The same air.

On perfect days, when it was sunny and the greens of the grass were too green and the sky was too blue and the birds were making too much noise and the cars were clean and they sparkled, on days like this one, when people were out and about wearing bright summer colors, I cried. The colors didn't seem real, they confused me.

On the day my third foster mother finally sent me away, there was a rainbow in the sky and this made me cry as well. After that, I let people call me Sammy again.

I had other foster parents, but I don't remember them clearly. In my mind, they all look like this third one, and she is a blob, a composite: fat but thin, tall but short, blonde but brunette, with a big nose as small as a button and a broad frown. They are both male and female, and yet they are neither but sometimes they're both and after the first and the second and the third one (who refused to call me Dorothy), each gave the speech about how *You're a good boy, and I really love you, but my kids, my own kids, are feeling neglected; I didn't realize how much . . . how much energy it would take to solve your prob—er, to give you a normal life; it's too much for me, so, um, you have to go—I've already called—they're going to find you a better match; don't feel bad, please don't feel bad, it's not you, it's me who has failed; keep in touch.* After three variations on this speech I stopped trying to comfort them as they kicked me out. I stopped trying to befriend them when they took me in. I stopped thinking of them as anything other than transient strangers loitering in my life, begging for proof from me that they were good people, valuable people, people deserving of all the stuff, all the junk that their lives had afforded them. They wanted angel wings and, having learned that I was a *nasty boy*, that I had no wings to give them, I didn't try. They couldn't give me what I wanted either: what I wanted was, when inevitably carted away from them, to be deposited somewhere other than with another family like them.

III.

This was the summer of asphalt and antiseptic. Of iodine. I was ten, double digits, beginning to think I would never wake up, beginning to believe that she was the dream.

This was the summer I darted in front of bicyclists. I was hit by Huffys and Cannondales. Giants and Treks. I was hit by a three-speed with training wheels and a banana seat. A ten-speed with an empty, hard-plastic toddler chair attached over the rear wheel toppled onto me and its handle bars slashed the edge of my eye socket—if it had hit half an inch to the left, it would have blinded me in my right eye. I was taken to the hospital.

I was awed by the cleanliness of the hospital. The floor was so shiny it looked wet. Even the emergency room, in spite of its chaos, its flailing bodies, and flung machinery, in spite of its blood, gave me an overriding sense of order. The interns and nurses running from opposite ends of the corridor never collided, but spun past each other gracefully, using each other as ballast. A hand on a shoulder, a cushion, a pivot point. They were going somewhere. They had purpose. They, like the blue and gunmetal machines—those machines coiled

117

in tubing turned yellow with age—which they sometimes wheeled in front of them, were functionaries of an institutional structure so carefully mapped, so minutely managed, so gloved in latex, that they were protected from the mess, emotions, and blood of their patients. Agony was tucked behind sliding curtains. Even the most massive hemorrhage of blood was contained on white sheets, on white coats, in white hampers.

A short blonde woman with perfectly round glasses knotted three nylon stitches to my cheek. She had me sewn up in less than an hour and sent me back to my foster mother's care. I searched for a reason to return to the hospital, to be admitted for a lengthy stay; upon my release, I was sure, the world would be changed, the hospital would have succeeded in transporting me to a more trustworthy, fathomable destination than the Seattle I had been released to this time.

When I peered out the side of my eye, the stitches grazed my peripheral vision. I imagined that instead of being attached to my body, they were attached to the city around me, that I'd found a seam in the sky, in the sidewalk, in whatever I gazed at, and if I worked my fingers into this seam I could rip Seattle in half. I wanted to jump through it like through construction paper and—having proved to myself that what I believed to be true in fact was true, that the somewhere else I belonged was hiding behind the somewhere I currently was, and this somewhere else could be reached simply by rending a hole in my current location and taking a couple of steps—I wanted to raise my fists high in victory. But knowing that, in fact, the stitches weren't holding the city together, they were holding my skin together, I strove to achieve the same transcendence, the same metaphysical transportation, by ripping myself into small enough pieces that I could sink like water into the surface of the earth.

I pounded my forehead for hours against the kitchen wall. The plasterboard dented and a blister formed under the flowerpot wallpaper, but my skin wouldn't split.

I dove repeatedly off the couch. As I descended, I flailed and squirmed, trying to position my body at the sharpest angle to the floor, the angle at which I was most likely to compact the vertebrae in my neck. My shoulder got in the way each time. It twisted and absorbed the impact. I did not have control over this. With each successive leap, I tried harder to concentrate on restraining my shoulder, but I couldn't—my desire seemed to stand in the way of its own attainment.

I punched plate-glass windows. I held plastic bags tight over my head and breathed deeply, the bag sucking into and out of my mouth with a rustle like leaves, until I felt light-headed and clawed at my face, stretching and tearing holes in the plastic. There was a joy in being so close to self-destruction, an intimacy. I lobbed kitchen knives at my feet, always missing. I jabbed sharpened pencils into my own thighs. I flirted with death. I was coy, like a virgin. I held my breath, let death's hand wander above my belt, and savored the feathery tickle on my skin until the sensation threatened to descend and penetrate and overwhelm me. Then I would swat death away and begin the flirtation over again. I was convinced that if I died I'd wake up later in my somewhere, but no matter how close I came to taking myself there, it always seemed to move farther away.

I played chicken with traffic. The tires would stop spinning before the cars halted. The doors would swing open with such velocity that they would bounce on their hinges. The women—always women— would leap from the driver's seats and grab my elbow and fling me out of the street. They would scream, *What do you think you're doing? You stupid kid. You'll get yourself killed.* I would stare at my foot and kick divots into the grass. *I should tell your mother on you, you dumb-ass kid.* I would try to pull my face into an expression of piety and fear and I'd say, *Jeez, sorry, lady. I'll try to be better next time.* They would place their hands on the tops of their heads as if holding in compressed air. Sometimes they'd cry.

This was the summer I failed to make music. I played the toy recorder and pranced around the house, pretending I was a maestro. The recorder was made out of plastic—baby blues and pinks up its spine, a yellow bell. If I blew into it long enough, spittle dripped out of the end. The noise I got from the recorder was inconsistent with the melody rolling through my head; the trills and arpeggios floated up from my lungs and spilled into the instrument, where they would bounce in the cylinder and squeak out the hole at the bottom in a reedy, mangled parody of the spellbinding sound I imagined. I could make the recorder honk and whistle. I could make the pitch wobble like water around the one I was after, but I couldn't get it to settle there. I blew harder in frustration, trying to beat the sound into a musical shape with my breath. I raced around the living room as if, by running faster, I might be able to catch the sound before it came out wrong. I was so consumed with my attempt to summon an aria that would be tender and fluid that I no longer saw the room I was

119

in, I only saw the joy that I couldn't conjure out of the instrument. I couldn't stop thinking that any second now—*in just one second*—my fingers would find the right holes, my lips would caress the mouthpiece, and the sound in my head would soar into the room. Legato. *Sorrento. Amorévole.* The music of love. I tripped over a throw pillow and tumbled forward, still struggling to compose. I belly flopped onto the living-room floor. The recorder pressed into the back of my throat and popped through my soft palate; it impaled me and my blood poured out of the bell like water from a drainage pipe. I was flung over some man's shoulder and carried to a car. My blood gurgled, bubbled with my breathing. As the car zoomed and leaned around curves, I watched the blood pooling in the ridges of the seat and saturating the foam cushion that bulged from the peeling corner of the Naugahyde. Then I was back on the man's shoulder and my blood splattered a trail in the pavement behind us. I recognized the polished granite floor of the hospital's foyer, and I felt safe and the wound in the back of my throat did not hurt. My blood fell to the floor in perfect circles and as it landed, smaller circles leapt up from the edges to settle concentrically—like dots of henna, like star-bursts—around the larger circle. The pattern my blood created as we sped forward related somehow to the sounds I had been trying to coax out of the recorder, whole notes on a staff, grace and beauty. Many hands grabbed at me, starched white fabric swept past my face, and when I could see again, I was looking at a small useless pillow and I was rolling down a hallway and I was in an elevator, moving up, and then I wasn't in an elevator, I had disappeared and the hospital was gone and the people were gone and all that was left was white and light and a soft wistful melody.

I woke in a sterile room, the music shallow now and wrapped in static. The thick burlap curtains were closed, their faded print of flowers backlit and dark. A bright rod of sunlight, so warm and crisp that it seemed to be a physical barrier, a plane cutting between two darknesses, sliced through the crack between the curtains. I wondered, where am I? I wondered, was I dead? Had I slipped from the dream I'd been trapped in for so long? A thin clear tube extended from my vein to a package of glucose hanging above me. Stiff bristles tickled the back of my tongue. I remembered the recorder. This was the same me who'd impaled himself. Someone had stopped up the hole. I gazed at the light cutting the room in half. I wondered, could I get out of this bed, walk through the plane, and be transported to my somewhere else? I was groggy. My body was heavy,

120

self-sufficient, no longer needing my help. It wouldn't respond when I asked it to rise and carry me across the plane.

I returned to sleep.

The room looked the same every time I awoke. I was in the hospital, cradled by nurses who all had soft touches. They straightened my leg. They replaced the tube attached to my arm. They emptied my bedpan. They told me, *Everything's all right now, you just need rest,* and they plunged needles into my thigh. After the morphine spread through my bloodstream, I did what they told me to, waking for the next shot, then sleeping again. Sometimes, when I opened my eyes, there was one nurse, sometimes two, sometimes three, or none. Time seemed to loop and circle over the same brief moments again and again. The reality that I had thought I'd be stuck in forever—the foster parents and hand-me-down clothes, the grimy toys missing parts—was gone. No one from outside visited me, or if they did, it was while I was asleep. The hospital, with its miracle workers, its morphine, its gleaming benevolence, took me away from the cold care of resentful do-gooders. It gave me access to the better place folded deep in my mind; once there, I could float, hazy and lazy, lost in contentment.

Waking and sleeping blurred into each other. I existed in a constant half dream, finally reconciling what was happening in my incorporeal life with what was happening in my physical reality, finally able to accept that both consisted of true events: I had bedsores and I adjusted my back on the hospital bed, I had gills and I swam toward the distant spiral of light at the surface of an unending body of water. I was in both places simultaneously; I could delineate between the two, split my focus and slide back and forth between them. Or, and this was more interesting, I could dwell in the dream state and gaze passively into the world of other people, noting the curious oval of leather holding the nurse's hair out of her face; the raw, peeling arcs of pink at the close-clipped tips of the doctor's fingernails; the way the clock on the wall's second hand quivered before it lurched forward, as if it were uncertain whether or not to continue the facade. Reality, time, human beings: these were abstractions—I no longer had to pretend I believed in them.

She was there, too, sometimes—once, at least once. I peered through my eyelashes, mildly interested in finding out if the room still existed, and she was there, shoulders jiggling, hands clasped and whitening, rounder, yet shorter than I remembered her, quivering in the wide plastic chair in the corner. I regulated my breathing, counted two, three, four, five as I inhaled and then exhaled one, two, three, four. Tears bubbled at the edges of her eyes and her face contorted as she tried to contain them. She murmured, *Sammy, my Sammy, don't die on me, Sammy.* Her voice was like rain, rhythmic and soft and surrounding me. *Baby, my baby, my meaning, my life, please don't leave me again, Sammy. I couldn't bear it.* She leaned on her haunches and reached for my foot, her fingers lingering, splayed, in the air before she changed her mind and returned her hand to her lap. *Mommy needs to know you're thriving.* The tears fell. *You probably don't care and don't want to hear this. I hope you don't hear this. I sit in my room all day because I'm scared of the crazy people that they make me live with, and I think about you, Sammy. I can see you, it doesn't matter where you are, part of me is there with you, watching you, holding your hand. You probably don't notice. You probably hate me and think I abandoned you. That's fine. That's OK. It's better for you to think that than to miss me the way I miss you—do you know that they won't let me out? I ask them. I tell them I'm not going to hurt myself, I won't hurt you. If they let me out I'll even take the damn pills. But no, we can't have that. We can't have Mommy healthy and caring for her Sammy.* The tears stopped abruptly. Her eyes seemed to sink deep into her skull. Her face went suddenly crimson. The plane of sunlight cut across the bed between us. She spit as she spoke. *You know why? Because we have secrets. We know things. They put you in my arms right after you were born and I looked in your eyes and saw it. You'd gotten the gift. You can see things. People's souls, people's—I can't say. They're listening. But I made sure to pass on those genes, don't you worry. You've got the powers. They tricked me, though. They forced me to tell them, and now we can't be together anymore. They're scared of what would happen. It would be the end of their . . .* she glanced around the room as if checking for a thief . . . *of their shenanigans.* Then, just as suddenly, she was soft and gentle again. *You know what? When I'm a good girl they sometimes let me have paper and crayons so I can draw pictures of all the fun things you're doing. That . . . I like that. I tape them to my wall and look at them and I just beam all day.* Her hands clutched her elbows and she rocked like she was holding a baby. *I smile and smile and smile and smile.* Though she didn't lift from the chair, though she held only herself, I felt her arms around me, she cradled me, slipping a nipple into my mouth, protecting, comforting, loving.

I was close to slipping away. I could see my somewhere ahead of me, just down the hill. I was gliding toward it. Before this moment, I'd imagined that when I arrived at my somewhere, she would be twirling on a pedestal there, like the dancer mounted on a music box. I'd imagined that it was she to whom I'd be returning. And now, in my groggy narcotic stupor, here she was, a play of light, invading the room as I twinkled toward extinction, a welcoming trumpet coaxing me home. But if I was finally entering my somewhere, why, when the nurse came to give me my shot, and told her, if she wanted, to hang around, why, when the nurse said my condition was severe, I might not make it, this might be her last chance, why, when the only thing I still needed was for her to place her palm on my cheek and say, *I'll take you with me now, everything's OK,* did she startle and tense up and snap at the nurse—*No, don't, I'll leave. Don't tell him I was here. I'm, don't, I'm, he's, I've caused him enough hurt*—and then disappear out the door?

No, she was not in my somewhere. She was leaving again, stepping out into the heat of Seattle, of August, of the very same world I was trying to escape. I understood, then, where she'd been all these years: displaced, hobbling from street to street, miles behind me, searching the sky for signs of my whereabouts, studying her veins as if they could provide a map of my trail, and listening, listening closely for my cracking voice among those that echoed in her head.

I hated her.

I had to live.

Three Poems
Donald Revell

GOOD FRIDAY

The clown is hurt between two trees.
His circus went far away, and they are happy there
With many animals, living by the sea.

Here, the low bushes are like little pigs,
And the flowers are fierce, with great teeth in them.
I see no animals in the sky, but my mother does.

I see lights under the ground at night.
I hear them digging sometimes, and I know
One morning, very early, when the house is sleeping,

Creatures no one has ever seen in this place
Will come up through the floors.
Their faces will be fires. Their fur will smell of earth

And of secret, white things, buried a long time.
If I go with them, I will never die.

MOAB

Where the later kids grow so tall
The talk is colors.
Avert your eyes, nary a vowel,
Avert your eyes.
Dying, like dirt reading a magazine, neither laughs nor cries.

I heard a hissing in the sun at sunrise.
Oh my Savior, this very morning
You must step out of the sun,
Colored in no color at all
But in the sound of grass stains

Waking the snowfields,
Waking even the crags and caverns
Whose simple pleasures are my destruction,
Against whose arrows my kids have nothing to oppose.

STORKS

Reading, I am,
As I find myself,
Praying for animals
One hundred years gone
And more sometimes, yes,
And a few men.

In cathedral towns,
Choirs of children
Gathered to sing to heal
The white storks ailing in the steeples.

In ancient Rome,
It was illegal to pay one's lawyer.
Cicero, for example. The money
Would corrupt the advocacy.

Singing to the sick birds heals them with a charm.
I mean as in the Old English—*caerm*—
Bells charming over the hay fields,
Finches charming in the trees.

The song is human
But unconcerned with the affairs of men.
So do bees love the bird-of-paradise tree
First thing in the morning sunlight
Striking in!

If one of a mated pair of white storks dies
The survivor stays on the nest,
Protecting the young, never leaving,
Not even to feed or to gather.
And so the young birds starve,
Their sharp cries becoming weaker all the time.

They need charming.
The children's choir is their advocate,
As the sun rising is an advocate,
Incorruptible, unconcerned in prayer with prayer
Or with the affairs of men, charming to honeybees
Striking in.

I was reading when my father died
Who could not read.
My wife was asleep,
And the baby slept beside her.
I went outside to see a house nearby,
A small house covered with green vines
Filled with bees.

I prayed and listened.
I prayed and heard
Nothing concerned with men, including my father.
He wanted nothing to do with them either.
He prayed so.
Once he said
My eyes and my sister's eyes were brown like those of deer.

The Distillery
Emily Barton

THAT VERY WEEK, DESPITE her father's lingering doubts, Prue's training at the distillery began.

Her mother's chief fear was that her hair would catch in a drive belt, so instead of dressing it, as she had always done, in two fuzzy auburn braids, she wound it onto the back of Prue's head and fixed it with a comb. Prue was pleased when she saw herself in the looking glass. The coiffure wasn't more flattering than the former one, but it made her look eleven or twelve, which she counted as progress. Roxana was also concerned lest some article of Prue's attire snag in the machinery, so she bought some sturdy gray linen from Mrs. Tilley and had Johanna make Prue a pair of close-fitting knee britches, such as boys wore. Johanna had to feel every stitch with her fingers, but her sewing was still expert, and the britches came out well enough. They fastened beneath the knee with tortoiseshell buttons, for whose fanciness Ben teased Prue, though he did not seem to mind the britches themselves. Between these and the new hairstyle, Prue no longer fully resembled a girl, and she knew this would be even more pronounced when the cobbler finished her long work boots. But she told herself she had never been popular with the Livingstons, the most feminine girls in the neighborhood. It was impossible to risk losing the regard of those who'd never held her in any; and Ben would no doubt value her more highly now that her clothes allowed her to run more quickly and fight like a boy.

Prue's father didn't worry about her hair or her clothing, having, as he did, at least some native faith in her common sense. Prue intuited, however, his concern about her aptness for the task she was undertaking. She was quick at writing and arithmetic, but she knew the prospect of teaching her the art and science of distilling daunted him, not only because of her sex. Even before she began her training, she understood the business was complex: there were raw materials to acquire and wastes to dispose of, machines to be kept in good order and on strict schedules of time and temperature, a few score men, of varying abilities, to be fed and clothed if they were slaves, and properly directed, kept off the bottle, and paid their wages if free; and there was the product itself, which sold only because it was of the finest quality. "But I'll tell you what the real trouble is," he told her the day they began. He sat down on his chair in the counting-house, so their eyes might be on a level. "The process is sufficiently arcane, even now I sometimes find myself surprised it transmutes grain into alcohol and not into gold."

"I won't be dismayed," Prue said, though when he spoke in terms of alchemy, she was.

He smiled at her with his lips pressed tight. "That's my girl," he said.

She nodded. She wasn't certain he meant this as a compliment.

"Good. If it suits you, I'd like to begin with the process itself, of distilling and rectifying spirits. Although it's the more complicated aspect of what you'll have to learn, I assume if you understand it, you'll apprehend the business side of things more easily. If not, we can always train up that little Izzy Horsfield. He'll make a good manager, mark me."

"He always seems worried about something," Prue said.

"Exactly my point. For your part, it's enough if you can make gin."

She inhaled a deep breath, took a sip of the coffee she was drinking despite its bitter taste, now she was a working person, and, wondering if she'd been wrong to volunteer for this task, followed her father down the open stairs to the mill yard.

Prue had always thought the buildings of the distillery were arranged in the most pleasing and symmetrical fashion possible, though now they did not look especially welcoming. The brewhouse, in which the distilling process began, sat at the southern end of the property, where Joralemon's Lane joined the Shore Road and raw materials might be most easily delivered. As the gin progressed through the stages of its manufacture, it traveled from building to building and tank to tank, heading northward toward the ropewalk and the ferry. The four long, narrow buildings in which most of the work was done—the brewhouse, cooling house, stillhouse, and rectifying house—were clustered away from the water, toward the foot of Clover Hill, to decrease the danger of flooding; and between the buildings and the straits was the hard-packed sand of the mill yard, in which the workers took rest and exercise, and in the center of which stood the countinghouse. Matty Winship and Israel Horsfield kept their paper-strewn office on the second story, and reached it via the outdoor staircase, against whose weathered planks their boots resounded whenever they went up or down. The office had windows on all four sides, so they might look out on any part of the works while seeing to other business. The ground floor was an empty room, swept clean weekly by a slave named Owen; there was thus always a suitable space in which to address the workers and give the wage earners their pay, regardless of the weather. (Prue knew neither the ropewalk nor the saw- nor the gristmill had an assembly room, but her father had once told her he'd been treated like a pig as a journeyman and had rankled under the indignity. "Mind, I don't provide 'em with French cravats or silken hose," he'd said, "but they do as they're told without grumbling if they can warm their hands by the stove of a winter afternoon.") At the northern waterfront edge of the property stood the casking house and storehouses, and those other buildings whose function supported, but was not integral to, the whole endeavor of making liquor: the cooperage, smithy, stables, slave quarters, privies, and cook shed. Past these, Matty Winship owned a stretch of open strand between his works and the Schermerhorn rope manufactory. If ever his business boomed enough to warrant it, he could expand northward.

From her visits to the manufactory, Prue had gathered the making of gin was hot, noisy, fragrant, and complicated, but she did not know how much so until her father led her down into the mill yard that morning. He began by asking her, "You know that I grow barley?"

"And Indian corn, vegetables, and juniper." She loved when the men hauled up kelp from the straits to fertilize the fields. It had a familiar, almost human stink.

He waved good morning to John Putnam, the brewhouse's foreman, who was hurrying past with a sheaf of papers in one hand. "Good. I grow barley for the gin, but not nearly enough to supply the works entire, and I'm no malter, either. I buy the remainder of my grain from Mr. Remsen and Mr. Cortelyou, and from a fellow in Nassau County, when the local supply won't suffice. Mr. Cortelyou has made his fortune selling malted barley to me and to the Longacre Brewery, up in Queen's County. And it all goes down to the Luquer mill to be ground. You know why it comes and goes in wagons?"

Some men were shouting outside the stillhouse, but her father didn't seem concerned. Prue had lost her train of thought in watching them, and didn't know the answer.

"So it doesn't get wet on a barge, monkey. Come, you've got a fine noggin there. Let's put it to use."

He opened the barn-sized door to the brewhouse, and Prue could feel the rumble of the great machines thrumming in her feet and her rib cage. At one end of the room, fires were lit beneath three copper cauldrons, each large enough, Prue thought, to hold a small outbuilding, and the moment the door was shut again, she began to sweat in her tall, heavy boots. Men were shouting to one another as they scrambled over the ramps and ladders surrounding the wooden mash tuns in the room's center; she had no idea how they could hear one another above the din. The agitators inside the first two tuns made a violent racket as they turned, and when boiling water spilled from the cauldrons down the chute to the third tun, it was loud as the river after a hard rain. Leather drive belts whirred and clattered over their wooden drums.

Her father leaned down close to her ear. "You know why it's called the mash room?" he asked her.

She craned her lips up toward his face. "Because they're mashing grain in there," she said.

"And you know why that's done?"

Prue thought a moment before giving her answer; she was anxious to get everything right. "To extract the sugar from't."

"Yes," he said. "We pump the water to the cauldrons from the liquor-back, which collects groundwater a good distance from the taint of salt in the straits. When it's good and hot, it spills into the tuns, as you just saw, there to be mashed for three hours. The fires beneath are just warm enough to keep things goin'."

Four men went running up the ramp to the third tun with paddles in their hands to prevent clotted grain from sticking in the agitators. They all had the necks of their shirts unbuttoned and their sleeves rolled up past their elbows.

"Are you ready to help?" Matty asked.

Prue was somewhat frightened by the noise and bustle but excited to be part of it, too. "Perhaps this first time, I can simply watch," she said.

"Nah." He gave her a courage-inducing rub on the arm, and she stumbled against him from its force. "You're going to be a distiller. You want to know simply by the smell how the wort is coming along."

So up the ramp to the first tun they went. The men made room, and a young fellow, whose florid mustache was already drooping in the steam from the tun, cracked a smile at Prue and said to her father, "You think she'll manage it, Mr. Winship?"

Matty took the man's paddle and gave it to Prue. "She's the best I've got, Mr. Southey. She'll have to."

Even above the din of the drive train and the moving agitator, she could hear the commentary this provoked. She wanted to run down the ramp and up the hill and take Pearlie for a walk, and she wanted to stay put and prove them wrong.

The lip of the tun stood shoulder high to a girl, and each spiked agitator within was twice as long as she. Prue had had no inkling how dangerous this process could be. If she fell in, she could easily drown, if her skull was not smashed instantly by the thrust of the agitating arm. She put the paddle's butt end on the ground and leaned into it as if it were a staff while she contemplated the roiling mess of the mashing. Her father leaned down beside her.

"Don't be afraid of it," he said, "and don't take it for granted, either. Whatever you do, don't go in. If the paddle drops, shout out. There's a warning bell over there"—he pointed to the northeast corner of the room, where a bell hung with its rope wound neatly around a cleat—"and the nearest man will ring it. As soon as he hears it, the windmill keeper disconnects the crown gear from the drive shaft, and the whole manufactory shuts down. It may seem a lot of fuss for a paddle, but it'll keep a whole batch of wort from ruination by splinters, and probably save your arm besides."

He taught her to watch the rhythm of the agitator, so she might put her paddle in and stir the mash without threat of injury, and she worked all morning alongside Mr. Southey, who seemed eager to catch her out in a fault. The sweat streamed down her face and arms and the channel between her shoulder blades. Her palms were rubbed raw, and her arms burned with exhaustion, but she determined she'd work as well as a man if it broke her. When the bell rang for lunch, she wished she could ask her father to carry her to the counting-house, but she clung to her pride, and once there, devoured her bread and cheese as greedily as would a coyote. She could hardly believe his collar hadn't wilted after a morning of such arduous work.

Prue spent a month in the brewhouse, sometimes accompanied by her father, more often working side by side with the men while her father saw to other business. The work brought out a deep, semipermanent flush in her cheeks, sinews in her arms, and calluses in her palms, but though Ben teased her about it, she could see he was jealous he had to spend his mornings in the domine's school. She began to notice subtle differences in the scent of the wort— the way it smelled light and sweet, like honeysuckle nectar, when

131

the mashing began, but nearly approached the odor of young beer when it was ready to move on. That first month, she had no real idea where it went when the mashers had done with it. One man would disconnect the agitator from the drive train, and another tripped a switch that opened a large screened valve in the bottom of the tun. The wort went cascading downward, who knew where, leaving the mash behind. Soon a second batch of boiling water would be let into the tank, so the mash might be reused for another, slower mashing. After this second mashing, the spent grains would be brought up in buckets, loaded onto a wagon, and sent out for the nourishment of Mrs. Luquer's pigs. Then came the enjoyable task of scrubbing down the tun, for which purpose the men let ladders down into it. Prue always volunteered to go inside, and often thought of Jack and the Beanstalk while she did the work, as if the tun might turn out to be some giant's butter churn.

By March, her father thought her knowledge of the brewhouse sufficiently advanced to move forward. "And I think she's an inch taller, too," he told Roxana one Monday morning over breakfast.

"I'll be sorry to leave the mash room, for all the hard work," Prue added. "I do love the smell of the wort."

Roxana flared her nostrils at her eldest daughter, but was too busy wiping porridge from Tem's face to reply.

"I've been amazed how much variation there is, from one mashing to the next," Prue continued, though she knew better than to prod her mother so.

"As if I haven't heard enough about wort in my lifetime?" Roxana said. "About wort and feints and gin?" Tem still refused to place her porridge spoon square in her mouth, and her mother took it from her and forced it in. "Christ, Reverend, while you're training her, you might teach her to raise less tedious subjects at table."

Prue was hurt by her mother's rebuke, but Tem shoved her wooden bowl to the floor and began howling, and there would be no further discussion. Prue could not decipher the glimmer in Pearl's black eyes as she sat primly eating her oats.

"Your mother's ill humor notwithstanding, it's a good-luck day for you," Matty told Prue as they walked down the lane. Indeed, it was a balmy March morning that could lull a body into believing winter wouldn't last until May. "The next stage of the distilling process is considerably less work—a perfect job for a little wool-gatherer like ye."

Prue smarted under the epithet, but knew it was true. Pearl was her own odd case, but though Tem was still well shy of her third birthday, Prue could already see she'd never bog herself down with reflection. It was Prue's own intrinsic nature, not everyone's, to wonder and brood. "I didn't mean to anger her," she said.

"No, you didn't," her father replied, providing little solace.

That morning, he took Prue down to see where the wort traveled when it left the tuns—deep into the brewhouse's cellar, into a cast-iron cistern called the under-back. The under-back's chamber was dank and noisy, as the power train kept two pumps whirring constantly to dispatch groundwater back to the sea, and the stone walls magnified their sound. The wort came cascading down the chute into the cistern, and a second set of pumps worked to draw it up and over to the cooling floor in the next building. A gruff, taciturn man called Hank Rapalje presided over this operation; his job was to check from time to time that all the pumps were functioning correctly. His skin had acquired a subterranean pallor, and Prue stayed as far from him as possible during her weeks under his tutelage, as he gave off a musty odor that reminded her of Johanna.

By contrast, the cooling house seemed like paradise. One climbed a short set of open stairs to reach it, as it was elevated on stilts some eight feet off the ground. The cooling floor was a shallow tank into which the wort was pumped from the under-back. This tank was as wide and broad as the room it occupied—twenty feet long by fifty across—and paved in cast-iron sheets to make it impervious to water. The room's pretty gambrel roof was supported by great unfinished beams, and its walls could open almost entirely to the breezes by a series of curtains and doors. A scant distance above the cooling floor's surface hung a latticework of planks resembling the top crust of a pie, and a balcony hung higher up the entrance wall, so the cooling house's foreman might stand aloft for a better view. Six men were ambling along the planks when Prue and Matty first entered, all holding paddles shorter than those in the brewhouse. Only two of the men looked to be slaves. The place was warm and smelled like rising dough, and a balmy breeze wafted in through the long, open walls.

"Quite the place, isn't it?" Matty said.

Prue only then noticed she had, indeed, been gathering wool. "What's the work to be done here?" she asked.

"You'll like it," he said, and took down a paddle from the wall and handed it to her. It was much lighter than the one she'd used in the mash room. "And it's perfect weather in which to learn it—it's less idyllic in December. D'ye smell the bready smell of the wort?"

Prue nodded her head.

"That's well and good, but if it ferments too quickly, we've got beer instead of spirits—and we can't turn a profit on beer. So the cooling men walk about the planks and stir. In that way, the wort at the tank's bottom is continually brought up to the top, where it can be cooled and freshened by the breezes."

"That's all the work?"

"That, picking out any debris that happens in, and helping wayward birds find their way back outdoors before they soil the goods with their excrement. And like the tuns, the thing has to be scrubbed down after each few batches to keep the product clean. How d'ye think you'll do?"

"Very well, thank you," Prue said.

"Then I'll leave you to enjoy yourself. Follow Mr. van Voorhees's instructions, if he has any to give you." Here a slightly built fellow raised his hand from across the room. "Mr. Horsfield or I'll be back to fetch you for lunch."

The cooling floor seemed incontrovertible proof there was a merciful God in Heaven. How else, Prue reasoned as she took up her paddle and began to walk and stir, could she explain work such as this existing in the world? It would leave her the entire day to dream. She held the paddle by its end and gingerly let it down to touch bottom; the tank, as it turned out, was less than two feet deep. One of the slaves laughed when he saw her do it. "Not so frightening, is it?" he asked her.

"No, not at all."

She would be able to amble along lost in her thoughts, with no danger whatsoever if she happened to fall in. The men with whom she'd be working also looked cleaner and more refined than Mr. Rapalje. She wagered they'd smell better as well.

"What's he, training ye up to manage the cooling floor when I'm a grizzled old man?" van Voorhees asked when they passed each other on the boards. "That's a nice bit of work for a girl."

"No," she said, and drew herself up to her full height. She was learning to brace herself against people's usual reaction to her undertaking. "He's training me to run the works entire."

He smiled and nodded, perhaps insinuating he'd already known what Prue was doing and believed she was bound to fail. She reminded herself not to take offense. This had been the response of the brewers as well, but she'd done a good enough job to keep them quiet.

134

Prue learned the business of cooling within the hour—the work was to wander and stir. Midmorning, a bossy jay flew in the west wall and Prue whistled and flapped her arms to shoo it out; van Voorhees told her that in autumn, there would also be leaves to remove. This was all, however. A batch of wort took most of a morning or afternoon to cool, and when it was ready, the men used their paddles to direct it toward a series of chutes near the north wall. Thence it descended to the fermenting-backs, which were housed belowground, exactly as the under-back had been. There, van Voorhees told her, the fermenting master introduced yeast to ferment the wares in a controlled fashion.

Prue would gladly have remained in the cooling house a year, and felt glad her father hadn't removed her the very next day, by which time she'd learned all there was to know. When, after a few weeks, she stood looking at the countinghouse floor and told him she'd imbibed all the lessons the cooling house had to offer, he lifted her chin and countered, "You're a diligent thing, but you're a child yet, too. A little more time enjoying yourself won't harm ye."

"Thank you," Prue said.

From across the desk, Israel Horsfield said, "Don't spoil her, now."

"I won't," Matty answered. "She earns her keep." He let her walk the boards of the cooling house through most of Lent.

In April, while the papers reported Ben Franklin was in Paris negotiating the peace, Prue moved on to help the fermenting master, the freeman Elliott Fortune, measure yeast and time the wort's ripening. News from the larger world interested her—she could not help hearing about it, either directly from her father or out on the streets—but Prue was far more concerned with learning to keep her eye on the clock, though she soon began to be able to judge her product's readiness by odor and taste. (The liquid that entered the fermenting-backs as wort left them as wash, which was pumped through pipes up to the stillhouse's copper wash-stills.) Matty Winship came down every few days to challenge her knowledge of the subject, but each time, he agreed with Mr. Fortune she was learning well, and might soon be able to manage a batch on her own.

Prue stayed in the fermenting room longer than she had in the other areas of the distillery; though the place itself was gloomy, she found Mr. Fortune congenial, and they agreed the process of making wash was as delicate and important as any she would need to learn to become a distiller. Near the end of May, however, he pronounced her ready to move on, and her father again came to oversee her personally. She had not known enough to value such supervision when she'd begun her training that winter, but now she knew how much else he had to attend to, and considered herself lucky when she could command his time and attention.

"Now, this'll be a fine spring for you," he told her, as he walked her around the periphery of the stillhouse, with its four great copper stills all shining and burbling, crowned with snaking copper tubes that reminded Prue of her own hair. "This is the real business of distilling, and the part that'll make or break ye. If you can't get proof spirit out of that wash, you might as well throw up your hands and jump in the river because river water's worth as much as the product will be. Do you think you can pay close attention and master it?"

Prue said, "I do." She had learned, in a few months at the distillery, that even when her confidence in herself wasn't strong, she could sooner or later make good on a promise by diligence.

"Hmm," he said, "I've almost begun to think so myself. But it's no use raising my hopes; it's not everyone can be a distiller. It's here in the stillhouse, you know, the alchemy begins."

Talk of alchemy continued to make Prue nervous, but she found even the most equivocal expression of her father's faith gratifying.

Each wash-still, she learned, had a thermometer attached to its side, because the heat of its contents was of paramount importance. "The men tend the still fires with great care, because the interior temperature must remain at all times above one hundred eighty and below two hundred twelve degrees Fahrenheit. For what happens at two hundred twelve?"

"Water forms blisters, and boils," Prue said dutifully. She hoped none of the men were listening to her catechism; in truth, they all seemed too absorbed in their work to notice her.

"Quite so. At two hundred thirteen degrees, all the wash would go bubbling up the pipes, and we be left begging for alms on the streets. But at two hundred eleven, the alcohol in the still vaporizes, without producing steam. Those alcoholical vapors ascend from the still into the copper worm," he said, pointing to the snaky tube overhead on the nearest wash-still, "and the worm makes its way down the inside of this tank."

Here he led her to a wooden tub as big as a mash tun. Water was splashing noisily in through its top, and equally loudly out through its bottom, into a chute in the floor. "This is called the worm tub," Matty told her, "and the water that surrounds the worm is constantly refreshed direct from the river. The alcoholical contents of

the worm are thus kept cool, and as a result, the vapors within con-
dense into liquid."

Here Prue's mind began to wander—she knew nothing of condensation except as it affected a jug of cool water or her house's window
glass; she couldn't say why it should become liquid. But watching
the noisy worm tub, a question arose to draw her back from her
peregrinations. "Where does the water go from the bottom?"

"The warm refuse from the bottom of the tub travels down the
pipes and out to splash over our water wheel, which provides ancillary power for the pumps here and in the rectifying house, as we're
far from the windmill, and a water wheel's easier to manage than a
whole 'nother mill." He watched her a moment to see if she'd understood, and went on, " 'Ancillary'—"

"I know," she said, "I remember. It's Latin, from *ancilla*, a
servant."

"Christ a'mighty. Your mother said the Latin wouldn't stick."

Prue felt awkward about her father's compliments, chiefly because
she knew his doubts about her would be confirmed if ever she bun-
gled a task. Whatever good opinion he had of her also seemed fragile
because she knew it would vanish if he learned what she'd done to
Pearl. As a result, she often dreamed up scenarios in which he uncovered her secret through stealth, or in which she herself accidentally revealed it. These fantasies made her skin creep, but she could
not force herself to leave them off.

The condensed alcoholic vapors went by the name of low-wine.
From the worm, it flowed into low-wine receiving-backs and was
brought back up again to the spirit stills, where it was redistilled to
increase its potency. "If any of the low-wine acquires a foul odor during the second distillation, we call it feints and give it up for lost, letting it run off into the river. The spirit proper, however, spills into its
own receiving-backs in the cellar, and there Mr. Horsfield and I test
the batches to bring them up to a standard strength. Until they reach
it, we keep sending them back for further distillation, and one never
knows how many trips through the spirit still will make a batch perfect. Sometimes only one additional distillation is required, sometimes three. And when it's strong enough—twenty times stronger
than gin—we mix it down with spring water and call it proof spirit."

"So when do you make the gin?" Prue asked.

"In its own due time," Matty answered. "But what gives gin its
particular taste happens in the rectifying stills; what we're making
here has no real taste nor smell a'tall." She must have looked vexed,

because he patted her on the head and said, "Never you fear—I'll do my best to teach you. But each thing in its turn. Manning the stills is a tricky business, and a great deal can go wrong in the worm. I'll learn you that, and then, God help us both, we'll get on to rectifying. Perhaps by the time you're twelve."

Prue's eyes widened—she hoped not to have to spend a solid year and a half in this hot noisy room. Then, too, she was fixing to spend her entire life here; she might as well get used to it.

"I'm only ribbing you," he said. "You won't surprise me if you move on to rectifying soon enough; you've been a quick study thus far. But for now, you work here."

Prue remained in the stillhouse through the summer, and indeed found distilling more complicated than the processes she had hitherto attempted. The art of keeping the fires at the correct temperature—which sometimes involved reaching briskly in with tongs to roll a flaming log, as big as she, out onto the tile hearth—required one to overcome one's natural aversion to fire, and she wondered if she'd ever master it. Being anywhere near the fires was misery, and made the beating sun outdoors seem almost a relief. Stills were finical: if the heat was to distribute evenly around their bases, the whole affair had to be shut down and polished every fourth workday. The worm sprang leaks, it seemed, as often as it worked properly, breeding lazy speculation while someone climbed into the empty tub with a lantern, searching for a hole the size of a pin; and the flannel at the worm's base, meant to trap any foul-smelling oils released by the process of condensation, frequently clogged the apparatus entire. Prue found the work frustrating, however, for a more basic reason: having spent six months in uninterrupted study of the distillery, she was beginning to have opinions about how things should be done. If she voiced them to her father, he'd hear her out, but in his absence, the men would wince as if she were imbecilic or speaking in French, then awkwardly return to their work. She had no doubt it was difficult for grown men to listen to a half-grown girl, but she knew her vision to be as clear as anyone's around her. She resigned herself to keeping her opinions private until she grew taller.

The rewards of all this work were threefold. First, in late July, her father began taking her down to the receiving-backs and instructing her in how proof spirit's potency was judged, both by objective measurement and by the way it burned the tongue. Prue delighted in any aspect of her appointed profession that smacked of science, and Israel Horsfield shook his head over Prue's glee the first time she introduced the hydrometer into its small glass vessel to measure the spirit's specific gravity. "She'll be a regular Galileo Galilei," he told Matty, scratching his pointy chin.

"Do you know what you've got there?" Matty asked Prue.

Prue examined the new instrument, bobbing in the vessel. "Looks like twelve-thirteenths the weight of water," she said, though she didn't understand precisely why the instrument should be calibrated in this way. "That's proof spirit, is it not?"

"Absolutely," Matty said. "But it's not off by a tenth of a point? Because it makes a difference here." He examined the vessel himself and pronounced her assessment sound. "I'll be damned, Israel, but she's as meticulous as we are." To Prue he said, "So we give it the second test. Remove the hydrometer, and take a wee sup from that vessel—but mind you, it burns, so no more than a drop to your tongue."

Prue felt flush with having read the hydrometer correctly, and tilted the beaker into her mouth. Her sinuses at once filled with fire, and the next moment, she was spluttering, with tears and mucus running down her face. Both her father and Israel Horsfield were laughing at her.

"Next time you'll know," her father said and brought her up, choking, into the mill yard and out to the pump for water.

But the day after this humiliation came her second reward: the new sign announcing the distillery's name. Scipio Jones whitewashed the words that had previously graced the side of the storehouse, but her own father climbed up the ladder to trace the outlines for the new letters, which Scipio then painted over the course of the next few days. Her father might yet have regretted his lack of a son, but Prue felt stirred when she first saw the black letters, shadowed in gray, gleaming out toward the port for all to see. Henceforward, those traveling across from Manhattan would see *Matt' Winship & Daught', Distillers & Rectifyers of 1ˢᵗ-Quality Gin*, and Prue felt sober and proud, knowing that everyone in Brooklyn and New York now knew a studious girl was learning to make spirits.

Prue's third reward was to be allowed to learn rectifying. She knew this was the place her father's art shone, and the part of the process he most feared she might be unable to master. "I don't mean to belittle you by saying it," he told her as he led her into the rectifying house—a building smaller than the stillhouse, yet similarly equipped with stills, and dominated by a looming iron hulk of a machine, with its great flat jaws yawning open—"but the truth is, when I was an apprentice, there were four others besides me, and none of them ever got the knack of it enough to start a place of 'is own. Everything you've learned until now is important, but it's all for naught if the rectifying goes afoul." Prue wondered why it had to be that everything could be ruined at each stage of the process, and she continued to stare at the gaping mouth of the machine. The men were piling up wood for a fire. "That's the press, little goat, the thing your mother most fears. Promise me you won't lose a finger in it; she'll never let either of us forget it."

"I promise," Prue said, but the press looked fierce.

"If you learn it right, rectifying'll be your great joy here," he said. She could not tell if he intended this to placate or frighten her. "There's no other task requires such knowledge and mastery, nor none that gives a man such pride in his work at day's end. From an odorless spirit, a gifted rectifier makes a product that delights the senses and buoys up the heart. Isn't that a fine thing?" She was too nervous and confused to answer. "That's all right, piglet," he said and worked his fingers into her tightly bound hair. "You'll see."

By means of this hydraulic press, he extracted the pungent essence of juniper along with various other berries and herbs. Their first day in the rectifying room, he showed her how the press worked—how he wiped down the lower surface, laid the herbs to be extracted on it, and used his whole body weight to depress the lever and bring down the top jaw. Prue was amazed a single man could operate a machine of such gargantuan size; Matty explained the workings of the hydraulic mechanism to her and showed her the place where the water dripped out from the hinges. The essence of the material— in this case, lavender plucked from their garden—trickled into a small vessel at the side of the machine, in an amount Prue thought disproportional to the quantity of herbs they'd placed in it. After unlatching and lifting the jaw, Matty once again wiped off the pressing surface and let Prue help him work the lever on the next batch.

"And attar of lavender goes into gin?" she asked, trying to enjoy the sweet fragrance wafting into the room and trying to dwell less on the danger of the work.

"Can do, but it needn't," he said. She knew her eyes must have widened, for he went on, "I'd think by now you wouldn't be surprised to find it all so complicated. There's no fixed receipt for gin, love, not in general. For Winship Gin, I've my own certain way, but I still make the slightest adjustments from one batch to the next. It's the great pleasure of the work, and the place a gin man proves 'is mettle."

Prue was shocked to know this whole manufactory was devoted to making a product whose recipe was no more precise than that for bean soup, and for the first time she sincerely doubted her fitness for the business. She could follow instructions well enough but the idea of having to invent them anew for each day's gin discouraged her. "What goes in it then?" she asked.

"The all-important juniper, of course." The Winships cultivated the evergreen bushes in their dooryard as other families tended roses. The sharp scent of the berries, ripening year-round, was so much a part of Prue's olfactory landscape she noticed its absence wherever else she went about town. "But one can flavor the liquor with a myriad other spices and sweets. I've used orris, angelica, lemon peel, cardamom, coriander, and the master I studied under used everything from sweet basil to China tea. But that was in England, of course; there wasn't any tea tax there."

"Soon enough we shan't be taxed any longer," Prue offered.

Her father began wiping down the press once more. "Not by the Crown, but mark well, wherever there's a government, an honest man has fees to pay. And you will, too, if you become a distiller."

Prue did not care for that "if."

That day, she watched him work and smelled the various extracts he produced and later in the week made some of her own, with his help with the lever. She came to understand how a gifted rectifier introduced these sundry essences in novel and harmonious proportion to the final distillation of spirit, such that their individual properties would be less evident than the balance of the whole. The product had to be recognizable to the palate and nose, have a taste that stamped it as *Winship* Gin, a thing a man would willingly plunk down his wages for when beer could be had at half the cost.

So into the autumn of 1782, Prue spent whole mornings roaming Brooklyn and asking if she might pick spices from her neighbors' gardens, or begging specimens of rarer varieties from Mrs. Friedlander. She knew this behavior—even more than her knee britches—made Mrs. Livingston click her tongue. She could not operate the press without assistance, but one of the slaves would help her crush whatever leaves and berries she acquired. And under her father's tutelage, she learned to taste and smell her herbs indoors and out, in the hot stillhouse and down by the cool river, by themselves on a fresh palate and in combination with other herbs and food. Her father brought her a small ledger from New York, and to its lined pages she entrusted inexpert drawings of plants, along with detailed notes on their tastes and interrelationships. Each week, she brought this book to her father for review, and though he chuckled over her sometimes zealous choice of adjectives ("The lemon balm was 'sprightly,' was it? I'll take your word, missy"), he seemed pleased, overall, to find her palate educable and her attention not yet flagging. He began to speak so often of her progress to the family that Roxana's eyes would glaze over when ginger and cinnamon came up at table.

"Might you teach her to cook and bake in the off hours?" she asked him one evening. "It'd prove a far sight more practical, and I dare say she already knows her spices better than I do."

Matty laughed. Tem, meanwhile, had finished her meal and began marching around the kitchen, hollering commands to invisible workers. She had never been to the distillery, so she'd copped most of her phrases from what she'd overheard on the wharves. Though Prue thought she herself should have had enough poise to disregard her sister, Tem's mimicry nettled her.

At the end of November 1782, a preliminary peace treaty was at last signed at Paris. Word did not reach Brooklyn until late December. The war had lasted all Prue's sentient life, and she realized that although she'd known it would someday come to an end, and had hoped with her father it would come to this one, she had always half considered it a permanent fixture, like a house. It would take some while, the men speculated down at Loosely's tavern, for the Crown to pack up its troops and send them home, so the Cortelyous had time left to grumble about pocked fields and poached pheasant, and the Winships might yet earn a tidy profit from the soldiers' love of the barroom. No one knew how long the occupying forces would remain, but to celebrate, Matty Winship put in an order for a doll-sized rectifying still, to be made to order at the English foundry from which all the original equipment had come. He had a talent for drawing, and when he explained the manner in which he thought she might practice her future art upon a gallon of spirit at a time, and showed her his delicate pencil sketch, she thought him as good as an old master. When the still arrived in early spring, she began to use it exactly as he had described, while the fires of the rectifying house roared and spat all around.

Prue had been using her new still a few weeks when Congress declared the official end to the war, and soon after came the order for those soldiers garrisoned in Brooklyn to return home across the sea. Those few remaining Loyalist families who had not yet left New York voluntarily began to pack up their homes to move to Canada;

Prue saw how awkwardly they were treated at Mrs. Tilley's or on the street. She had imagined there would be general jubilation, but there was little; the process of making peace had dragged on so, most of the neighbors seemed weary. After all the complaints the occupying forces had engendered, Prue had thought the Livingstons and Cortelyous would rejoice to see them go. But the soldiers had been in Brooklyn a long time, which made their parting bittersweet. White women and Negresses were suddenly to be seen crying in the streets—the mistresses and whores, many of them holding babies, or with small children clustering around their skirts and shrieking for their papas. Prue asked her mother and Johanna what would become of them, but found them both, conveniently, stone-deaf. Many of the neighborhood boys, including Ben, were also heartbroken at the prospect of the troops' departure.

"There won't be any more quoits, or shooting lessons, or card games for money," he complained to Prue as the neighborhood children watched some of the enlisted men tie up their bedrolls with hempen twine. Ben had his hands tucked under his armpits as if for warmth, though it was a balmy spring day.

"But it's a good thing they'll finally go," Isaiah told her. "And I, for one, shan't miss the gambling."

"Because you've been too much of a girl to take part in it," Ben said.

"Because I've been stalwart in the face of temptation," Isaiah corrected him, "which we shall all be better off without."

"I should knock you senseless for saying that," Ben said, but he kept his arms folded and his eyes on the soldiers.

Later in the week, the officers hitched their carts to the farmers' horses and went in clusters down to the waterfront, where they waited with long faces to begin their journey home. When at last they were all gone, Prue could see the full extent to which they'd devastated the landscape of Brooklyn—hewed down the forests, furrowed the fields with trenches, eaten up most of the livestock, and riddled the sides of barns with holes from their countless drunken games of darts—and the quiet that reigned in the village at night seemed unnatural.

When Prue wrote to her daughter, Recompense, about that period, she described it thus:

> A few prisoners had survived the fœtid English prison
> ships in Wallabout Bay and were set free, but most

succumbed soon thereafter to putrefaction or despair. A score of the natives of Brookland, Bedford Corners, Flat Bush, & Midwout were found among the dead, but only one Brooklander was recovered among the living:—Ivo Joralemon, a grandson of the farmer who'd sold my father his land. I had only a vague recollection of Ivo as a quiet, slender boy in the years before the war, but he came home skinny as a hoppergrass & seemingly more aged than his parents, with one leg so gangrenous, Dr. de Bouton had to amputate it. The Joralemon house stood close by our own, to the opposite side of the Ferry Road; and when Ivo's cries pealed out across the countryside, my own leg could feel the pain in sympathy, & I gritted my teeth till at last he must have fallen unconscious. I should not have been surprised had people heard his shouts all the way to New-York, where I half imagined his soul would soon be bound. Ivo Joralemon recover'd from the surgery, but limped around town hunched over his crutches, and never again spoke. The neighbourhood children joked he would marry Pearl. I pretended not to hear them.

My parents, the Looselys, & the Philpots had profited from the war, but the rest of the village was hard hit. When I took breaks from my work at the distillery, I sometimes saw fathers in their best suits of cloaths, standing together in threes or fours on van Nostrand's landing. I was not close enough to read their expressions, but their postures were glum; and I knew they were going to beg the bank for new mortgages on their properties, or for leniency on the terms of their current liens. Joe Loosely, who during the war had run his auctions only sporadically, now advertised one almost every week. On any given Saturday, the hammer rang on his block as carefully husbanded stores of lumber & seeds sold for pennies. Even the cost of a hired laundrywoman had grown prohibitive, and my father & Joe Loosely were the only men in Brookland who still had clean linen on workdays. All the other men wore starched collars out on Sunday, then grew progressively sootier till the Saturday next. One could tell in an instant who was too poor to have his razor ground.

And yet Brookland as a whole did not succumb, as I had thought it might do, to melancholy. Many families,—the Joralemons, Remsens, Rapaljes, & Cortelyous,—had lived on the land under Dutch rule, and their ancestors had weathered the change when the English arrived; they rebuilt after the long occupation with what must surely have been the same doggedness & faith. The king's officers had purchased the far western portion of Mr. Remsen's fields,—the area whose boundary everyone in the village knew to be pounded by the waves,—for a cemetery; & now, instead of crops, their dead were planted there in neat rows. Some of the westernmost were almost immediately unburied by the tide, but the rest slumbered peacefully. After a decent interval, Mr. Remsen returned the field to the cultivation of asparagus, and the resulting shoots are still counted the most succulent in King's County. (Do you shudder, dear Recompense, to hear what you have et?) As farms were parceled off on the auction block, some new arrivals bought up land for the Friends' meeting a short distance out the Jamaica Turnpike. From the way the men had long griped about the ravages of war, it had seemed to me my village must be doomed; but appearances spoke otherwise.

And for me, the pleasures of working with herbs, concocting recipes, & trying them upon my father's sensitive tongue were legion. My mother's attention yet wandered when I spoke of my progress and discoveries, but my father could no longer doubt my aptitude for the business, & he rewarded this with high praise. I held on to this knowledge when I approach'd him to ask if my next task might be to learn the workings of the mill's machinery.

—What, you want to know how the drive train works? he asked. He could not disguise the condescension in his voice.—You've already learned how to *make gin*. It's a far sight more than anyone thought I could teach a girl.

I felt smaller than my years, but I made my self hold my shoulders square.—I know how the drive train works, I said, looking out the countinghouse window toward the wharf, as if the direction of my gaze could lessen the strength of my impertinence.—The crown wheel hooks into the lantern pinion, and it sets the whole thing spinning.

My father went over to the shelf & poured him self a nip of the wares. It was early for this; he ordinarily waited until operations were complete for the day.

—If I'm to run it someday, sha'n't I have to know the mechanicks of everything?

He drank his cup down, and placed it carefully on the desk he shared with Israel Horsfield.—I suppose. But it might be thirty years from now.

—Even so, I said.

He shook his head at me & said,—Gears an' drive belts it shall be, then. But I warn you, I'm condemning you to a life of spinsterhood. No man in 'is right mind will share his bed with a woman knows so much of machines.

I faced my father as bravely as I could. At that time I didn't care about marriage. I could see plain enough what it had made of my mother;—but I could not dream of saying such a thing before him.

Reading this, Recompense thought how well her mother's knowledge of machines had served her, and smiled to see how incorrect her grandfather had been. The world contained at least one man who, looking around a village of girls trained in the domestic arts, preferred the distiller. Now that she was so far from home, Recompense thought perhaps she did, too. She curled deeper into the smooth cushions of the divan, and did her best to picture the machinery her mother spoke of, truly to apprehend, for the first time in her life, how her mother's manufactory worked.

Two Incidents
From Exist to Kiss You
Howard Norman

I.

I SAW MY FATHER ELEVEN times that summer; the number I think means nothing, except that it wasn't more or less.

The poet William Bronk wrote, "Happiness passes in a vague state, an inkling, an echo through one's memory, whereas sadness! Sadness plaits itself into memory." The poet Amichai wrote, "The precision of pain, the blurriness of joy." The Japanese writer Akutagawa wrote, "What good is intelligence if you cannot discover a useful melancholy?" Here are a few facts of my childhood. I had no books in my house save for a set of encyclopedias. I was for the most part raised in Grand Rapids, Michigan. The dominant population was Dutch Reform; there was an Afrikaans newspaper published there; the "twin city" was Holland, an hour away on the coast of Lake Michigan, where you could catch enormous lake perch right off the docks. During the summer of 1965 I worked in a bookmobile. The driver's name was Pinnie Oler. I had turned sixteen the previous March 4. For working as "library assistant" I was paid sixty cents an hour and worked forty-four hours per week. I kept ten dollars per week; the rest went to my mother, Estelle, which was all right with me, I suppose: "You're helping support us," is how she put it, "seeing as your father's mostly out of the picture." So these are facts, but then, of course, there are the emotional dimensions of childhood and young adulthood, perhaps more difficult to calibrate yet more rewarding to ponder, and which possibly contain more gravitas than does any "merely factual" (Chekhov) testimony that basically purports that a person lived and tried to feel things deeply.

When I say that I can truly recall only one conversation with my father with any confident degree of accuracy, I mean it. Others I can "reconstruct." For this conversation, however, I believe I became a stenographer. He had been away for about a year. My mother had said, "Your father now lives in California," a demographic assertion unaccompanied by any other information. Take it or leave it.

Perhaps I would have preferred that he was living in California, but the fact was, he was living across town somewhere, but certainly in Grand Rapids. How else might he have heard over WGRD radio that I had won $666 in a contest? I had not entered this contest; my older brother's best friend's girlfriend, Paris Muldovy (I quote Paris: "I was named after the capital of France"), had entered it on my behalf. The process was simple: she had called in the license-plate number of my 1965 Corvair, which of course had Michigan plates. Hundreds of people submitted their license-plate numbers. These were put into a hopper, and on the morning of June 23, the DJ Marty Sobieski— "Mad Marty," whose trademark exclamation was "Mad Marty's throwin' a party!"—reached into the hopper and plucked out my license number. A separate list matched car owners' names to their license numbers. Paris had tuned in, and when Mad Marty announced the winner, she telephoned, then I telephoned Mad Marty, who said on the air, "Well, Howard Norman of 1727 Giddings Street Southeast here in the Furniture City, get on down to the station and we'll cut you a check! And then you can ask the girl of your dreams out to dinner!" (The girl literally of my dreams that summer was Paris Muldovy, but no way could I ask her out to dinner.) Then he played "Sherry," an incredibly popular hit by the Four Seasons, replete with Frankie Valli's falsetto croon. I had only two months earlier obtained my legal driver's license. However, I had been driving the tan Corvair, purchased from my brother with no questions asked, for $150; this, of course, was the very Corvair featured in Ralph Nader's first book, the diatribe against the car industry, *Unsafe at Any Speed.* As it turned out, my brother had also heard me win the contest on WGRD, from his "work detail" under the auspices of the Kent County Correctional Facility, where he was serving thirty days for breaking and entering Hibbet's Apothecary on Division Street. When he went before the judge, my brother claimed that the heat had finally got to him and he was desperate for a root beer float. Not without humor, the judge had sympathized with the thirst but could not condone how it had been quenched.

Basically, except for Division, Cherry, and Giddings streets, the map of Grand Rapids is vague, but I do remember pulling into the A&W Drive-In, with its individual speaker phones (like at a drive-in movie) on poles, and waiting for Karen Eldersveld, my self-proclaimed love interest, to roller-skate out and take my order. Let me be direct: Karen was not really my love interest, and had she really been, it would have gone unrequited, but I had to declare one to my brother, his best friend, Tommy, and to Paris, an attempt at obfuscating my obsession with Paris Muldovy; all of this was part and parcel of the irrational calculus between fantasy, preoccupation, and erotic contingencies loosed in my heart and soul that summer, and I think it is fair to say that the irrational can provide as adhesive a purchase on life as the rational any day. Weeks and months at a time, even, or a complete summer.

When Paris Muldovy died in late August, instead of attending her funeral, I crawled back into the backseat of Tommy's black Buick and fell asleep.

Karen's father was a policeman. Every time I ordered a hot dog and root beer, or chili dog and root beer, she would say, "You're not supposed to be driving. You wouldn't want me to tell my dad, would ya?" This was, of course, when I was driving my Corvair without a license. Enunciated with slow charm (she was busy; no time to repeat herself), this was her standard bribe for an outsized tip. Clipped to my belt was one of those dorky press-down change dispensers with individual metal silos for nickels, dimes, and quarters, the kind people hawking magazines and cabdrivers had. I always left Karen a painfully extravagant dollar tip. One night, less than two weeks before obtaining my driver's license, her father pulled his police cruiser up directly next to my car. He looked over, registering my face and countenance, until Karen skated up between our cars and said loud enough for me to hear, "Hi, Pop! Hey, look, that's Howard Norman in that car. He's a year behind me at Ottawa Hills. He kind of supports his mother." Her father then reappraised me with a somber, sympathetic look and nodded a greeting. After he got his hot dog and root beer—no, I think it was a cup of coffee—he backed the cruiser slowly out of the parking lot. Almost immediately Karen skated up to my window and said, "For the 'kind of supports his mother' bit, that'll be two dollars, please." I always thought of her as a good businesswoman.

When I drove without a license I mostly learned Grand Rapids at night. Though it was a midsize city, I suppose, my nightly rounds were composed of stopping at places not especially associated with urban life. From the get-go I had kept to a precise, unwavering order. First I would park near the faux Mississippi steamboat at Reeds Lake in the wealthier part of the city. Summer gulls always attended the steamboat, having migrated in from Lake Michigan. At night they would roost along the chipped railings, deck chairs, calliope pipes. They flew in and out of the shadows. Sometimes the weight of four or five dozen seagulls noticeably moved the paddle wheel.

From the steamboat I would drive to the Thornapple River and park near the quintessential make-out lot, where, one stifling hot night, I saw Tommy's Buick with its windows down. His radio was playing. The area ironically was demarked by a symbol of domestic order, a white picket fence. You could, I was told, hear the river from your car. Anyway, I studied Tommy's car, which I seem to recall with a kind of binocular detail, though the imagination enhances even in retrospect and I hope it always does and I rely on that. At one point on that particular night, in that particular time and place in the universe, and with an illuminating assistance from the full moon, I saw a pair of feet atop the front seat—red shoes still on; Paris Muldovy's red shoes—and marveled at the geometric inventiveness of lovemaking in a car. "Sherr—eee, Sherry bay-ay-bee, can you come out tonight? Come, come, come out toni-i-iyee-ite."

Navigating past love cars, I would work my way down a steep path on foot to the riverbank. There I would shine my flashlight on the river's surface, hoping to lure the ghoulish, whiskered face of a catfish or bullhead. (There was a rumor when I was a kid that catfish had a kind of electrical circuitry, and if you got cut by a catfish's razor lips, a terrible shock befell you.) Mostly, however, I shined the light out onto the river for ducks, geese, the occasional loon; waterbirds were active at night more often than people knew. I liked being in the spectral world.

Next I would drive upriver about a mile to the elevated osprey's nest, on a pole about ten yards out into the river. Looking back on it, I realized this setup was an early example of ecological protection; on shore was a sign warning that any damage to the roost or the ospreys themselves led to a thousand-dollar fine. One night I saw an osprey glide in to the roost, and its body seemed illuminated from within, like a lamp shade, though of course it was the effects of the moon, and the moon's reflection off the water. The osprey had a fish in its bill. I remember saying the word *magic* out loud, feeling embarrassed right away, even though I was alone. However, if magic is a conjunction of rare, disparate, and vivid elements, the sight of that osprey with pale moonlight igniting its chest feathers and wings qualified as magic.

Last, I would drive to see the swans at Ebbets Lake, which, in every dimension, was a subsidiary of Reeds Lake, but the place the swans preferred at night.

This, then, was my nocturnal gazetteer of bird life and is what I remember with the most intense affection.

So birds provided a kind of aesthetic sustenance and pleasing memories and such. One Saturday morning in early August, I happened to be looking out my second-floor bedroom window at the very moment my father drove up and parked in our driveway. I remember thinking, "Where'd he get that car?" He had left driving a Ford and about a year later now returned driving a Pontiac. He stepped from the car, looked at the house a moment, walked to the back of the car, popped the trunk, reached in, took out a ball-peen hammer, closed the trunk, flattened his left hand against the slope of the trunk, took a deep breath, then slammed the hammer against his left hand, purposely, it looked to me, striking his thumb. A wince of electric pain contorted his handsome face. This was immediately followed by a bemused grin I later associated with a certain "See what I'm capable of doing?" sneer perfected by the actor Richard Widmark. Possibly because I had done well that school year in geography and suddenly desperate for irony, I thought how Michigan was shaped like a mittened hand, thumb slightly extended, and how people said, "I live in the thumb."

I heard the side door open and close. My mother was at work taking care of children at the orthodox shul near downtown. My two younger brothers were at my aunt's. My older brother was no doubt along some highway clearing weeds or putting down tar; he had already committed crimes but was on the verge of committing serious ones. I went downstairs and stood in the kitchen doorway. My father was sitting at the kitchen table with its red plastic table cover. He looked over at me and said, "You're too skinny. You're a skinny goat, son."

"I'm your son. So does that make you a goat, too?"

"Ha-ha and ha."

"Why'd you do that, Dad? To your thumb there?"

He held out his hand as if beholding some object entirely separate from himself. "Oh, that," he said. "I accidentally slammed it in the trunk door. Get me some ice cubes and a towel, will you?"

But I stood my ground, staring at him. I was dressed in a black T-shirt and light green shorts and I was barefoot. I was the only one of my friends—in fact the only young man I knew—who had a ponytail.

"What's that on the back of your head?" my father said. My father was nothing if not well groomed. He was five feet eight, slim, with

151

beautiful blue eyes, curly brown hair cut in what he called a "businessman's cut." What he did for a living I had not the slightest clue.

"Cat got your tongue?" he said. He walked to the Kelvinator refrigerator, opened the door, opened the small freezer door, punched away at a few stalactites of ice, reached into a drawer, and took up a butter knife, took out an ice-cube tray, and pried out a half dozen or so cubes, which he wrapped inside a dish towel, then he sat down at the table again. He swathed his thumb in the towel.

"Slammed it in the trunk door, huh?" I said.

"That's what I said."

"Yep, that's what you said, all right."

"What's that on the back of your head?"

"Where's the hammer? Still in the trunk?"

"What hammer, exactly, are you referring to?"

We stared at each other a long, silent moment.

"I guess that's a badge of individuality, that ponytail, or is there something you want to tell me? Is there something you want to tell me?"

"Like what?"

"Such as you aren't the kind of young man interested in having a girlfriend. Something along those lines."

I could hear the refrigerator humming.

"I have a girlfriend. Karen—that's her name."

"Karen the girlfriend. Is the ponytail her idea, Karen's?

"If you've been living in California, how come you've got Michigan plates, Dad?"

"It's a borrowed car."

"Borrowed from whom?"

"Oh, I like your diction."

"Whose car is it?"

"Someone you don't know. Someone you'll never know."

(Since it was his car, he was right in that.)

"What color is a California plate, anyway? I've never seen one."

"It's blue with a palm tree on it."

"That seems more like Florida."

"California might've copied the idea from Florida, how do I know? What's so important about it to you?"

"Nothing."

"Maybe you just need money for a haircut. Maybe that hairdo's the result of financial constrictions around this house in my absence. Is that it? I could give you a haircut right now, just with the kitchen scissors."

"No thanks."

The ice cubes were melting onto the table.

"Speaking of license plates—," he said. He adjusted the towel and winced.

"What about them?"

"Let's reverse the situation here, shall we?"

"Whaddaya mean?"

"Let's reverse the situation. Say you dropped by my place of residence and said you were temporarily not flush. Do you think for one minute I'd hesitate to reach into my pocket, snap out my wallet, and hand you a roll of five-dollar bills, or tens, or twenties, peel off a few fifties for you? Right on the spot for my son."

"I'm sixteen, Dad. I work in the bookmobile. Maybe you didn't know that. Maybe that news didn't reach you in California. I'm never flush."

"Speaking of license plates, you're pretty flush now, though, aren't you?"

"You must have had the radio on in your borrowed car, huh?"

"Imagine how proud I felt—just flew into town and the first news I get is my boy's a millionaire!"

"Imagine."

Then came the turning point in the conversation. I did not recognize it at the time, but it definitely was the turning point. I knew where things were heading now, that my father wanted my WGRD prize money. Right then and there I was fully resigned to it. But asking for the money was not the turning point.

My father sensed that it was exactly the moment to punch his right thumb with his left fist, and instead of loosing a howl of pain, he more or less threw his head back, crying out, "Sher-r-r-eee, Sher-e-bay-ay-bee, Sher-er-ee, won't you come out to-night?" in a falsetto voice that would match Frankie Valli's in pitch and intensity any day. He was forty-four at the time, a decade younger than I am as I write this. He had quit smoking. He was living somewhere. Anyway, I cracked up laughing to think of him listening to the Four Seasons on the AM rock & roll station WGRD.

It was some connection, at least.

My laughter was a mistake but I could not help it. And he further seized the moment. "Hey—I could drive you over to the Old Kent Bank and cash your check or be right there when you cashed it.

Did you cash it already?"

"No, it's upstairs."

"I'd've thought your mother might've cashed it."

"She didn't."

"Well, you don't need an adult to go with you. Not at age sixteen, I imagine. But I'd volunteer."

"Where've you been this past year, anyway?"

"Mostly California."

"Oh, sure."

"Mostly."

"What happened, Dad, all the support checks get lost in the mail?"

"You know how I feel about the postal system."

"Yeah, well, Mom's not exactly flush."

"Whoa, now, son. Hold on. Hold on, there. The adult finances— no, that is not your business. That's not—"

"I'll give you a hundred dollars of my money."

"How about half? How about a two-way split, $333?"

"I'll give you a hundred dollars. How long are you here? You going to see Mom? Mike's in jail. You going to see Mike?"

"Actually, your mother doesn't know I've come over today."

"Dropped in from California—out of the blue."

"No need to tell her, really. Now that our business transaction is completed. It's a loan, mind you."

"I'll get my shoes on."

"Old Kent Bank's open till noon Saturdays, I noticed."

"I'm giving the rest to Mom."

"Well, maybe keep some for yourself, kid. You won it fair and square. It was your license plate, wasn't it?"

"I'll do what I want."

"Fine, do what you want."

"Nice to agree with so disagreeable a person, as Mom would say."

"Oh, that's a saying of hers, is it?"

"Yes."

"Look at this mess, ice cubes melting all over the place, and what kind of son do I have, not a smidgen of sympathy for a man who's slammed his thumb in a car door? There's pain involved with this." (Well—enough sympathy, looking back on the moment, to offer a hundred dollars from a windfall. But that was my fault. He was just practicing his craft. He was working the room, and I happened to be the only other person in it.)

"We could stop at Blodgett Memorial. They could look at your thumb."

"No, no—life's generally an emergency, isn't it, but this thumb's not."

"I don't know what you mean."

"Let's drop it. Let's drop the subject. The bookmobile, that's your summer job, I take it."

"My summer job, yeah."

"What's your wages?"

"Six hundred sixty-six dollars an hour, Dad. That's what I'm making. Since you asked. Since you're so interested all of a sudden. I file cards in the card catalog. I dust the books. I fill out overdue notices. I do everything there is to do. You used to read books. You should drop in there, find a book to read."

"I've got to get back to California, truth be told. So just imagine how overdue that book would be, huh? How would you explain that?"

"You'd have to explain it. I'd just send out the overdue notice. But for that I'd need an address, wouldn't I?"

We drove in his Pontiac to the Old Kent Bank. I cashed the check. The teller had heard the contest on the radio and commented on my luck. While still in the bank I handed my father ten ten-dollar bills. There was no more bargaining or conniving. "I'll walk home, thanks," I said.

In the parking lot, he said, "Yes, it's a nice day for a walk. A nice summer's day to be sixteen, out walking, some cash in your pocket."

"OK then, Dad. See ya."

He slid into his car and drove off. I noticed that he adjusted the rearview mirror. But then he screeched the Pontiac into a U-turn and stopped next to me. He stretched his arm out the window. "Men shake hands when they part company after a business deal," he said. We shook hands—a handshake is a form of complicity—and he drove off. I had $566 in my pocket. I walked directly to the Buy Right, a drugstore, where I purchased a notebook and pen. I sat on the bus-stop bench and wrote down the conversation as best I could remember it; even in that amount of time there had to be emendations, a sculpted sentence or two, perhaps, even in immediate retrospect, but I think I got it down with a large amount of accuracy. I've kept the notebook for thirty-seven years; surely it registered one of the earliest moments, perhaps unbeknownst to me, when writing became something.

When my mother dragged in from work, she said, "I'm beat." I had already cleaned up the kitchen spick-and-span. I handed her the $566. "So you went and cashed the check," she said. She counted it out on the kitchen table. "So, what, you kept a hundred dollars for yourself, honey? That's a lot of money, sweetheart. Use it in good health. It's only fair. Well, one way and another, it all goes for household upkeep, doesn't it? Being grateful and in good cheer, that's household upkeep, isn't it? I'm going to have a lemonade. Then I'm going over to pick up your younger brothers. Then I'm going over to visit Michael if possible. Want to come with?"

That night, again, as I would most every night that summer, I toured the bird haunts and was quite successful, seeing what I had come to see.

II.

In 1965 the Vietnam War was occasionally on the radio but not really on television yet. Tommy Allen was the first man I knew to volunteer for the military. He wanted to fly helicopters. He eventually served two tours in Vietnam. He left for basic training in September. Anyway, that summer I sort of "studied" Tommy. He was often at our house. So was his girlfriend, Paris. Paris Muldovy. At the time you didn't see that many T-shirts with writing on them; however, it seemed that Paris was always wearing a black T-shirt that read EXIST TO KISS YOU. (The utmost erotic existential presentation possible; Paris, as my mother noted, was "well endowed.") One sweltering afternoon in July I accidentally discovered her alone in our basement, naked from the waist up, watching her T-shirt tumble in suds behind the oval window of the washing machine. When she sensed that someone else was present, without looking over she said matter-of-factly, "Hey, a girl needs some privacy, you know." Then she looked at me. "You want me to tell your brother?" I went upstairs and for some reason fed my goldfish.

I had been impressed that Tommy had begun to drive at age fifteen. In effect, he had turned the street map of Grand Rapids into a grid of illegal sojourns. At sixteen he passed the driver's test with flying colors. Later, his father gave him the family's 1956 Buick, a black hippopotamus of a car. The word Turboglide flowed in silver cursive lettering across the dashboard. The car had a plush gray interior with a pull-down armrest in back, five ashtrays, side-view mirrors adjusted by knobs from inside. Tommy lived with his father, Woodrow

Allen, who referred to his former marriage as "my war wound." Woodrow had served in the marines and had fought at Iwo Jima. He claimed to know "the guys who are depicted on the famous statue." Once Tommy asked if his father would like to go to the art museum. (Tommy had taken a fancy to a part-time museum guard from Ottawa Hills High School, Marcia, who worked weekends.) His father said, "Speaking for myself, the test pattern on the TV at 6:00 AM, after half a bottle of Jim Beam, is art enough for me." That, I believe, is verbatim.

Tommy had poise, confidence, attitude. I am sure that on some days my admiration scarcely fell short of hero worship, which I did not feel toward my brother. I was vigilant around my brother, physically intimated, but I did not admire him. From my first experiments with inwardness, I knew that resident in my love for my brother was the foreshadowing of that love departing and probably for good. I definitely loved the idea of Tommy Allen, the phenomenology of him; I looked up to him because Tommy epitomized a kind of beatnik cool. Stylized slouch, pompadour hairstyle, black chinos in any weather, boots with Cuban heels, hipster vocabulary—he used the word daddy-o—and sneering intonations. It never seemed he was approximating a "look" as much as embodying it. "Cool" was something you yourself felt or recognized in another person but it could not be defined. To define it would be to cage it; "cool" exacted a restlessness from the calmest of moments. Cool was a kind of agitation; it forced a heartbeat between regular heartbeats, it changed the natural syncopation. To put it another way, Tommy was not "like" anyone else; he was fully resident in himself. Though he had a poster of teen matinee idol Sal Mineo on his bedroom wall, and though he had seen *Rebel Without a Cause* umpteen times, it was as if Sal Mineo were imitating him, not vice versa.

My mother picked up on the physical resemblance and expressed a judgment on it. "Your brother's friend Tommy reminds me of that young degenerate actor Sal Mineo," she said one evening before going to work babysitting. That was one of my mother's employments, babysitting. ("Here I am in my forties and I'm having to compete with thirteen-year-old girls. Well, what can I expect? I'm lucky to find the work. No husband at home, what am I complaining about? And I don't pay taxes on what I make.") She was away from home a minimum of three nights a week. "Tommy's got those same Mediterranean good looks. Though I always got the feeling that Sal

Mineo's mean as a snake in his private life. Is Tommy Allen mean as a snake?"

"I don't know how mean a snake is," I said.

"That's your contribution?" she said.

"I guess so."

"Well, I'll have to trust you and your brother to be a good judge of these things, especially since you spend most every evening with Mr. Tommy Allen. I suppose it's nice that your brother takes you along. That's not always the case between brothers, now is it?"

(I never told my mother, of course, that my brother decided that the lecture on "the facts of life" would be for me to sit in the front seat of the Buick and watch in the rear-view mirror while Tommy and Paris were screwing in the backseat. That actually happened.)

This was memorable. One morning in July Tommy picked me up in the Buick. My brother was at summer school—that turned out to be a euphemism; in fact, he was already married and had a daughter, but had not revealed this to even my mother. "Yeah," he said, "I'm in classes all day—and I'm taking a night class, too." I have no idea to this day how he supported a young wife and baby, but my best guess, based on his subsequent criminal résumé, is pawning stolen goods—not in Grand Rapids, possibly Kalamazoo, Detroit, Muskegon, Holland—I believe he had some sort of percentage "arrangement" with a friend who worked on the loading dock at J.C. Penney.

The morning in question, Tommy honked the horn of his Buick until I came out. "Get in," he said. "You're in for a good time." We drove downtown and he parked in front of WGRD, a popular AM radio station, which broadcast out of a building next door to the Pantland Hotel. Tommy considered WGRD "a station for squares." He held a morning DJ—"Mad Marty Sobieski"—largely responsible. "Sobieski is chickenshit," Tommy said, a serious indictment in those days. "He don't play any music that's risk-A, you know what I mean?" I followed him as he sauntered through the lobby past the reception desk and went directly into Sobieski's studio without knocking. Sobieski was short and chubby with thick black sideburns; he was about thirty-five years old and when he said, "Who let you in here?" I saw he had bad teeth. Tommy said, "Here's a letter from hell" and flew a paper airplane directly onto Sobieski's desk. A record was playing. Sobieski picked up the paper airplane, unfolded it, and read Tommy's letter—it was a list of songs that Wolfman Jack regularly played on his outlaw program rumored to be broadcast out of Mexico. "If these are requests, buddy, I can't play 'em," Sobieski said. "I can't put these on the air. Not here. Not in Grand Rapids. I know my audience." He crumpled up the list and tossed it in the waste basket.

"You don't know shit," Tommy said. "But I know something."

"Yeah, what's that?"

"I know I feel sorry for you. Because you're a DJ who isn't cool and doesn't know shit. It upsets me so much, I'm gonna smoke a cigarette."

"You're going to get out of my studio is what you're going to do," Sobieski said, lifting a phone from its cradle, as if about to call the police.

Tommy reached into the hip pocket of his jeans, took out a pack of Marlboro cigarettes. Tapping the pack against his open palm until a cigarette slid out, he put the cigarette in his mouth and lit it with a blue-tipped match flicked against his zipper. He had perfected this method.

Later Tommy said, "I had him mesmerized." And truth be told, it looked that way, because Sobieski simply observed Tommy smoke the cigarette down to the butt. He played a few songs during this interval. Then Tommy ground the butt into the carpet with his heel. When Tommy turned to leave, Sobieski said, "See you in jail."

Tommy had something of an epigrammatic way of talking. "Some nights," he said, a certain gravity and edginess in his voice, "I sometimes go to this one place where they do certain types of dances. Your brother used to go with me. He doesn't go anymore." He was not inarticulate; he purposefully composed his sentences in such a manner as to impart provocative information while at the same time maintaining a reclusive aspect. While driving, he often revealed the deeper agitations. For example, he would dial the car radio frantically, his hand moving with the sort of flicking impatience you might associate with a card shark. "Shit, I can't find anything," he would say, and now I see that phrase had a great deal of existential angst about it. "I need it to be night. I need to tune in to Mexico."

Tommy's loyalty to and reliance on Wolfman Jack could, I think, be accurately categorized as religious, insofar as he would say, "I hear his voice in my head day and night, radio on or not." In fact, Tommy had invented a prayer: "Now I lay me down to sleep / but I can't sleep / because the Wolfman is coming through / loud and clear." He would utter this prayer in the car, then stick his head out the window and let fly the trademark Wolfman Jack howl. "An am-bu-lance has got nothing on me."

Tommy was legend, in the sense that in eleventh grade he forged a permanent association between himself and Wolfman Jack. This occurred at Ottawa Hills High School during history class. It was the third- or fourth-to-last day of class and the teacher, Mrs. Britton, foolishly attempted to impose order on students whose restlessness was a kind of insanity. It was near to unbelievable that she conducted an oral quiz based on the last section they had studied, "The Cultures of Ancient Egypt." Here is how I heard it: "Class," Mrs. Britton had said, and a black eraser ricocheted off her desk, exploding chalk. "I'm going to ignore that. Now—you have your notebooks. Each of you choose any figure from the historical period we've been studying, and ask that figure any question you wish. We'll pass the question around, and then each of you will answer the question you receive. Understand?"

Tommy's hand shot up. "Will miracles never cease?" Mrs. Britton said. "You haven't raised your hand all year, Mr. Allen. Of course, I haven't yet asked you a question, have I? Still, Mr. Allen, proceed."

In an astonishingly accurate imitation of Wolfman Jack's gravelly, Negro-jazz, smoky-room, sexually besotted voice, Tommy said, "Cleo-pat-ra, are ya nekid? Are ya wearing only that snaky necklace, are ya nekid? If yer nekid, I'm drivin' my camel right on over and ooo-ooo-ooo, baby, I'm yer back door man!" Then he threw his head back and let loose the iconic howl.

The room went crazy, for who among them could deny such absolute perfection? "The principal's office—now!" Tommy was suspended; he therefore did not have to attend the last three or four days of class.

Tommy's most oft-quoted song lyrics were from John Lee Hooker, the Detroit bluesman, whom Wolfman Jack himself had knighted "Mr. Down and Dirty, God of the Underworld." He was Paris Muldovy's favorite, too. The lyrics were: "I got a girlfriend / I ain't never seen / what I mean / what I mean / she's the onliest coffee / in my midnight cream."

When it came to love, John Lee Hooker was an agent provocateur, for when his songs were not directly elegiac ("You done left me"), they equally moaned and wounded with a sense of elegiac anticipation ("I know you done gonna leave me"). And of course John Lee had a voice like the very baying hellhound on his trail.

Tommy took John Lee Hooker's words to be a kind of resignation, a fait accompli. "I know how it's all gonna turn out with Paris and me, from listening to John Lee," he once said.

"What do those words mean exactly?" I asked him.

"What words are you talking about?"

" 'I got a woman I ain't ever seen,' " I said, "and all the rest."

We were driving along at night. Tommy immediately pulled the car over to the side of the street. Apparently my question required his full attention, because he turned off the ignition as well. We both stared ahead through the windshield. Again in the intimate, disturbing, visceral, suggestive growl of Wolfman Jack, Tommy said, "You don't decipher, you just squirm and smile." (I had heard Wolfman offer this same advice late one night.) He turned on the ignition, put the car in gear, and had driven a few minutes when he rejected one alley for the next. Navigating the Buick like a barge through the Panama Canal, Tommy nodded his acquaintance with the brick corridor of fire escapes, garbage cans, rectangles of dirty light through window shades. "Many a night I've ended up here," he said, "and pictured myself standing in the shadows of love."

As for what he meant by that bit of autobiographical wistfulness, I did not even ask. Later that night we huddled in Tommy's own basement inches from his Grundig-Majestic shortwave radio. It was raining cats and dogs, wind lashing rain against the basement windows. Like a safecracker, Tommy worked the broadband dial in minuscule calibrations, trying to pick up Wolfman through the weather and distance. "Shit, shit, and shit—it's every kind of static," he said. "Lots of interference between Mexico and Michigan." He lit a cigarette. And suddenly, as if the cigarette smoke had helped the reception, we heard Wolfman Jack deliver these sentences with perfect clarity:

> Listen up, darlin', to Wolfman's advice,
> I'll give it once, but I won't give it twice,
> Remember, whatever else you might do,
> Every night you got to arrange a *rendezvous*.

"The Wolfman is fluent in French," Tommy said.

And this thing happened that I cannot ever thank him enough for, though it was very disturbing at the time. One night he drove me across town to a bowling alley called Avenue Lanes. "I'll wait in the car. You go on in, but don't go all the way in. Just stand by the soda machine near the door and look down the lanes. Look down to Lane

161

Three. The lane closest to you is Lane One. Look down to Lane Three and see what you'll see. Don't worry, you'll see it."

My heart was pounding but I went into Avenue Lanes. There were a lot of people bowling and a lot of people watching the bowlers. I counted down the lanes and when I got to Lane Three, I looked at a blonde woman sitting at a glass-top table, keeping score. The scorecard was duplicated on an overhead screen. There was a man and woman sitting on a bench behind the scorekeeper. My father was holding a bowling ball and stepping slowly toward the beginning of Lane Three. He sent the ball down the alley and it knocked down—this definitely is accurate—seven pins. He was supposed to be living in California, I thought. That is what I was told. And yet at that moment all I could think of was, "Seven out of ten is not bad. Not bad at all."

If you lower your expectations in life, your disappointments square better with reality. Or something along those lines.

When I got back to Tommy's car he said, "I bring Paris here sometimes. One night she bowled 125. Course, if you bowl three hundred, it's considered a perfect game. But Paris called her 125 a perfect game. I said, 'No, no, darlin', you didn't bowl a perfect game,' but she said, 'Yes I did.' 'Why do you say that?' I asked. 'Because I felt so good bowling it,' she said. 'I felt so good being with you and bowling the game I bowled. It was a perfect game.' I am telling you, you hear someone say that and you don't decipher, you just squirm and smile."

We sat in the car not talking for about ten minutes. Then Tommy said, "Your father's a world-class shithead, and I'm not going to lie to you about any of that. I don't lie to your brother about that and I won't lie to you about it. One other thing, too. I've seen your dad here bowling oh maybe five-six times and he never once bowled over 170—tops."

Ten O'Clock
Micaela Morrissette

I.

CHILDREN ARE UNDER the table, hidden behind the tablecloth. Children are in the kitchen cupboards, inside pots all over the floor. Children are twined around the coat racks; they have lost their feet inside our giant galoshes. Children are under the bed and under the covers. Children in the field impart no movement to the grasses. Children cling to the underbellies of our cars. Children press their noses to the windows and draw the curtains closed behind their backs. A child has locked himself inside the refrigerator and will not open the door. A child has wedged herself into a dresser drawer and is stuffing sweaters in her mouth. A child is in the garbage can and another peels potatoes onto its head. A child is curled up inside that pillowcase. A child is braced inside this chimney. They brush against our legs and their breath stirs our hair.

What are the children up to? We sent out spies to watch them, but these came back hobbling. We tried to tell them we believed they were playing a game and that we wanted to join in, but the children were having none of that. Even though they are not wise children, they seem canny. *That's why we've got teeth and fingernails, and hot tea and pushpins,* they say. *So as not to have to worry about wisdom.*

We discovered the children on the occasion of their initial raid, the one in which they stole all the beautiful pictures we had drawn. They hung their headquarters with the booty and now live in a splendor of artworks the majesty of which is unsurpassable. Initially, we could not understand our loss. Later, we came to realize they had done it because they had no windows. Now we are happier than we were before, because with all our pictures on their walls, we can see clearly what they are up to, even if it's totally unclear what this is.

163

Only that they first engage, always, in fantastic revelries, drinking and puffing on fat cigars, blowing smoke rings in huge, hideous shapes and collecting these shapes in lockboxes. On the upside, they've stopped asking after their parents. When, after all, they know very well!

In battle they wear dunce caps. Undercover, they sneak into the cells and into the halls of suspension. Thieves from their ranks steal lollipops, razorblades, necklaces, and our deeply personal keepsakes. They are all pedophiles. Their leaders call for a wholesale corruption of their elders.

The cruelty of the children is not as shocking as their gaiety. As when they all begin at once to clap their hands together, and continue doing so until their palms are red enough to burn us. Several of us have the marks of children's hands permanently on our cheeks. Although this makes us infinitely more attractive, it is the indignity of it we cannot bear. We have decided that our revenge will take the form of suicide, as is always the case, as this is the only thing the children cannot stand. We don't understand why, since there is nothing they like better than blood, but it may be that, like everyone else, they hate a missed opportunity.

II.

The child peered up at me out of the ooze and sharpened its teeth on a brittle bone. *Where is my present?* it asked.

I emptied my rucksack out onto the stone. The child poked through my offerings. A pocket knife, a shrunken head, a soft terrycloth straitjacket smelling of damp hands. The child snarled its disapproval.

Listen, I said desperately, *I implore you! Your wasted youth! Your wilting days! Won't you leave this awful place? Won't you join us in peace? Think of all that you are missing! Matinees, chilblains, chlorinated water, hot asphalt, copper batteries. All the joys of childhood, and you here in the murk!*

The child ignored my pleas. It asked me to pull out its baby teeth. Its gums, it claimed, were tender. There was a rash on its tongue from rubbing against the poison tips. Point-blank, I refused. I would not put my hand in that mouth. I could hear the child swallowing a throatful of hot saliva. It splashed idly about, glancing at me sideways. I could feel its thoughts poking around inside me, like hard little tumors.

Violently, I requested that the child behave itself at once. Inside me was no place for it, I insisted. I was full of knowledge the child was too young to learn, I explained. If the child discovered my secrets, I told it, it would cease to be a child and would lose all its special powers, and it would tremble before me.

The child snarled and scratched at itself in deep frustration. I offered the child a deal. I would bring it down to the city and take it to the school where it could find others, weaklings to do with what it would, or strong specimens like itself. In return, the child would wash its hands and comb its hair and put on shoes and dance for me. At the thought of the child dancing, blood suffused my head and I felt my mouth grow soft and slack. The child could smell my desire, but it did not know what this meant. I trembled, and tried to pull myself together.

The child crawled toward me, licked my hand, and bit deeply into my thumb with its jagged, rotting teeth. I kicked the child in the chest and quickly stepped on its head with my heavy boots. Noises of cracking and sucking. I bore down on the child's soft head with my heel until the child was quiet a long time. Then it reached up and put its small hand in mine and I could feel fingernails reading the lines in my palm. The lines were short, and the child's nail traveled back and forth in the shallow grooves, digging deep.

Micaela Morrissette

III.

One child said to another, *Would you like a piece of my candy?* Wily, the second child declined. The first child said to the other, *Do you want to get married?* Brutally, the second child scoffed. The child said to the other child, *Can you come to my treehouse when the sun goes down?* The other child sent its regrets. The first child pouted and chewed at its lip. Then it pointed its finger and brought down its thumb. *Pow!* The second child tumbled to the dry ground and soon enough was gone.

The child left the child disappearing in the dust and continued on its way. Before long the child met a witch in the road. They cackled at each other, rubbed noses, bit tongues, and the child gave the witch a sixpence. *God bless the cheerful giver,* said the witch, and the child made the sign of the hex, touching lightly the witch's cracked, smiling lips.

The child continued on its way and before long it met a cat. The child cheered and pulled the tail of the cat so hard the tail came off in the child's hand. The eyes of the cat rolled like paylines in a slot machine, then closed. Golden coins poured forth from the ass of the cat. The child cheered and bit into one of the coins. The tongue and teeth of the child became golden and its breath turned rancid as it ate one coin after another. It ate until its stomach swelled and clanked and then it lay down in the sun with the cat for a pillow and napped until it ran out of dreams. Then the child continued on its way.

Before long it met a dog with eyes as big as saucers. The dog licked and licked at the child until the child's eyes fluttered and its bony chest heaved and parts of it melted away entirely under the frantic tongue of the dog. When the dog had its fill of the child, it laid down and napped in the sun and dreamed of the child's fingertips, kneecaps, earlobes, armpits, and eye sockets. When the dog had dreamed of each of the child's thirteen hundred small, sharp-smelling parts, the child rose from the ground, kicked the dog in its sharp ribs, and continued on its way.

166

The child came to a ruined city. Saltwater washed over the gray stones of the buildings and made them soft as sugar cubes. Sodden piranhas flopped awkwardly along the sidewalks, sucking and burbling at the child from their toothless mouths. Jellyfish were stuck to the walls, left clinging there by a faithless high tide, and they bubbled in the sun, and the child stuck its finger in their soft, sweet bodies and sucked at it. Another child walked toward the first child, through an avenue of blighted saplings. *Hullo,* said the first child. *Hullo,* said the second child. *Have you got any candy?* said the first child. *Have you?* said the second child. The children hacked at the crooks of their elbows with bits of shale and seashell, and they pressed the cuts together and mixed the blood, and then they licked themselves clean. *I know a game,* said the first child. *I know a game,* said the second child.

IV.

There is nowhere the children are not weeping. They weep walled behind the cinderblocks of basements and they weep perched atop the rafters of attics. Caught in cobwebs, they weep; at the bottoms of wells, they weep; in coffins, they weep; in brick ovens, they weep; in fridges, in junkyards, they weep; in hollow tree trunks, they weep; under aprons, they weep; in haystacks, they weep; in sandboxes, in spaceships, in cages, in ditches, in classrooms, in bedrooms, in forts, in igloos, in church pews, in elevators, in garment racks, in night forests, they weep, they weep. They scream. The children howl. They bawl. They sob and they bleat. They plead, they lament. The children mourn. They snivel, they sniff, they wail, they blubber, they cry. The children hiccup, they pant. They tremble, they quaver. They press their fists against their eyes so that their eyeballs strain to bursting. They hold their breath until they fall in a faint. Their red faces, their wet lips, their eyes swollen shut, their inhuman keening. Thousands, millions of children fall lightly at our feet like moths from a porch light. They pile up and begin to stink.

The children weep and weep and we do what we can to placate them, to comfort them, to resist them, until in one wrenching instant, across the continents and the oceans, we all tear the hearts from our chests. Our hands full of blood and muscle, the empty cavities of our bodies, our shocked, staring eyes—a pause comes over the children's weeping as they regard us. They begin to giggle.

The children are laughing. Their laughter is the twittering of birds, the groaning of corpses, the shrieking of the mad, the tinkling of bells. The children laugh with bright eyes, pink cheeks, sweating and wiping their brows. They pinch their lips together to suppress their laughter and it comes out choking. The children are bent over double. The children clutch one another in hysteria. They pound one another on the back, slap one another across the face, punch one another in the stomach. The laughter quiets, recedes, lulls. Then a giggle, then a snort, then a shriek of delirium. We roar at them, our voices shuddering down from the heavens like rain. *Quiet!* Their eyes fly open, their mouths clamp shut.

A quick gasp. A low moan. The children are weeping.

They weep so that they cannot eat and they cannot sleep and they weep until it kills them. All night we labor, burying the bodies, smoothing closed the eyelids, folding the small, pale hands on the hollow, rigid chests. We rake over the traces, plant the lilies as the sun comes up, and all the next day we sleep, our faces slack, blank with pleasure, the breeze beating in our empty ears.

V.

The child looks in on the mother as she sleeps.

The vague shapes of her limbs under the blanket do not match the shape the child knows. Here is an extra leg, there is a missing arm. Which is the impostor, the sleeping mother or the waking mother? The child covers the mother's face with a pillow.

The mother looks in on the child as it sleeps. The child's eyes race beneath its lids. One hand is curled into a fist and will not reveal what it holds. The mother forces open the child's fingers. In the middle of the palm is a bottomless hole. The mother leans into its depths and is sickened, dizzied. Something bright and deadly flashes deep within the abyss. The mother takes the child's stuffed animal from the floor where it has fallen and places its paw in the child's hand. She closes the child's fingers around it. The animal hisses in the dark.

In the garden, the father turns over the earth with a spade. When the hole is deep enough, he throws himself in. The child smiles in its sleep. The pearls of its teeth. A flytrap grows from the father's chest and the flies crawl in.

VI.

Children are slithering through our hair, twisting the tendrils around their fingers, digging their toes in the warm flesh of our scalps. Children are inside our mouths, rubbing themselves along the lengths of our tongues, cleaning the scraps from between our teeth. Children are beneath our skin, scratching at the undersides of our scabs, wedging themselves through our tunnels of pores.

Children sit cross-legged in the dark spaces of our pupils, and wave to each other from one eye to another. When they want us to look at something new they pluck out an eyelash and poke it at the optic nerve. Children curl in our ears and whisper dirty words. There are many, current in the schoolyards, that we had never heard before. Children wedge our thighs open and push themselves between our legs. Some get their arms in up to the elbow; one wedged a whole head in, and the doctor had to be called. When we wake up, gasping in horror, to discover them there, they bow in their small brown suits and curtsy in their pinafores. *Look what the stork has brought,* they crow. Their smiles are lopsided with our lipstick.

We send them back to the orphanage, and beg the headmistress not to spare the rod. *Oh, but the rod is no longer au courant,* she smiles, and lights one of her long cigarettes. Our children shudder with soft convulsions and whisper to us of a certain machine. The headmistress invites us to throw the switch any time. Most of us decline, as the treatments are very expensive, and are printed in a gaudy, festive red, in foul taste, on every bill.

VII.

The children are asking for seconds. The children are taking thirds. The children demand dessert before dinner. They receive it—chocolate cake, bricks of Neopolitan ice cream, sopapillas, canned peaches lumped with cottage cheese, caramel creams, tiramisu, Turkish delight, pistachio pudding, date compote, saltwater taffy, strawberry mousse, Mississippi mud, trifle, sugar cookies, baklava, eclairs, lemon meringue pie, gingerbread men, blueberry cobbler, ambrosia salad, praline fudge, crème brûlée, rock candy, pear tart, macaroons, madeleines, baked Alaska, jelly doughnuts, Italian ices, apple slices spread with peanut butter, petit fours, shortbread, Rice Krispie treats, hazelnut truffles, lady's fingers, biscotti, bananas Foster, tall frosted Shirley Temples lousy with cherries, handfuls of Boston baked beans, cheekfuls of Mary Janes, scalding throatfuls of hot cocoa, gutfuls of saliva the children swallow as they slaver for more, these, the insatiable, voracious, fat-cheeked, slack-jawed, yellow-toothed, puffy-eyed children.

The children bounce off the walls. They tremble, their small hearts race, their knives and forks clatter against their plates, their tongues flop helplessly in their mouths. Their lips, coated with sugary slime, smack, and their eyes roll. Their teeth chatter. Their hands grope blindly in delirium and they glower and grow and bellow and their voices deepen, roughen, with pain and with need. We bring vats of ice water and they wade in and wallow, and soothed, they belch evilly and stagger back to the buffet. At last, they begin to totter and to fall, and we see their eyes close and hear their gluey breath slow with our usual deep despair.

We rub their swollen limbs, chafe their sweaty palms. We lay cool cloths against their brows, poke them with clean, bright needles, slap their faces, swaddle them in coverlets. Anything to keep them with us, awake. We brew thick teas of ipecac, we press on their stomachs, we tickle inside their throats. Anything to take back the offering we made them. Still they swell, redden, bloat, snore, moving into their hibernation, and we lift our hands in helpless horror, knowing, when they emerge, what they will have become, and how little time remains in which to save ourselves.

VIII.

On the child's birthday all its special powers awaken and its abilities delight it. At the child's behest, the sun rises and the house fills with the warm maple smell of its rays. A breakfast feast is served: silver dollars, blood oranges, and thickly clotted cream. The child writhes with pleasure and blesses all at the table with small pricks of its fork.

In the garden, the sun smells like a lollipop and shimmers in the sky like something deep underwater. The child jigs from foot to foot and pinches its arms and cheeks, marveling and humming and grinding its teeth.

Now the birthday treasure hunt begins. First the child's own presents to itself, to be safely gathered again for the birthday quest to come. The rusty knife, buried under the squash patch. The fishing line, wrapped around the gutter spout. The cap gun, in the tool shed behind the coffee cans of turpentine and oil. The all-seeing glasses, sunk in the goldfish pond in a black rubber sack. Then the presents that reveal themselves to the child as it casts itself about. From a black-and-purple butterfly, a ragged wing, for flying with. From the deepest ditch, a jagged white stone, for drawing secret signs. From the high grass across the black asphalt, a gauzy plastic bag, smelling of lemons and powder, to go over the face for invisibility. From the gleaming silver trash can, a chicken bone, for showing the right road.

The child croons and spins like a falling leaf. Cars pull up in the drive; the child's birthday guests are beginning to arrive. Other children descend from the cars. The birthday child wonders what they know and it crushes its secrets close in its hands, deep in its pockets. A balloon drifts idly out the front door and begins its journey toward the sun. *Soon,* whispers the child longingly. A call from the house, the squall of a noisemaker. The child's stomach rumbles and it licks its lips and casts a lascivious glance at the sun and then it begins to make its way inside.

IX.

The children's season is nearing its end and already we dare to walk with firmer steps through the rooms of our houses. Our eyes dart slyly toward the corners where the children collect in little dry heaps. The children breathe in short, quick gulps; their hair is thin and brittle and strands of it float in the air around our faces like ghosts of sunlight. The children's lips are chapped; they lap thirstily at the shallow, thick bloodslicks that well up from the cracks. The children are loveliest by far in this time of their passing—their pale, stumbling legs; their thin, groping arms; their milky eyes. How we love them, now that we can draw near enough to see the perfection of their many small parts and smell the strange, heady tang of their fear. They snap feebly at us and we are moved by the flushed, violent pink of their long tongues.

The first symptoms. A stubbly, itching rash that rushes across their cheeks, foreheads, and bony chests. Small swellings lodge in their throats and deep within their stomachs, in their groins and in the damp crooks of the arms. Light, delicate pains shiver up and down the lengths of them, and their eyes flicker, flick, flick.

The second symptoms. A painful sensitivity to light attended by a terror of the night. A parched throat, an inability to swallow. Hands that clench involuntarily, inexorably. A series of small heart attacks. These are highly contagious and will travel through a pack of children like a purr down the knobs of the spine of a cat.

The third symptoms. A hectic speaking in tongues, bouts of graceful swooning, the ruthless ravaging of scabs, the compulsive, painful curling and uncurling of their long, bloodstained toes.

X.

The children's graves are spick-and-span. They leave no sign behind. When they die, they vanish, and our mourning is bitter and fierce. Weeping, rocking, rending, etc., we wrap ourselves in our own arms. *Our lost children, our own cruel babes, spilled like milk, our spoiled brats, the rotten apples of our eyes! Their bite was cruel, their nails honed to a deliberate point, but oh! whose eyes should they scratch if not ours? before what should we tremble if not before them?*

The black stone of their fortress is bleaching and crumbling in the midwinter sun. The birds that fly unwittingly into the air above their territory no longer lose their grip on the thin and breathless arches of the children's sky.

When our mourning ends, we begin our fortifications, however vain, against the coming season. Great vats of sweet poison to butter their teacakes. Thin needles we practice concealing in the soft pads of our inner cheeks. Jacks-in-the-box primed with dynamite. Rings that will squeeze their fingers till they weep. Dolls with porcelain heads that will shatter sharply in their hands. Stuffed bears that withhold comfort in the dark.

When the spring mud begins to stink in the streambeds and the first bitter herbs knife their way out of the earth, the children will return. That their lives will be brief and their beauty, tarnished!

Nuts

Gahan Wilson

175

Mikky Waze
Gilbert Sorrentino

THE NARRATOR IS discovered insisting, by implication, on a regular-guy childhood for himself on the famed mean streets of the Big City. His hope is to create the "ring of authenticity"—so treasured by readers—in his tale. His childhood was, however, spent in Glen Cove, Long Island.

THE IDIOT

The Brooklyn neighborhood in which I was born and brought up during the years of the Depression had the usual New York complement of maniacs, drunks, and garden-variety psychopaths, who ran the gamut from inventors of superatomic fountain pens that would write forever to potential salesmen of pop-up get-well cards that dusted their recipients with disinfectant powder to tire repairmen who sprinkled the streets outside their dim and filthy shops with nails and broken glass, in the great tradition of honest business initiative, usually called "drive." The neighborhood also contained a man afflicted with—or, to employ the current cant—challenged by Down syndrome. In those benighted days, such people were known as Mongolian idiots. No one understood the term with any degree of accuracy or precision: What was a Mongolian? For that matter, what was an idiot? Many of the children who attended the local schools, both public and parochial (read: Roman Catholic) were, more or less regularly, called idiots by their teachers, but none of them resembled Jo-Jo, the name by which everyone called the idiot. Our parents called Jo-Jo a Mongolian idiot, and we followed their experienced if not jaded lead. Jo-Jo, the Mongolian idiot! Fine. It had a whiff of Coney Island's freak-show emporiums to it, those creaking buildings on Surf Avenue and the Bowery, which housed attractions like Morris, the Dog-Faced Boy; Lucille, the Human Reptile; and Grace and Georgy, the Pinhead Twins: why not add Jo-Jo, the Mongolian Idiot? So all was comfortably in place.

Nobody knew how old Jo-Jo was, the guesses ranging from twenty-five to fifty and all ages in between, but he acted as if he had not reached his tenth birthday—that is, when he was at his best; at his worst, he was infantile. His mother, an old, gray-haired Irishwoman of perhaps seventy, who went to mass every morning without Jo-Jo (the accepted wisdom was that she tied him to the bathtub while at church), held her son's hand during her—or their—daily shopping trips, during which Jo-Jo would be given little gifts by the shop-keepers—a slice of baloney, a raw clam, a few grapes or walnuts. It sometimes seemed as if the donors were warding off Jo-Jo's bad-luck influence (for idiots were almost on a par with those who had the evil eye) rather than expressing affection.

The other women in the neighborhood, all of whom made their daily shopping rounds like Jo-Jo's mother, were, I believe, oddly pleased that Jo-Jo had turned out to be an idiot boy, irritated as they perhaps were at what they took to be the sinful sexual activity of his mother, in what was, shamefully, an act of fornication at an age when she should have known better. They may have been angry at the thought that she might have found pleasure in the perverse and unnatural act. Not, oh no, not that a Just and Merciful God was punishing her for her brief middle-aged spasm of delight, oh no. But, well, God *was* Just and had given her a Cross to Bear—as well he might! So they'd glance at the old, frail, wispy-haired woman and her drooling son, who would amuse himself on these excursions by pulling his hair, punching himself in the face, and pissing in his pants. He'd ask his mother, again and again, "Candy, candy, candy?" until she'd buy him a penny marshmallow twist or a two-cent Hooten chocolate bar. But what Jo-Jo really wanted was a Milky Way, which he called Mikky Waze. They, however, cost a nickel, and so Jo-Jo rarely got one. He'd grind up his cheap candy with his green teeth, melted chocolate slobbered on his lips and chin, and staining his already stained shirt. Disgusting, the women said. Poor boy! God bless the mark!

Now that the narrator has posited his main character, if character he may be called (he doesn't seem to be "fleshed out"), he suspects that his story, to be a story, needs conflict or confrontation in order to be, ah, marginally successful. He consults certain "model stories," here to be nameless. And so:

Gilbert Sorrentino

ENTER BIG MICKEY

One of the recurrent dangers of the neighborhood was the presence of a boy of fifteen or sixteen, known to all as "Big Mickey." He was the perfect thug and sadistic bully, swaggering, vicious, cruel, careless of his own and everyone else's well-being, and thoroughly brutal. His mother, a tramp and drunkard, had left her son more or less to his own devices from the age of six on, although he had a grandmother in the neighborhood at whose place he could get an occasional meal, a bath, and a place to sleep. He rarely stole much from her, and hit her only once in a while. He'd been in reform schools for truancy, petty theft, and some unnamed sordid delinquent behavior in the rail yards with a brother and sister about Mickey's age, at that time about twelve.

He enraged the neighborhood superintendents by urinating and defecating in their buildings' hallways and lobbies, breaking ground-floor windows, setting mailboxes on fire, and dumping garbage cans down areaway steps. The beatings he occasionally got, when caught, were no deterrent, and he always got even with his assailants. He was tall and slender, with a tough yet handsome face—spoiled a little by a sullen, outraged expression—black hair and eyes, the latter shielded by the bill of a gray tweed cabbie's cap, pulled low. He always had a cigarette in his mouth, a Bull Durham handmade or a cheap loosie—Wings or Sweet Caporal. He disliked or held in contempt or injured virtually everybody, but he especially loathed Jo-Jo, nobody quite knew why: Jo-Jo had never done anything to Mickey, whom he looked upon as another wandering piece of flesh. Mickey's hatred of Jo-Jo manifested itself in relentless taunting and petty torture: yet none of this worked, since Jo-Jo took these assaults as evidence of Mickey's fondness for him. When Big Mickey, in crude imitation, drooled, bugged his eyes out, and hit himself and then Jo-Jo in the face, Jo-Jo laughed delightedly at these delicious antics, this wonderful entertainment: he began to think of Mickey as his *friend.* Mickey was, of course, well aware of this, but no behavior on his part, no matter how mean or cruel, could now change things. When Jo-Jo saw him on the street, he would howl and laugh, punching his mouth and screaming, "MICKEY MICKEY MICKEY!"

It will be recalled, of course, that Jo-Jo's favorite candy—his favorite food, if it comes to that—was Milky Way candy bars, his fabulous Mikky Waze. Someone in the candy store suggested that perhaps Jo-Jo identified Mickey with Mikky Waze. Well, perhaps.

179

Gilbert Sorrentino

The candy-store analyst further theorized that, to Jo-Jo, Big Mickey was the Candy God, was, in effect, God, and that God was now his ally and friend. Summer days were long, long in the somnolent thirties.

These aberrant notions were, of course, but exaggerations of the fact—that Jo-Jo reveled in what he took to be Mickey's attentions, which were anything but what Jo-Jo thought they were. But now that Mickey *was* God, there was nothing he could do that was not construed by the Idiot Boy to be the effects of sublime friendship, a relationship wholly different from the neighborhood's aloof disgust and his mother's worried fussing. "MICKEY MICKEY MICKEY!" Love.

As the situation became ever clearer to Big Mickey, he became ever more enraged, and although no one who valued his well-being had the foolhardy courage to hint to Mickey that he had created this, ah, friendship, the very fact that none of this was said made it all the sweeter to the neighborhood. "The fuckin' idiot prick basted!" Mickey would say, to silent delight. "I'm gonna clean his fuckin' clock for him!" Then he'd throw somebody to the ground or spit in his face or tear some girl's dress down the front. Yet he was demeaned and humiliated by the Mongolian Idiot Boy, yes indeed, and the absolute silence enclosed a message that all, including Mickey, could easily read: YOU'RE STUCK WITH THE IDIOT, YOU SON-OF-A-BITCH SHANTY-IRISH TRASH!

We now have a "situation." What, muses the narrator, to *do* with Big Mickey and Jo-Jo? Create a strange and unlikely friendship à la George and Lennie? Redeem Big Mickey as he realizes innocent Jo-Jo's strength in the face of adversity? Posit other positive resolutions? Or simply get rid of them both and allow the story to sit uncomfortably but perhaps happily in the great midden of neighborhood lore? Read on.

IN THE COURTYARD

Late that summer, Jo-Jo was found dead in the courtyard of the tallest apartment house on the block, a six-story yellow-brick building put up just before the collapse of 1929. His arms and legs were broken in many places, his internal injuries massive, and his great

180

stupid melon head smashed open. He had, apparently, fallen, or so the police guessed, while chasing sparrows, one of his pastimes when he slipped away from his mother. His pulverized mouth was sickeningly decorated with chocolate, caramel, teeth, and blood, and in his pocket were two Milky Way wrappers.

Jo-Jo *never* had any money, which the narrator has more or less made clear. Now he sees the end of his tale.

JUSTICE PERVERTED

Big Mickey was arrested later in the week after breaking a display window in the Owl Men's Shop, inside which window the police found him at 3:00 AM, stuffing shirts and socks and ties into a paper bag. We discovered, courtesy of the *Brooklyn Eagle* and *The Spectator*, that Big Mickey's true name was Michael Xavier McAnamee, and that he was almost eighteen. He was sent away again, to Lincoln Hall, where he was to remain until he reached the age of twenty-one, when he would be released into society, but the boys in the neighborhood expected to see him appear any day, cigarette in his mouth, cap pulled low over his eyes, his swagger sending his message of banal cruelty, and, as everyone but the police knew, more than that. He would be back momentarily, back to throw them all off the roof.

Nizi Goes to Market
Yan Lianke

—*Translated from Chinese by Karen Gernant and Chen Zeping*

NIZI HAD WANTED to go to the market all by herself for a long time. She wanted to walk here and there, look at everything, slip in and out of the crowds, buy whatever she wanted to buy, eat whatever she wanted to eat. It wouldn't be at all like going with Grandma when she had to let Grandma know even when she had to use the toilet, so that Grandma would wait for her at the roadside or stand at the door to the toilet. It seemed that if she were away from Grandma, away from adults, she would surely get lost. Going to market made Nizi happier than anything else: she was like a lamb on a vast grassy hill. She hid in the cracks between people, just like a lamb hiding in the grass. She loved smelling people's sweat. She loved seeing grownups with the third button unexpectedly buttoned into the second or fourth buttonhole: then their clothing flapped against their bellies. Yet, they still thought they were smartly dressed: they walked with their heads high. Oh, and when young women went to market, they dipped their wooden combs into water and combed their hair until it shone. They pulled new clothes worn only at New Year's out from the bottom of the trunk, but didn't wear them—just draped them over their shoulders. That was just how clothes were displayed in the shops: these clothes weren't meant for covering up or keeping warm, but for attracting people's attention and appreciation.

Nizi knew that she was still little. She wasn't old enough to paint her fingernails and powder her face as the young village women did. The young women bamboozled their kids into staying home while they—all dressed up—went to market to buy this and that. They enjoyed it when men's gazes slid back and forth between their hair and their new clothes, although they didn't dare stare back at the men. After the men passed by, more often than not the women would comment cheerfully that men were all pigs. Actually, Nizi didn't approve of this. She secretly looked down on the young village women. She thought, *You're dressed gorgeously in order to be eye catching. But when people do look at you, then why do you curse them?* She thought to herself, *When I grow up, I also want to get all dressed up just like them, and let people look at me. But I'll smile at whoever looks at me. And I'll just stand there without moving while they look at me. Or I'll turn around, or spin around, so that they can get a good look.* She even thought, *I'll give a little money to whoever looks at me. If I have some money, I'll give it to the men who say I'm pretty and fashionably dressed.*

Still, the important thing was that she wanted to go to market all by herself. If she didn't go by herself, never mind letting men look at her, Grandma wouldn't even let her look at the fashionable men and women at the market. Nizi had already told Grandma lots of times that she wanted to go to the market alone. Every time, Grandma had looked at her and said, "What did you say? Wouldn't you be scared? Would you dare go all alone?" One time, Nizi lied and said she wanted to go to the market with a few other girls. Holding some of the dishes she'd washed, Grandma stood dumbfounded in the courtyard. She asked, "Who else?" Nizi said, "Yang, Caozhi, and the neighbor girl Xiaoli." Telling lies like this made Nizi feel naked in front of Grandma. Her face was hot and her heart thumped, but Grandma didn't notice. Grandma said, "All right then, go ahead." Then she took the rice pot to the kitchen. Nizi was almost screaming with happiness as she ran from the courtyard to the village street. But at the kitchen door, Grandma turned around and, narrowing her eyes, she said, "Nizi, wait a moment while I go next door and ask Xiaoli if she's really going."

Grandma left. She put the rice pot on the ground and walked on bound feet over to the neighbors'. She didn't care if the chickens pecked at the rice from the pot. When Nizi saw that Grandma really intended to go and ask, beads of impatient sweat appeared on Nizi's thin little forehead. Just as Grandma was about to go out the door, Nizi suddenly squatted on the ground and shouted loudly, "Grandma, my tummy hurts. It really hurts. Quick, come and massage it for me."

Nizi never knew where her parents had gone. There were two yellow plaques on the table at home. Pointing at one, Grandma had said, "This is your daddy," and pointing at the other, she'd said, "This is your mama." But Nizi wondered, *How can these be Daddy and Mama? They're just yellow-lacquered plaques with black writing.* Nizi had thought about it for a long time, but never figured out how the plaques could be her father and mother. She stopped thinking about it. Anyhow, she had Grandma and food, clothes, and toys. Grandma saw to it that she didn't lack for anything. But Grandma wouldn't let her go alone to market. She wouldn't let her go all by herself to the mountain ridge to cut grass and tend the sheep. She wouldn't let her go to other villages to drop in on relatives.

Grandma was protecting her, just as if she were protecting a young seedling from being nibbled by sheep or dug up by pigs. But this morning during the autumn vacation, when Grandma was still in bed, she woke Nizi up from a dream. "Nizi, didn't you want to go to the market?" Nizi sat up excitedly in bed and said, "Is this a market day?" Grandma said, "This is the ninth. Go off to the market by yourself. Grandma won't go with you. Grandma feels a little dizzy." She said, "Get started soon, and come back soon. When you get there, buy a spool of yellow silk thread for me."

Nizi walked around the market three times before she finally understood why Grandma had let her come to the market alone. It was because actually no other villagers had come today. Previously, Nizi and Grandma had come to the market when the farmers could take some time off work. And so it was that every few steps they had run into a fellow villager. At the pig market, they'd run into village men selling piglets. At the timber market, they'd run into young married men buying wood for home building. At the egg market, they'd run into young wives selling chickens or eggs. At the clothing stores, groups of young village girls dropped into one shop after another. To buy one pair of trousers, they had to go to at least five shops. To buy one length of cloth, they had to drape ten different kinds over themselves so that others could offer advice and make comparisons. In the end, they were usually totally confused. All the pieces were attractive in different ways, yet none was perfect. But today, Nizi walked from one end of the market to the other and back again. She even looked more than once at the wood market, which she didn't like at all. To her great surprise, she didn't encounter even one person she recognized.

It was autumn harvest time. People had to pick the corn. All the grown-ups were busy farming. The ones who'd come to market were those who wouldn't need to pick their corn for a few more days and those who had been busy with other things the last few days and now suddenly had discovered that they needed some farm tools. They had to fix the tires on their carts so they could get the corn to market; they had to sharpen their shovels so they could dig up the corn stubble; they had to get baskets and crates on hand for moving the corn from the fields—and so they had rushed to take advantage of this last market day before their really busy farming season. They went directly to the place selling what they needed, bargained, dickered, and, after making their purchases, they simply left.

In the whole market, it seemed that only Nizi had time on her hands: she didn't need to buy sickles for cutting the corn, nor did she need to buy spades for turning the earth, much less did she need to think about planting wheat right after the corn harvest. Grandma had said it would be a few days before the corn was ripe and she wanted to take advantage of these few slow days to get her funeral clothes ready. She said she was doing fine. She couldn't leave this world until she had seen Nizi grown up and married, but she also said that she would get her funeral clothes ready just in case. Grandma had already been making these clothes for a winter and a summer. Everything was ready. Now she just needed lace for a funeral robe. For that, she needed a spool of yellow silk thread. Nizi had come by herself to the market today especially to buy a spool of yellow silk thread for Grandma. Not nearly as many people were on the road to the market as before. There wasn't even the noisy and confused sound of people selling clothes. It was desolate. This market day was not much different from any other day.

Nizi had already located the silk thread shop in a small building next to the town's department store, but she hadn't gone in right away to buy the thread. It wasn't easy to get a chance to come all alone to the market: she wanted to look around to her heart's content before buying the thread. It would be a bother to carry it while wandering around. She might even lose it on the street. Grandma had given her ten yuan and said that a spool of silk thread should cost two yuan at most and if she bargained she might get it for one yuan six jiao. *After you've bought the thread, you'll have eight yuan left and you can buy whatever you want with it or eat whatever you want. But whatever you do, don't lose the money.* Nizi had put the money in her pants pocket. That pocket held a wallet she'd made by folding paper from a pictorial: it was shiny and pretty. At first, it had held only a little loose change—at most not more than one or two yuan. But today it held a ten-yuan bill, and so it was heavy. With each step she took, the wallet patted her thigh. And that's how she knew that the wallet was still in her pocket, and the money still in the wallet, so as she walked along the street, she wasn't like those

185

hopeless village women. When they saw a toilet, they went in not to relieve themselves, but to take advantage of a place without other people nearby to see whether their money was still stuck to their chest or their thighs. Nizi wasn't afraid of losing the money; she was just afraid that the paper wallet wouldn't pat her thigh again. The pictorial paper was stiff and shiny. When it patted her thigh through her pants pocket, it was like someone's hand touching her body. She felt relaxed and secure, the way she felt when she was almost asleep on a summer evening and her grandma fanned the mosquitoes away from her—safe and comfortable and relaxed.

Nizi had already walked all over the main street several times. She'd been strolling from early morning until the sun was in the south. At the vegetable market, she'd looked at cucumbers, eggplants, and chives; at the wood market, she'd looked at purlin wood, rafters, and trees that had just been logged. None of that had anything to do with her. She just wanted to look—get fleeting glances of lots of things in order to prove that she had really come by herself to the market. She looked at everything. There wasn't a corner she didn't look at. But she didn't go into the livestock market: it was a very large yard, so she just stood at the entrance. Those sellers were too insensitive: *year in and year out, you plow the land with an ox. Now, when it's old and can't plow any longer, you lead it here and sell it. Somebody will then lead it home, butcher it, and cook beef stew. And then there are the sheep. They've never had anything delicious to eat. The springtime grass is the best thing they've ever had, but in the end you sell them to people who sell mutton soup.* Nizi hated the people who came here to sell oxen and sheep. She felt sorry for the animals. She didn't have the heart to go in and look at them. She just took a quick look from the entrance to the livestock yard, and then got away from there as fast as she could.

What took up most of Nizi's time was the newly opened free market in the southern part of the town. Almost two acres of farmland had suddenly been packed with facilities built with flimsy walls and asbestos ceilings. Some of the free enterprises sold shoes, some sold hats, some sold all kinds of cloth and all styles of clothing brought in from the city. There were plastic toys, cloth dolls, and toy pistols. There were also tailors who would make up clothing on the spot. There was everything anyone could possibly want in these simple shops. Nizi felt as if she had entered a pigeon cote. She went from one shop to another. All the shopkeepers were smart: at a glance, they could tell that she wasn't a potential buyer, so they just went on drinking tea or playing cards. They didn't even give her a second look. But that was OK with her: Nizi was like someone walking alone in a zoo. If she liked looking at something, she looked a little longer. If she didn't, she just left. After she'd looked at the last shop selling bowls and chopsticks, she glanced up. Before she'd realized it, the fiery autumn sun had burned its way up to the highest point.

Nizi had to take care of what she'd come to do. She was satisfied. She'd seen shops selling straw hats and socks, shoe and lock repair places, dentists' offices and beauty salons. It was like the children's book she'd read last year and the year before: she'd read it over and over until she was thoroughly familiar with every single page. She had memorized all the stories. Now, after walking all over the market, she knew exactly which shop sold what and where each shop was located. She had no reason to keep strolling on the streets. She had to buy the silk thread and eat some lunch, and then take the thread home.

The silk thread shop was next to the department store. It was near a small privately owned restaurant called Eat for Less. The first time she'd looked inside the shop, she'd seen only the silk thread there. When she went back, she not only saw the shop but also noticed that the shop was nothing but a sheltered space between the restaurant and the department store. Taking advantage of the red brick walls on both sides, someone had piled up earth in back and had built up the front with broken tiles. They'd left an opening for a door and had whitewashed the door frame and written the two words "silk thread." So much for the silk thread shop. Nizi was disappointed. She'd made the rounds of so many bright shops, and now finally she had come to a tiny shop only as large as two mats. Not only that, but the floor of the shop was sunken; probably water would come in when it rained, so a step had purposely been placed in the doorway to keep the water out. When you climbed up the step and entered the shop, it was as if you'd taken a sudden leap and jumped into a black well.

The shopkeeper, a woman a little more than forty years old, had a broad face and short hair. She was wearing a short-sleeved embroidered blouse with a high neckline. Her face made her appear to be from the countryside, but the way she dressed made her seem like a townswoman who'd experienced a lot. Without knowing why, as soon as she jumped into the shop, Nizi didn't like it very much. She thought she'd buy a spool of silk thread and leave right away, so she went up to the counter made from an old table, looked at the walls

on both sides, and glanced sideways at walls pasted with old newspapers, but she didn't look carefully at the woman shopkeeper sitting
down and cooking in a corner of the room. Yet, the woman had long
since sized her up.

"Little girl, may I help you?"

The shopkeeper was actually welcoming. Needless to say, a silk
thread shop was a specialty shop. Someone not interested in buying
silk thread wouldn't come to her shop just to pass the time of day.
Because the shop was low lying, Nizi smelled a musty odor. She also
smelled the dye on the silk thread, as well as the noodles that the
proprietress was cooking. She rested her gaze on the bin leaning
against the wall next to the counter. The bin was on a bench. It was
divided evenly into more than a dozen compartments, each holding
a different kind of colored silk thread—red, yellow, green, black, and
also light yellow and dark purple, pink and silvery white. Each kind
was wrapped in paper: the visible part flashed with light. It was especially brilliant under the lights in the daytime. A few leftover compartments held some old wool and the woman's bowls and chopsticks. Quickly scanning the displays in the shop, Nizi said, "I want
to buy a spool of yellow silk thread."

The woman said, "This kind?"

Nizi said, "That light yellow one."

The woman asked, "Just one spool? Is one enough?"

Nizi said, "My grandma's funeral clothes are all ready. She just
needs some yellow silk thread for the border of the robe."

The proprietress didn't hand her a spool of yellow silk thread right
away. Looking at the clock on the wall, she saw that it was already
past time for lunch. She said, "Little girl, have you had lunch yet?
I cooked a lot. Come and have a bowl of it." She said, "I knew right
away that you weren't from town. You came from a village a long
way away especially to buy silk thread, didn't you? I can tell at a
glance if a child is good or bad. I could tell at once that you were the
sort of good little girl who dotes on your grandma. You're tired and
your shoes are dusty: you must have come at least three miles. How
could your father and mother let you come alone to the market?
They should take better care of you. What? What did you say, little
girl? Oh, so that's the way it is. I thought so. I feel really sorry for all
the little boys and girls who come here alone to buy silk thread:
they've all been brought up by their grandmas and grandpas. I saw at
once that you'd been brought up by your grandma, so I didn't dare say
anything about your not having a father and mother, I just asked why

Yan Lianke

your father and mother let you come all by yourself to the market. Come over, little girl, come on over, and choose whatever silk thread you like for your grandma's funeral robe. Choose whatever color you want. Take out however much you need. If you have money, pay me something. If you don't, I won't charge you.

"Little girl, come over, come over and choose whatever you wish."

Nizi just stood at the counter. She hadn't imagined that a shopkeeper could be so nice, inviting her for lunch, letting her pick out the thread herself, and even saying if she didn't have any money she could just take the thread with her. For a whole morning, she'd gone to several markets and dozens of shops. They'd all realized she wouldn't buy anything and so not one person had talked with her. It made her eyes tired, and her tongue was numb from being idle. But when she got to this shop, the proprietress, whom at first she hadn't even liked, had talked so much with her. She was like an auntie to her or even a mother. Nizi felt a little moved. Nizi felt a little as if she'd been walking to and fro all day on the main street looking for someone whom she hadn't found, and then when it was dark and she wasn't looking, she'd suddenly looked up and bumped into the person. Timidly, but also a little intimately and sorrowfully, she looked at the proprietress and said, "My—my grandma said she just needed one spool of light yellow silk thread."

The proprietress turned off the honeycombed coal stove, removed the pot of food, and placed an iron cover on the stove, and then put the cooked noodles on it. She did all this very carefully and slowly, as if she was afraid of ashes flying into the pot. Because she was paying so much attention to this, she wasn't looking at Nizi, and because she was unhurried, she could keep talking with Nizi. "Did you say your grandma's funeral robe just needs a border?"

Nizi said, "Um," and nodded her head.

The proprietress hung the tongs on a nail on the wall, and said, "Little girl, you are really still very young. You still don't quite understand things. Have you heard that if a grandchild buys a package of tobacco for a grandpa, the grandpa can live past the age of eighty-three, and if a grandchild buys an extra spool of thread for a grandma, the grandma can live past the age of ninety-four?"

Nizi opened her eyes wide and shook her head.

As the proprietress picked up the bowls and started dishing up the food, she asked, "Are you really not going to have something to eat, little girl?"

Nizi nodded her head again.

189

The woman put a scoop of food into her bowl and then added another. She said, "OK, then, just one spool if you don't want your grandma to live a long time."

Nizi's face flushed with terror. She didn't know what to say.

Holding her bowl, the woman mixed the long, fibrous noodles.

"Come over here and choose the thread, little girl. Choose whatever color you wish."

Nizi stood there blankly without moving.

The proprietress ate a mouthful of noodles and said, "Are you going to buy it or not?"

Nizi said, "If I buy an extra spool of thread, will she really be able to live past the age of ninety-four?"

The woman took another mouthful of soup, and said, "It isn't so much a matter of whether she will really live that long as it is a matter of whether you want your grandma to."

Nizi said, "Then I'll buy a few extra spools of thread."

The woman said, "Wearing a robe embroidered all over with phoenixes, the old person will go to heaven. Your filial piety will bring your grandma a long life." She asked, "How much money did you bring?" Nizi said, "Ten yuan." The proprietress said, "Ten yuan, right? Then why not buy five spools? If she doesn't need them all, you can bring the leftovers back to me the next time you come to market." She set her bowl down, and helped Nizi choose five spools of colorful thread. Each spool of delicate thread was only as big around as a chopstick. The five together weren't even the size of a sparrow, but the thread was so light and so glossy that when Nizi took out her pictorial paper wallet and paid the ten yuan, she thought she had really bought a wild sparrow, and after taking the five spools of thread wrapped in book paper, she didn't immediately leave the shop. It was as though she were afraid that the bird would suddenly fly out of her hand. The proprietress figured out what was going on, and took five jiao out of the counter drawer and gave it to Nizi. She said, "Little girl, if you aren't going to have something to eat here, then go over to the butcher shop. With five jiao, you can buy two biscuits and get a free bowl of beef soup. If you want more soup, just ask. It's free, anyway."

Nizi didn't want the beef soup, even though it was free. The ox had plowed land its whole life, and in the end people had butchered it, taken out the bones, and cut up the meat. Nizi couldn't drink the beef soup. Instead, she ate a bowl of noodles with eggs. She hadn't imagined that she could get so much for five jiao. It was an extra large bowl, although there wasn't much of the egg in the soup. After eating, she felt satisfied and full. When she left the street with the five spools of thread in her hand, she felt grateful to the woman selling thread. She'd suggested that Nizi buy five spools of thread and she'd also given Nizi the money for an extra large bowl of noodles. Although there was a little too much thread, Nizi thought she could keep whatever was left over: when she came home from school, in her spare time, she could learn how to embroider from her grandma.

Nizi left the town and headed home.

She'd walked four miles to get to the market, and it was also four miles home. That hadn't changed. But the road home always seemed shorter. Going to market, she could never figure out why she wasn't there yet. But going home, in the blink of an eye, she reached the persimmon tree that marked the halfway point. This tree was short and lopsided, one side flourishing and the other with only a few branches, but anyhow, this was the year it would produce little fruit. In the past in this season, fruit hung all over the tree, but this year, one could see only the half-yellow leaves. Generally, in previous years, when villagers carrying heavy loads of small packages came back from the market, they rested their feet under this tree. But Nizi didn't want to rest there. It wasn't that she wasn't tired, but rather that the sun was already in the west. Grandma had told her she must, she absolutely must, get back to the village before sunset. She'd bought five spools of thread for Grandma and she wanted to get home right away. But when she got to the persimmon tree, someone who'd gone to market was resting there. She glanced at him, and just then the person spoke to her. She felt she had to answer him, if only out of politeness. The person said, "Little girl, rest for a while." She said, "I have to hurry home before the sun sets." The person asked, "Which village?" She said, "Straight ahead, below the mountain ridge." He said, "That's so close it won't take you long to get home. Rest a bit, and then we'll go on together. I go past your village any-way." Then he said, "Are you thirsty? If you are, I'll go over to the field and get you a juicy, tender cornstalk."

Nizi hadn't been planning to rest, but as the man talked with her, she stood in the shade of the tree at the roadside to respond. She hadn't been thirsty, but when the man said he'd get her a juicy corn-stalk from the field, she realized that her mouth was a little dry. She stood on the grass in the shade of the tree and licked her lips. She saw that, sure enough, the man was standing up. He said, "I'm also

191

awfully thirsty. Watch my things for me while I get two cornstalks."
Now Nizi could see that the man was more than thirty years old. He
was wearing black pants and a white shirt. He had short hair and the
bridge of his nose was high. Under the tree were two empty baskets
with a layer of straw and some pig turds. She guessed he'd gone to
market to sell piglets. He'd sold all of them, and now was returning
with a pair of empty baskets. Nizi didn't know why she liked people
who sold pigs and didn't like the ones who sold cattle and sheep. She
didn't like pigs, so she didn't mind if people sold them. She was
watching him walk step by step into the cornfield. A cloth bag was
hanging close to his bottom, slapping him with every step he took.
Needless to say, the money he'd taken in from selling piglets was in
the cloth bag that was slapping his bottom. Nizi was amused: she
didn't know why other people didn't do as she had done and fold
some pictorial paper to make a wallet. Why, instead, did they hang a
cloth bag on their bottoms? It was vulgar and silly. Also not very
convenient. Nizi really wanted to make a stiff paper wallet for him
to replace the bag. But as she was thinking this, he was already in the
cornfield: he had disappeared like a sheep going into a deep grassy
ditch.

The cornfield was exceptionally large and sloping below the ridge
path. She looked down at the cornfield: the corn seemed quite ripe.
The field was an expanse of earthen yellow. The scent of ripe corn
wafted over the mountain ridge. Nizi couldn't see where the man
had gone to look for the sweet stalks, but she could hear the hot dry
huala sound of the plants. She couldn't figure out why it was taking
him so long to come back. She was suddenly so thirsty that it
seemed as though a wad of rough cloth were stuck in her throat. She
wanted to chaw on the juicy sweet stalk as she walked home, just
as she usually did when she walked to and from school. She thought
she'd go find some sweet stalks by herself, but after taking a few
steps, she saw the man's baskets under the tree. She stood still. If
she looked for sweet stalks in the field, it would be like picking up
a stone from the streamside—nothing easier. But she didn't know
what was taking the man so long.

She was getting a little worried as she stood there.

Finally he came back.

He was empty-handed, and a layer of red was frozen on his face. He
stood there as if he wanted to ask Nizi to do something, beg her to
forgive him for not bringing any sweet stalks. Sweat hung on his
face, as though he wanted to say something but couldn't get it out.

His face reddened from suppressing what he wanted to say. Nizi didn't know where his stream of talk just now had gone, where it had been lost. Looking at his reddening face, she spoke up first. She said, "Didn't you find any sweet stalks?" He said, "Why don't you come in and look? I don't know where they are."

How could a farmer actually not know how to find the sweet stalks? Weren't they the ones that were thinner and taller and still green, rather than those that had long been ripe and yellow? Nizi was staring at the man: she suspected he was stupid. She felt a little sorry for him for being stupid. She didn't say that, though. She drew her gaze away from his tense, wooden, sweaty face, and went into the cornfield. She was walking in front; he was following her. She said, "Stay back and watch your things." He stopped and said, "I'm following you to learn how to find sweet stalks." When he saw that she wasn't hinting that he shouldn't follow her, he began following her again. Deep into the cornfield.

In the west, the sun's brilliant yellow had turned weak red. Fragments of it were falling among the corn plants, like countless bits of shiny red glass falling into the field. The hot, sweet fragrance of the ripe corn was flowing like water among the plants. People had long since picked and eaten the sweet stalks closest to the road. Nizi kept walking deep into the center of the field. There, in the shade of a chinaberry tree, she suddenly saw a few stalks that had been stripped of their leaves and husks. The leaves, which had just recently been pulled off, had been thrown to the ground. They were emerald green. Nizi knew at once that they were sweet stalks that had been picked and peeled just now. She went over and picked up a few stalks, and then turned to look at the man. "Aren't these the sweet stalks you were looking for?"

Flustered, the man was looking at Nizi's face. Unexpectedly, he squatted down and grabbed the sweet stalk. He also seized Nizi's hand. His face was flushed a dark purple. His hands were so sweaty it was as though hot water had just been poured over them. He was trembling so much that it seemed it wasn't Nizi's hands he was holding tight, but two lumps of red-hot soft iron. Nizi didn't know what he wanted to do; she didn't know why his body was so paralyzed that he couldn't seem to either stand or squat. Why was he kneeling before her? She said, "What's wrong with you? Just now, your face was red for an instant and then it paled. Are you sick?" He wanted to say something, but couldn't get it out. He opened his mouth, and then couldn't close it again. His mouth wide open, he licked his

193

upper lip, then his lower one. Then, little by little, he moved his hand to her face and stroked it, as though touching something he'd lost years ago and suddenly found again; it was as if something had been returned to its original owner. Nizi was staring at him close-up, staring at the sweat on the tip of his nose. It was muddy white like river water. She said, "What do you think you're doing by touching me?" Stuttering, he said, "I want to look at you. My entire life, I've never seen a woman's body."

She wasn't very happy as she said, "Women are grown-ups. I'm still a child."

He said, "You're pretty. Your face is as delicate as grapes." She laughed and said, "Under my clothes, I'm even more delicate. Paler, too."

He said, "Can you take your clothes off and let me look at you?"

She asked, "If I do, are you going to touch me?"

He shook his head. "No, I won't touch you."

Sure enough, she took her clothes off as if getting ready for bed: first her shoes, then her colorful blouse, and finally her trousers. She was now wearing only the underpants that Grandma had made for her. The wind was blowing in the field, brushing over her like silk thread. It was velvety and cool, as pleasurable as if she'd plunged into cool water for a bath. He was trembling all over and panting. He touched her all over. Nizi was watching this pitiful man kneeling in front of her: when he touched her, he trembled as if he were cold. She heard his teeth clatter like a lot of cobblestones colliding in the water. Whatever part of her his hands traveled over, they felt like rough wood being dragged over her. The sun was now much lower. He touched her body for a long time and finally suddenly squeezed his thighs tightly together and fell down—sitting as if paralyzed on a cornstalk. When he broke the stalk by sitting on it, it sounded like bones breaking. Then he looked down and, head on his knees, he asked in a muffled voice, "Little girl, how old are you? Are you in school?"

She said, "I'm twelve. I'm in fifth grade."

He said, "Get dressed and run along home."

She said, "Am I fair? Am I pretty?"

He said, "You're fair and pretty. Run along."

She got dressed and, holding the five spools of thread, walked away from the field. After a few steps, she turned around and looked at him. "Aren't you going? Look, the sun is about to set." Then she asked, "Would you like to have my wallet that I folded out of pictorial paper?" The man was staring at her idiotically, as if staring at a lamb.

The sun had just set when Nizi got back to the village. She'd gone all by herself to the market. She'd been gone a whole day, and although she was a little sleepy, she felt content and happy. At last, she'd gone to the market all by herself. She'd gone all over the downtown streets: she'd seen everything. And she'd also bought five spools of thread. And she'd run into a man who'd said she was fair and pretty. The village was just the same as usual, sitting quietly in the sunset. Smears of sun red were spread out in the alleys, looking like red gauze floating above the village streets. Grown-ups were coming back from the fields with the corn they'd harvested, carrying it on poles or pulling fully laden carts of it. They passed by as if they hadn't seen her. She wanted to talk with them, but they were all so busy they didn't have a moment to talk. Nizi really wanted to find a grown-up to talk with. She wanted to tell someone that she'd spent a whole day at the market. Just then, an empty-handed adult walked across unhurriedly. When she saw that he wasn't carrying anything, she guessed he had some free time, so she stood in the center of the road, blocked it with her arms, and said, "Uncle, I went to the market. I went to the market all by myself."

The man was stunned. He said, "Nizi, hurry on home. Your grand-ma is gone."

Nizi didn't understand. Eyes wide open, she was staring at his mouth.

He went on. "Hurry on home. Your grandma had a dizzy spell. When she fell over, she stopped breathing."

This time, Nizi understood. She repeated, "Your grandma had a dizzy spell. When she fell over, she stopped breathing."

The grown-up said, "Oh, Nizi, you silly child."

The grown-up went on his way. Nizi went home through the alley. She hadn't walked far when a woman she called auntie came walk-ing up with a bowl of food. When she saw that Nizi had five spools of colorful silk thread, she said, "Nizi, your grandma is gone. She died. She can't use the thread you bought. Could you lend me a spool of the red?" Nizi stood there blankly for a while, and then suddenly ran toward home. She dropped the paper packet of colorful thread in the alley. The woman with the bowl of food squatted down and picked up all the spools of thread.

Fourteen Prose Poems
Ben Lerner

ALL WE REMEMBER OF OUR CHILDHOOD is sliding down inclined chutes mounted by means of ladders, down slick chutes terminating in pools of water, across wet tarps laid atop the lawn, across hardwood floors in our socks, on short boards equipped with wheels, on roller skates, on ice skates, on ice, on gravel.

DEAR CYRUS, HE PUTS DOWN, DEAR CYRUS, yesterday while taking the, he puts down, air in the company of M. Charlus, your cousin, the Baron, that is, while taking a spin, he puts down, in the motorcar, which respects no mystery, to Thun, he puts down, to the town of T, and the children trailing the, he puts down, which respects no, and the children playing with smoke on a string, frozen smoke on a stick, your cousin the Baron, drew my attention, my attention, you understand, was drawn, there was a silver, and the children screaming, flying machine, in terror, he puts down, with pleasure, and in the eyes of the cousin, your Baron, who respects no, who is no, displayed like, longer, objects, tears, of price, remain your, humble servant, I

THE DOG IN THE CARTOON shoots a gun, overtakes the bullet in a car, and awaits it with an open mouth. Slight, continuous changes in the shapes of the scenery give the illusion of motion. In lieu of erections, sprouting cephalic contusions. Otherwise reduced to a pile of ash, the eyes of the mischievous cat remain, blinking. Contiguity substituted for substitution: flatten the duck with a frying pan and he becomes a frying pan. The bear indifferently fingers the holes in his chest. The giant ham around which the episode is organized weighs nothing, appears slippery, and is ultimately swallowed by a mouse. The popular breakfast sandwich is made of cartoon flesh. The child actor who worked opposite the dragon is scarred for life. Open your eyes. You're still holding the dynamite.

THE GIRL PLAYS with nonrepresentational dolls. Her games are devoid of any narrative content, amusements that depend upon their own intrinsic form. If you make her a present of a toy, she will discard it and play with the box. And yet she will only play with a box that once contained a toy. Her favorite toy was a notion about color. She lost it in the snow.

DEAR CYRUS, HE PUT DOWN, DEAR CYRUS, what you experience as an inconsistency in tone, is, in fact, the Montessori method, in which we practice abstinence during the period of ovulation, in which we move across the plane of fracture, where adjacent surfaces are differentially displaced. Dear Personified Abstraction, he put down, dear Counterstain with Safranine, I am writing to describe a perfect circle, the sudden sine curve of a fleeing deer, and to request your absence at my table, with quakes of lesser magnitude to follow. Dear Reader, he put down, Dear He Put Down, when the golden parachute failed to decelerate your cousin, The Baron, the first dog in space, the kids fanned out across the field and screamed *I've got it*, mistaking the shower of sparks for bedtime, the luminous obligate parasites for a lecture on film. Dear Lerner, he put down, Earth to Lerner, throw three damn strikes and get us out of this sentence, but the runner had long since grown into his base.

CHILD ACTORS are not children, that much we know. Their reputation for viciousness is, by all accounts, deserved. Napoleon and Liszt were child actors. In situation comedies, child actors are black. Some child actors have never been off camera. If you build a set and start filming, a child actor will come downstairs. Some doctors believe it is the constant surveillance that stunts the growth of the child actor, the pressure of the viewing public's gaze, while in fact a child actor off camera is like a fish out of water. He cannot breathe.

A GREAT BOOK must be frozen and fractured along its faults in order to lay bare internal structure. Anna Karenina touches the paper knife to her cheek. When a child dies in a novel, he enters the world. And writes the novel. The calories in a great book equal those burned in its reading. Or its burning. Even if there are no great books, argues Levin, we must act as if there were. For the sake of the peasants who work the paper. A gentleman may only fight duels with

Ben Lerner

other gentlemen. A reader may not demand satisfaction.

WE CAN FEEL THE CHANGING of the tense. The sky distends six inches. Like a parachute opening inside the body. If you don't secure your own mask first, you'll just sit there stroking the child's hair. In the dream you form part of the wreckage you pick through: an allegory of reading. Who knows how many hijackers have been foiled by an engrossing in-flight movie. This one seems to be about symmetry, about getting yours. Its simplified geometrical forms recall the landscapes of our simulators. It's not just the pilots who have to be trained. When you ask the stewardess for another tiny bottle, she says, This is neither a time nor a place.

THIS IS NOT YOUR FATHER'S BOREDOM. 1986: the year in pictures, the year in tears. Out of the ordinary emerged the first, doomed shoots. In my honor they will one day name and electrify a chair. Wind in my hair, windshield in my teeth. A grammar derived for an early death. Mere wit is the new wailing; black, the new black. My best friend went to Mexico and all I got was this lousy elegy. As easy as taking context from a baby. I'd like to say a few words in memory of Memory, an all-state wrestler who left teeth marks on the median. I can't help feeling that it should have been me. It was, whispers the priest.

A STUDY OF A CHILD [ERASED], a study of erasure [Child], the swiftness of pencils repeating a theme until it achieves the illusion of enterable space. Rake me, she said, with a moral light, but the luster of her ostrich-feather fan had dimmed her eyes. For the purposes of study, we have removed those figures attributed to disciples, yielding a string of visual commas and the inscription *Turn away.* We work with a found vocabulary, working backward from the detail to the richly textured blindness of Parmigianino's gaze. Anyway, as a child, I was thrown from my Powell Peralta, and when I came to, my left brain had been erased. No street, no land, no sky—just scape.

IN THE COMMERCIAL she just stabs a straw into an orange and sucks. We tried that at home and lost massive amounts of blood. When I was little, she confessed, beginning to cry, we were forced to race in sacks, to race in pairs with our near legs bound. Coach was finally fired for rewarding each good hit with a sparkling article of porn. His slow-pitch team was sponsored by AA. His house was always already egged. It was when I tried to eat a straw through a straw that I learned my first important lesson about form.

THE INHERENT DIFFICULTY OF THE GAME rests exclusively in the obscurity of its object. Points are taken away for killing civilians, but points are irrelevant. Gold earns you extra men. Children, if questioned, deny the mediation of the joystick or fail to hear the question. Often we are permitted to return to levels we've surpassed to search for mushrooms.

SPUN DOWN FROM AND REELED UP TO the hand by a flick of the wrist. In what sense is it a toy, she asks, if it catches real fish? Like soldiers carrying popguns and switchblade combs. At first, the elephant could only fly when he held a feather in his trunk. Would you rather live during the ascendancy of a civilization, asks the top-hatted cricket, or during its decline? Pygmalion or Pinocchio? Then he learned to hold it in his mind. Not every off-screen voice is the voice of God. But we must act as if it were. For the sake of the rabbit who has run out of landscape and plugged the shotgun with his finger. Do rabbits have fingers? I don't know, do chickens? The hunted confounds the hunter with a sudden change of gender.

DEAR CYRUS, HE PUTS DOWN, DEAR REPETITION, while you were driving home from, how shall I put this, Mexico, driving dark pales into the panic grass, the kids got into the Roman candles, the ginger vodka, the Bible I gave your daughter was hollow, contained a, how shall I, pistol, two kinds of people in this world, do I smell incense, swimmers and nonswimmers, a child with puppy-dog eyes asks if puppies go to heaven, the pistol proves untrainable, ruins the carpet, a no or no question, I guess I just assumed dogs dog paddled, Dear, Dear, he puts down, Dear Me, when a dog drowns an angel gets its wings, and a long proboscis for sucking blood, no self put-downs, she screamed, I pretended it was alive so I could pretend to put it to sleep, how shall I, sweetheart, no doggy heaven, put this, without a doggy hell.

Four Stories
Diane Williams

SATISFYING, EXCITING, SUPERB

IT MAY EVEN BE her real name. Lucky I called to Gumbo. I was in the bedroom concocting rocket fuel. I had a fold-down bed and it was in the fold-up position. It had like a long shelf and the bed was tucked in underneath and the shelf was fairly high and when it ignited it was just one bright white-yellow flare—the rocket fuel! I used the shelf of the bed for the laboratory. I went into the hallway where there was a full-length mirror. I looked at myself, at the little scraps of thrushbeard peeling off my hands and my face.

We should all attempt to send rockets into space. Maybe it would be a good idea to ask someone how to do it.

There was a wooden shelf. There was a wooden shelf and there was a curtain over the bed, so that the curtain caught fire and the wood caught fire but I was able to put it out. I didn't feel this was serious.

I was the one who got blown up.

I tried it a number of times and sent off a number of rockets. I tried to improve on the fuel mixture.

I may have put too much magnesium in my mix.

Well, the whole thing was like my mother used to say.

So we attached fins at the bottom and made it heavier so it didn't tumble.

I say it too!—our mother used to tell us—"A burnt child smells bad."

But after that incident I gave up my career as a rocket builder. How far did it go in the air? I try to figure that out.

Magnesium—it is not controlled, nor is sulphur and today you can buy it. OK, and then I'm going to blow myself up.

EAT THE DEEP TOO!

Some of us are very good and some aren't. You know, some did their homework and got good grades. Likely they'd get a blank stare from you.

"I have to put in the medicine," the girl said. "I have to brush my teeth."

"I told them you do everything better than I do," the other girl said.

"Who did you tell?"

"Bett!"

"Bett! Bett!"

Bett started to cross her mind. Bett hung there waiting to be helpful and then Bett groaned.

In any event, people show you there is a way to have pleasure.

CUTTING AND DRESSING

The doctor said, "Then you have a wonderful night."

The term *wonderful night* is used to refer to the inner sanctum that has sex feeling in it.

There is a widespread misconception about the look, feel, and texture of a doctor's waiting room. The doctor asked me did I want to give him my co-pay now.

For the handover, I wore toreador pants and bone leather shoes with little heels—backless and strapless. I did not bend my knees, but instead stiff-walked to my sitdown in a chair. My feet I kept up parallel to the floor and I crossed my legs at the ankles.

Back at home for a cold lunch in my house with a red-tile roof, I sat in my own chair for sitting stiffly.

People are lovely things. People must have seen that my hair was in flat knuckled curls and really inconsiderately arranged. My walls are papered with a moiré pattern. My floor is covered by split brick pavers. I've got a tea cart set out with plastic cups, lime green drink, and a plate of dry baked products.

My tot Silvanus—with bad habits and suddenly—we had set the boy free!—pulled himself up onto our lyre-back side chair. Completely frenzied, the chair fell—and, because this child has never been significantly maltreated, he was stunned by the fall and he's dead.

201

Diane Williams

EVERY DAUGHTER SHOULD HAVE A NICE
MOTHER LIKE THIS

She told me she was very brave. I was envious and angry. She was our servant who was a lost princess who had a pretty nose, small brown eyes, and a personal smell like a flower—she belonged to us and she did what I told her. I don't know when I am overdoing it. I have gone on for three minutes, actually two and three minutes. She always surprises herself with how excellently and easily she can do things. We liked the house she worked in. Over the top, between the roof and blue sky, a tree was brown and had a knob in the middle. The house looked as if it had a hand sticking up through the roof because the princess could get worked up. The house's body was poured into a thick pink stucco.

It's a lot to ask a person to go too much further—to describe her reassuring pat.

The Big Betty Stories
Lois-Ann Yamanaka

BIG BETTY

BIG BETTY LIVES next door. Big, fat Betty. My best friend Big Betty. She takes care of Dominic. She takes care of me. Never mind that Dominic rides the small yellow bus to and from school with all the retarded kids. Never mind that all the kids in our class call him the Mento Boy or Double-Dick Dominic or Dominic Who Has No Dick. Never mind.

"He's your big brother, damn it," she says, shoving me, then shoving a handful of *arare* in her mouth. *Crunch, crunch, crunch.* "You are so lame, Linus." *Crunch, crunch.* "Help him off the bus. Oh, get outta the damn way."

Big Betty with the big, bad attitude:

"I heard somebody call me FAT. Who called me FAT? Speak up, panty-ass wimps. Well?" She scans the hallway. No one moves or speaks. "That's what I thought, wimps."

Big Betty with the big, bad mouth:

"I tell you, Linus, she was so f*****g smelly. I said, "S***, girl, you are butt-f*****g skanky. You must wipe your s*** stinky f*****g a** with your hand and rub it all over your armpits in the morning."

Big Betty with the big, fat butt.

"Move over, Linus, give me some space, man. You breathing all my air."

Big Betty, my best friend.

Babachan likes Big Betty.

"Betty-chan, you li-kee coconut cracker with Hi-C?"

Or "Betty-chan, you so very nice to Domee. No, Domee-chan, Betty so ni-cu to you. Betty goo-du friend."

Or "Betty-chan, you take bag lychee home, OK? You tell your Mama that Ri-noosu Baba gi-bee you, OK?"

Big Betty who walks with Dominic to the Special Ed classroom, which is way, way in the back behind the Shop and Band rooms. Big Betty who puts his backpack into his red cubbyhole on the second

Lois-Ann Yamanaka

shelf. Big Betty who saves all of her Happy Meal toys for him. Mean old Big Betty who never gives up.

"What's this, Dominic? Ti-ger. You say it. C'mon, use your words. You can say it. Ti-ger. Tiii-gerrr. It's a f*****g tiger, right, Linus?"

Big Betty always says it's us against the world. She writes it on Dominic's Marble Composition tablet:

BB, Linus, and Dom vs Everybody Else
Winner = Us
Loser = Them

I don't know if she's right.

"You dunno nothing," she says to me.

Dominic sees the crowd of boys coming toward the bus stop. It is morning. The aide straps a girl with leg braces into her wheelchair. Dominic stops on the bottom step of his small yellow school bus.

"Double-Dick, Double-Dick," they call.

"Thass why he gotta ride the handicap bus. 'Cause he got a Double Dick, the big dummy."

"Mento Boy, Mento Boy."

He screams, small at first, and then a loud, pitiful wail.

I turn to walk away from the small yellow bus, away from their calling, away from my wailing, screaming brother.

Big Betty places her hands on my shoulders.

"He's your f*****g brother. Don't be a panty-ass wimp, Linus."

She turns on her heels. "C'mon, step up. You got something to say to Dominic, step up, and say it to me first." She takes Dominic by the hand. He holds on tightly. He reaches his other hand for mine.

"C'mon m*****f*****s," Big Betty yells, "say something so I can call my big brothers come here and kick your a**."

The sidewalk is silent. The wind stops. Cars idle. The trees and J.P.O.s stand still. The world is silent.

"That's what I thought, wimps," she says, walking toward the Special Ed classroom way in the back of nowhere.

I take my big brother's trembling hand in mine.

Us vs Them

Just me, Dominic, and Big, fat Betty, my best friend with the bad mouth who lives next door.

SWEAR BOX

She needs help. She needs help now. She has been in detention seven times. For swearing. She has been suspended twice from school. For swearing.

Big Betty with the big, bad mouth.

It's her grandfather's fault. He was a mechanic at Fat's '76.

It's her grandma's fault. She's a Joe Mormon of Latter-Day Saints.

It's her father's fault. He's a stevedore at the docks.

It's her mother's fault. She's a beautician at Venus Victorino Hair Shoppe.

It's her oldest brother's fault. He plays varsity football and wrestles.

It's her second oldest brother's fault. He had sex last year.

It's her third brother's fault. He hangs with Puerto Ricans.

It's her fourth brother's fault. He flunked seventh grade twice.

"It's your fault, Linus. If you were my true friend, you would help me cure my mouth of swearing."

My father decides to help her. He makes a Swear Box from an old Band-Aid can and lots of duct tape. BETTY'S SWEAR BOX, he writes with a Sharpie. A dime for every swear word.

"Ten cents for every swear word? No f*****g way," she grumbles. Cha-ching.

Big Betty has eaten Ivory, Cashmere Bouquet, Dial soap, and chili pepper water for swearing. She has picked up dead leaves from the school yard, swept roach and mouse dodo from the janitor's closet, and scraped gum from underneath desks for swearing. She has been banned from Sunday school and Kai Store for swearing.

"I don't give a s***," she says.

"S***," Dominic says.

We all gasp. At the same time. He can hardly say his own name. All this time, we've been trying to teach him to talk. And this is the word he repeats?

"It's all your fault, Betty," I tell her.

"Shut up, Linus," she says. "Don't say that," she tells Dominic. "It's a bad word. You not suppose to say bad words."

"S***," he says.

Big, old Betty stares at her big, old feet.

She carries BETTY'S SWEAR BOX in her backpack. It's heavy with coins. She's treating Dominic and me to fudge revel cones at Kai Store since the owner's son Paul Kai lifted the ban on Betty. He felt pity for her standing outside the door with her nose pressed to the glass.

Dominic and me help her Ajax the desks after school in Mrs. Saiki's class. "And then you clap all the erasers, clean the sink, close the windows, put up all the chairs, and wet wipe the blackboards, Betty," Mrs. Saiki says from behind the piles of paperwork on her desk.

The word forms on Big Betty's lips. A wet snake sound. A fizzy, furry sound. She looks at Dominic. He looks at her. And *those* words don't come out.

"Shoots, Mrs. Saiki," Big Betty says. "Fine. All right. Whatevers."

"Shhoots," Dominic repeats. "F-F-F." He looks at Big Betty.

"Good talking, Dominic." Big Betty doesn't even look at him when she says this. She just keeps clapping the dusty erasers.

SCHOOL PICTURE

It's the most stressful day of the school year. The day we take our school pictures. And it starts in kindergarten.

Mama gave Dominic and me a haircut a week before so that our hair could grow into our faces properly. She bought us new shirts. She pomaded our hair. She made me practice my smile in the mirror all the way to school. "Smile big, Linus," she said, even the year I had no front teeth. "Smile big, Linus. Nice and big, OK?"

She always bought the big Package C for Dominic and me. One 8 x 10, two 5 x 7s, four 4 x 6s, 16 wallet size, one class photo. And every year, she'd put our school pictures in wood frames on the Haruno Wall of Fame above our TV.

I'd trade my wallet-sized pictures like precious baseball cards with all of my friends. Have pictures of sixteen classmates to put inside the plastic sheaths in my wallet. Sign each of mine to each of them on the back:

To: (Name of a classmate)
Sorry
SO
Sloppy
Frenz 4-Eva,
Linus H.

To: (Name of a classmate)
Keep it cool.
Have a safe summa.
Stay the same.
Luvs,
Linus H.

It was Dominic's school picture Mama worried about. He would not smile on cue after the photographer counted, "One, two, three—" He could not even sit still on the tiny stool surrounded by bright lights in front of the photo studio's backdrop of the sky.

So Mama waited in the cafeteria for Dominic's Special Ed class to arrive. She would make him smile. She always made him smile. She sang silly songs to him that made him laugh. She said silly phrases that he liked to hear over and over again. She told him funny stories at bedtime. When Mama danced with him, he laughed. When she chased him in the yard, he laughed. When she made funny faces at him, he laughed. When she startled him on purpose or accidentally, he laughed.

I have not heard Dominic laugh like that since she left.

I try to be like her sometimes. But it's not the same. He knows it. I know it. He looks at me like a bewildered puppy and sighs. *Nice try.* I don't blame him. Nobody could ever be like our mama.

She'd greet Dominic's class in the cafeteria then sneak up onto the stage area where the photographer set up his equipment. She'd comb Dominic's hair while he waited in line for his turn. She'd fuss with his shirt. He'd be watching the heavy velvet curtains sway in the light wind. Or blink-blink-blinking when the flash went off with a *Poof!*

When Dominic's turn came, she'd squeeze her way behind the photographer and make goofy faces, sing goofy songs, jump up and down to get my brother's attention. Dominic always looked her way with a big, happy grin on his face. *Poof!* And she'd clap and hug him. "Nice job, Dominic! Nice smile for Mama!"

In every photograph we have of Dominic since he was born, he is smiling. Because she is behind the camera, making him look, making him laugh. Dominic at the beach. Dominic's birthday party. Dominic at Christmas. Dominic on Uncle Rico's pony. Dominic on the slide. Dominic at the church bazaar. Dominic with the ducklings. Dominic with the bunnies.

She is not in any of the pictures.

I can't remember what she looks like. Even when I try.

Tomorrow is school picture-taking day. Babachan went downtown to Ah Mai's to buy aloha print shirts for Dominic and me. My father looks at the bright prints and winces.

"You're going to have to make Dominic smile," he says to me, putting his glasses down.

Me? I point to myself without saying a word.

"Yes, you. I can't take off from work just to make my damn son smile in his damn school picture," Father says.

"I can't do that. I don't want to. I won't go. I have a project due. I don't know when. I will not—"

"Linus, you big baby," Big Betty says. "It ain't that hard." She had come over after school to do math homework with me and to eat Babachan's chocolate *chichi dango* covered with fine rice powder and individually wrapped in waxed paper. "He's your damn, I mean doggone, brother." She pops another *chichi dango* in her mouth.

"Paht-nah—," Jichan says, "you better listen yo' daddy."

"Bumbye Domee-chan get uga-lee pick-cha," Babachan says, refilling Big Betty's glass with more Tang. "And poho yo' daddy money."

Guilt.

Nobody says Mama's name. She's the one who makes him smile. I can't do it.

The next morning, I watch Dominic get on the small yellow school bus with his bright aloha print shirt from Ah Mai's. "You smile bee-gu for the camera," Babachan tells him as he waves good-bye.

Big Betty and me get into Jichan's Valiant. I'm holding my father's handwritten note to my teacher:

To Who It May Concern,
Please excuse Linus Haruno from your class to assist his
brother Dominic Haruno who is in Special Education to take
his school picture.
                    Thank you,
                    Melvin Haruno

We're in third period. Mrs. Kurokawa's math class. Big Betty's signaling me, jerking her head toward the clock and whispering to me through gritted teeth, "It's time, Linus. Go. Give the teacher your note, you f%#@ing idiot."

I don't move.

She snatches the note from me and takes it to the teacher's desk.

Mrs. Kurokawa reads the note. "I think you'd better go now, Linus. According to my picture-taking schedule, the Spe—"

I get up to cut her off. I don't want the mean boys in my class to hear her finish, ". . . the Special Education class is taking their picture now. Hurry, Linus, go make your retarded brother smile."

I hear somebody say, "He gotta go help his mental brother Dummy Dick."

I grab my backpack and run down to the cafeteria.

Dominic is sitting at one of the cafeteria tables. He waves at me when he sees me. He's holding the complimentary black comb that the photographer's assistant gives to each student. I take it from him and comb his hair. Then I fuss over his shirt, straightening it out, fixing the collar.

"You smile, OK, Dominic," I whisper to him as he gets up, holding my hand. We get in line on the stage. He's flapping his hands whenever the photographer's flash goes *Poof!* He's watching the curtains move in the light wind. "C'mon now, Dominic. You have to smile," I beg him, squeezing his hand. "Just like you did for Mama."

"Mama work?" he says. And then he does not say anything to me. He lets go of my hand. He doesn't even look at me.

I can't do it. I'm sorry, Daddy, Jichan, Babachan. I'm sorry, Mama. I blew it. Dominic didn't smile for me. I want to run away from the cafeteria full of Special Ed students, the strange sounds they make, the strange faces they have, their strange bodies, their strange movements, my strange brother, my strange life.

It's Dominic's turn. I get him to sit on the small stool. It swivels. So Dominic swivels. The photographer gets irritated. He has so many more pictures to take. Let's get it over with. What's the holdup? He starts counting. One. I'm not even behind the camera. Two. Dominic's going round and round. Three. Who's this other kid? Hey, get this other kid out of the way.

"Dominic! Look at me. I'm Sandra Dee," someone sings from behind me. I turn around. Dominic stops swiveling. I move behind the camera. "Hey, Cinderelly, Cinderelly, night and day it's Cinderelly!" It's Big Betty. Making goofy faces, singing goofy songs, my brother's favorite goofy songs. "I got no strings to hold me down," she starts. And then I sing and dance with her. "To make me fret, to make me frown!" Dominic laughs at us. "Snap the picture, you f@#$ing idiot," she tells the photographer. *Poof! Poof! Poof!* He takes three shots for good measure.

"Good job, Dominic," she says, high-fiving my brother. He smiles at Big Betty. And then he goes back to swiveling again.

"How did you—," I begin to ask.

"What are friends for?" she says to me.

"I was trying—," I start to tell her.

She gives me a shove. "Nice try," she says, "but no bananas. And if you must know, he was laughing at me, not you. You brought any of your Baba's *chichi dango?*"

I don't know what to say to her. How to thank her. I dig out a couple of the waxed paper–wrapped *chichi dango* from my backpack. I follow my big, bad neighbor out of the cafeteria.

A month or so later when we get our school pictures, Dominic looks so happy with his big smile and bright aloha print shirt. It's a smile as big and bright as when Mama jumped up and down behind the photographer all those other years.

"You did good, Paht-nah," Jichan tells me as Babachan puts the 8 x 10 in a wood frame. She puts it next to my 8 x 10 school picture on the TV.

I take one of my brother's wallet-sized pictures. He'll probably keep the other fifteen. I make Dominic sign the photograph in his sloppy, baby handwriting:

To Betty
Thanx.
Frenz 4-Eva,
Dom H.

Fretless
Peter Gizzi

We're off the grid, mother
sweep aside the lightning.

Then every gigantomachia
the day was:

a blue blue event
and still one wants to know.

Wants to be free of it
to be touched

and held again' it.
To regard oneself in the glass.

To regard oneself.
To be on the ground

always at the base of it
to say there I am.

Everything gets to him
from the edges

of the thing.
The dense lilacs

coming in
on the page.

But I wanted this
to be a narrative

I still do
want a holiday in reality.

The air alive with style
want style

a hundred percent fiction
a hundred percent fact

its blurred registration.
To be on the ground

in my lanes
lifting off

did I say flight?
It's shitty to reckon

the end-of-day
shapelessness.

A rabbit in moonlight
a dirty patch of snow.

Twig diorama
lit from afar.

Such emanations
made vast

like all goodnight stories.
The bear slept in the porridge

and we skated off
into a bed of honeysuckle

and away we are
when in your room

we say belonging
to a name

if belonging
to anything.

It's late, mother.
The house is a noise in my head.

The house is not empty alpha
late omega.

How much longer?
How much more radiator clank?

I have come to regard
the winter fly.

To regard
electricity.

To regard its purpose
and charge

regard life
no matter the voltage.

A voice comes to one.
A voice becomes unreasonable

when spoken.
Unspoken

maybe the sun
controls these walks, dreams, talk.

The body teaches, mother
its slow arc

attraction to a good
every good

this stereoscopic depth.
Call it cellular.

Remarkable things went on
in each place

no time to remember
unless it be words

before him
in open air

at ease with company
with all things green.

The day before him
shadows, midearth

time and its weather.
To imagine

air spanked clean
to think of everything.

To say my age, blown
as vapor on the glass

evaporating, reflected.
To read the lace curtains

and figures in cut glass
a deep focus

invariable as weather.
These choices

swallow you.
The snow unspoken.

A little cardinal
through the air

at the edge
of night.

Then the edge
of everything.

Girls in White Dresses
Mary Caponegro

THE PURPOSE OF AN AUTOMOBILE at an airport, especially at a major international airport, is an obvious one, a transient one. Its earth-bound transport is a mere warm-up for the glorious act of flight—for once at the terminal's parking lot, what use is a car? It is to be exited so as to permit its driver and/or passenger to enter the much more mysterious machine called the airplane. But the powder blue Chevy Impala parked near Terminal 1 is in this sense an anomaly, and its clean lines are not vastly inferior to any jet's in the eyes of its young passengers, who are content to be swaddled in its interior. The anonymity airports tend to breed is transmuted to intimacy behind the little pink hat whose brim is held sideways by the boy in his left hand and by the girl in her right, and at times it seems to levitate all on its own, with the invisible assistance of Mr. and Mrs. McGil-licuddy in the front seat, who voluntarily facilitate the preteen romance with the aid of the improvised round pink wool screen.

Thus the nearly-nine-year-old girl and the just-turned-nine-year-old boy continue their conversation.

"What's your middle name?" the birthday boy asks. "I get my wish since it's my birthday, right? You have to tell me."

"If you promise not to make fun." The girl adjusts the hat to reach his ear and whispers, "Fiorenza. Now tell me yours."

She feels his warm breath tickle as he mouths, "Carruthers." Even his first name is special, but he doesn't want anyone else but her to know that Gary is actually short for Garrison.

"But that's such a neat name! I wish Ginny stood for something interesting. When I'm old enough to be confirmed I'll take the name Teresa for St. Teresa the Little Flower so I can go by Terry instead of Ginny."

"So what's wrong with Ginny?"

"Well, Ginny's OK, I guess, but Virginia? It's so . . . stuffy."

"And Garrison isn't?"

"No, not at all! Besides, your last name isn't something that would end a spelling bee."

"Ginny, it's almost as long as yours."

"But the vowels are short and . . . smily. Mine sound . . . angry!" He laughs.

"And *you* sound silly! But here, I'll show you something else the letters can do: I, Garrison Carruthers McGillicuddy, on this day, April third, hereby cheer up every single letter in the name Virginia Fiorenza Postodellafuoco."

And then he makes one peck for every syllable of her entire name, coupled with the ones in his name, and with the final press of soft lips to soft lips she feels the vowels and consonants disintegrate, as if there were only one syllable left to her; then even that evaporates, as if all of her were a length of balloon released into air. That is, until Steven Dunlop brings her back to earth by saying, "Are you two done smooching yet? If you're not, I'm gonna go watch the planes take off myself. Your dad's already there with Matt and Brady." And when no one stirs behind the pink hat, he adds, "We're not eating cake and ice cream in the car, ya know."

And then Mrs. McGillicuddy says, "Mustn't ignore your other guests now, Gar." This was many years before the nuns conspired to shame Ginny and her peers into awareness of the backseat's tainted nature.

Despite the presumed etiquette of reciprocation, at Ginny's party there is not a single boy. Salvatore and Rose Postodellafuoco have discussed the matter extensively, and they consider it inappropriate, at least premature, to have boys—plural or singular—present at their daughter's ninth birthday party. As compensation they are more than happy to accommodate all her special girlfriends, seven of them, and lest there be any residual disappointment over their verdict, they make a bona fide excursion of it: a special lunch at a fancy restaurant in the old neighborhood followed by a specially reserved viewing of *The Sound of Music!* The restaurant is owned by a man who does business with Salvatore Postodellafuoco. All the letters on one side of the menu spell Italian and all the letters on the other side English, and the waiter helps Ginny pronounce the fancy consommé called *pastina in brodo*, which means tiny macaroni stars in chicken broth. The waiter says the birthday girl can have any specialty of the house, meaning of the restaurant—funny words like *vitello, osso buco, linguine con frutti di mare*—and patiently explains each one. "But, *bella*," he says, "*bellina* should have whatever she wants

218

on her special day," and she says shyly, "Turkey, I'd love turkey," already seeing a hint of disappointment, but it's too late to change course now. "Just the white meat, please, and no dressing or gravy either, please."

"*Allora, tacchino.*" He writes on his pad all her specifics, takes all the other girls' orders, and then her mom's and dad's, and leaves them enough time to open the beautiful presents: the Jean Naté bath oil, the pink Snoopy pillow, the blue fuzzy slippers, the cream-colored satiny half-slip—which she oohs at when she opens, but frowns when Dad asks her, "What's that one?" and then *he* frowns when she instead shows him the box full of shiny new John F. Kennedy silver half-dollars. Fortunately, they are interrupted by the waiter bringing Ginny's consommé, the consumption of which is followed by more presents, which are in turn followed by the serving of entrées. After the entrées have been eaten and the dishes cleared, the waiter returns with a beautiful cake and ten candles (one for good luck) and spumoni and special Italian cookies.

Amidst these high spirits and full bellies, Salvatore Postodellafuoco does a dangerous thing. He indicates in his ancestral tongue his appreciation for the wine, as it was with the waiter's counsel that the bottle was chosen. This gesture is an amalgam of appreciation, vanity, and generosity. It is not unprecedented in the family's experience, and the causal chain is a predictable one. The waiter initiates an exchange more complicated than Ginny's father bargained for. He begins to extrapolate, offering more technical information regarding the vintage, complimenting Salvatore's palate, inquiring whether the food has been as satisfactory as the wine, in essence turning a discourse of pidgin-Italian shorthand pleasantries into an actual dialogue requiring comprehension and response, a certain mastery of vocabulary and verb forms. It is unclear whether this is born of sheer exuberance on the waiter's part or mild sadism, but at a certain excruciating point, when Salvatore Postodellafuoco's face has become a shade brighter than Ginny's pink coat, the waiter turns his attention back to the birthday girl and her guests.

"*Allora,*" he declares and proceeds to perform a magic trick with an amaretto cookie wrapper and a cigarette lighter—the former sails up in flame and disintegrates. All the girls applaud and on the way out he says, "*Buon compleanno, bella,*" which is like a compliment, Ginny is pretty sure, and then they pile up all the presents into the car just in time to get their seats at the movie—at which point Salvatore Postodellafuoco does what he considers a sensible thing.

As sensible, in his mind, as purchasing the block of tickets in advance lest the matinee be sold out, as sensible as making, a full two weeks in advance, a reservation at Bellini's for his daughter's party. As sensible as relocating to Queens from Brooklyn, then to Long Island from Queens, as each borough outgrew its promise, and the city around him grew increasingly alien. Salvatore now declares that it is too risky to leave all the lovely presents in the car for the duration of the movie because these days you never know, and remember this isn't Long Island, it's Queens, and wouldn't it spoil this perfect day if someone broke into the car and stole all these nice gifts?

Rose Antonucci Postodellafuoco says, "I'm sure locked in the trunk they're just fine, Sal. It's broad daylight." He still looks worried and then decides that they should carry them with them across the street to the movie theater, so every girl takes back her present temporarily, which makes for an impromptu procession and makes it a little cramped in the seats, but nobody minds in the end because they spend the afternoon with Julie Andrews singing to them from the big screen of the fancy theater. Nor does anyone notice that three hours have passed, so engrossed are they in the high-spirited, music-laden, marital mathematics of solving a problem like Maria. On the way out, snow starts to fall like magic, as if Queens itself had become a movie set, and all the girls tilt their faces up toward the sky to see if they can make the wet flakes fall on their noses and eyelashes just like in the song, while they wait for their parents to pick them up in the parking lot—at which point Salvatore places his hand on her shoulder and says to his daughter, "Maybe we'll all go sing in the Alps someday, whaddaya say?"

"I say," begins Ginny, and then whispers into her parent's ears, "I say these are a few of my favorite things." Even with the awkward interaction between waiter and father, even with the back and forth of presents, even without the presence of one Gary McGillicuddy, it will have been a perfect—well, a nearly perfect—day.

On the way home, to pass the time in an animated fashion, the Postodellafuoco family goes through the customary motions of striving to amass, through visual ownership, a complete roster of states via license plates, but they start to lose steam at twenty-eight when, after a completely unexpected windfall of Nevada, New Mexico, and Oregon in sequence, they are mired in the familiar yellow/blue of New York with nothing more exotic than New Jersey and Connecticut for garnish—whereupon they redirect their energies to singing

"Ninety-nine Bottles of Beer on the Wall," subtracting digits incrementally through yet another rousing chorus, but only make it to fifty-six bottles. At a loss, and knowing full well that the closest they may get to the Trapp Family's musical mastery is a monotonously repeated round of "Row, Row, Row Your Boat," they initiate a contest among themselves to convert the *Sound of Music* theme song from Austrian to suburban.

"How about 'The lawns are alive,'" suggests Mrs. Postodellafuoco, when, having exited the expressway, they pass by Roosevelt Field, whose airportlike expanse gives Ginny an inspiration.

"I know, I know: 'The malls are alive ... with the sound of ... Mu-ZAK!'"

"That's a good one, Gin Rummy," says Daddy.

Far south of the Alps, in Calabria, two years later, Virginia Postodellafuoco is miserable. She knows the plumbing is unavailable after midnight and thus devises elaborate rituals using vast quantities of scratchy Italian toilet paper, which she then scoots out to the single minuscule wastebasket behind the fabric curtain by the door, the path to which is in plain view of everyone. "Please God," she prays, "make a minimiracle to part my red sea and let it flow discreetly, directly, into the Ionian, sweep my body's excess under a liquid rug." Sleeping padded, pinned, and belted, barely moving, Ginny is nonetheless afraid of staining the sheets, and by dawn, finds her fear confirmed. When the water comes on at eight, she ejects herself from the narrow bed to quickly flush the blood she couldn't prevent from tainting the pristine white porcelain of the house's only toilet, then returns with a dampened cloth to try to scrub the soiled sheets, until Nonna appears and says, "*Non ti preoccupi, niente, cara ... figura ti.*" Ginny thinks *figura ti* maybe means *figure something out to fix this mess,* and so she takes fresh linen from a big basket, but Nonna says, no those are *lenzuolo matrimonio,* and Ginny is all confused, since there was so much talk of marriage the night before, so why are they the wrong ones? Maybe they were only for a wedding night.

"*Troppo grande, troppo grande, capito?*" Ginny nods her head but doesn't yet quite understand. Later, relieved to have things more or less under control, she announces to her relatives that it's all Greek to her, what comes out of their mouths, and everyone laughs as if it was an original remark. This leads to a discussion on the adults' part of how much of southern Italy is in fact Greek, archaeologically speaking, and it is decided that they must take several excursions in the days to come. In fact, why not today?

"*Oggi,*" Nonna says, "*come non?*" And her cousins say, "*Non oggi, dai, la spiaggia invece. Dai, dai.*"

And after Virginia Postodellafuoco, with the help of her mother, ascertains that these relatives are not in fact telling her grandmother to die, she votes for today, too, because any excursion is better than having to face the beach with this new physiological issue. So they travel to a city of white caves, and Ginny is only too happy to dwell in their mysteries in lieu of the Red Sea's.

"Are these the caves the Mafia bring the stolen children to?"

"*No no, non ti preoccupi, cara.*"

"*Un'attrice,*" says Nonna, "*lei e un'attrice!*"

And Ginny wonders why God wouldn't rescue the children, wherever it was that the Mafia took them to after kidnapping them. Maybe because their parents were rich and stuck on the way to redemption like a camel in a needle's eye. But wouldn't that be canceled out by their being Catholic, and wouldn't they, especially the children, automatically merit assistance—an innocent young boy or girl saying prayers every night before bed, saying their act of contrition: *Oh my God/ I am heartily sorry/ for having offended thee.* Or was salvation only available to souls?—the saving of mere flesh and blood not as legitimate a concern, no matter how dire the circumstances? But the act of contrition would be in Italian, of course.

"How would you pray it," she asks Nonna, "in Italian?" Her mother translates the question sufficiently.

"*Mio Dio, mi pento e mi dolgo . . .*"

"Nonna, that's five o's in a row!"

"Don't worry," Dad says, "the Postodellafuocos ain't rich enough to be of interest to the Sicilian Mafia. I'm not that successful—yet."

But why wouldn't God at the appropriate time simply pluck them from the cave, rescue them like Superman would? That wouldn't be strenuous for him: a much more modest miracle than parting the Red Sea or sending the manna from heaven to the Israelites or, for that matter, than sticking a soul in a monkey just in the nick of time so evolution wouldn't have to seem completely sacrilegious, doing so as deftly as Vicki's hero Rusty Staub getting the ball to home plate just before the runner slid to home: a deftness Ginny

222

found unfathomable but for God apparently was standard issue. Though sometimes he chose to keep his deftness dormant—if, for instance, his children had to learn for themselves, like Adam and Eve did, by weeding the hitherto weedless garden, or had to prove themselves to him, like Abraham with a knife clutched in his trembling fist, held high over the heart of his long-awaited firstborn. Or if they exercised their free will, like the no-longer Brooklynite Dodgers, who traded, instead of a player, one coast for another—although Ginny and Angie agree that if God ever considered any of his children's choices as offensive as Dad and the rest of the Brooklyn-born citizens considered the Dodgers' defection, then forgiveness was hardly a foregone conclusion.

The caves' history captures Ginny's imagination sufficiently that her worries for the children dissipate, and by the time they return to her grandmother's house, she is ready to sleep, more prepared for the exigencies of her novice womanhood, being now a veteran of one night. The entire extended family attends the beach the next day, and Ginny is almost as uncomfortable but at least she gets very tan staying out of the water, which seems to increase her status, because her cousins and everyone keep on exclaiming with admiration, *"Sei bronzata,* Genie!"—always pronouncing her name as if long e, not short i, as if she were a spirit emerged from a bottle or, better still, the blonde Barbara Eden in harem pants and midriff top, whom they would never see here on TV, given that the box ubiquitous at home was nonexistent in the tiny but utterly tidy white stucco house. And the next time, aching more from lying on the stones with only a thin beach towel for padding than from the internally induced cramps, Ginny decides maybe Bridget Callaghan had the right idea after all and dives right in, red sea be damned.

After Gary McGillicuddy's party, Ginny and Gary convene every weekday at recess, exchanging secrets and bags of Cheez Doodles and *Man from U.N.C.L.E.* magazines, secluded in a private huddle, oblivious to the jubilant chaos around them, while the other children jump to the beat of a rope, or bend and unbend their knees while seated on seesaws, or push against the small of one's back as the other grips with her fists and sticks her legs straight out for momentum, a mere curve of canvas beneath. The children form teams that extend almost the length of the playground and shout one to the other, *Red rover, red rover, let Gary come over,* then, *Red rover, red rover, let Ginny come over* and, getting no response, send a scout or two, who, if they spy their ardent classmates, report back to the others, who spontaneously begin to chant, *Ginny and Gary sittin' in a tree, k-i-s-s-i-n-g, first comes love, then comes marriage . . . then comes . . .* Fortunately at that moment Sister Cordelay rings the bell that signals the end of recess.

Two Stories

Scott Geiger

THE FRANK ORISON

MAX ORISON EMERGES from the garage pulling the type of red wagon forever popular with children his age. Frank Orison, his father, rides squarely in the wagon's bed, mute as a chessman. A primitive daylight shines low in the sky. Morning comes slowly up this way, climbing the broad pine trees along the drive. Through patches of sunshine and over long shadows cast by the trees, Max and his father go. At the drive's end, they turn to make their way through the neighborhood. The wagon wheels clatter over broken slabs of sidewalk. They pass houses set back behind yards of low shrubbery and maples. Two familiar shapes stir in their windows. They keep pace with the Orisons, leaping from one window to the next. The figures reappear in the windows of each house as Max and his father pass. But Max doesn't notice. He whistles an improvised tune for happy Saturday adventures with his father.

It's either up to the airfield or down to the jetties.

This Saturday morning custom defines the Orisons. Without it, could it be Saturday? Could Max still be Max? Could Frank Orison still be his father? How Max loves to watch the jets and the biplanes pull themselves off the earth and over the horizon. He thinks of a windy Saturday last summer at the airfield, the morning they saw men use cables to pull a red-and-white dirigible down out of the sky. This scene reminded Max of the fishermen on the jetties, of their excitement, their pointy smiles, and their shouts as they reel in their perch. The dirigible lay down gleaming against the black tarmac in the end, and men wove cables along its belly to fasten it down. The "when-I's" and "if-I's" conventional to boys' talk played out of Max's mouth for hours afterward. Max would have a jet and if not a jet, a biplane; if not a biplane, a blimp; and if not a blimp, a fishing rod would do for now, though he would fish only in the spring since the sea lions nap on the jetties on summer afternoons. Max thinks of them as halfway dogs, and dogs scare him.

It's down to the beach and the jetties, Max decides. The year's too young for sea lions. But not for blue jays. One lands on a crab apple tree nearby and chirps inquisitively. Max grins at the bird with a dreamy, feline smile. Everything tries its best to come to life for the summertime, to attend a warm, green world.

A silver sedan drives by doing the speed limit. For an instant, the Orisons and the wagon are reversed on the side of the car. The name on the wagon flips like a sock turned inside out. When it comes to mirrors, Max knows how they pervert details. Still he cannot help but stare. He's the sad story dog, the one holding a bone between its teeth as it stares down the well. Mirrors remind Max of how things fall short, how the world performs below expectations. Could this be because the world is very old? Each time the Griers' station wagon struggles down the block, fuming blackly, he's sure that that will be its last voyage. But inside the jalopy, Mr. Grier seems to know better. He holds the steering wheel with his fingertips and looks resolutely out at the road ahead of him, while lower on his face, his lips sculpt words. Is it prayer, Max wonders, that keeps the station wagon moving? Max's mother has said the Griers are ruined. So isn't it likely then that the present imperfection of mirrors, like today's sputtering engine, is only an early symptom of worse things to come?

Max wishes his father had something reassuring to say.

They travel through the morning down the boulevard and out of town to the beach and the jetties. Below a landscaped park, the beach begins amid rolling dunes seeded with finger grass and sleeping plant. The wagon performs poorly in the sand, but in the end Max and Frank Orison arrive at their destination: the last stone block of the farthest jetty. At high tide the waves will break against the stones where Max now spreads a blue-checked beach towel. The last tide left a dark green vein of seaweed in a crevice. Max is leaning down to stroke it with the back of his fingers when the sound of wings surprises him. He stands up to find a fat gray gull preening itself on his father.

Shoo!

Frank Orison remains calm, absolutely still.

Shoo, stupid bird! Max says.

He swipes at the gull and it flitters off into the breeze above the gray-green water. The same breeze plasters Max's hair over his eyes.

He removes his shoes and socks, and sits facing his father. He lets his right leg dangle over the side and his left foot rest on the edge, his left knee raised; his left elbow rests on the knee so his left fist can prop up his tilted head. Fishermen cast silently against the offing. He takes in the pale blue sky and the freighters out at sea. But just then there's a blinding bit of the sun bouncing off his father's face, straight into Max's eyes. He winces and, shielding his eyes with his left hand, uses the big toe of his left foot to turn his father just enough.

Were any evil to befall Frank Orison—theft, for example, or the ever-present threat of discovery by his mother—Max will rely on replicas. One rainy day, he found that sugar cubes could be carved in his father's image. He took an emery board to a cube and shaved one corner flat. This became his steady base, his foot. With the cube standing upright, he drew the emery board over what was now the topmost corner, pulling it lightly toward his chest and downward at an acute angle. He worked gingerly, and in time the pentagonal asymmetry of his father's face revealed itself. Max keeps dozens of such miniature fathers in his dresser drawer. Most he shaved from sugar cubes before his mother had the chance to plop them in her tea. A few he cut from cork, four he molded from white beeswax; one is balsa wood, one is a fragment of cinder block he ground for weeks against a piece of callous steel. Many of the replicas fathered poorly. The sugar dads proved especially defective: they crumbled too easily in his palm or out-of-doors on humid April days. They tempted the birds and the squirrels and the ants. Ants captured two, a fly licked another, and there was one Max ate in a moment of doubt. Others fell to everyday hazards and carelessness: one wax father was smooshed in the back pocket of his blue trousers, and he lost a balsa wood replica somewhere in his desk at school.

Max has learned over the course of months how to protect his Frank Orisons. Errands with his mother, for example, call for either a balsa wood or a cork father. But Saturday adventures require *the* Frank Orison, the original, which he found at the airfield on that Saturday morning he left the house alone. His father was too heavy to carry, so he went home and got his red wagon. Max has not been able to create a replica on that scale, nor one so strong and resilient, so confident and handsome. He's lucky to have found such a worldly father, too, who so brightly reflects everything around him. But his attempt to make a backup miniature from one of his mother's hand mirrors failed. The blood ran in threads between his fingers down

Scott Geiger

onto the Oriental rug. Should evil befall the Frank Orison, Max knows he will never be able to replace him. Should the worst happen, he will make do with his pocket Frank Orisons until at last he's too old for fathers.

At a sleepy corner where two streets merge into a third, Max Orison passes the Griers' house on his return from the jetties. It's a shabby dark place with a yard of willows and sprawling rhododendron. Max sees Edgar Grier and his twin, Sly, loitering between weedy flower beds with Sam Treble and his fearsome dalmatian. The handle of the wagon dampens inside Max's grip. These older boys and the dalmatian preside over the neighborhood. Edgar, Sly, and Sam weave in and out of yards as they please, picking this way and that, throwing off their teenage noise. Their oily skins and disproportionate limbs make the boys a tribe unto themselves. The dalmatian is probably their leader. Wherever the Griers and Treble go, they slink doggishly in imitation. Whenever they stand still, their shoulders droop like the dalmatian paused in a prowl. And sure enough, the dalmatian notices Max first. The boys follow the barking.

The three saunter up to Max and surround him. Sam looms in the shade of a willow bough.

Jamie Tyson's older sister jogs on Saturdays at noon sharp, says Edgar. We saw her in a sports bra.

It was black, adds Sly Grier. His eyes, expectant, pendulum from Sam to Edgar.

Max's feet spread apart and his arms cross.

What's that in the wagon? asks Sam.

My father, Max says.

The boys chortle.

You idiot! Sly says. The joke is "Your mamma," not "My father"!

The same silver sedan drives by doing the speed limit. A tableau peels off its side: four boys, a dog, leaves, grass, a red wagon with a shining metal polyhedron on board.

Your dad left to be on television, says Edgar.

No.

No, what? Edgar asks.

Max shakes his head. The palms of his hands turned upward, he says, No, he's right here in my wagon.

The boys step closer. Even Sly Grier, whose language is always on the tip of his tongue, has nothing to say about the polyhedron. The

228

Frank Orison stands two smooth and metallic feet tall. There are eight sides to him. The largest is defined by five edges, a pentagonal diamond-shaped slope almost half his total height. This could be his face, and this is where Max looks for the sort of help sons seek from their fathers. But the Frank Orison isn't that kind of father. He rests squarely in the wagon, rigid as an urn. Max sees instead his own head framed between the five edges. Reflections move vaguely all along the Frank Orison's skin: the new leaves swaying slowly overhead, the dappled coat of the dalmatian. The boys' faces appear, too, though weakly, as if faded in memory.

Max knows that there is a man called Frank Orison. Max uses memories of him all the time. But memory fathers cannot go up to the airfield or down to the jetties.

A garage door opens across the street.

Edgar, impatient, flicks the Frank Orison on the side. A low bell chime echoes through him. The dalmatian cocks his head.

You've got to be kidding, says Edgar. He does it again, the dalmatian barks.

Sly cannot be contained. Mr. Orison is hollow! he says.

Max's arms unfold, his hands drop into his pockets. He wants to laugh.

Then something new arises or intervenes in Sam Treble.

Where are you going? he asks.

Home.

Where were you?

The beach.

Why?

To watch birds and ore freighters and the fishermen, says Max. To look at the sky and water. Don't you do that sort of thing with your dad?

So what, says Sam Treble. You don't either.

The afternoon is soundless in the moment before Max takes his first step. He pulls the wagon around Sam Treble and past the Griers. Edgar takes one last flick at the Frank Orison but misses inexplicably. He begins to follow the wagon, to try again, but Sam Treble calls him back into the willow shade. Max and his wagon go off down the street, the Frank Orison glinting all the while in the afternoon light.

Max is reckless: he takes his father to Dads-in-Class Day and pastes on his side a red-and-white label that reads HELLO, MY NAME IS . . . MR. FRANK ORISON. The other fathers are ordinary sorts. Wrinkled men in cardigans and ties, bearded ones in T-shirts under flannel, the young and fighting kind in olive green uniforms, and suited elites with clear complexions and compelling smiles—they all disbelieve. Max hoists his father onto the corner of his desk. Murmurs rise and beady looks are brought to bear. Someone laughs once and others follow. Melodramatic Emma Friese throws her hands toward the ceiling. She slouches down in her chair and lets her forearms tumble back onto her head as it shakes from side to side in exasperation.

When will it end? says Emma. Where will it end?

Max slides the Frank Orison into the middle of the desk. Max hides.

When Miss Jupiter comes in, she thinks the Frank Orison is a kind of prank.

She calls Mrs. Orison. There's a meeting at four o'clock. The Frank Orison sits alone in a brown paper bag beside Miss Jupiter's desk. Max rolls and unrolls the cuffs of his pale blue sweater while his mother and teacher talk as if he weren't there.

A cry for help, Natalie, if you ask my opinion, Miss Jupiter says. Stunts like this always are. It will necessitate a memorandum in his permanent record, I'm afraid. But no larger conclusions will be drawn. I know you're concerned about that, naturally. Nothing that could become public. You have my assurance. The entire staff here is just so proud of Max's father and we all wish him the best.

Yes, says Mrs. Orison. Thank you.

Max's mother confiscates the Frank Orison. She bags him up with the asparagus stumps and a green-glass chardonnay bottle.

After dinner, Max poses the Question to his mother.

Don't torture me again, sweetie, she says without looking up from her paperwork and calculator. I've already told you that he's away, traveling all over the country. He wants a new and very important job, but to get it he has to be away almost all the time. Sometimes he comes home while you're asleep and leaves before you wake up. But I can't say when he'll be home next. I just don't know.

Max says, I could swear—

Pranks in school reflect poorly on me, Max. Remember that hurts my business reputation and your father's reputation in the community. If people see you playing with *that* and calling *that* your father, he may come home without getting his new and very important job.

*

All of his traveling would be for naught.

Max uses his silence.

His mother looks at Max over her glasses. Her skin is soft and creased around the mouth, and the shape of her hair is failing late at night like a spent candle. Her lips are very red and her sharp teeth show as she starts to speak.

Please try to understand, she says. Please.

She touches Max's hand, the one with the bandage. She kisses it.

Come nightfall, Max cannot help but retrieve him from the garbage can. He tiptoes back through the house and in the bathroom spritzes him with blue window cleaner. He wipes down the Frank Orison, the original and still the best, until he can see himself in his father. Once he's finished, Max quietly carries him into the bedroom and locks the door. No one knows more about the world than Max's mother, but still he cannot bring himself to accept what she says. Max does not necessarily believe the Frank Orison to be his father, not in the conventional sense. But he has come to admire and value him in ways different from the father seen in his memories. The Frank Orison sparkles expertly in sunshine. He warms in the afternoons and cools in the evenings, like the wind and the water. His faces are smooth, his corners crisp. There is no scarring nor any outward indication, like soldering, for instance, that his father is in any way provisional or contrived. Nothing on him droops or sags. There are no wrinkles or smells or softness to him. The Frank Orison is pure as a wheel on the wagon in which he rides when they go down to the jetties or up to the airfield on their Saturday voyages.

Max speaks soft words to the Frank Orison by the nightlight's butter yellow glow.

Halfway off to sleep, however, a yearning for a more permanent father begins in Max. Such a father would be wrought from huge stone blocks or erected like skyscrapers out of steel and glass, titanium and bronze. He imagines a city rising up around such a patrimony. How silent it would be. How weather would pass over and around him. There would be no stores nor trades to speak of, so no coins to jingle nor currency to fold, no street names, no signs. No one would go to such a city, except Max Orison, to play alone in his father's compassing shadow.

WALPOLIANA

Elizabeth Walpole wore her marriage of twenty-three years like an emigrant's last old-world frock. She said nothing while the airline's computer assigned her to 18A and her husband to 12C. They passed through the checkpoints and down the navy blue carpet to their gate. It was an hour before midnight. The wide windows along the concourse were dark but for the running lights on the planes and the headlamps of service carts. At their gate, to look out over the plane's silver body, Elizabeth stepped close to the glass. Her own image, dull and semitransparent, rose up in the window to meet her. Slender of limb and narrow about the hips and shoulders, her body had borne a daughter reluctantly. Round shadows masked her eyes in the window's reflection. Robert's face now appeared beside hers in the dark glass. The years had drawn down his earlobes, thinned his hair, and set a paunch on his belly. Yet her husband persisted over time, an iceberg loosed to the open seas. Gathered over his eyes, too, were shadows in the shape of a mask.

They had met in Gainesville on the brightest day of 1980. He selling insurance, she selling syringes. Ride up to Charleston with me tomorrow, he had said. Love, she had hoped, was about surrendering yourself to someone. That's why you *fall* in love. Their eyes met now in the glass without causing a quiver in either face.

He reminded her to take her pill and Elizabeth said she would.

You'll need your sleep, said Robert, for the movers.

She put her eyes on the plane, the pilots working in the cockpit.

Sleep, he said. You didn't sleep at all last night.

Cool air streamed from a duct overhead as the central system activated.

Midnight came and the plane taxied out over the crisscrossed runways. The turbines spun and wind traveled against the wings at the requisite speed. The dark stiffened to yield lift; the world fell away. Elizabeth saw only the moon and stars as the plane turned for a long time. When they leveled off, she saw Los Angeles through the port, nothing more at this altitude than a luminous signature. The man beside her in the dark cabin smelled of mouthwash and tossed in his seat.

Elizabeth Walpole deliberately did not take her pill. Alone with her thoughts, she watched the wingtip's white light for hours. A flight attendant came with tomato juice and took away the empty cup. She felt the aircraft's slight adjustments and listened to the turbines. Her cheek pressed against the port's cool plastic. She felt in her jawbone the vibrations of the accelerated fuselage. The black sky and the slight turbulence called to mind how—years before Robert— she paid the gondolier to take her through the back canals, where only the lusterless water's splashing broke a silence many centuries thick. The gondola slipped by houses and tiny piazzas, round sudden curves and past unforeseen, still narrower canals leading off to untrammeled precincts. In and out of sunshine and shadow, she coasted. Elizabeth saw windows visited only by seabirds and ornamented metal doors under which the canal water flooded. Her memory had held dearly to this sense of drifting alone, or practically alone, through the lagoon city. She had planned to take Sidney someday under the Rialto to those canals, just the two of them, alone as mother and daughter. They would speak solemnly if at all in the gondola, their voices echoing between the sapped foundations. Sidney would ever afterward associate her mother with the bridges and palazzos sinking in the tides.

The man in the seat beside her was speaking in his sleep, muttering what might have been the name "Meriwether" or "Mary Weather" but might have also been "merry weather." The sound haunted his mouth. Each time he said it louder until he startled himself awake. The man looked anxiously around him and, seeing that Elizabeth was also awake, apologized.

For what?

I've tried to help it, he said.

The man folded his arms and closed his eyes. A moment later they blinked open again and he seemed to have a thought spooled for saying. But he kept mute. The man closed his mouth and his eyes and went back to sleep. Elizabeth slid down in her seat and leaned against the port. Dawn in the distance was a girlish pink ribbon stretched tight from one end of the sky to the other.

The owl was most severe when Elizabeth didn't sleep. That's what Robert Walpole thought. As she came off the jetway that morning in Ohio, he saw on her face the worst case yet of the owl. Her lips pursed, her broad cheeks paled, gray circles hung under her outrageously dilated black eyes.

It had been since Sidney that he had held her, years since sex.

Any sleep? he asked.

Elizabeth Walpole shook her head. Off and on.

Sleep in the car?

You know how I am in cars now, she said.

It was the last day of August. Cirrus clouds patched the sky. They drove the black rental coupe ninety minutes to an old ore town many storefronts long but few deep. One street like a cord led through its heart. Over this crescent of stores and homes rose the smokestacks of smelting furnaces, dormant now for decades. Very much awake and taller still was a ziggurat of smoky blue glass, the Cusco Mutual Building, which loomed between the town and the interstate.

Where's your office? asked Elizabeth.

The seventeenth floor, he said. Northeast corner.

Is there a view?

Robert said there was plenty to look at but nothing to see.

A memory came back to Robert uninvited. Elizabeth poised on her knees in his black leather Eames chair long ago in Kansas. Did she remember? he wondered. Could the memory be invoked?

They passed the new hospital under construction near the interstate. They passed rowhouses built to look like brownstones and the billboard advertising them for sale. They passed a pond and a small park where children stood in the wind atop climbers and dangled from a silvery jungle gym while their adults watched from the benches. Then neighborhoods filled up either side of the road. Old houses lined streets with Indian names and flower names and number names. Huron, Amaryllis, Seventeenth. There were streets with famous last names and old-fashioned names for girls. Webster, Fulton, Venetia, Una. The Walpoles had bought a house on a rise at the edge of town. It had a master bathroom with a skylit double shower. From their front lawn, Robert could look one direction down to the Cusco Building and then in the other straight down into a blue-green valley of old farmland where corn was almost over for the year.

We're late to meet the movers, she said. I know it's been bothering you but there's nothing to do about it.

We'll be fine.

Robert Walpole hadn't even thought to look at his watch. The movers had beaten them to the house and now stood smoking cigarettes and drinking soda from cans in the shade of two dollar green semis. He had lived in the house for a week by himself, sleeping on an air mattress in the smallest of three bedrooms. That week in the new office had been easy and he came home early to his

Scott Geiger

empty rooms. He had toyed with the notion of having nothing in the world at all, nothing that could be collected and carried away over the horizon.

He told the men to begin unloading. They called him sir and lowered ramps from the truck.

Something's broken, I'm sure, Elizabeth said. Like the Waterford last time.

Robert got out and hung his hands by the thumbs from his pockets. With the truck's side and rear doors already swung open, Robert Walpole saw their property swelling beneath quilted tarps. It was scrambled, inverted, compacted. But there was the scarlet leather ottoman and the crimped lampshades. There in a roll was the Persian rug that had paled in the bright foyer of the California house. Out of boxes and blankets and Styrofoam peanuts, the Walpoles' home began to reappear in the skin of an Ohio house.

Their past unfolded and came back to them in the form of accumulated possessions. End tables, candlesticks, silverware bought in Antwerp, Tupperware, sweatshirts, jackets for all seasons, framed watercolor seascapes, two golden putti, a Japanese screen, pink silk carnations, a white wooden table with four green upholstered chairs, pewter plates from Bruges, and countless smaller things like ties and magnetic pots for paper clips. Hidden in one of the boxes, wrapped densely in newspaper, Robert knew there was a magic item: a blue china serving bowl that lived in the breakfront. It had been a wedding present from his grandfather. He wasn't sure why he had started in these past years to open the breakfront and touch his thumb to the bowl. The movers brought in a series of seven brown cardboard boxes marked with an *S* for Sidney. Robert moved them himself up to the smallest bedroom. New things were coming, too. A new burgundy leather couch and two plasma televisions to hang on the walls. This is the sum of it then, thought Robert Walpole: a rummage pile.

Wherever his insurance company asked him to oversee the expansion or contraction of activities, Robert Walpole went. Often he imagined his life could be expressed in units or irregular segments based on these transfers. Robert could say to himself: my daughter, Sidney, was born in a July of the middle Georgia Period, got her braces in the early Maryland, and one Saturday morning at the close of the California was killed with two girls and one boy at a misty curve on I-15 when a truck hauling polyvinyl chloride pellets jackknifed. And because the Ohio Period succeeded the California, the

235

Scott Geiger

Walpoles sat very quietly at their kitchen table that night eating Chinese takeout.

Elizabeth fell asleep twice between forkfuls.

Let me, he said. Let me put the bed together.

I can sleep on the floor.

You deserve a bed.

Robert climbed the stairs and put together their bed frame and settled the mattress and box springs onto it. Elizabeth changed into a pale yellow nightgown and lay down on her side of the bed. He covered her and then flipped the lights off. A diamond of sunset shone orange on the bedroom's white walls.

I'm sorry there are no curtains, he said.

Robert couldn't resist touching her throat with the back of his fingers. He led them softly over her chin and across her lips. They traveled over her cheek and behind her ear. But she was already asleep.

Robert walked down the hallway past the stairs to the room that would have been Sidney's. He sat down in the folding metal chair he had placed by the window last week. Spread before him were the brown cardboard boxes, dimpled and creased in the move. Some of the tape had lost its grip. Green stickers the size of thumbprints numbered the boxes 57 through 63. As Robert leaned over them, his elbows set against his knees and pocketknife in hand, a noise at the window paused him. In the dark of the yard, a wind was up. She would've liked the trees outside, he thought. The way the leaves rake the window in the breeze. She would've listened for the rain in the leaves, too. He opened a box with his knife. Without knowing what to look for, Robert searched the boxes. Knowing what was in each box, he expected no discoveries. The postcards followed the tiny plastic dolls; scented candles lay on their sides below the black marble dish she'd kept jewelry in. Because he knew what came next in the boxes, he felt a sequence of relationships between Sidney's things. An illusory pattern, a constellation, emerged. He looked at each article of clothing, even her socks and black underwear. He found the powder blue T-shirt with dark blue ringers on the sleeves and collar. There was a horse's head on it advertising a stable in the desert. He held the shirt's underarm to his nose and breathed. It was clean and smelled nothing like Sidney. There was too much left over from her. Too many things over which her memory spread too thinly. Each item could not be an emblem of his daughter's life just because she had owned it. He had no sense of what had been most

236

important to her. Sidney had liked softball and horses, though the latter only as an idea. Actual horses frightened her. They're so big. She had no dominant passions, no firm goals, no sense of destiny. She was just starting out as Sidney Walpole, so far as he knew, and then she was abruptly over. Yet the Sidney Period of Robert Walpole's life continued without end in sight. He was the citizen of a failed state, whose customs and traditions he would perpetuate without understanding.

Two hours passed and Robert Walpole repacked his daughter's things. He piled the boxes in one corner of the room, four on the bottom, then two, and then the one with the T-shirt. He left the door a little open behind him.

Elizabeth Walpole slept for twelve and a half hours. When she woke, she went into the bathroom and checked her eyes in the mirror. She could go on sleeping for years to come. She put on a robe and went downstairs. Through the kitchen window she saw Robert talking to a pretty woman in the backyard. He stood with one hand in his pocket and the other straightening his hair. His untucked Sunday shirt rippled in the breeze. There had been days when Elizabeth had wished Robert would run away with another woman. The mettle wasn't in him for it; he lacked the magnetism. A doctor had discovered polyps in his colon once and she had fantasized about life without him until the polyps were pronounced benign. Her thoughts precipitated guilt. Elizabeth Walpole had never believed herself to be a good person. Her own mother had called her a squanderer, a breaker, a dolt. As a girl, Elizabeth had used solitude like a tent. Alone inside, no one could criticize her. As a woman at large in the world, however, Elizabeth wondered if love couldn't be a kind of boat you board, a cruise ship. For a while it was like that with Robert, until she let herself get pregnant. She had wanted someone to hold up in the wind, evidence that she was someone altogether different from the foolish Elizabeth of long ago. But her hopes had ebbed over time. It looked like her daughter only proved that she had gotten worse with age. "Witch" is what Sidney had said during one of many fights about eating modest, smart meals.

She was at the table drinking water when Robert came in.

Who was that? she asked.

Ellen Mungo. Her husband, Sean, is the chief adjustor at Cusco.

237

They live in that house with the brick patio and gaslight lamps behind us.

She seemed very friendly.

They want to have a little something for us next weekend, he said. To meet the neighbors. Cusco folks will be there, too. Might be a good chance to get our feet on the ground, don't you think? We have to start somewhere.

Elizabeth Walpole had no organ with which to sense the invisible boundary lines in her life. When her husband announced that Cusco would transfer him again, and to Ohio, she did not say to herself, "This life will end and another will begin." Instead she rewound, the way a clock is rewound, a colorful idea she had cherished for years: "There are many Elizabeth Walpoles," she could say to herself. All at once and everywhere. In Kansas another Elizabeth Walpole continued to work as an interior designer's assistant while in Maryland another went on watching a white-haired little girl smear fir pitch between her fingers. But today in Ohio, after all those other Elizabeth Walpoles, the most recent felt the thinnest, the most depleted. Violence had stripped this Elizabeth of her Sidney, the evidence by which she could prove emphatically her merit and goodness. She felt blasted and purposeless. She felt blown from hinges, torn from her mast.

You slept.

Not well.

But for a long time.

But not very well, I don't think.

Maybe you should try again, he said. Why don't we both.

His hand moved along her side.

I want to go to church, she said. It's Sunday.

You've never gone to church, Beth.

I'll start, she said.

Maybe I'll come, too.

You should unpack.

Robert Walpole sat across from her at the white wooden table. He picked up her glass of water and drank half of what was left. Religion is a conventional recourse at a time of grief, he said. So is the love of your family.

His hand, set palm up on the table, was an invitation.

Let's take a shower, he said. And go to church.

Elizabeth's eyes looked askance. She said she would just like to sit here for a while.

*

Robert Walpole told himself he was a simple man. He no longer entertained hopes or expectations. These he imagined were like the pair of blue-eyed cockatoos he'd kept as a boy. Shrill and dusty beside the open window in the garret of his Uncle Bert's house. For two summers he spent all his time with John and Richard. During the school year, they called day and night for him. When Robert learned how to appease them with squeaky toys, he also began to find excuses. He visited them less and less. When Richard died, John plucked out every feather he could reach and then began stabbing himself with his bill. Atop the Cusco Mutual Building, Robert looked at his black leather Eames. He knew intuitively that the feelings he had felt for and the actions he had performed with Elizabeth in the past would not recur. That version of Elizabeth had expired, somehow subsumed by this impostor, this half wife. He strangled his cockatoos.

White feathers fell across the room.

Robert Walpole put his elbows on his desk and folded his stiff hands. Though hidden behind his right middle finger, he could feel the band's cool metal. Behind him in the wide windows were the rooftops of the town, the highway bridges, the blue-green farmlands. The sky, a diffuse smear of curdled blue light. There was no need for such a view. To others, a view like this means something. It inspires, it stirs. But it did nothing for him. If anything at all came to him while he looked out from those windows, it was the years that had passed and how hard he had worked for Cusco. And if he thought of the daughterless, wifeless years ahead, words like a single curl of smoke from a trimmed candle came to mind: I have entered the Ohio Period, landfill for all previous periods.

The new Elizabeth Walpole decided to grow her own flowers. She saw the sunny slope in bloom behind the Ohio house. Contemplative Chinese yellow mingled with Roman Catholic violet. She cut a piece of foam from the spare mattress pad. It would be a selfless life of light and air, soil and water. Her work would be in plain view; she imagined the neighbors complimenting her irises.

On her knees lodging the bulbs in the soil, Elizabeth heard the whine of a decelerating jet overhead. A passenger plane glimmered on its course through the midday air. Minutes later another came over the house, this one a little smaller and porcelain white. Others followed. Traveling over her shoulder they each vanished behind the maples in the Mungos' yard. This is how she learned that her new house and the future sanctuary garden lay below an approach path to the distant airport. The sound of voyages concluding would fill her life in Ohio. This pleased Elizabeth.

There was a gale the night of the Mungos' party.

It's a fête champêtre, Sidney Walpole's father said.

A *what?*

They're the guests of honor, Sean Mungo told his wife. They get to call it what they like.

You have to call things by their proper names, Sidney's father said. A fête champêtre.

You two are just so worldly! said Ellen Mungo.

Bob, let me introduce you to some special people before I take you around.

I love this white sweater, Elizabeth. It's angora, isn't it? How long do you think an angora piece lasts? Doesn't it just start falling apart from the minute you put it on?

This, said Sean, is Benjamin and his brother, Stephen, our boys. And Beckett Brescia, their friend from school.

I think it's all just a matter of how you care for it, Sidney's mother said.

Gentlemen, said her father to the boys. How old are you?

Well keep clear of the sangria, said Ellen. You'd never get over a stain like that.

Seventeen, said Beckett.

A flock of napkins took flight from a table under the maples.

The rustle of crepe-paper decorations was her signal. She brushed the lawn where the setting sun cast long and deformed shadows against the hillside. She wiggled loose the leaves from the maple trees, urging them toward her mother's head. She fizzed the Campari sodas and wafted the scent of scotch. The smell of prawns toasting blew with her across the yard. She coursed through Beckett Brescia's earring and allowed herself to pool in his mouth. His lungs tugged at her wantonly. Robert breathed her, too: she went back to him like a wave curling back to the sea, to be his jokes and laughter. She played in Elizabeth's black hair and found the spots graying along her temples. She wove between each eyelash and wrapped herself like a

boa around her mother's shoulders. Sidney Walpole sang in the gut-
tering tiki torches and the crackling sparklers the children ran with
in their fists. Around the patio she winked the gaslight lamps in
secret semaphore. She feathered Robert's lapels the way she had
when she used fingers. She flushed against his gray Saturday evening
stubble and mixed with her faint Indian summer humidity the
famous smell of his cologne.

Sidney Walpole swooned inside her costume of air. What was left
she spun between Robert and Elizabeth like the Cusco blue and
white crepe streamers overhead.

Younger
Brian Evenson

YEARS LATER, SHE WAS STILL calling her sister, trying to understand what exactly had happened. It still made no sense to her, but her sister, older, couldn't help. Her sister had completely forgotten—or would have if the younger sister wasn't always reminding her. The younger sister imagined, each time she talked to her sibling on the telephone, each time she brought the incident up, her older sister pressing her palm against her forehead as she waited for her to say what she had to say, so that she, the older sister, the only one of the sisters with a family of her own, could politely sidestep her inquiries and go back to living her life.

Her older sister had always managed to do that, to nimbly sidestep anything that came her way so as to simply go on with her life. For years, the younger sister had envied this, watching from farther and farther behind as her older sister sashayed past those events that an instant later struck the younger sister head-on and almost destroyed her. The younger sister was always being almost destroyed by events, and then had to spend months desperately piecing herself together enough so that when once again she was struck head-on, she would only be almost destroyed rather than utterly and completely destroyed.

As her mother had once suggested, the younger sister felt things more intensely than anyone else. At the time, very young, the younger sister had seen this as a mark of emotional superiority, but later she saw it for what it was: a serious defect that kept her from living her life. Indeed, as the younger sister reached first her teens and then her twenties, she came to realize that people who felt things as intensely as she were either institutionalized or dead.

This realization was at least in part due to her father having belonged to the first category (institutionalized) and her mother the second (dead by suicide)—two more facts that her older sister, gliding effortlessly and, quite frankly, mercilessly through life, had also sidestepped. Indeed, while the younger sister was realizing to a

242

more and more horrifying degree how she was inescapably both her mother's and father's child, her older sister had gone on to start a family of her own. It was like her older sister had been part of a different family. The younger sister could never start a family of her own—not because, as everyone claimed, she was irresponsible, but because she knew it just brought her one step closer to ending up like her mother and father. It was not that she was irresponsible, but only that she was terrified of ending up mad or dead.

The incident had occurred when their parents were still around, before they were, in the case of the mother, dead, and, in the case of the father, mad. There were, it had to be admitted in retrospect, signs that things had gone wrong with their parents, things her older sister must have absorbed and quietly processed over time but which the younger sister was forced to process too late and all at once. The incident, the younger sister felt, was the start of her losing her hold on her life. Even years later, she continued to feel that if only she could understand exactly what had happened, what it all meant, she would see what had gone wrong and could correct it, could, like the older sister, muffle her feelings, begin to feel things less, and, in the end, perhaps not feel anything at all. Once she felt nothing, she thought, knowing full well how crazy this sounded, she could go on to have a happy life.

But her older sister couldn't understand. To her older sister, what the younger sister referred to as *the incident* was nothing—less than nothing, really. As always, her older sister listened patiently on the other end of the line as the younger sister posed the same questions over again. "Do you remember the time we were trapped in the house?" she might begin, and there would be a long pause as her older sister (so the younger sister believed) steeled herself to go through it again.

"We weren't trapped exactly," her older sister almost always responded. "No need to exaggerate."

But that was not how the younger sister remembered it. How the younger sister remembered it was that they *were* trapped. Even the word *trapped* did not strike her as forceful enough. But her older sister, as always, saw it as her role to calm the younger sister down. The younger sister would make a statement and then her older sister would qualify the statement, dampen it, smooth it over, nullify it. This, the younger sister had to admit, *did* calm her, *did* make her feel momentarily better, *did* make her think, *Maybe it isn't as bad as I remembered.* But the long-term effect was not to make her feel calmer but to make her feel insane, as if she were remembering things that hadn't actually happened. But if they hadn't happened the way she remembered, why was she still undone more than twenty years later? And as long as her sister was calming her, how was she ever to stop feeling undone?

No, what she needed was not for her sister to calm her, not for her sister, from the outset, to tell her there was no need to exaggerate. But she could not figure out how to tell her sister this—not because her older sister was unreasonable but because she was all too reasonable. She sorted the world out rationally and in a way that stripped it of all its power. Her older sister could not understand the effect of the incident on the younger sister because she had not let it have an effect on her.

For instance, her older sister could not even begin to conceive how the younger sister saw the incident as the single most important and most devastating moment of her life. For her older sister, the incident was nothing. How was it possible, her older sister wanted to know, that the incident had been more damaging for her than their mother's suicide or their father's mental collapse? It didn't make any sense. Well, yes, the younger sister was willing to admit, it *didn't* make any sense, and yet she was still ruined by it, still undone. *If I can understand exactly what happened,* she would always tell her older sister, *I'll understand where I went wrong.*

"But nothing happened," her older sister said. "Nothing. That's just it."

And that was the whole problem. The sisters had played the same roles for so many years that they didn't know how to stop. Responding to each other in a different way was impossible. Every conversation had already been mapped out years in advance, at the moment the younger sister was first forced to think of herself as the irresponsible one and the older sister had first acted as a calming force. They weren't getting anywhere, which meant that she, the younger sister, wasn't getting anywhere, was still wondering what, if anything, had happened, and what, if anything, she could do to free herself of it.

What she thought happened—the way she remembered it when, alone, late at night, she lay in bed after another conversation with her sister—was this: their mother had vanished sometime during the night. Why exactly, the younger sister didn't know. Their father, she remembered, had seemed harried, had taken their mother somewhere during the night and left her there, but had been waiting for them when they woke up, seated on the couch. He had neither slept nor bathed; his eyes were very red and he hadn't shaved. Somehow, she remembered, her sister hadn't seemed surprised. Whether this was because the sister wasn't really surprised or because, as the calm one, she was never supposed to appear surprised, the younger sister couldn't say.

She remembered the father insisting nothing was wrong, but insisting almost simultaneously that he must leave right away. There was, the younger sister was certain, something very wrong, but what exactly it had been, she was never quite certain. Something with the mother certainly, perhaps her suicidal juggernaut just being set in motion—though her older sister claimed that no, it must have been something minor, a simple parental dispute that led to their mother going to stay temporarily with her own mother. And the only reason the father had to leave, the older sister insisted, was because he had to get to work. He had a meeting, and so had to leave them alone, even though they were perhaps too young—even the older sister had to admit this—to be left alone.

Her older sister claimed, too, that the father had bathed and looked refreshed and was in no way harried. But this, the younger sister was certain, was a lie, was just the older sister's attempt to calm her. No, the father had looked terrible, was harried and even panicked, the younger sister wasn't exaggerating, not really. *Do you love me?* the younger sister sometimes had to say into the phone. *Do you love me,* she would say, *then stop making me feel crazy and just listen.*

So there was her father, in her head, simultaneously sleepless and well rested, clean and sticky with sweat. He had to leave, he had explained to them. He was sorry but he had to leave. But it was all right, he claimed. He set the stove timer to sound when it was time for them to go to school. When they heard the timer go off, he told them, they had to go to school. Did they understand?

Yes, both girls said, they understood.

"And one more thing," the father said, his hand already reaching for the knob. "Under no circumstances are you to answer the door. You are not to open the door to anyone."

*

And after that? According to her older sister, nothing much. The father left. The sisters played together until the timer rang, and then they opened the door and went to school.

But that was not how the younger sister remembered it. There was, first of all and above all, the strangeness of being alone in the house for the first time. There was a giddiness to that, a feeling they had stepped beyond the known world, a feeling the younger sister never for a moment forgot. A feeling that made it seem like not just minutes were going by, but hours.

"But it was just a few minutes," her older sister insisted.

"*Like* hours," said the younger sister. "Not actually hours but *like* hours." All right, she conceded, not actual hours—though she knew that when it came down to it there was no such thing as *actual* hours. But for all intents and purposes she had already lost her sister, once again had rapidly reached a point where she could no longer rely on her sister to help her understand what exactly had happened. But she kept talking anyway, because once she had started talking what could she do but keep on?

The point was, time slowed down for the younger sister and never really sped back up again. There was a giddiness and a sense that anything could happen, anything at all. There were only two rules: the world would end when the timer rang and under no circumstances were they to answer the door. But within those constraints, anything could happen.

What did they play? They played the same things they always played, but the games were different, too, just as the girls, alone, had become different. Her older sister, as always, went along with what the younger sister wanted, playing down to her level, but this time anything could happen. The small toy mustangs they played with dared do things they had never done before, cantering all the way across the parents' bedroom, where they gathered and conferred and at last decided on a stratagem for defeating the plastic bear, which, once bested, was flushed down the toilet and was gone forever. The two girls watched with sweaty faces and flushed cheeks as the bear disappeared: anything could happen. The younger sister pulled herself up on the bathroom counter and opened the cabinet and used the mother's lipstick on her own lips, something she was never allowed to do, and then used the lipstick to paint red streaks on the horses' sides, which was blood from where they had been gashed by the bear in battle. The most injured mustang limped slowly away and found a cave to hide in. He lay down in it and hoped that the cool and the dark would either help him get better or would kill him. At first the cave was just the space under the couch, but the mustang wasn't getting better so the younger sister stuck him in her armpit and called that a cave and held her arm clamped to her side. When, later, she reached him back out, the blood had smeared off all over the cave and the horse was miraculously healed and allowed to return to the pack.

"It's not called a pack," her older sister told her over the telephone. "It's a herd."

But the younger sister knew they had called it a pack, that anything could happen, and that *herd* was part of it, too. They had known at the time it was a herd but they had called it a pack, and they had said it wrong on purpose. They were building a whole world up around them, full of things more vivid and slippery than anything the real world could offer. Just because her older sister couldn't remember didn't mean it hadn't happened.

And the sisters had become mustangs as well, had joined the *pack* as well—couldn't she remember? They took the two biggest rubber bands they could find and stretched them from their mouths over the backs of their heads like bridles. They took old plastic bread bags their mother had saved and filled the bottoms with paper napkins and rubber banded them to their legs and then slipped shoes over their hands. And suddenly it wasn't just pretend but something was happening that had never happened before. Couldn't she remember? It was ecstatic and crazed and like they were fleeing their bodies—it was the only thing like a religious experience the younger sister had ever had, and she had had it when she was six.

And then suddenly it all went wrong.

They heard the timer go and ran to turn it off but they were still wearing shoes on their hands and neither of them wanted to take the shoes off, so they tried to stop the timer by trapping its stem between two shoes and turning it, but the timer stem was old and too smooth to turn like that. So while the timer buzzed on, the younger sister had neighed at her older sister and together they had cantered to the dining-room table and taken a chair, supporting it between them with their hooves, and brought it to the stove. The younger sister stood on it and leaned over the burner, feeling the enamel warm in one spot from the pilot light, and turned the timer off with her teeth, by twisting her head.

That was, the younger sister knew, the sign that the world had come to an end, that it was over, that now they had to go to school. Only it wasn't the end, for as soon as the timer was turned off, the doorbell rang. It froze both of them and they stood there, bread bags on their feet and shoes on their hands, and kept very still and very quiet. They were not to answer the door, their father had been very clear about that. But they were also supposed to go to school. How could you go to school when someone was at the door, ringing the doorbell, trying to come in?

My older sister, the younger sister thought, will know what to do.

But her older sister was standing there not doing anything. The doorbell rang again, and still they waited, the younger sister nervously rubbing her hooves together.

They waited awhile for the doorbell to ring a third time. When it did not, her older sister leaned close to her and whispered, *Come on.* But they had only taken a few steps when they heard not ringing but a hard, loud knock: four sharp, equally spaced blows right in a row. And that stopped them just as much as if someone had yanked back on their bridles.

It was like that for hours—for what, anyway, seemed like hours. Her hands were getting sweaty in the shoes. Her feet in the bread bags were much, much worse; the napkins at the bottom of each bag had grown damp. Her mouth, too, hurt in the corners because of the rubber band. Her older sister took a few steps and the younger sister, not knowing what else to do, followed. Her older sister, she saw, had taken the shoes off her hands without the younger sister noticing and had gotten the rubber band out of her mouth and was now creeping very slowly past the door. The younger sister followed, trying not to look at the curtain-covered window beside the door, trying not to see the shadow of whatever was on the other side, but seeing enough to know that, whatever it was, it was big, and seeing, too, when the knocking started once again, the door shiver in its frame.

In their bedroom, her sister helped her get the shoes off. They had been on long enough that they felt like they were still on even once they had come off. The rubber-band bridle got caught in her hair so that her sister had to snip it out with scissors, which made the bridle snap and raised a red stripe of flesh across her cheekbone and almost made her cry. The rubber bands holding the plastic bags to her legs had left purple grooves on her calves and her feet were hot and wet and itchy. She dried them off on a hand towel and put her shoes on while her older sister stood on a stool by the bedroom window and tried to see out.

"He's still there," she said.

"What is it?" asked the younger sister.

"I don't know," said her older sister. "Who, you mean."

But the younger sister had meant not who, but what. She wanted to climb on the stool beside her sister and look out as well, but was too scared.

"What do we do?" she asked.

"Do?" said her sister. "We play until he's gone."

So they had begun again, with the plastic horses again, only this time it was a slow negation of everything that had happened before. Before, it had seemed like anything could happen; now all the younger sister could think about was how they were trapped in the house, how they couldn't leave, how they were supposed to leave but couldn't. The mustangs were just ordinary horses now and could no longer move their plastic legs but simply stayed motionless as they were propelled meaninglessly across the floor. The bear was gone for good and she and her sister weren't horses anymore, just two trapped girls. Everything was wrong. They were trapped in the house and she knew they would always be trapped. The younger sister kept trying to play but all she could do was cry.

Her older sister was comforting her, telling her everything was fine, but the way she said it, it was clear nothing was fine. Everything was hell.

"What is it?" she asked again.

"He's probably not even there anymore," said her older sister. "I bet we can leave soon."

And, to be truthful, it probably was soon after that, though it didn't feel that way to the younger sister, that her older sister went back into the bedroom and climbed up on the stool again and looked out and said that it was safe now and everything was fine and this time seemed to mean it. They gathered their books and their lunches and opened the front door and darted out. The whole street seemed deserted. Her older sister, who hated to be late, made them both run to school, and the younger sister reached her class even before

249

Brian Evenson

Mrs. Clark had finished calling roll. When you looked at it that way, almost no time had actually passed. When you looked at it that way, as her older sister in fact had, really nothing at all had happened.

But as for the younger sister, there was less of her from there on out. Part of her was still wearing shoes on her hands and a rubber band in her mouth and was somewhere, sides bloody, looking for her pack. And part of her was still there, motionless, trapped in the house, waiting for the door to shiver in its frame. She was still, years later, trying to figure out how to get back those parts of her. And what was left of her she could hardly manage to do anything with at all.

"So what do you want me to do?" her sister finally one day asked, her voice tinny through the telephone. "Play mustangs with you again?" And then she laughed nervously.

And yes, in fact, that was exactly what the younger sister wanted. Maybe it would do something, it was worth a try, yes. If her sister would only do that, perhaps something—anything—could happen.

But after so many years, so many telephone conversations burning and reburning the same paths through their minds, so many years of playing the same roles, how could she ask this of her older sister? She knew her role enough to know she could never bring herself to ask this of her older sister. Not in what seemed like a million years.

Life Drawing
Ilona Karmel

—Translated from Polish by Fanny Howe and Arie A. Galles

CHILDHOOD

This story begins like any other.
A childhood story as ordinary
As milk and flowers. A world so small
That it could be contained within four walls.

The tale begins in an aura of tenderness
And calm though also in a world
So huge that Mother's
Hands had to protect us.

There was a children's room
With blue walls and ceilings
And when the day broke open
Outside the window the sky
Merged with our ceiling

And everything then was golden blue.

That day—my God—was short.

We couldn't fathom all its wonders
Before the light began to fade
And the sun disappeared. The lamp
Flickered sleepily, darkness trailed
From its hiding places out in the town.
It glued itself to our windows—
It was stifling—and we tossed.

And then that darkness became something else.

251

Whispers, rustles, chatters
From a primeval woodland
Joined the silver patterns on the wallpaper
And became forty thieves.

Bad dreams, black covers, light walls.
Unknown folk. Alarms.
Until a milklike river of light
Poured between you and that,
And you were safe enough to run
Into your mother's arms. . . .

There were stickers in a hundred colors,
Butterflies, flowers slick as a rainbow,
And big bonbons with a surprise
Inside their sweet chocolate shells.

The world was glutted with secrets.

Written into the blue walls were elves,
Water nymphs, slender and skittish,
Hampers, baskets, naughty gnomes,
And spirits hid in the corners of the room.

Every day, my God, was too rich
To fathom. Brimming with miracles.

Mother's room, pale lilac, held
Enchantments deep in large drawers
Among ribbons, blouses, and veils,
Yellow lace (ecru) scented

With the rolling press. Violets
Decorated the broken fan,
And peacock feathers. Yes,
Silk and taffeta and satin—

Too lovely to be described!

Ilona Karmel

Number 16 Dluga Street is still there,
I am sure, crammed in
Between the same houses
That were standing when I was a child.

In the park the maples bloom and droop.
But childhood is gone
Fast and for good, who can say
Where it went? The world around

Shriveled up and grew small.
I don't know how. Now
Nothing is mysterious.
Nothing survived the pogrom

Of time, not the elves
Sprites, gnomes, or little folk.
They were not saved
Any more than the secrets in the drawers.

The fantasies fell slowly, heavily
And brutally.
The tub is no longer an ocean,
The whale nothing to fear

And the chestnut is just a chestnut.
What is good fortune, I ask. . . .

Now fear doesn't lurk in the dusk.
Darkness is tempting instead.
The dangerous unknown
Looks good. A mother is superfluous.

Farewell, childhood! Hello, youth!
A splendid, gigantic
World of stories and adventures
Awaited me at fourteen
When we still counted the years.

Ilona Karmel

And before a new way of computing
Time began—by days, hours, fears,
Minutes, menace, ashes,
Ruins, pain, despair, terror, suffering, murder.

Yes, that became the way
We measured time when I was fourteen.
No words to explain
Without weeping.

YOUTH

Hush. Close your mouth.
Raise your hand
Into a clenched fist.
This is youth.
Another story altogether.
Bitter and sad
Hard and unavoidable.

These memories won't quit.
They even hurt.
It was the autumn of '39.
How to describe (in what language?
Fire?) that time.
When she arrived, she, youth,
She, without romance,
Or poetic introductions.
Distant reader, she came
With thunder, soldiers,
Cannons, machine guns,
Youth. No more fables.

I see the dark ditch and us in it.
Overhead, horrible wings.
Shock, screams, smoke, sun,
And a shaking ground.

What was The World to us
Crashed down. Gray petals
Of smoke unfurled
Into a red conflagration.

From that moment on,
It would always be the same.
A mother's terror
And still her comforting hands.

Both of these, and that avalanche.

Time staggered forward
Without mercy
Carrying each person with him.
I grew from fifteen to sixteen.

The days were voracious,
Like creatures that clawed
At whatever we took with us.
The closest, the most loved.

They clawed until they dug
A horrible void into
Our childish faces!
We grew old, dull-eyed, dry.

Only hate stayed strong.
Little, but quite sufficient
To get us through the graveyard days
And give us more bitter knowledge.

The art of the closed fist
The clever closed fist.

Don't scream from pain.
Don't express rage.

Cut from your lexicon
The words happiness, laughter,

Ilona Karmel

And change love to hate.
Words that would be a waste.

The simple and difficult art
Of self-censorship is to ensure
That no heart exists.

Mother's hands, once capable
Only of arranging flowers in a vase,
Were now hard, she learned
How to deflect a blow with them.

Love made them tough
While her face grew yellow,
Her eyes lost their life,
Until her heart gave up the struggle.

So, friend, that is all
I can remember. You count.
How many graves? How many days?
It is now 1945.

Blood, a taste of morphine,
Bad dreams, no more mother's hands. . . .

This is the epilogue, friend.
From my life inside four walls.

I have no childhood dreams, only
Visitations from the fearful
Nightmares of those years.

Worse for being known
But now with nowhere to run
For comfort from them.
No maternal hands.

The story ends here
When I am twenty.

Ilona Karmel

Ilona Karmel

TRANSLATOR'S NOTE

Ilona Karmel entered the Krakow Ghetto with her mother and sister when she was fourteen years old. She spent her teenage years being moved from one labor camp to another, ending up finally in Buchenwald. She and her sister, Henia, composed poems on work sheets stolen from the factories where they spent their days and hid them in their clothing. They and the poems miraculously survived the war. Ilona Karmel's masterpiece, *An Estate of Memory*, gives an excruciating account of those years in Poland and Germany. A few of the 140 pages of poems were published in chapbook form decades ago. Now many of them have been translated from Polish to English. This poem, "Life Drawing," was written in a hospital bed in Sweden at the end of the ordeal.—*F.H.*

Five Stories
Kim Chinquee

HALFWAY

TORI AND BESS SIT in their room, inventing new names for their father. "Turkey. Chicken. Baby," Tori says. She looks at her lips as they move in the mirror.

"Slimeball." Bess tries to flatten her back on the mattress, which sags in the middle. She and her twin sleep in the same bed. At bedtime, each gets on her side, but by morning, they'll be cuddled up together in the middle.

At dinner, after prayers, their father spilled the Kool-Aid. He blamed it on their mother. She'd filled the pitcher past the halfway that he liked. The mother said sorry, wiping the sticky grape up with her apron. The girls sat looking at their father.

In the room, they get a rope out from their closet. Bess ties Tori to a chair. It's a game they play when they're angry with their father. Tori takes off her clothes, and as they pretend Tori is their father, Bess whips Tori's shoulders. They stole the whip from their father. They got it from the barn. Their father whips his cows. He has lots of whips. He will never miss it.

Tori plays her role. "I'm sorry, sorry, sorry," she says.

Bess tells her sister to be nice. She tells Tori to repeat after her. Bess hits Tori. They have a code word, Father.

Tori is bleeding, saying Father. Bess unties her. Music plays from the speaker in their room, a hymn, but they don't know the title. They are supposed to memorize the verses. They play it loud. It drowns out lots of noises.

The sisters lie in the middle of the bed together. "I feel better," Tori says. Bess says, "I do, too." They are eight. Their mom is making brownies. They can smell them.

258

PAPER DOLLS

Sara sits on the carpet, cutting out of catalogs: cribs and pets and houses, a swing set for the yard. People. Sara cuts out of the Wish-book, making her inventions: Ken and his wife, Barbie, and they have a lot of siblings, and they might have seven children. Sara rearranges, spreading the households all around the floor, decorating with the cut-out items: furniture and bedspreads, hampers, trampolines, and treadmills. Some even have pianos. Sara pretends the people can afford things, although their sole careers are caring for their children.

Sometimes her father strips her naked. He whips her if she forgets to do things, like today: wipe the dinner table.

After she gets tired of her families, she cuts off all their heads. She tells them to make friendly conversation. They don't listen, so she throws everything away.

Later on, she'll get their heads out of the trash can, taping every-thing back where it belongs. Or maybe she'll forget. She will not recall that anything existed.

OVERALLS

In the morning, my sister's spot was vacant—we slept in the same bed. I could smell the bacon my mom made, could hear the cartoons my sis was always watching. Her favorite was *Scooby-Doo*, but that morning, at my waking time, I could hear *The Jetsons*. I heard the buzz, the song, and I imagined George getting in his saucer.

I looked in the mirror. I was six, a girl, although my hair was brown and messy, like a boy—when my mom took Amanda and me to the grocery, strangers would tell my mother how adorable a boy I was. They would say my sister and I made the perfect twins. She was one year older. I always held my mother's hand, afraid of losing her, yet my sister was running off, her pigtails flopping like a pom-pom, shooting up like a baton.

People said I looked like my father.

My sister came into the room and asked what I was doing. I ignored her.

"You dumb?" my sister Manda said.

When she left the room, I donned the clip-on earrings that had been my grandma's. I changed into the hand-me-downs I got from Cousin Teddy. Then I went to breakfast.

My father watched the dairy channel. We watched what he wanted. He didn't say much. My mother always told us what we should do around him. He only talked when he was yelling. She helped us to know what to expect. I was very good at listening.

I was eating eggs and toast and bacon. I had a glass of milk. The TV blared something about Holsteins. When we folded hands, I mouthed the words, but I didn't say them.

After breakfast, when I lay on the sofa, Manda talked, but I would only listen. She told my mom I wasn't talking. My father was outside, and my mother was baking fudge. "Mom," Amanda said. "She isn't talking."

I thought she would tell my father.

"Maybe she doesn't feel like talking," my mother said, calling from the kitchen.

My sister tried to tickle me, looked at me as if I were a creature at the fair. As she stared, I pretended to be an attraction at the zoo, and I tried to imagine how those animals felt, how people looked at them and pointed, making comments about their hygiene or their habits. I remembered watching all the pandas when I went on a field trip. I tried to talk to them. I didn't understand them.

Later on, my mother took a picture. She smiled and said it was good that I could be so quiet. She put her camera in the drawer, and then she asked Amanda to help her with brownies.

I went to the barn and fed the calves. I almost talked to my favorite heifer, Kitchen. But I petted her instead. Later on, I went to bed, and Mandy kicked under the covers. She asked me if I was OK, and I smiled at her and nodded.

I wanted to tell my sister that I wanted to race the field, then go to the creek and catch minnows. I wanted to cycle down the lane and feel the movement, the wind against my face, riding against the force, gripping the handlebars, pushing the pedals with my toes. I wanted to go barefoot. I wanted to wear a golden dress. I wanted to grow hair as long as my sister's. I wanted to go to the barn and walk in the manure, feel it warm and sticky, making stains between my toes, splashing on my polish. I wanted to be bigger. I wished that I could shout.

TIRE

Jenny swung from a tire that hung from an oak in her grandparents' backyard. It was almost summer and yesterday Jenny had taken the school bus to her grandparents' farm, since her mother was at a Tupperware convention. She didn't want to stay there. She was promised a surprise.

She was almost seven. She missed the way her mother smelled: like polish, Mr. Clean, and powder. Her mother would sing while wiping Jenny's tears, holding her and rocking. Jenny cried after beatings from her father.

Jenny was swinging high. She almost started crying, thinking of the kids at school who talked badly of their mothers, telling jokes that ended with "Yo Momma," jokes that included things like truckloads, smelly, fat.

Oh, how she loved her mother!

Jenny saw her grandmother approaching, still in barn attire, limping lopsided, crooked kneed. A red scarf covered her head, looking like an apron. Her grandmother stopped, leaned over, picking rhubarb.

"Grandma?" Jenny said.

Her grandmother stood erect and asked Jenny what she wanted.

"Do you have my surprise?"

Her grandmother grabbed her stalks and said she'd be right back. She went into the house, the screen door flopping.

Jenny swung high, trying to imagine what the surprise might be. Jenny pictured a pink ring or silver earrings, or maybe a note her mother had left, telling Jenny that she loved her.

Her grandmother returned with her hands behind her back.

"What is it?" Jenny said. She watched her grandmother's hands emerge. She knew her mother would not let her down. She hoped for something lovely. When she saw, she didn't believe it. She kept on looking, then she looked again. The present was a Kit Kat.

"That's not it," she said.

"What?" said the grandmother.

Jenny headed for a tulip. She pointed to the reddest. She felt the petals.

"Oh yes!" the grandmother said. The grandmother went inside, then returned with scissors. She cut the tulip, giving it to Jenny.

Jenny was feeling right, and wonderful, and pretty. She would tell her mother thank you. She thought of all the nice things she would say. In two days, her mother was returning. She put the flower in her hair. She went higher and she waited.

COW

They didn't move like they used to. The older cows moved slowly in the pasture, flocking through manure, Jenny's father whipping on their rumps when it was time for milking. There was no hurry getting to the parlor, Jenny's father emptying their udders with his fanciful equipment. Jenny noticed this. She noticed a lot of things about the animals, how just out of their mothers, they were ragged on their legs, and then, after being calves, they grew into heifers. Later, after offspring, they'd start what they were bred for. That was milking. Jenny was only ten herself. She watched the Holsteins and she fed them. She watched them die away. Some left on crowded trucks. She never asked where they were going.

She was in 4-H, and her parents said she needed to take dairy as her subject. She clipped the heifers, calves, and cows that she would show at the coliseum, at the fair, and she combed and brushed them, cleaned them, leading them around, clothing them with halters, pulling them with ropes, spraying them with hairspray to keep the flies away. She even trimmed their hooves and pulled their horns, burning off the roots with a clunky iron made just for the occasion. She groomed them with preciseness and perfection. She'd be wearing white. She apologized to the animals for having to put them through this, saying she was sorry when her dad was not around. She befriended cows and heifers, calves, and she imagined them following her around, as if they were her puppies. The first cow was Iona. That was four years ago, and Jenny showed Iona at the fair, along with all the others.

On a Saturday, Jenny wore her cutoff jeans and a flowered halter top, her hair up in a ponytail, and her mother drove her to a farm twenty miles away for the annual Junior Judging Contest, where a big man with a John Deere hat gave the 4-H members a lesson on how to judge a cow, pointing to the udders. He said the udders shouldn't be saggy. He talked about bone structure, stressing the importance of a Holstein's upright posture. He pointed to a cow so white it was borderline albino. He talked about her legs, saying that the longer the cow's legs were, the better off she'd be. He didn't mention anything about color, about black or white, about the shape and pigmentation of her eyes, about a sweetened nature, or a cranky disposition.

Jenny saw no one that she knew, but that was fine because she was very busy. She walked about the barn with all the others: nearly fifty children aged seven to eighteen. Jenny figured she didn't know what she was doing, yet it seemed very simple in a way, to look at a cow and measure what the man had said to look for. So she walked about the barn, ranking each set of cows based on the animals' appearance. Everyone carried pencils, writing on the paper on their clipboards.

Later on, while the judges of the contest graded, the children ate ham and cheese on bread, and drank milk that was provided. Jenny sat by another girl who said she didn't know what she was doing. "My first time," Jenny looked at her and said.

Then the children went out to the yard and hung around the farm equipment. Jenny found a hay-bale sorter like the one she had at home. It reminded her of an escalator that she'd seen once at the mall. She grabbed the sorter's pole and lifted herself up, then dangled, hanging upside down. The other girl copied her and they hung like that together.

"What club you from?" the other girl asked Jenny.

"Go-Getters," Jenny said. She looked at her new friend's face, and she realized that she could feel her own blood rushing to her head.

"I live in Shawano," the girl said.

A few boys ran around them, playing with a squirt gun.

After the meal and the assortments, the judges made announcements. Jenny won. She got a trophy and her picture taken for the local paper. The other girl congratulated her.

"I didn't deserve to win," Jenny said, sort of in a whisper. "I didn't try very hard. As hard as I should've."

When her mother picked her up, she put the trophy in the backseat of the car. Her mother said she couldn't wait to tell her father. Jenny figured that tonight, maybe her father wouldn't beat her. He was actually nice to her one Saturday last year. She'd won a spelling contest. She got a trophy. She had spelled "incipient" correctly.

Kim Chinquee

After thirty minutes of riding with her mother, she was home. She ran out of the car, almost forgetting that she had won the trophy. She ran out to the pasture, like any other day, and she looked for her favorite cow, Iona, seeing if she might want to be petted, even play. When she spotted Iona, resting in the distance, chewing on her cud, Jenny yelled out her name. Iona looked up briefly, as if to scare a fly. The cow looked ahead, maybe even upward for an instant, and she kept on chewing. Jenny approached Iona, scaring the other cows away. Jenny stepped through all the manure, getting to Iona. She couldn't wait to talk about the day.

Jenny sat on a patch of grass, and told Iona about the man with the John Deere hat, how she thought it was so bizarre that cows had to have good udders. She told Iona she just wanted someone she could talk to. She told Iona about the girl she had just met. Jenny reached in her pocket, pulling out a lilac that she'd picked earlier that day. She set it on her palm and put her hand out to Iona. She wondered about Iona, if she was really listening. She felt the cow's saliva. Its muzzle touched her hand. The tongue was rough and felt unique, like wood and gold and sand. Iona was a cow. Jenny was a girl and she was watching.

Memoirs of a Boy Detective
David Marshall Chan

THE BOY WHO DISAPPEARED

IMAGINE THIS: A BOY IS running down a road, and then the boy disappears. His friends see him just before he vanishes, spot the car speeding down the road, hear the terrible moment of impact, but they do not see a body. They do not see any trace of the boy—no blood, no shoe, no shy smile, no strand of hair over the eyes, no awkwardness that may one day disappear or calcify to become a trait of a man, no laughter bubbling like soda. They walk up and down the road, but find nothing. Puzzled to no end, they do not know what to believe. Are they blinded by their grief, or did the missing boy disappear into that moment of impact, vanishing in broad daylight? This mystery needs answers, and so they look up to the trees.

They search for clues to *The Secret of the Boy in the Trees*. Was he hiding there, nestled in the swaying branches, covered in leaves? Was the impact so horrible his body flew that high, now resting fragilely with quail eggs and the colors of the fall? Was he up there—or did he fly away?

The friends and soon the mother and the father and more friends come to the trees to search for their boy. They want answers. They look up, looking until the sun blinds their eyes and they can see no more. Do they care that the sun's rays are really light from a dying star that has traveled here from the past? Do they care about the possibilities that starlight reveals? If we feel the presence of another star each day, then why couldn't a boy be hiding in the trees, waiting to return? Why couldn't he have survived?

Why couldn't we wait for the boy in the trees to come back to us one day with all the stories of his great adventures during his time away?

Time passes slowly in his absence. How many years would he be gone? Who would bring him back alive?

*

In the end, it was not the trees that he disappeared to, and the story would not have him hiding among leaves and quail eggs and the colors of the fall. When that speeding car struck him, the impact was so great and so horrible that he flew into the windshield and remained there as the car continued along its path. In a hastily dug grave of dirt and stones miles from where he was struck, his body was found, millions of shards of glass in his arms and face. The driver must have continued along for miles with the boy embedded in the windshield, stopping to bury him only after taking the body so far away. That's why there was no trace of that boy on the road, why those he left looked up to the trees for answers. When bloodhounds finally located the body, the solution to the mystery of the boy in the trees became known. The boy was no longer missing. Everyone knew the answer to that question: *where had he been all these years.*

How much better would it have been for the boy to just be out of sight, away for a while, so the mystery could live on: *Was he up there in the trees or did he fly away? How many years would he be gone? Who would bring him back alive?*

Why couldn't he be found again years later, like a fondly remembered book from childhood rediscovered one day in an old bookstore? After moving to New York, I came across a book like that—better than any clue—in a used bookstore off Prince Street. It was hiding there, on a shelf among Alice and *Goodnight Moon* and *The Cat in the Hat* and Edward Gorey's dead alphabet children—not missing, not gone, but waiting to be rediscovered. The story still moved and fascinated me like it did when I was a boy—there was no damage to that tale in the passing of years. The book was about a town, its people, and the weather—wild, crazy weather like the kind we faced in our youth in Bayside or the kind in the skies of a Henry Darger painting. Only in this story the weather was intertwined with food, creating a wild phenomenon. One day it rained meatballs. Another day brought a storm of spaghetti, then a fog of pea soup, then a hail of jelly beans. What was at first comical soon turned horrific. Monsoons of applesauce. Tornadoes of condensed milk. Floods of New England clam chowder. Devastation followed. The town became overrun with food, and the food got larger as the days progressed: enormous meatballs, colossal eggplant, humongous apples, Gigantor-sized waffles—all falling from the sky. In order to survive, the townspeople had to leave, abandoning the city they built. They created their means of escape from the devastation

266

surrounding them, building boats from giant slices of stale bread, held together with peanut butter. They took to the water on sails of cheese. In the book's illustrations of their voyage into the unknown, the townspeople are pictured clinging to their makeshift vessels. Sharks nibble on their boats, but the survivors ignore the terror in the water below, all eyes straight ahead, staring into the future and what lay there before them. It was like our ghost ship mysteries— like mysteries in general and the possibilities they invoked, or the exit in the Henry Darger painting *Lost in a Cavern*. Possibility lay in the unknown land beyond the caves or at the end of the ocean or in the convolutions of a mystery. There was something like hope there.

Eventually, the townspeople arrived on a new shore and like immigrants forged new lives. They dismantled the boats they arrived on and used the slices of bread to build roofs and walls for their new homes. Without exception, each survivor knew that something strange and utterly unique had happened to him or her. Those days of wild weather were like our mysteries. We boy detectives understood that something weird and wonderful and horrible happened to us when we were kids, when we were chosen by the mysteries. Their force was like a tornado or a hurricane: once in their path, we couldn't escape. For the storybook townspeople, their survival would become a tale told repeatedly, in time by grandparents to their grandchildren, an unbelievable story of survival described again and again until transformed into a kind of truth. That's how the book began, with a grandfather recounting to disbelieving grandchildren the comical first signs of the phenomenon, then how comedy turned to horror, and how the survivors made a decision to leave, heading out into the unknown, finding a new place to call home, and then having to build new lives out of, literally, the stale ruins of the old one. For the children it becomes their myth of origin, explaining how they came to be in a town with houses built from giant slices of bread. In part, that's what we grown-up detectives were faced with: the process of discovering our own myths of origin, and telling it as an elegy to those years lived in caves and tunnels and forests and other dark places—and to those who were with us in that darkness.

When I think of the survivors of that wild storybook weather, I imagine that some of them never spoke again about what happened, and others who survived could do nothing else but recall and retell it all the time. I know because I've been in both places. I know the feelings of those who bury the story deep inside, turning themselves and what they lived through into a mystery. And I understand what drives those who are forced to tell the story again and again, telling it with humor and pathos and exaggeration and fear—fear that what happened could happen again. That the wild weather could return. And they entertain that notion with anticipation, because as much as they want to walk away, they long for the weather's return, the same way once touched we were always in the thrall of the mysteries. There's something more I want to say here, about how we boy detectives survived the mysteries and how that changed us, but it would take me my whole life. I know we became addicted to the danger, like heroin, or lithium, and once pricked we could never shake the hold those mysteries had on us. Our futures were set. If we ever strayed away, we'd return in time to the fold, filled with a desire so intense, so undeniable, like a starving person before a buffet who returns to the table again and again, never sated, plate empty, hungry for more.

SKY MAPS

We used to read the sky like a map once, when we were younger. I distinctly remember one mystery, *The Secret of the Apple Orchard Keys*, where silver keys were hidden inside apples. The secret keys opened lockers at the Bayside Train Station where rare and valuable smuggled coins were left for pickup by the bad guys, and so that season old Mrs. Crandall who owned the Bayside Apple Orchards was bemused to find all sorts of foreign types coming to her orchards to pick her apples. The bad guys told the other evildoers what type of apples contained the keys—they inserted them into old worm-eaten ones and marked them with an X. While surveying the orchards, Frank Hardwick saw two German suspects about to drive off in their truck, so Frank signaled to his brother Joe and me to follow them. There was no way we could match them on our bikes, so Joe smirked and motioned to me. We dove into the back of their truck and lay down next to one another, carefully so that the bad guys wouldn't see us. We had no idea where we were headed—we watched the sky for clues, searching for answers in the clouds and the overhanging tree limbs and the butterflies and birds that flew by. From his pockets Joe produced two shiny red apples—one for each of us. On the road, going fifty-five miles an hour, not knowing where we were heading and not caring, just laughing and talking quietly, eating apples and watching the sky overhead—those were some of my best days as a boy detective.

MYTHOLOGIES

Move fast!!! Joe Hardwick yelled. He grabbed me by the collar of my shirt and pulled me out of harm's way. Behind us massive rocks, displaced during the sudden cave-in, smashed to the floor of the underground cavern! We turned around and saw rubble sitting in the place where, moments ago, we'd been standing. White dust filled the air. Cadmium and dysprosium were in our hair. Joe had saved my life once again, the same way he did when he discovered me in that grave of leaves so many years ago. We were always saving each other—it was the boy detective way. Joe appeared shaken, sitting on the floor of the cave, staring down at the ground. *I thought it would be like Mexico all over again,* Joe muttered. He was thinking back to that case that killed Tommy Tomorrow and destroyed Biff Hoover. I wasn't with them that day; Joe and I had never spoken about it except in allusions. *The only good thing about Mexico was you weren't there,* he said to me once, at the end of some brutal case when the memories of that time returned to him. That was a dangerous space for us, I knew: it was scary to remember things. It was so much easier to just be swept away by the endless stream of cases—to be consumed by mystery instead of by memory. In our bright-eyed youth we spotted things no boys were meant to see. We knew that monsters exist—monsters roam free. In ancient times our coming of age would have been to go out on journeys to slay them— that's what, in part, the mysteries were, even though we didn't live in an age of myths. Our cases became our secret history—there was no way our families or teachers or our normal friends could ever understand. Amongst our tribe we understood we were brothers of the lightning, struck in our youth by something . . . unknowable. To this day I still wonder what it was that hit us, and why only now we are beginning to try to understand it. Why didn't we ask these myriad questions back then, back in those days when we moved so fast, the rest of the world appeared like statues?

David Marshall Chan

CHILDHOOD MEMORIES

Those years in Bayside, we were always running through some farmer's cornfields, our faces beaten bloody by the tall stalks of corn brushed aside by the running body ahead of us. It was always best to be the lead runner, to be the first when running for your life. The others behind you would get all the hits, the hard corn stalks propelled backward slingshot fashion by the one ahead.

And those poor farmers: what must they have thought the next morning, waking up to find the footprints of teen detectives and their assailants throughout their property, an escape path etched into the field of corn? *Those damn mysteries!* they'd mutter, before moving on to milk the cows, to repair the barn, a life touched by but outside of the mysteries.

BONES

"We need a light down here," Jim calls out. "I think I've found something."

"I know," I respond. "Let me get my flashlight out." I reach into my backpack and pull out a flashlight—*the* flashlight—the one I thought had been lost forever. The brightest light on earth. I turn it on, illuminating the whole place—a cavern? a cave? a tunnel? I see my old friend Jim Fong kneeling down on the ground and an outline traced there in the dirt. Jim begins digging, creating little pyramids of dirt beside him, uncovering bones.

"Do you th-th-think th-that's him," I say, my voice shaking with fear. And then it's raining inside the place, raining.

"Yes, it's me," my missing brother Frank says, appearing from nowhere.

"What happened to you?" Jim asks, rising up to approach the ghost.

And then he's melting in the rain, gone, or maybe it's us—Jim and me—who are melting away.

270

David Marshall Chan

SECRET GARDENS

"Shh. Be quiet!"

"Wait—not so fast."

"Hurry up then!"

We were walking fast, almost running. Anticipation quickened our steps and we were tense with excitement. There were more than half a dozen of us—me and Frank, Nancy Blue, our pals Chet Moran and Tommy Tomorrow, and I think Jim Fong and Nina Sorrow were there, too. We all headed to Mrs. Weatherby's old house, to the garden where we were promised the body would be.

Nancy had a nose for these things, literally. Like a bloodhound, she could sniff the air, catch a scent, and follow its trail to where the mound of dirt was newly displaced, where the ground was freshly dug, where the stones were recently moved. She knew the smell of shallow graves.

The garden was overgrown, thick with weeds. Mrs. Weatherby had died a few months earlier, and her garden grew wild. Vines hung like hangmen's nooses, and the flowers bloomed monstrously large, petals opened obscenely. Hundreds of bees buzzed wildly in the air, moving in a frenzy from flower to flower in an orgy of pollination. Large and isolated, on the edge of town, the garden was the perfect spot to bury a victim. Recent rainstorms rendered the dirt moist and soft, and we left footprints in our wake. Chet carried a shovel and began digging. The grave was hastily dug, the outline of the body clear in the ground among the roses and grass and leaves. It didn't take long to unbury the body. The smell of decomposition lingered with the scent of the flowers, that and the smell of our own sweat, too, our excitement.

In the course of our mysteries the discovery of a body was special. Finding a body was like a holiday, like Thanksgiving, and once we were through with it, the body often resembled the unfortunate remains of a holiday turkey. It was not a pretty picture. Parts ended up strewn all over, and some went missing, kept to further examine in our makeshift labs at home. It was a necessity: to know as much as possible, to piece together a chain of events. There would be a story in the details, a poem in the splattering of blood, a plotline in the direction a body was dragged. The measuring and weighing and examining of limbs and organs revealed a life story, now in its final

271

chapter. It was a palpably erotic feeling to find a body before the police and coroner got to it, to be the first to explore a victim's wallet, to tenderly undress the victim, to gather the wristwatch, the jewelry, the shoes, to pluck a single strand of hair from the head, to delicately open the eyelids to discover the color of the eyes—and to piece together a story. We were careful and prepared, our hands sweaty inside gloves. The more medically inclined among us carried scalpels and knives. In those moments there was an obscene closeness between us and the body. It was like that line from old detective novels: we had to completely know the victim in order to solve the crime. We explored the guts and heart and brain, and afterward, after we had washed up and left the remains of the body for the police to find, we knew a little of how cannibals must feel.

We all collectively gasped at the sight that day—after uncovering the body, after digging it up, after pulling tangled weeds from it with gloved hands, brushing the dirt and leaves off the face. It was a young boy, our own age: a cautionary tale. We went through the body, silently, delicately, and in all our minds passed the same thought: What was he doing, underneath the mud and grass and leaves? What fate brought him here? We would walk away afterward and resume our lives as young detectives, and still the question remained: *Why him?* Why was he underneath topsoil and not out in the world solving mysteries?

A trail of footprints of young detectives.

The smell of excitement, of curiosity, of fear.

These were the things the police would not find when they finally came, after another shower, stepping into new mud. By then we were gone, grown a little older, and all of these things had long ago been washed away by the rain.

DIRT

"Come on, little brother, let's explore this hidden cave!" Frank exclaimed, venturing into the darkness.

"Follow me, Joe, there may be a clue in this basement!" Frank

David Marshall Chan

called out, stepping down the creaky old stairs.

"Watch your step!" Frank warned, moving down into the tunnel.

I like to remember those old adventures and all that could be found buried in the dark. I like to remember that anything could happen in unfamiliar places. In those dark underground places there were hidden things. Maybe Frank simply disappeared through a door while investigating some cavern, passed beyond to somewhere else, somewhere safe. I like to imagine that: he's gone through some portal, been swallowed up by time. He's wandered across a hidden underground railway and hopped aboard a train and ridden it away. I like to think of all these possibilities—I want to believe that that's where he went, why no body has been found.

But in my own mind I'm being buried underground, drowning underneath it all—I'm a boy detective wanting to get out from all the darkness.

After I left Bayside, I realized all I wanted was to lead a life free from the mysteries. I wanted nothing more than to be able to walk out in the world and be carefree; to remember what it's like to go out, to pass the dark woods, the forest, the swamp, the lake—and to not see unnamed things hiding there. I wanted to know what it feels like to pass a mound of dirt without worry, to recall a time when that mound of dirt was not a body buried, a clue hiding, a mystery needing to be solved—but just that, dirt.

BAD WEATHER

Once upon a time a band of boys and girls found themselves on a very bad adventure. When the story turned and they realized they could never go back, they were lost in a forest. They ran, bleeding, cut from branches and falling over rocks. Around them piles of leaves lay waiting, like hungry graves. They could not hope to outdistance the weather, but this was familiar: to be on the run, with no time to scream or think or try to remember when they lost themselves so long ago. The dark skies followed them, making daylight seem like night. "Keep running!!!" one yelled to the

273

David Marshall Chan

others. *"I think my ankle is broken!" another cried out, bleeding, half carried and half dragged by his comrades as they attempted to flee the black clouds. Electricity filled the air, along with the noise of crying birds and other animals howling with agitation, and footsteps passing through fresh dirt, and leaves trampled, and heavy breathing, and a sound like scratching on paper, and the smell of secret gardens and new graves and fear. The world would never be the same again, they knew. They could see it coming: the darkness in the sky swept above and over them. All the lessons learned with time . . . that sometimes the search for answers might be as rewarding as the actual solutions . . . that clues come with time and patience . . . something about saving what you can and coming back alive . . . all erased into nothing. Mysteries vanished in time. Stories became lost. Everything was ending. They couldn't get out of the way . . . their world turned to grey. Every person and every thing touched by the weather changed, some frozen solid, immobile, some transformed into dark ash, others fallen like leaves to the ground, lying in a heap, others becoming just shadows in the forest. Lightning struck, and thunder roared overhead. A deer caught in the weather during midleap changed into ash, a whole deer turned grey and frozen in the air for a moment before falling and disintegrating upon hitting the forest floor, crumbling little by little, first the layer of skin, then the meat, then the bones, each layer a color of grey ash darker in hue than the previous, until finally the heart, the darkest grey in the world, dropped to the forest floor, trembling and crumbling. The only sound remaining was violent rumbling in the sky. All the bodies were as still as coffins. Everything was dead.*

THE BOY DETECTIVE AT THE END OF THE ROAD

He didn't try to run when they finally caught up with him. By this time he was on the outskirts of Angeles National Forest, and after leading his pursuers around the web of freeways and highways for hours, Joe Hardwick finally ran out of gas. His car rolled to a stop and he just sat there as the patrol officers approached him with guns drawn. He didn't step out when they ordered him to. He didn't seem to even hear them. I could only imagine what was running through his head, the images clouding his mind—the ancient map, hidden;

274

the broken locket, lost; the old key, rusted; the secret treasure, smuggled away; the house on the cliff, fallen to ruin; the old elm tree, withered; the hidden passageway, blocked; the bulb in the porch light, unlit; the old manuscript, lost or burned; the secret signals over the bay, shining no more; the ghost ship, disappeared; the last boy detective on earth, dead; the gun, aimed; the police sirens, wailing; the highway, ended; and the body in the road, still burning.

Five Poems
Danielle Pafunda

DEAR CLASSROOM, NO WINDOWS, TWO SLIDE PROJECTORS, HUMMING

Here is where Zorba recorded my measurements. The chalkboard
rinsed and the numbers frisked. Pinkly. Prickly. Here
the eraser clapped. The clap of thunder. Under the desks,
and Zorba tolled the log truck.

Here is where a ninety-degree angle. A hummingbird knocking.
Too late in the season, I measured the red syrup, I ran the funnel
to the vial, to the window where we seated. In a row. Zorba,
her little nephew, her shotgun, myself. Bubblegum. Bubblegum.

THE UNHOMELY KINDER

For the first time ever, I felt my tentacle flex,
curl and uncurl in he loves me, loves me not fashion,
in party favor timbre, in a mile of shoreline friction.
That slick green tube, that horn of plenty.

In the vestibule once were wellies, were welsh poppies
and weltschmerz. In the vestibule of that Wendy house,
that matched its swatches to Zorba's lesser looms.
The household was all clothespins and on each finger,
each furled. Each yarn hair, and the smudge mouth.

And soon thereafter I stiffened.

WHAT HISTORICITY

Or, Zorba, let me do what I want. Zorba the Greek told me,
when I was a little girl, "Don't stand like that." Don't cock
(blasé!) your hip like that, don't limp your wrist, your
tip, your chew. She said.

Zorba, get off my back. Repeat. In the small closet,
in the small creature. Under the stairs. A tabula rasa.
A break in the spindle results in a headspace. A margarine tub.

Where we hung the ovary of homestead.

WADING THROUGH THE HOPE CHEST, A BLEATER

I was up to my lungs in Zorba's time line. Flecks of charcoal
in the water glass, the bellwether. I had been advised
to position a keen little stone, or a ragged bit of glass, not
so fragile as to shatter, in the toe of my riding boot. Advised
to knot my own toes thusly, to relieve them precisely, to weave
a pattern of discomfort.

If questioned, I would have said that indeed I soaked the petal
of a large-mouthed bloom against a wound I'd given myself shaving.
Indeed buried it in the southern corner of Zorba's vegetable garden,
near the radishes, the ravishes. Indeed I thought it would produce.
Indoctrinate. I was a year off from menses.

Zorba's nails, in those years, were the grim of gasoline. Her weeds
were hired out, her little yellow cushion cuddled beneath the knees
of neighbor girls. The willow trees a dirty pest, a skirt shifting.

NÉE PROVIDENTIAL

My little mommydaddy, my little broken rib. My little sterile
strip. You gave a sister with a wig that looked like you.
A transistor. You made a sister look like you. You had
a little pocket watch.

A hired house to haunt me. I had a house ghost. You hired.

I searched your suitcase for a jewel you sewed. I searched for
tickets, penmanship, sick tags, permanent. A whiff of home.
We hid your picture in my lining.

Digging to the Devil
Julia Elliott

THE SPINE OF THE DAY HAD SNAPPED, and summer sprawled like a fat man on a lawn, the pines ringing with cicadas. Cabbage was in his hole, in his Superman Underoos, hacking at the earth with a silver serving spoon. He'd gotten down to the blood, to the red reeking clay. And I gazed down at his dusty head. I held a plate of food in one hand and a dirty string in the other. I rolled a Kraft single slice into a scroll, tied it to the end of the string, and lowered it down into the hole. Cabbage took it, peeled off the plastic skin, and bit his way clean through the cheese until he held two orange strips in his hand. He stuffed these remnants into his Underoo waistband and gazed up at me with sad frog eyes. I lowered a floppy piece of baloney. I lowered a big dried booger of deer jerky. I lowered a Pop-Tart, an enormous cheese puff, a Little Debbie Star Crunch. Cabbage made me fill his old Tommy Tippy cup with Kool-Aid and ease that down, too. Purple juice squirted from the lid slit and dripped on his bony chest, making rivulets through the dirt. I sat on one of the big stones Cabbage had hauled over to kill the Devil with. He'd toted bricks and rocks and heads of broken hoes. He'd mixed bleach with Lysol and peroxide, and filled his entire water gun collection with poison that would burn the Devil's filthy goat fur off. Pistols and AK-47s and laser-spitting space guns sat cocked and propped behind arsenals of broken brick.

"What if he jumps you while you're down there?" I asked Cabbage.

"I'll feel him," he said, "rumbling up."

"What if he sticks his hand up through the dirt and grabs your ankle and jerks you to hell?"

"He ain't."

"What if you hack through the ceiling of hell and it crumbles and you fall down into the flames?"

"It's got to get hot first," said Cabbage, squatting to test the clay under his feet. "A little bit hot, then more and more hotter the deeper down you go."

The twins came trotting from behind the shed where they'd been

279

busy inflating tadpoles with a bicycle pump. Yesterday they'd made T. W. Stubbs, a Russian spy, eat a dog turd dissolved in Mountain Dew. Back there behind Cabbage's stinking turtle pen, where honeysuckle strangled the gardenia bushes, they'd set up their torture chamber.

"We're gone bury you alive, Cabbage," said Little Jack. He grabbed a clod of dirt and threw the bomb at Cabbage's chest.

"You won't be able to breathe," said the Runt. "And worms'll come slithering up against you, eating you bit by bit with a thousand snapping needle teeth."

Cabbage gazed off toward the broken-down dog cage, where a magnolia rose crooked from the wreckage, then picked up his serving spoon and resumed chopping.

Daddy was in the kitchen, hunched over a sheaf of typed pages, a butt with an inch-long ash clenched in his grimacing teeth. Scribbling in the margins, he pressed so hard his pen tip sliced paper, then he cussed and held the sheet up between his good eye and the light. Smoke and roasting venison mingled in the heat and cicadas rattled beyond glowing window screens. Daddy sucked whiskey from his glass of ice. Daddy peered down his huge oily nose at me. Daddy smiled like the Grinch.

"Sit down and let me read you how I lost my eye," he said.

Perched on the counter, I fished through Mama's bloated purse, rattling a bottle of painkillers as big as snake eggs.

And Daddy read from his memoirs, unfolded epics as familiar as Bible stories, words swarming up from the page like locust clouds and ringing in the air. Daddy never started from the beginning. He started at the surface, then dug down to the hot beating guts of the tale, pausing on the way to give history lectures about his ancestors and to explain things: how to clean a quail, how to find a catfish bed, how to evade a deer by sprinkling raccoon pee on your pulse points just as you would Stetson cologne. I'd zone in and out, flip through the DHEC calendar stuck to the fridge, visit secret parts of my head.

"The black mammy lunged at me with her broom," said Daddy. He looked up, pegged me with his grape green eye, which I feared would pop out and hit me. His dead eye drooped in its scrunchy socket. "You listening?" he said.

"You're right in the thick of the BB-gun war. Little black boys against little whites."

Daddy splashed Jim Beam into a tumbler of hissing Coke and started over. Little whites chased little blacks into a dilapidated shack. Whites tossed smoke bombs. Blacks screamed. A woman burst out with a broom.

"What's she doing out in the woods by herself?" I asked, suddenly curious about this stock character.

"I don't know," said Daddy. "But that's not the point. We thought that shack was abandoned." Daddy read on and on, foreshadowing and foreshadowing and foreshadowing. I wanted my mama to give me a home perm but she had a broken leg. I kept picturing myself in a leopard-skin bikini, greased up with baby oil, my long curly hair gelled and highlighted with Sun-In.

"Your great-great-grandfather," said Daddy, "the first surgeon to successfully remove a cancerous jawbone."

I caught a fragment about a slave named Cicero, lurking around the woods without a jawbone, eating grits and custard and applesauce.

"What did his face look like?" I asked.

"I don't know," said Daddy, "collapsed, I guess. The skin hanging loose like a turkey wattle."

"Did he get a new jawbone?"

"I don't think so, but what I'm doing is building thematically up to the climax when Cousin Duval shoots me in the eye."

I snorted at the word *climax* and read about Obesity Awareness Month on the DHEC calendar, listening to the drone of my father slipping deeper into the hot iridescent murmuring of old Dr. Stukes's pigeon house. A hundred dozing birds with rainbows in their feathers were too much to take. My childish little daddy felt the tug of greed. He grabbed a sleeping creature in each hand. "Go get some pillow-cases," he told his younger brother. And they plucked the soft dreaming idiots from their perches, dropped them into sacks, took them out to the back lawn of their house without a clue as to what to do with them.

"I smell burning," my mother said, poking her head out from the dark hallway. She surveyed the wreckage of the kitchen, where my father had scattered a dozen bowls, each bowl crusted with something going rank.

"I'm making deer jerky," Daddy said.

Mama hobbled into a gush of light from the kitchen window, her eyes wild from painkillers, her nylon housecoat stuck to her sweaty spots.

"What the hell are you doing?" said Daddy.

"Somebody's got to clean up this mess."

"I'll get to it, dearest." My father grinned his gargoyle grin.

"They need something decent," Mama said.

"Fighting Dick Anderson survived a whole month on rattlesnake and pokeweed."

Mama rolled her eyes. "Quit piddling with those goddamn memoirs and give them something decent to eat," she said. "It's your fucking fault I'm in agony."

Mama pointed her crutch at Daddy. Daddy plucked a page of his memoir and hid his scowl behind it. "We erected an old pup tent and dumped the slumbering fowl into it," he said. "We grew bored and went out to the fragrant moonlit fields to shoot rats."

I wanted to ask my mother about the home perm before she limped back to the living room, but she was too pissy. She'd bedded down on the velveteen sofa and covered Daddy's plantation coffee table with pills and magazines and sweating glasses of Coke. Daddy liked to putter in there, polishing his historical knickknacks, but Mama had marked it with her perfume-spiked sweat. So Daddy manned the kitchen in his ruby red robe, cooked up what he called huntsman's feasts, took deep drafts of whiskey, and pecked out his memories on an old typewriter with a broken G.

Cicadas swelled, lapping at the heat with their metallic drone. I heard little boys screaming. I listened to the thatch of noise that dwindled where my world ended: sirens, cars, planes, lawn mowers, kids, birds, bugs. I studied the split ends of my limp red hair. If I didn't get a home perm soon, I would die. I owned the ugliest bathing suit in the entire county. My breasts were mismatched lumps that wobbled like peach pits under the skin. And beyond our cedar fence, a chain saw started up, grinding away at my misery.

"We opened the tent and the smell of death wafted out," Daddy said. "In the hot miasma, birds lay in piles, their claws clenched. We tossed them out onto the lawn where they sparkled in the sun. We paced in panic around piles and piles of iridescent pigeons, bright and rancid in the broiling sun."

Yesterday my best friend, Squank, had come over, and we'd stuck to our summer routine: slipping out to the shed where rusty fishhooks prickled and worms burrowed in paper cartons and a jug of wine lay hidden under a moldy tarp. Squank, a plump boy with huge buttocks, was always squawking and fretting. Squank oinked. Squank stank sweetly like a pond. Squank pinched bruises all over his arms when he felt guilty—and he always felt guilty—about everything he did. He had huge shining eyes the color of tarnished silver, damp pale skin, and fine black hair. We'd drink and smoke and spy on my brothers and their idiot friends. They carried on their dramas out by the turtle pen, torturing each other in the swelling heat. Yesterday they'd tied T. W. Stubbs to a lawn chair to interrogate him.

And we got drunk, listening to T. W. carry on about nuclear war, about which he knew diddly-squat. He thought Russia was a city in England; he said *nucular* for nuclear. We laughed until our spines started buzzing and we feared we'd float up off the floor. Squank couldn't take a sip of wine without thinking about Jesus, and he'd punish himself with a pinch on the arm after every sip, even though I reminded him that wine was the biblical drink *par excellence*, or so said my father. But I think Squank *enjoyed* punishment. He'd pinch himself into a frenzy of drunkenness and pain. Then with glowing eyes he'd bumble against me, snatching at my arms and tainting my skin with his clamminess. And yesterday, after an endless laughing fit, Squank'd lunged at me with wine-stained lips. He'd grabbed me in a bear hug, pressed his fat mouth to mine, and slipped his tongue in and out like some kind of probe. My stomach flipped over. I thought about insects unrolling their long slippery tongues and slithering them down into the secret places of flowers. But, still, something deep in me liked the kiss just enough to keep going—until I heard Mama screaming her head off at Cabbage, and I opened my eyes and saw Squank's giant silver shark eye looking right at me. We jumped apart and I spat on the floor. Squank slapped himself in the face three times—once for the Father, once for the Son, and once for the Holy Ghost. Then he stumbled out into the garish day, blinking and pinching his arms blue. I heard the dogs raising hell as he scrambled through the secret hole in our fence. I crouched down by Daddy's Fishhawk Depth-Sounding Module, smoking one cigarette after another, fiddling with knobs on the mysterious control panel as Squank's kiss replayed in my head and T. W. Stubbs screamed, "I don't know a goddamn thing about the Nazis, I swear."

It was that time of day when Squank was wont to show—so hot our frizzy Boykin spaniels wallowed in holes to cool their fat bellies. In search of clay, the dogs dug and dug like squint-eyed moles, and

Julia Elliott

that's how Mama had broken her leg: falling in a hole dug by my
father's curs. Bred for swamp hunting by one of his ancestors, the
matted idiots had never seen a swamp in their life. That's what
Mama always said before reminding my father that it was his goddamn fault she'd broken her leg. And now Cabbage was outdoing the
dogs at digging. He was down so deep he'd disappeared. I walked over
to his hole. An assortment of Daddy's fish-skinning knives fringed
the mouth of the chasm, their blades stabbing the grass. And down
in the dank coppery gash, Cabbage still toiled—steady, wordless,
sneezing every now and then, his spoon chopping.

"What if the Devil isn't even down there?" I said.

"I'll get him," said Cabbage.

"He was an angel once, so he must be able to fly. Why would a flying creature live down in the ground?"

"Trapped," said Cabbage, "like a lightning bug."

"Well, what do you think will happen when you let him out?"

"I'll stab him and burn him and crush his bones."

"The Devil is weird," I said. "In the Bible he's all over the place,
popping up in disguises and hissing inside people's heads."

"He's down there," said Cabbage. "I feel him."

"How?"

"Teeny-tiny electric shocks."

"What if he's in a cocoon and he hatches like an orange butterfly
and flies up into the sky?"

"I'd shoot his wings off."

"What if his snake head pokes through the dirt and bites you on
the ankle and you get a big fat infected Devil bite?"

"Mama'd put peroxide on it."

"You think peroxide'll cure a Devil bite? They'd probably have to
amputate."

"What's amputate?"

"Cut your foot off."

Cabbage gasped and stopped digging.

"Where would my foot go?"

"I don't know; in the ground, I guess."

"To do what?"

"Rot. Get eaten by worms. Turn to slime."

"I'd dig it back up," Cabbage said.

"It would stink."

"Why?"

"It would be dead."

*

In the kitchen Daddy had Squank pinned to a chair with the drunken gaze of his good eye. When I walked in from the yard, Squank gulped and giggled and went pale. A big splotch of pink spread across each cheek. He twirled a piece of jerky in his hands. Daddy took a bite from his own withered tidbit of deer flesh and washed it down with a splash of whiskey Coke.

"What I was saying, Squark, is that the Imp of the Perverse is perverse precisely because you know that what you are doing is the absolute worse thing you can do, and you do it anyway, as though a secret death wish lurks in your blood. Do you follow me, Squib?"

"Dad," I said, "it's Squank."

"That's right, Squank. Do you follow me, Squank?"

"Yes, sir. I think so."

"Because putting pigeons in a pup tent was not fun, served no purpose, was rather tedious, in fact, but I think we secretly long for our own destruction. What do you think about this theory, Squirp?"

"I don't know, I . . ."

"Because, Squab, I knew, deep down in my bones, as my dear old Mammy, Vic, used to say, that stealing Dr. Stukes's pigeons and stuffing them into a pup tent would end in disaster. But the Imp of the Perverse whispered in my ear."

"Is this imp thing the same thing as boredom?" Squank asked.

I poured Squank a glass of deep red Kool-Aid and set it on the sunny table where it glowed.

"Not exactly, Squat. It's like jumping into a poison oak patch. Even deeper down in my bones I think I knew that Dr. Stukes would hate me forever, would exact revenge upon me one day, excruciating revenge, Squirm. He was an agent in my tragic destiny as a half-blind man. Do you follow me?"

"I don't know. What did he do to you?"

"That, Squint, is a long and sordid tale, captured here in my memoirs, which, if you're interested, I could read to you."

"Well, OK. Yes, sir. Thank you." Squank looked resigned, as though he'd just sat down in a dentist's chair. And Daddy started reading—not at the point where he and Cousin Duval ran off into a day burning blue like a pilot light, BB guns strapped to their backs; not where they slipped into the humming wet gloom of the woods, mosquitoes thick as hair on their arms; not where they climbed twin magnolias and shot at each other from perfumed boughs. No, Daddy circled around the pigeon story, a synopsis of which Squank had already tucked away in his memory with Bible verses, the planets of the solar system, the grasshopper's digestive tract, and interesting facts about President Lincoln's assassination.

Squank drained his Kool-Aid and slumped at the table. Cicadas drummed. Daddy droned. Little boys screamed outside. And pulsing beneath words and images and noise and laziness was the hot knowledge of what we had done yesterday in the shed. Squank grossed me out and the thought of kissing him squirmed in my stomach. But something deep in me ached for the sick giddiness that surged like a volt of poison in my blood.

"And because of some neural damage, I was temporarily blinded in both eyes," said Daddy, "wandering in complete darkness through the woods, the wilderness, the valley of the shadow of death, stumbling on toads and serpents and jagged rocks, until my mother finally found me hugging a cypress stump and weeping. And when she asked Dr. Stukes if I was blinded for life in *both* eyes, the old man, who called my mother daughter, said, *No, daughter, it's only temporary; the right eye should be fine.* But when she left the room to call my father, the doctor's stinking old mouth dipped toward my ear, and, spattering my cheek with spit, hissed, *You're gonna be blinded for life, son: in both eyes. I didn't want to upset your mother. But it's true; you'd better buck up. When you get to Columbia, they're gonna stab a foot-long needle into your eye.*

"I screamed and kicked," said Daddy, waving his cigarette at Squank. "Old Dr. Stukes, who had prescribed phenobarbital for my hyperactivity the year before, gave me an extra dose intravenously, breaking three needles in my arm before he struck a vein. And they strapped me down and drove me to Columbia, where a thousand voices echoed in the sterile air, and the optometrist's huge disinfectant-smelling hands plunged a needle directly into my retina with no anesthesia. No anesthesia, Squid, imagine: the needle sliding deep into the wet nervy heart of the eye."

I was drunk, submerged in gauzy gray shed-light with the funk of worms and earth and mildew in my nostrils. We were half pretending that Daddy's depth sounder was the control panel of a nuclear submarine. Squank, a sketchy aquatic creature, floated too close. A person was so many things—a smell, a warm body, a pale glow, a croak of voice on the hot hum of day—and when you're near a person in strange light your mind plays tricks on you. I wanted a boyfriend more than anything in the world, more than a perm, more than a new bathing suit. At night when I sat alone on the back porch, gazing up at the twisted clouds, I could feel this boyfriend moving closer in the soft air. I half expected him to spring from the bushes or burrow up from the ground or flap down from the sky on doves' wings. Squank had nothing to do with this person I dreamed about. I knew Squank so well that he'd become strange again. His delicate monkey ears looked too precious for his fat-cheeked head. His eyelashes were twice as long as mine, crow black and straight as broom straw. Squank sniggered. Squank pinched himself. Squank sat strangely in the ashy light.

We'd stopped talking. We drank and darted looks at each other, listening to the interrogation.

"I admit it," said T. W. Stubbs, "I'm a commie spy. Now let's go get some Kool-Aid."

We heard the tart sound of a slap.

"What do you want from me?" T. W. cried. He sounded sincere, his voice a plaintive note in the heat. The interrogators were digging deeper and deeper, wearing him down to the bone. Under the concrete floor of the shed where the dogs had a secret nest, a single cricket chirred, a night sound that brought a dreamy feeling to the afternoon. Squank crept closer, sliding on his huge butt. He took a sip of wine and pinched himself softly on the arm. He shivered. He rested a damp hand on my thigh. The hand lay there like a sleeping animal.

"I've told you everything," shrieked T. W. Stubbs.

Squank's fingers moved. My heart felt swollen.

"I don't know a motherfucking thing about the goddamn Japs, how many times do I have to tell you?"

Squank's hand walked like a tarantula up my thigh and crouched near the hem of my shorts.

"They got squint eyes. They don't speak English."

Squank's pale face loomed. I closed my eyes.

"They kung fu fight. They make cars."

I was tasting the strange mouth again—slobber and mucus, wine-tongue and bone of teeth.

"They the ones that bombed Pearl Harbor?"

I was not me and Squank was not Squank.

"No, please, Lord, have mercy on me."

Julia Elliott

I'd forgotten about Squank's fat spider-hand until I felt it, fingering the elastic edge of my underwear, not like a lover, more like a doctor. And I opened my eyes to find him studying me with his shark eye once again. And he was Squank. Fat and gross and giggly. He was too familiar and I wanted to slap him in the face.

"Get out of here, you butthole," I said.

I couldn't stop.

"You moron," I screamed. "Retard. You stinking scuzzy freak. Pansy-ass space-cadet slime-ball dork."

Squank pinched himself. Squank slapped himself. I couldn't look at his eyes. I turned to the wall with my arms crossed as he stumbled out into the light.

T. W. Stubbs screamed.

The day was a swollen balloon, bobbing, and I was looking around for the needle that would pop it. I stalked around Cabbage's hole. I sprinkled dirt and twigs and dead insects on his head. I ran the length of our shrubbery plucking shreds of leaves, and kicked one of the dogs when it tried to flick its tongue over my face. There was poison in me. The sky looked green. I needed a cigarette, but my stash had dwindled to the filthiest of stolen butts, their filters bearing dents from my father's gnashing teeth. I ran into the kitchen and let the screen door slam.

Mama and Daddy sat at the table, clawing idly at each other, waiting for something to catch. A jazz of insults blared in the summer air. Daddy was an idiot for keeping our worthless flea-bitten mangy mutts. Mama was too low class to recognize the nobility of a purebred dog. Daddy lived in fantasyland. Mama had a martyr complex. Daddy was a tyrant with a big head. Mama was a yapping Chihuahua. Daddy couldn't hammer a nail into a board if his life depended on it. Mama came from a tribe of redneck leprechauns.

They sat there, nibbling deer jerky, throwing out insults between bites.

Daddy's sisters were spoiled-rotten obese hypochondriacs without a lick of common sense. Mama's brother was a rude illiterate midget. Daddy's daddy was a mean drunk with a nose like a lump of pork liver. Mama's daddy was a p-whipped pip-squeak who wore a size-five shoe. Daddy's mama had no spine. Mama's mama resembled a bulldog. Daddy was a conceited idiot who spent hours every morning plastering six hairs with Aquanet. Mama's new haircut made her

288

look like a Chinese man.

Their eyes were on fire and they lit their cigarettes at the same time. I stood with clenched fists, ogling their half-smoked pack of Dorals.

"You one-eyed ape," said Mama.

"You shrieking spider monkey," said Daddy.

"You're both full of shit," I said.

Their heads swiveled in perfect time and they drilled their eyes into me.

"What did you say, young lady?" said Mama.

"I said: fuck off, bitch."

Daddy winced; Mama gritted her teeth. "Jack, you're going to have to beat her."

"Me?" said Daddy.

"I certainly can't do it." Mama pointed at her cast.

"Isn't she getting a little old for beatings?"

"She said the F-word."

"Go get my belt," Daddy barked at me.

"You must be out of your fucking mind," I said.

Something licked up my spine and I surged forward, snatched their cigarettes, and ran laughing out into the yard. Daddy lurched after me, toying with his bathrobe sash and squinting into the glare. A flock of starlings had swept down, and the air felt charged and wild as they fluttered up into the treetops.

Drunk, barefooted, his comb-over torn to pieces and waving on his head, Daddy chased me around the yard. Little boys emerged from behind the shed to watch. Cabbage's head popped up from his hole. Mama stood shouting on the back stoop. And I zipped toward the sandy part of the yard where a crop of spurs had grown. Daddy plodded after me on his tender feet. When he hit the spurs he clenched his fists, threw his head back, and roared up into the sky. Then he limped over to the back stoop and sat down to pick the stickers out of his soles.

"You're gonna get it!" screamed Mama, and my heart revved in my chest. I scrambled up our crooked magnolia, sending spirals of starlings into the sky. I sat on a branch and swung my legs and lit a cigarette with the lighter Daddy kept tucked in the cellophane wrapper.

Poison hit my lungs and danced in my blood. My father was up and raging again, fury radiating from his glistening, tic-wracked face, and I thought that was exactly how the Devil might look if you dug

down to his bedroom and woke him up. He'd come spitting and fussing into the cooler atmosphere, sparks jumping from his wings like
water from a swimmer's back. He'd stomp around the grass just like
Daddy did, except he'd leave a singed black footprint every place he
stepped. The air would rumble and the sky would flash orange. And
you would be completely alert, your spine rippling with electricity,
your brain on fire.

Walking Hand in Hand with Dinah
A Book without Pictures or Conversations
Lucy Corin

1.

HER FIRST IDEA WAS that it might belong to a pleasure, wrapping itself up very carefully. So they got thrown out to sea, every now and then treading on toes, and felt dreadfully puzzled. As soon as they had a little recovered from the shock of being upset, she drew her foot down as far as she could, throwing an inkstand into their simple joys. The only one who got any advantage from the change found it advisable to go.

I can see her trying to invent something. Trees in which she had been wandering just grazed her nose. In another minute there was not even room for this, so I went in without knocking, fancying the sort of thing that would happen. She said the last word with such violence; I fainted in coils, and, half expecting to see it again, fell past it. It's no use going back to yesterday, because I was a different person then.

Let me think. What nonsense I'm talking. A great girl like you, such a dear quiet thing trembling down to the end, bristling all over. I've tried the roots of trees with a shiver. Oh *please* mind what you are doing. Run back into the wood for fear, making such a noise inside, and do not venture to go near the house until you have brought yourself down.

2.

Once she peeped into the loveliest garden you ever saw there seemed to be no sense in waiting. She looked up, but it was dark overhead. She could see this quite plainly. I think I could go around and get in her window, if only I knew how to begin. Perhaps she won't walk the way I want to.

Lucy Corin

A number of bathing machines in the sea seemed to her to wink at her. I went on eagerly, afraid I'd offended, and making quite a commotion. She set to work, and very soon finished off washing. A large pigeon had flown into her face while she was looking about for some way of escape and wondering whether she could get away without being seen. She seemed too much overcome with this beautiful thimble of promise, and so with an air of great relief, put one arm out the window and dropped the kid gloves.

And now for the garden, a frog or a worm still in sight. She just succeeded in curving down into a graceful zigzag and was going to dive among the leaves. She ought to have wondered at this, but at the time it seemed quite natural. Beautifully printed in large letters, she'd fallen into a cucumber frame, and what a number of cucumber frames there must be, taking one side and then the other. I never left off staring, digging for apples, and waited patiently until she spoke again.

She looked all around her at the flowers, stretched herself on tiptoe, drew back in a hurry, hardly knowing what she did, tumbled head over heels in a hurry to get hold of it, ran wildly up and down looking, and ran around the thistle again. After a series of short charges she looked under it, and on both sides of it, and behind it, and I must have changed several times since then, quite safe in a thick wood at a short distance. I felt that she was losing her temper. She made a snatch in the air, but did not get hold of anything.

But suddenly she came upon the pleasure of making a daisy chain. She kept her eyes fixed on it, looking down with wonder, tried to fancy to herself what an extraordinary way of living would be like.

A general clapping of hands at this.

For her to speak first, using it as a cushion, would generally take some time. Yet she balanced, living in that poky little house, a good deal frightened at the change and immediately suppressed.

You promised to tell your history, you know. You should have run away when you saw me coming.

In another minute there was not even room for this. Our curls got entangled together, full of smoke from one end to the other. We were the only two creatures in the kitchen, nibbling first one, then the other, certainly too much of it in the air. Pebbles came rattling, and quite a crowd of little animals. Last came a little feeble voice; she fancied she heard it just under the window. This was a new idea, with the patience of an oyster. She tucked it away under her arm.

The lowing of cattle in the distance—quite a chorus of voices— paused as if somebody *ought* to speak. And what a clear way you have of putting things. Just think what work it would make with the day and night.

Nobody moved. She half believed herself, a little startled when she heard her voice by her ear. No one attempted to explain. She could hear the very tones of her voice feebly stretching out. Everyone said, "Come on!" but she frowned like a thunderstorm. I am so *very* tired of being all alone here, wondering why I don't put my arm around your waist.

I am sure those are not the right words. Speech caused a remarkable sensation. I wonder if I've changed in the night, made out the proper way of all sorts of things. I growl when I'm pleased, an eel on the tip of my nose. Still, her hair has become very white.

All this time I kept my limbs very supple. Now, I'm opening out. Will the roof bear?

3.

Yesterday, things went on as usual, but to her disappointment, it was empty. It was too slippery. She soon made out that she was a person of some authority and, producing from under her arm a great letter, discovered the cause of all this. As soon as she had recovered a little from the shock of being upset, she ate a little bit and said anxiously to herself, "It doesn't sound at all right." She felt she was dozing off. There was nothing else to do, so she soon began talking again and sulkily crossed over to the other side. I tried to make out what she was coming to. At last she sat down a good way off. Her voice sounded hoarse and strange.

She went on planning to herself how she would manage it. It was as much as she could do, to look through with one eye. There seemed to be no use in waiting, but to her disappointment it was empty still, and still she was in sight. She began to feel uneasy, to be sure, her chin pressed closely to her foot, yet she balanced. We were getting so far off, and she felt so desperate that she was ready to ask help of anyone. She took courage and tried again, solemnly presented the thimble, waited patiently until it spoke again.

I did not at all like the tone of the remark, but the low, trembling voice persisted, not taking notice of her or anything else. She went timidly nearer, to make out what it was, to make out who was talking, to see what was the matter with it, to keep herself from being run over, but it kept doubling itself up and straightening itself out again, fluttering down from the trees into her face. She had not a moment to think before she found herself, still in sight, hurrying down it with some alarm.

She ran across the field, burning with curiosity. Then, turning to the rose tree, she went on, though she could think of nothing better to say than her first remark. She was considering, in her own mind, the opportunity of showing off her knowledge, but did not drop the jar for fear of killing somebody.

A bright idea came into her head, reminding her of a globe of goldfish. She kept tossing the little thing up and down. She looked down into its face and found her way in, hurrying into a tidy room. She called softly after, looking down with wonder. She felt very curious to know. It seemed a good opportunity for making her escape.

In another minute there was not even room for this. She only does it to annoy.

It flashed across her mind. Got up in great disgust and walked off. At any rate a book of rules for shutting people up like telescopes. This piece of rudeness. Nice grand words anyway. I'll kick you downstairs into a house with gently smiling jaws.

4.

It was hard to make out exactly what they said, but I interrupted in a great hurry. I should frighten them out of their wits. It'll be no use putting their heads down, flat on their faces; that's done by everyone minding their own business. Everyone will be surprised when she finds out who I am.

I should like to hear her try and repeat something now. Tell her to begin. Hand round the refreshments. She'll be sending me on messages next, very neatly and simply arranged, almost certain to disagree.

"Come, there's no use crying like that." She tried to curtsy as she spoke. "You know, you make one quite giddy." A pencil squeaked. She could not, could not, join the dance. "Pray, don't trouble yourself," she said at last with such sudden violence it must have been that she felt she could box her own ears for having cheated herself in a game she was playing against herself.

Presently she began again, and it all came different, but in a piteous tone. Oblong and flat, with hands and feet at the corners, we never left off quarreling. If one only knew the right way to change.

More sounds of broken glass had just grazed her ear and I hadn't the smallest idea how to set about it. "You might like to try the thing itself some winter's day." As she said this, she looked at her hands, trembling down to the end, bristling all over. This she would not allow.

No wonder we felt unhappy in this pool of tears. Hastily, she put down the bottle, saying to herself, "Do you think I can listen all day to such stuff? Take off your hat." I never left off staring, and very sulkily crossed over to the other side. She walked sadly down the middle, wondering how she was ever to get out again.

A likely story indeed. I am *not* a serpent, but I have tasted eggs, certainly. And so I will tell you how I managed it, though I advise you to leave off this minute, as I'll soon make you dry enough that there will be no sense in knocking. I'll try the whole cause and condemn you to death, which would *not* be an advantage, for a

Lucy Corin

red-hot poker will burn you if you hold it too long. If you cut your finger *very* deeply with a knife it usually bleeds. I hadn't to bring but one advantage and I'll set it on you.

5.

As she stared violently, the two threw themselves back again.

In despair, for she felt very lonely and dispirited as well, she put her hand in her pocket and said, in a melancholy tone, that everything seemed to have changed since her swim. I looked for some way of escape among the bright flowers and cool fountains, feeling very glad that it was over at last. It was much pleasanter at home.

I think I should understand this better. This sort of life, put it to your lips, and how are you getting on now, dear? The words don't fit. If any one of you can explain it, please take this head outside.

The party assembled on the bank, wet, cross, uncomfortable, exactly as if nothing had happened. *Everybody* has won and all must have prizes. More sounds of broken glass called out. Perhaps after all it might tell us something worth hearing.

Conversations with Fountains
E*laine* E*qui*

—*For David Trinidad*

While still a child
I discovered
the fountain of youth.

It kept me small
in all the right places,

insuring some part of me
would always be incompetent
and dependent,
impractical and silly.

Under its watery umbrella,
I stood spellbound for years,
trying to decipher its murmuring

and mimic the poses of pigeons
gathered round its basin,
one preening and one scholarly
and one flirtatious

like a cross section of society
from a Balzac novel—with wings!

Yes, part of the appeal of fountains
is how they make everything,
even water, seem to fly.

To be in love
is to speak and listen
to a fountain.

Elaine Equi

*

My mother had a mural
of a fountain sketched
on the living-room wall
in charcoal and violet.

It was always dusk
no matter the time of day.

Our sofa curled beneath it,
a velvet cat, and I played
a chubby stick figure
in search of perspective,
lonesome as de Chirico.

Eventually we sold the house,
but the fountain did not disappear,
sprang up this time in the entrance
of my father's new Italian restaurant.

A statue taller than me
who poured water endlessly
from a stone jug.

Hebe, they called her,
goddess of youth,
companion of adolescents.

I worked as a hatcheck girl
stationed opposite her;
the customers would throw us
each a coin.

Gradually, I came to see her
as a kind of stepmother, wise aunt.

Fountains, I realized, are thirsty, too—
for company.

FOUNTAINS I'VE SAT BY

Trafalgar Square, London

where I studied a map,
bronze lions looking over my shoulder,
as I tried to decide if there was time enough

to visit Freud's house,
see his collection of tchotchkes,
and get his blessing on ending my therapy.

As it turns out, there wasn't
and so I'm still talking.

After I finished with one analyst,
went on to another.

Just when you think you're done with the story,
the fountain says, "Go on."

Trevi Fountain, Rome

where Jean Peters, Dorothy McGuire,
and Maggie McNamara found love
to the memorable, if schmaltzy, theme song
sung by Frank Sinatra and written by Sammy Cahn.

There I made the necessary offering
with my mother, but so far have not returned.
Something about the place evaded me.

It's as if past and present are so intertwined,
they almost cancel each other out.

The city cannot be said to exist fully
in either dimension. Only the taste
of its hazelnut gelato proved eternal to me.

Elaine Equi

Buckingham Fountain, Chicago

It was a musical without need of music.

Arpeggios of spray crashing, floodlit,
then separating into juicy bands of fruited air—
droplets of lemon, lime, raspberry, grape.

Angelic Swedenborgian conversations
between gradations of light.

The ur-psychedelic experience before drugs.

Pretty but a bit over-the-top dramatic.
After a few minutes my attention would wander.

Give me a quiet, a shy fountain—
one content to sit in a small square gathering shade.

Washington Square, New York

If you must consult a liquid compass,
this isn't a bad one to keep in your back pocket.

Living around the corner from it, I feel its presence
even when I completely forget it's there,
look up and see its white plume wave a frothy hello.

There is something blatantly vagrant about it,
protective of free time and speech.
In an ultraprofessional city like New York,
one could call it an amateur fountain,
a perpetual open mike.

Many times I've sat along its meridian
caught in the crossfire of klezmer and blues,
surprised by the variousness of the variety show
in the green room of the park.

300

It's a good place to practice being yourself
or better still, put off that duty for another day.

CODA

Fabulous fountains of the future

Cooling whirlpool for funky feet

Photo op for minor actresses
looking to make a splash

To you I'll crawl
from the shipwreck of one moment
to the next

Oasis to oasis calling

(adult movie
late afternoon

    ghost ejaculating

        time loops back on

            the trees in black and white)

Latona Street
S. G. *Miller*

THIS MUST ALL HAVE BEEN just before Latona. We must have been living in the place with the two dark rooms. There must have been only one lamp and the light from the television on in the living room. There must not have been many windows. There must have been only the one window behind our heads in the bed in the bedroom. The head of the bed must have been against the wall, with the window behind and above us. There must not have been a headboard on the bed with the window so low and so close to our heads. It must have been a double or a queen to hold the three of us. It had to be. It had to be all three of us sleeping in the one bed.

It would have been the light of the sun that would wake my mother up. There would not have been a curtain or a shade or a blind covering the window. If the window had been covered, the covering would have been thin or sheer or torn for the light of the sun to come through it. That is, if there had been any covering there at all, whatever the covering was. That had to be why my mother covered her head with the sheet when the sun came up. That had to be why I covered my head with the sheet, too. That had to be why so did my sister.

Didn't I do what my mother did?

Didn't my sister do what I did?

Didn't my mother say don't do what I do? She probably said don't cover your head up or you won't get air enough in, if she had said anything about it at all. Or maybe she was still asleep and talking to herself or to somebody else that wasn't me? It would not have been easy to hear what she said with her talking to me with her head under the sheet, when my head was not under with her, but out without her. If my head was out, I would have had to talk louder to get her to hear me. I would not have been able to talk to her in a whisper. But at my age at that age, I would like talking in a whisper to my mother.

There must have been a question from me, whether whispered

under in with her or said aloud out without her. I must have said how come you can put your head under the sheet and get air enough in, and if I did it, I would not? I suppose she told me about air pockets or air holes or air cracks, or air something like that with a name she might have not said right. Or maybe she told me there were ways to breathe through the sheet that she knew from cheating and practicing at, but if I didn't know yet, I might catch my death in my sleep.

If she had said this, would I have looked for an even billowing in the sheet? Would I have thought to lift the sheet up to check for the rising of her chest? Would I have gotten under it with her to feel for the warmth of her breath?

They will fold my hands on my chest,
And cover me up with the sheet,
They will remember to number my bones.

Didn't my mother watch us race through the words on our knees? Didn't she teach us all the wishes and the sorrows we needed to keep in us always? Didn't she tell us to say the same thing every day in the morning when we waked and again at night before going to bed again? Though it could have been my grandmother who taught us and told us when to. Didn't our grandmother tell us this was the way to be safe, if we should happen to be taken away in our sleep? Who was it that made me think I would be lifted up and carried away from the bed? What was it that made me believe I would be taken to a place I had never been to by a man I had never seen? But I do believe it was my grandmother who gave us pennies for every verse we learned to remember for her. Or it could have been as much as a quarter. But it would not have been my mother, would it? I cannot see my mother giving coins to us, especially at our age at, at that age. Though I can see and hear my mother going to my grandmother and asking for money. And I can see my mother walking in and out of rooms through all the rooms of my grandmother's house. And I can see my mother looking for something she had dropped, or maybe she had lost. That is, if she hadn't been pretending. If she had been looking for anything at all.

My mother probably worried a lot about what my grandmother thought of what she was and what she wasn't doing. But she must not have worried about it enough. My mother must have put her head under the sheet to forget about everything. She must have wanted to go back to the places and the people that came to her in her sleep. I imagine my mother learned how to breathe with her head under the sheet a long time before us. My guess is it all started

S. G. Miller

back when she was as young as we were then.
Angel of God, My Guardian Dear.
Go to sleep.

II.

We would have been put in the back through the opening of the gap in the seats. My sister would have been kneeling, or maybe standing, to see out the window. I must have stood riding up on the hump. My mother must have been up front and moved toward him in the middle. That would have made her hair within an easy reach for me. That would have put her ear within a whispering distance.

My words must have brushed against my mother's cheek and echoed out through the hollow she made with the man. The man must have picked them up and said something to my mother about what it was I had said. I can see my mother speaking with her head still forward, her gaze out the front window on the road and far ahead.

Where is the place we are running away to?

Didn't I ask?

What were the words lost to me traveling back to me in the backseat? Whatever my mother's words were back to me, they must have been something to get us talking about something else. She probably tried to get us talking about what to think of in the days or the weeks or the months to come, instead of just thinking about right then and only about what was. Or it could be the radio was on and she began singing along. Because didn't she stop her singing to tell us?

Didn't she say, what do you think of me getting married again?

Those were her exact words, I am almost sure.

My sister probably said, oh, yes! oh, yes! But I know I can hear me saying no. And if I had said no, I know my sister would have repeated a no after me.

But my mother said, well I am, didn't she?

Ever this night, be at my side.

What did the man say? Likely nothing. It could be he just hit the packet to the steering wheel or maybe against the bone of the wrist. I see him freeing the cigarette out the rest of the way by the teeth. He would have beat the end of it against the metal of the lighter. I can hear the whiff of the flame and the snap of the lid that came after. I can see him giving the lighter to my mother to hold, and she looking over at him, or maybe resting her head on his shoulder. She might have held the warm lighter in her palm for miles, thinking of the faces and the words and the places she had hoped for before her. Did she feel herself being lifted up and carried away? Were we going to a place she had never seen?

This must have been the time I asked to hold the lighter, too. This must have been the time my mother said, yes, to me, you can, to me. The window had to have been rolled down on my side in the back. The force of the wind had to have pressed too hard on my arm, opening my hold and making me let go. That must be how I let the man's lighter fall out of my hand.

But why, later, would I have dropped his wallet into the toilet?

And why would I have opened the gate to let his dog run away?

And why did I try to choke him from behind, another time he was driving?

Or was this only something I dreamed I did?

To light and guard.

To rule and guide.

Why did all the days seem to happen mostly at night?

III.

This must have been soon after the place with the two dark rooms. My father must have come to get us, from wherever it was we were living at. He must have picked us up in the car I have seen in the photograph, the car parked in the driveway along the side of a house. This had to be the house on Latona Street. Wasn't there grass to mow that grew in the split of the driveway there? Wasn't there a hill for rolling down on the lawn in the front of the house? Weren't there bushes that grew on both sides of the porch steps? What were they, with the glossy leaves and the clusters of flowers in spring? What was it the other wife called them?

What was it we called the other wife?

I can see my father sitting tall, his arm rested on the top of the seat, his shoulder and head twisted back as he backed the car out. He probably had a map along to find us by, to find whatever the street it was my sister and I were living on then. My sister and I were probably outside in the front, of wherever it was, chalking the brick walk up, playing some kind of game during our waiting. We must have looked up and into the front of every car that drove by us on the street. We must have looked at every face that came toward us on the walkway. But it would have been me who first ran to the stranger, thinking I was seeing my father. And didn't my sister follow and call out mistakenly with me after?

Oh! Yes, it's him!

My father would have pulled up alongside the curb to parallel the car and park it. The other wife probably stayed in the car while my father went out to get us. Then again, it could be the other wife stayed back at the house on Latona and waited, taking a nap on the sofa. I can see her curled on her side with her face toward the dark of the back, maybe with the kitten tucked into her hold. But whether she was sitting in the car, at wherever the place was we were living at, or napping on the sofa back at the house on Latona, it would have been my father going in alone to get us.

He might have stood outside on the step waiting for us to gather whatever it was we had to pack up to take with us. Wasn't there a door screen for him to peer in through? Would he have looked inside and seen the gray and sepia colors of what seeps from the mind during sleep? Or did my father open the door and come into the place we were living at, wherever it was, letting all the colors of day turn hard all at once? Would he have stood waiting in the middle of the living room? He must have looked across the room and seen my mother's husband seated on the davenport, looking back over at him. Wasn't that davenport a hard thing that could be folded out of its halves to lay flat? My mother's husband probably sat with his head tipped back against the hard back of the davenport with a hard look on his face, staring at my father. I can hear the way my mother's husband is breathing, that hiss or whistling sound, as if air got stuck coming out. I can hear him tamping the cigarette against the metal of the lighter, hitting it deliberately, six or eight times at least. He probably kept his eyes on my father the whole time. Or maybe he wouldn't even look over at my father. Maybe instead he just kept his gaze straight ahead on whatever it was that was on on the television, pretending my father was not even there in the room.

Wasn't there barely air enough and light enough in there? Wasn't it the time of day when you don't know what the something is that is wrong, but it is? Wasn't it the kind of waiting that beats the life from the hours you are only trying to live in?

There would have been ticking.

My father must have looked at his watch. He must have stood there in the haze of the smoke and dark air. He must have needed a cigarette. He must have put a hand to his heart and patted it to find a packet. He must have fumbled in the pocket of his coat or of his pants for a match. He probably wouldn't have had a lighter. And I can't see or hear my father spitting tiny bits of tobacco out the way I can my mother's husband. But I do see my father striking a match to light the cigarette up and maybe having to strike more than one match because of some trembling in his hands.

Should I believe there was a gun on my father's hip? Should I believe my father stood in the middle of the living room and touched his hand to the gun and said words to my mother's husband? When was it the policemen came with the lights flashing off and on on the top of their car? Who was it that would have told me this? Or was it only an image coming from the television again? Or was this what I had seen?

Everything could so easily be me.

IV.

What was it we called the other wife?

I doubt we would have called the other wife Mother, since we called our mother Mother. I doubt my father even wanted us to call the other wife Mother, since he didn't want us to call my mother's new husband Father. You already have a father is what he said, or words that were somewhere close to this. He would have made it perfectly clear, whatever the words were, even though what he said had to have been confusing for all of us. But what name would we have called out, if we needed help with a reach or an answer to a question? Wouldn't we have called the other wife by her name? Maybe I tried to use the other wife's name, but found it too hard to say. Didn't the lettering of whatever the name was trip my tongue up? Or was it the sound of it that would stick in the back of my throat? Or was the name stuck down lower than where I even swallowed from? Where was it in me that it wouldn't come up out of?

We must have had to wander room to room to find the other wife if we needed her. We must have touched a finger to a cuff, or tugged at a hem, or pulled on a button, to get her attention before we began speaking. And if we had had to speak of the other wife to my father, we must have just said her to him, or she to him, or maybe even them to him.

I must be saying we, because didn't my sister do what I did?

I must be saying them, because wasn't there another other woman at the house on Latona?

It must have been the other woman the other wife would have

been talking to. Didn't the other wife talk about a tremoring in the fingers? Or was it a fluttering under the ribs? Or was it a wringing in the uterus she was talking about? I can see the other wife sitting talking in the hall space with the telephone cricked into her neck. I can see her with the pad in her lap, practicing at fingers and lips and ears, maybe as a way of erasing some picture she had of the future of things. Maybe that's why she went into the dining room and shaded fruit shapes? And maybe that's why she opened the book and looked at the body inside? Maybe she hoped to find all the roots and the joints and the tiers there are in us?

Would she have gone for a pill or a drink? Or would she have gone to the kitchen to fetch the kitten asleep in the basket next to the stove? Would she have gone to the sofa for a nap, with the kitten held in the cradle of her hips, while she lay curled on her side, her face toward the dark of the back? Maybe sleep wouldn't come and she got up to hunt for bedding and linens and pillows? She might have been in the guest room, making it into a bedroom for us, when she heard the car pull up in the driveway. She would have come out to help us carry the sacks of our clothes or the rolls of our blankets or the piles of our stories or whatever else it was we had, from wherever the place we had been living at was. Or was it not the other wife, but the other woman helping us at Latona, who did?

That had to have been the twin.

V.

There was an archway, it seems, that opened into hall space, that then split off into bedrooms. There would only have been the two bedrooms in the house, the one bathroom toward the north of both. That would have been my father's and the other wife's bedroom across the hall space from us. Didn't the place for my bed let me see out our bedroom door and in through the door of their bedroom?

Didn't my sister and I sleep in twins set against opposite walls? And my father and the other wife had only the one double—or it could have been a queen—the center of the head of the bed seeming close to the middle of the wall of their bedroom. There must have been a lamp on the table by the far side of their bed that lit the bedroom up the way I'm remembering it. The other wife may have draped a scarf across the shade to color the room in warm amber. Wasn't that the light my father walked out of during the day in the middle of the day one day? Otherwise, how could I have seen in?

Didn't he come out buttoning his trousers up? Or was it a buckle he was buckling up? Or was he tucking his shirttail in?

All I know is they must have had the blackouts closed to cut all the daylight out. And it must have been the other wife lying on her side, all the naked back of her toward the door, her head toward the light.

Would she have snapped awake when I put the pillow over her face?

VI.

The other wife could have been her twin. Isn't that what people often said? Or words that were somewhat close to that? That must be why the two of them took to wearing different scents and lengths and frames. That must be why they had their own patterns and colors, their separate brands, and the other wife with the holder, though it could have been the other wife's twin who used the holder. And on some days, didn't the other wife pull her hair back in a knot, and the twin did not, the twin instead leaving her hair to hang down long and straight, the wisps of which would sometimes stray into the eyes or catch between the lips? Or it could have been the other way. Didn't the other wife and the twin like playing the being-the-other-wife and the being-the-other-twin games?

Where is my father in the house among us in all this? Why do I see myself wandering room to room, looking for him as if lost? I must have found him in the kitchen making us pancakes, because didn't my sister and I like pancakes most of all back then? And didn't we like the little ones best my father called dollars? I must have asked him why they were called dollars. I must have asked him why the other wife was always asking for dollars, even though she wouldn't eat them the way we did.

I must have asked him who is the other wife and who is the other wife's twin?

Why don't I remember asking where is my mother again?

All my questions and all his answers must have led to other questions I would have asked him. It might have been the answering that tired him. It might have been fatigue that made his voice get deeper and quieter. It could have been what made him not look at me when he was speaking and not look at me when he was not. Didn't he talk to me, or not talk to me, as he watched the pan for over easy, or looked out the window at the cat leaping from tree to tree?

Or was I not looking at him?

Didn't he get up and cross away to the other side of the kitchen? Might this have been the time I came out of the bathroom with the other wife's cherry red lipstick all over my lips and my teeth? Or was the cherry red lipstick the other wife's twin's? Or maybe he didn't like the way I had cut my hair and my sister's hair all the way down to a stubble, like his, with the other wife's kitchen scissors. Though it could have been the words that made him quiet to me. It could be my father stopped looking and talking to me when he caught me racing through the words on my knees. Wouldn't he have said, get up off the floor and get into your bed, or something that had to have been close to that, that is, if he had said anything about it at all? And if he had said anything at all, wouldn't he have said, the only father you have is the father in front of you standing here now? Wouldn't he have said there is nothing more than the more of only this you see?

Where is the place I will be taken?

Where is the place I have never seen?

I must have asked about beyond the stars and after. My father probably shook his head to everything. Or maybe he just changed the subject to get me off it. Maybe he said something like, let's go fry some bacon up. Or he might have said, why don't you go see if you can help the other wife set the table. Maybe he called out for the other wife by name? Or maybe he sent me away to go and find her? She could have been in the dining room, tracing bones or shading flesh again. Or was it the book with the tubes and the womb she drew from? Weren't there pages of fetuses to see? Or were the pictures pictures of the lining being shed?

Maybe I don't remember it all very well in the dark.

It must have been the mahogany on the walls and the light on on the sideboard that made the room seem dimmer than it was. If I see us in light, I have to put us at the table in the booth at the window in the kitchen. The other wife and my father would have been sitting on the one side across from us in the booth. My sister and I would both have been side by side across from them on the other side. My father would have been looking out the window, chewing and thinking. He might have been thinking about pruning the hemlock back or going out to split more kindling up or maybe when would the other wife's twin be coming again. The other wife might have been cutting my sister's food up small enough for her to eat it with a spoon. It would have been my father who would have shown me how to hold my fork and my knife right. He would have explained the way to cut the meat. He would have said cut only one bite at a time and then put your knife at a slant on your plate this way. He must have said the napkin gets tucked under your chin only if you are a baby. At my age, at that age, he must have said you are not a baby anymore. Even my sister, at her age at that age, wasn't a baby anymore.

Didn't we leave baby age long before we ever got to my father? Wouldn't I otherwise have remembered the time and the place? Or was it my father who forgot it?

VII.

We must have had a garden on Latona. If there had been a garden, it would have been in the yard in the back where the earth was flat and wormy. There must have been flowers budding and dying back there. Or did the flowers bloom in the sun along the side of the house? Weren't there tall stalks that grew there and vines that would tendril and climb the twine up the siding? Or did we walk down rows to pick the pods and eat the pea raw to see if the pea was sweet yet or not? Weren't there berries that grew plump in the summer and stained our lips and our fingers bloodred? Maybe the berries were wild berries and not growing along the house or in the garden at all? Didn't they root by accident and spread by neglect? Didn't they grow by a choking clinging? Didn't they grow into a wall of brambles along both sides of the house and the alleyway behind us? Was it the thorns that kept me and my sister fenced in? Didn't their stickery shoots reach as far as the garden? That is, if there had been a garden at all.

But there had to have been flowers for knowing.

He loves me.

He loves me not.

If there had been a garden, it must have been a small garden. Not because the yard was small—I remember the two big apple trees in the back that would bud and bear fruit, or could they have been cherry?—but how would my father have had the time to keep a garden up? And would he have dug the hole to bury the cat in in the garden, instead of another dirt spot in the backyard? Would he have buried the cat with the flowers or maybe instead in the peas? Or was it someplace else he buried the cat at, maybe out in some empty lot someplace? Or did he just put it stiff into a gunnysack and leave it for the garbageman?

S. G. Miller

Was it the cat that was stiff inside the gunnysack?

But I don't see any cat after.

And I don't see the other wife, or the other wife's twin, on her knees in the dirt with a spade or a hoe. It must have been the weight that made it hard for them, for either the one or the other of them, to bend to plant a bulb or a seed, or crouch to fork a weed from the ground. Though you might find the other wife drawing the garden in chalk in the garden. And you might find the twin sitting in the garden, and the other wife drawing the twin in chalk in the garden. Or you might find the twin asleep in the hammock. Or could it have been both of the twins in the hammock? Which of the two would have asked me for a push for a swing?

Didn't it seem one of them was enough to be both of them?

Would that have been my sister out in the grass rolling, practicing for fires with me? Or would it have been the girl who lived across the busy road, at the end of Latona? I don't know. But didn't I used to think the twin was the other wife and the other wife the twin? Didn't it often seem like there were two other wives we lived with back then?

VIII.

As far as any memory goes, if you asked my father about the past, wouldn't he have claimed he couldn't be counted on to remember a thing? But didn't I keep asking? Didn't I ask him questions about back when I was baby age? Didn't I ask him didn't he want to carry me again? He might have just changed the subject to get me off it. He probably said, can you show me our state on the map, or who has seen the coal man lately, or isn't it now time for bed?

Or where is the twin again?

I don't know. All I remember here is flicking my father in the nose with my thumb and my finger. This had to have been the last time my father ever let me sit up on his lap. Wasn't it in the armchair across from the sofa he was sitting and reading the newspaper in? Would he have lowered the newspaper to turn a page, and that's when I decided then to flick him? Or did I move in on his side of the newspaper and flick him inside there with him? Didn't he flinch? Didn't he grab hold of the end of his nose? Didn't he look me right in the eye? Or both eyes? Or one eye and then the other eye? Maybe this was the last time he looked me in any eye? Or maybe it was the only time?

312

S. G. Miller

IX.

What was it the other wives did when I was sent home from school
with the note? It was probably my friend, the girl who lived down the
hill at the end of Latona, across the busy road, who said we should
do what it was we did. And it was probably this girl, my friend, who
told me to bring the matches to school. Didn't the basket of papers
go up in a burst of flame before dying out and settling into ash?
Didn't we run down the steps and out the door long before the bell
rang? And wasn't it this friend who said it was all right to cross the
busy road at the bottom of the hill at the end of Latona? Was it my
father who told me, or maybe the other wives did, that I was never
to cross the busy road at the bottom of the hill on my own? What
must the other wives have said when my friend's mother called up
to say would it be all right for me to stay the night, and with ice on
my head? All I remember is the smell of a kind of soft candy and
falling, but there is no memory of the car when it hit at all. Maybe I
got home on my own and walked upright enough to be sent to my
room without supper? Would the other wives have come in to ask
me what I knew of the time and the place? Would they have lifted a
lid to check the size of the iris? Would they have watched for the rise
of my chest, or counted a minute of my breathing?

Would my father have called from out on the road or wherever he
was when he wasn't with us, to check up on us? Wasn't he out selling tents and camping supplies and all of what a person would need
to live in the woods in? Or would he not have called so as not to hear
about any trouble at home? Wouldn't he have wanted the other
wives to take care of what was on their own? Why do I think he
would not want to think about any of this?

Or is this all again just me again?

Was the headache lingering from the falling? Or did I not have a
headache and only thought I did? Or maybe I thought I should? Or
was it one of the other wives complaining of a headache? I don't
know. But someone must have had one the day I fell on my birthday.
And my father was home, is what I am guessing. Maybe he was in
the kitchen when they called him. Or maybe he was doing something in the locked room off the kitchen; the room, I believe, had to
have been the twin's. Or would he have been down in the basement
loading the furnace with kindling and coal, the coal that when it
came would slide down the chute of the bin?

Wherever it was my father was, he must have been close. Didn't he have to jump in the car and rush to the school? He must have rubbed at his neck or his forehead, his eyes fixed on the broken line ahead of him. He must have thought how could anybody honestly really want to be a father or a mother or an other mother? He must have been shaking his head in regret when he got to the school. What was the look on his face when he saw me sitting in the sickroom with my hands wrapped in the wads of towels? Why can't I see it here? He must have wondered how could my child have fallen up the steps? Because how often do you hear of someone falling up? But that is what they say is what happened, didn't they? I fell up.

It must have been a step that tripped me. It had to have been the glass dish the other wives baked the cake in. Wasn't this the first time I saw a gush of blood? When would I ever have seen so much blood?

My birthday would have seemed almost the death of me.

I wonder what my father thought when he saw all the blood? He must have turned white. He must have told me not to cry. He probably said let's get in the car and get to the hospital up at the top of the hill. He would not have explained what the people up at the hospital would have to do to me. He would have said they are just going to wash you and bandage you up. Because if he had told me about losing the tip of my finger and the stitches I would be getting in the folds of my hands that might have told my story, I would have been better prepared for the needles and the dish they call a kidney to put the fingertip into.

I must have been quick jumping off the metal table and running out the door and down the hallway. Why did it take the nurse and the doctor all the time it did to catch up to me? How fast could I have been running? Didn't I run out and call out for my father?

Please, oh! please, come and carry me away.

Would I have called out Father for my father? Or would I have used a more childish name? Or might I have said a name I might have used at baby age, even at my age, at that age?

Or might I have not called him at all?

Why was the hallway in the hospital empty? Shouldn't there have been stray beds and metal poles and wheelchairs somewhere in it? Shouldn't there have been people busy or noisy or limping in it?

Where did my father run away to?

He must have been frightened. Or he could have been tired. Or maybe he just needed something to eat. Maybe he walked out to the lot at the hospital and tried to rest in the back of the car. Or he might have gone across to the coffee shop while they were picking the slivers of glass out. Because he couldn't hold my hand, either one, could he?

What was it that made everything change the day my father and I came home to Latona from the hospital at the top of the hill? Weren't we all eating at the table in the dining room and not at the table in the booth in the kitchen? And why would we not be talking about the tip of my finger missing or the stitches in the folds or what I still had of my story to tell? No one seemed to want to speak. Except me, probably. I was probably asking questions about a new way to eat. Would my father have cut my meat up for me, even at my age at that age, with the clumsy bulk of the bandages I had on my hands? Probably not. He probably would have encouraged me to figure a way out for myself by myself. Maybe I complained. But if I had complained, my father would have explained what life was going to be like with something missing, wouldn't he?

Why don't I remember the words?

Why can't I remember the gift or the cake?

It must be me who has forgotten it all.

Could this have been the early months of the baby?

There must have been too much my father and the other wives had on their minds. Could this have been why everyone was so quiet? Or are people always more silent inside memory? Maybe they were all thinking about where will there be room enough in the small house here on Latona for a crib for a baby? Maybe they were thinking about where would all the baby things go—the piles of diapers and bibs, the bottles and nipples, the bassinet, the bath, the baby crib? Where would there have been baby space enough when there was so little space for playing in, or sleeping in, or breathing in, as they say, in the house on Latona?

Did my father buy the pickup truck to move the baby things in? Or did he think about the other wives maybe needing the car to get to the store to buy milk with? Maybe he just borrowed the pickup truck and it wasn't his to keep at all? Or maybe he hadn't owned it all that long and we were not in it often enough to remember it. Because the only time I can see us in the pickup truck was the night we all got up and left the house in the middle of the night.

Didn't my father tie my sister and me into the back? The tail of the bed must have been up and deadbolted shut. He must have made pillows for us by stuffing our coats into tent sacks. We must have

315

rested the pillows up against the tail of the bed. He must have given us the flashlight for light, in case we were frightened by the smother of dark above us or a voice calling out of the night in the lot. Wasn't the cover he covered us with a large sheet of canvas with metal holes in it? I must have asked him how we could get air enough in with the canvas pulled tight across the edges of the bed and cinched up so close over our heads. We must have only had inches above us to breathe in. Would he have said something about having air enough? He must have said he would come back during our sleeping and check on our breathing during the night. Would he have loosened the rope from the rivets and lifted the canvas to see us? Would there have been light enough from the pole lamps in the hospital lot to know if we were breathing or not? Would he have lifted the canvas to let air enough in for us? Or were there air cracks or air holes or air something like that in the bed of the truck or in parts of the canvas we didn't know of?

Weren't we back in the lot at the hospital at the top of the hill? Would this have been the night of the birth or the death? Was it the night of the baby or the baby after the baby? How long was it later? is what I am asking. Because all I see next is the dining room again, and all of us sitting at the table in it. Because if we had been in the kitchen, I would remember the light coming in through the window, wouldn't I? And I could have looked out to the garden at Latona, that is, if there had been a garden at all. But it must have been in the dining room, because both of the other wives were there, weren't they?

Which of the other wives told my father the story, the other wife or the other wife's twin? Or both? I don't know. But she, or the other she, or both shes, told him I had run down the hill with the baby in the stroller. They must have told him I stopped and let the stroller go and I watched the stroller roll down to the bottom of the hill on its own, straight down Latona toward the busy road.

My father must have looked across the dining room and out the living-room window during the telling, maybe chewing during his thinking again. We must have heard him swallowing in the quiet, wasn't it that quiet? He must have taken one last bite and wiped the crumbs from his lips and folded his napkin up to put back in its place on the table right. He must have had everything already ready. He must have thought to pack the canvas tent and the cookstove up. He must have thought to put the cot and the bag in the back. He must have checked things off from the checklist, reminding himself of matches and utensils and compass, tin cup and canteen and tarpaulins.

Why do I doubt he would have forgotten anything?

Why can't I remember what he said? Did he get up without uttering a single word to us? Wouldn't I have remembered the word or the words if he had said it or them? Wouldn't I have remembered a kiss for good-bye, or maybe a wish of good luck?

He must have got up from the table and walked to the front door and gone out and got into the pickup truck. He must have started it up, then fixed the sideview and the rearview mirrors, letting the engine warm up before he opened the clutch. Would he have taken one last look back in a mirror? Would he have paused and thought of reverse instead of first, first?

The other wives must have stood at the window. I can see them standing in the dusky light, maybe waiting until the taillights faded out at the bottom of the hill and disappeared after he turned onto the busy road at the end of Latona. My sister and I must have stayed at the table watching the other two watching. But who would have been watching the baby? Where was the baby? Why have I no memory of a baby inside the house on Latona at all? Would the baby have been in the master bedroom, maybe sleeping? Could there have been a crib in there I had never seen, or had seen, and now am not able to remember it? Or would the baby have been in the room I had never been into, the locked room off the kitchen?

Or had there been no baby in the house at all?

Maybe there never was any baby?

X.

Suppose my father made a right and drove to the pier, taking the long way along the cut from the lake to the sound. Suppose he parked on the dock and waited with the next load to board. Maybe he stayed in the car, parked below deck, and he dozed on the ride. Maybe the car behind in line had to tap the horn to shake him awake from his daydream or sleep. He might have waked with a start. It might have been the rattle in the unlocking and the clunk of the drop of the chain that put him back to where he was again. He would have sat up and rubbed the stubble on his head and put his hat back on. He would have put the truck into gear and driven off the ramp and taken the road toward the coast. It could be he had to wait for the draw when he got to the bridge. What must he have thought, gazing at the red light pulsing at the stop? Would he have thought about was there room enough for making a U from his place on the span? Why do I think when the drawbridge closed and the wood guards lifted, my father drove over the floating bridge, feeling himself buoyed, aloft? Why do I see him driving, knowing he was going nowhere, or thinking he was going anywhere, or maybe not caring about thinking of going or where you went when you did at all?

Wasn't it some time in autumn? The light might have bled out of the woods too fast for him to see to make the tent up by. He might have left the stakes swaddled in the canvas and the canvas left bundled and strapped in the tent sack. He might have relied on the light of the dome to roll his bag out out in the truckbed. The woods would have blanketed him in black, all the light pitched out and lost into time and sky. He would have needed to strap the flashlight around his head, with the beam set against his forehead to guide him. He must have been reading maps and the names of new places, looking at possible routes he would take. He was probably wearing the gloves with the tips snipped off, following the roads with an index finger, maybe pointing random towns and ferry crossings out. He must have known all the ways to get to wherever it was he was going, to the onwards and the forwards he was heading toward.

I suppose he folded his maps closed and lit one last smoke up for the night. Maybe he put the light out and inhaled in the dark and the quiet. He probably rubbed the hot stub out on the swell of the metal wheelwell up next to his head. He probably lay on his back, his head rested on the stuff sack he had stuffed with his clothes for a pillow. He must have looked up through the tree holes and seen clusters of stars and pieces of spiraling galaxies. He must have shut his eyes and breathed in canvas and sea air and evergreen. He must have breathed in the pure empty space before him. Maybe a tree groaned and he thought it the sound of the rapture in him. Or maybe he groaned, and he thought it the give of a tree.

Whatever he thought, he must have thought everything enough as it was. I would like to think he lingered in his falling. I would like to think he opened doors or entered rooms he had not known before. I would like to think he slept until the sun came up to wake him up.

Three Poems
Malinda Markham

TO HUNT IN THIS LANDSCAPE

Two figures crouch in the corner
and wring music from stones. Pebble by petal
by peal of something
like asking, they do
what they were born to. Outside,
a woman screams in a field.

From the shape of her mouth,
we know there are words,
but we cannot discern them.
Children push honey
through a sieve to search
for small gems. If stones are in water,
why can't they be culled
from the air? The smell is sweet
and takes the place of food.

We stood in a field where butterflies mated.
The more I spoke, the more I tasted
the curled leaf of fear, the more
butterflies swarmed. Not far away,
two people sang in fury. They spat
notes at their feet, hoping for wings.
Harvest, they still sing, but fruit
softens on the vine all the same.

I remember a chemical smell,
an empty house where apricots
blacken each year and draw flies. Here,
men force the stones to speak: someone

has to. Women grieve before a banquet,
thinking it a cliff. We know
there are words from the shape
of their mouths, but we cannot
deter them. Children hunt lions
for the sweet they contain.

THOSE WHO CAME RUNNING WERE CHILDREN

A lantern left of the outstretched
Hand here is a blade

Fingers cocked the bird
Held straight from the chest

Like a mourning device
Speak boy this is your moment

Your mouth is fit to choose
Something helpful

A name do you know
How it feels now to break

The bird to spare
Its awful speech this is

Relapse another intrusion
A day to sing a hole

Back into the ground
Sister on the roof at night another

Armed in bed they do
Adult things with no words

To describe them this
Is the mercy

Malinda Markham

Of children
The world outside still

Almost untouched it curls
Around shoulders

Too narrow not to be grateful
For warmth

IN WHICH THE CITY IS TAKEN

Metal in the milk, the youngest wake into mist.
The horizon is no longer
bare tongued and harmed. Trees billow
like weighted sheets on its line. Colors
are wrong today. The dancers' torsos
are bathed in persimmon. As they move,
their hems lacquer
to obedient curves. Figures beckon

then turn. On this morning, like no morning,
all the sharpest eyes are numb.
Sentry dogs curl like warm shells
on the pavement. They should bark, should bare
their teeth like fortune machines.

A flash of one bare foot
so translucent the veins steep
themselves in pale. Children sleep,
their brittle bones inside them,
like secrets held
so unfortunate and bold
the body curves to protect them
and cannot unfurl.

Trees along the horizon
did not hold the breaking back and thus
are accountable. When a tin bird note
catches the sun, its simplicity

Malinda Markham

could blind a whole city of men.
But no one will witness. Even the mapmakers
doze at their compasses—like children,
no danger to anyone but themselves.

Thunderbird
Mark Poirier

IT'S JULY, THE SUN'S HOT and white in my eyes, and a dirty kid named Peter rides up, thinking he can use the jumps we built from old real-estate signs. We spent all of June clearing trash and tangled barbwire from this dirt lot behind Taco Bell so we could have a good place to ride our bikes. Jay even had to get a tetanus shot when he cut his arm on an old mattress spring. And Peter just shows up. I think, *Go away, go away,* but Jay and Phil don't say anything.

Peter has crooked bangs like his mom cut his hair in their kitchen, and his teeth and lips are stained purple from juice. He has a crappy bike—a Huffy, from Gemco or Zody's. We have Diamondbacks from real bike shops. Jay even has hundred-dollar Tough Wheels. I didn't go near Peter at school last year. He's the type of kid who'd shove me into a urinal or wind a rubber band and let it loose in my hair or start a rumor that my mom's a lesbian, all for no reason.

But Peter hits the jumps and soars way higher than any of us ever has. His front and back wheel hit the dirt at the same time. He looks over at us and smiles, knows we're watching him, knows he's good, better than us, even though he has a shitty bike and we have good ones.

"My dad was runner-up to be an astronaut," Peter says. The four of us share a plate of nachos covered in bright orange cheese, sitting at a faded plastic picnic table in the shade of a truck. Jay bought the nachos. He always does. His mother gives him five dollars a day because she feels guilty that his dad ran off like my dad did. Jay's dad ran off with their old neighbor, a lady named Deborah who Jay's mom says has a drug problem.

I know Peter's lying about his dad almost being an astronaut, but I don't care. I like his froggy voice. It makes my stomach feel nervous and my neck tingle in a good way.

"Bullshit," Phil says. "Your dad was a realtor, and he couldn't sell any houses, so now your family's poor."

I stare down at the stained cement, my dumb, too-skinny ankles, my new sneakers—blue slip-on Vans. When I finally look up, Peter's pedaling away toward Bear Canyon Road, his heavy bicycle rocking back and forth between his legs. Peter has hair on his legs already.

"It's true," Phil says. "They had to drain their pool because they couldn't afford the water bills." Phil snatches the last two chips and stuffs them in his mouth with a loud crackle.

"How do you know?" Jay asks.

"My mom," Phil says, still chewing.

Phil's mom dresses like a teenager in tank tops and really small running shorts to show off her tanned skin. She never wears a bra and I've seen her nipples twice: once when she was driving us to Skate Country and she twisted around to reach in the backseat for Phil's skates and the other time when she leaned over to pick up a penny on their kitchen floor. She looks at me like she knows all of my secrets, and whenever I go over to Phil's house—every time—she asks me, "What do you hear from your father these days, Craigy?" I have to tell her that I haven't heard from him in a long time, then she pretends to be on my side and says, "Men . . ." as she shakes her head, like she can't believe it. She does the same thing to Jay. Behind Phil's back, Jay and I talk about what a bitch she is. Jay's seen her nipples three times and says he saw her scratch her pussy with a spatula out by their pool. She didn't actually stick the spatula in her shorts or anything, but we joke that the hamburgers she grilled tasted like fish burgers that day. If Phil knew this, he'd kill us.

Peter lies to us all summer. He says he spent two nights in the tunnels under Tucson Mall and caught an albino cockroach, says his uncle invented Pac-Man, says he was colorblind in fifth grade and now he isn't. Each time he lies, I brace myself for Phil's response, but Phil doesn't say anything, and I let Peter's voice go through me like a chill and ask him questions to make him talk more.

Peter and I stay at the track longer than the others, jumping our bikes until the sky goes from orange to purple. My arms ache from jumping, but I'm getting better. Better than Phil and Jay, not as good as Peter.

We sit on the warm curb and eat thirty-nine-cent bean burritos, and Peter grabs my hand. Peter's hand is dry and rough and my retarded hand is sweaty. "Your life line is long," he says. He traces the line on my hand and it tickles into my wrist and up my arm. "My mom taught me this." He smiles right at me, the right side of his smile hooking higher than the left. "This line means you'll be rich."

All I can say is "Cool" and hope that he examines every line on both my hands and that my hands stop sweating so much.

"Your love line is short, but you'll be rich so who cares?"

"Not me."

"You can tell someone's fortune from their head, too," Peter says. "From their scalp. My mom said she'll teach me."

"You believe it?" I ask. Peter still holds my hand.

"No," Peter says, then he squeezes my fingers together, hard, until all the good feelings stop and I pull my hand away.

It's the second Monday since school started and everyone wants to talk to Peter because he was on the news. He found a dead homeless lady on our dirt track next to the third jump. He was on all the channels and on the front page of the *Arizona Daily Star.*

"Did you touch her?" Lacy Clark asks him at lunch. Lacy has big tits and she French-kisses us at parties. She always wears tight Izods and Jordache jeans. Her purse is grubby, made of pink parachute material.

"I poked her with a stick," Peter says. "Just to see if she was alive."

"I would have freaked out," Lacy says. Her hands are in her back pockets and her eyes are bugged. She looks at Peter like he's a star and sticks out her tits. "Is it true she was covered in beetles?"

Peter smiles at her like he's embarrassed and shy, but he's not. He's faking it. I can tell.

"There were some bugs on her," Peter says, "but not tons."

Peter got to meet Steve Fogleman, the reporter from Channel 7 who has a thick mustache and curly brown hair. Steve Fogleman called Peter's discovery of the dead lady "gruesome" and Peter "courageous." All Peter did was poke her with a stick and call 9-1-1 from the telephone booth at Taco Bell. I want to ask Peter if Steve Fogleman wears makeup, but I don't because he and Lacy are talking about Mademoiselle Rosenblatt, our French teacher and Lacy's and my homeroom teacher, and when I try to add something, Lacy looks at me like I'm annoying her, like I should go away, so I do.

Mark Poirier

It took less than a week and now Peter and Lacy are officially a couple. They sit together at lunch and write notes during social studies. They're so popular that girls besides Lacy have written *Peter + Lacy* on their notebooks. During homeroom each morning, I listen to Lacy brag about what she and Peter talked about on the phone the night before. The girls gather around her like what she has to tell them is important. "He was totally imitating Mr. Thone. I was cracking up! Then he started to imitate Mademoiselle Rosenblatt. It was so funny."

Peter's hair is combed in a new way: a perfect part down the middle and lightly feathered on the sides—like Orioles pitcher Jim Palmer. All the girls love it, especially Lacy, who raved about it all morning in homeroom. I wanted my hair like that last year, but I have a cowlick and I can't get it to part in the middle no matter how much of my mother's hair gel I use, so I comb it to the side.

I'm glad my hair won't part in the middle like Peter's when Phil calls the style "disco fag hair" at lunch. I watch Lacy's face go slack as she glares at Phil. Peter looks at Phil through half-closed eyes, like he wants to fight.

"What?" Phil says. "It *is* disco fag hair."

"We all decided it looked really good," Kim Fenster says. "So you guys better shut up about it." Kim Fenster has a wide gap between her two front teeth and she only wears concert T-shirts. Her older sister who Phil's mom says is a druggie brings her to see every group that comes to the convention center downtown. Today's shirt is Pink Floyd's *The Wall:* a creepy cartoon of a monster-teacher looking over a pile of bricks. The only band I've ever seen is Styx, and my mom made us leave after like half an hour because my older brother started coughing from all the smoke. He's asthmatic.

"I didn't say anything," Jay says. "God."

"Me neither," I mumble. I kind of want to say how good his hair looks, how I want to have the same style.

"All three of you are jealous," Kim says. "Losers."

We play a game of two-on-one that we invented where the guy without a teammate can't be guarded outside the key. It's mainly a shooting game, lame and boring, and I can tell by how slow Jay and Phil move that they think it's lame, too, but no one else will play with us

326

because of what Phil said about Peter's hair. It's hot on the dusty courts under the noon sun and our sneakers squeak on the cement with every move. If Phil weren't such a dick, we'd be inside, hanging out in the common room with everyone else.

The next day, Kim Fenster calls me Alpo Mouth during break, because Lacy told her I had bad breath when we kissed at Jay's party in July. Two other girls call me Alpo Mouth as I wait in lunch line. Phil and Jay bark at me and tell me to sit at another table, that my breath's making them sick. I don't feel like pretending to like the stupid basketball game anyway, and it's over a hundred degrees again, so I hide in the library and flip through this week's and last week's *Sports Illustrated* for articles about Jim Palmer or the Orioles. There's nothing good, only some stats, so I read *Rolling Stone* instead. Someone drew tits and a dick on a photo of David Lee Roth. Someone draws tits and dicks on almost every magazine in here.

Phil and Jay find me in the library, and they start barking at me from behind the glass display of Kachina dolls, until Mrs. Rydell threatens to write them up. When they finally leave, Mrs. Rydell walks over to me.

"Do you know those boys' names?" she asks.

"No," I say.

She looks down at the magazine I'm reading and points to the picture of David Lee Roth. "Did you do that?" she asks, thinking I drew the dick and tits.

My throat bunches up and I feel like I might cry. "No," I say, and my voice cracks. "I swear I didn't." I know she doesn't believe me.

Instead of going to pre-algebra after lunch, I walk across the tennis courts in front of a PE class, leave school, and no one says anything. I hike along the Rillito riverbed to the mall, and I spend my last two dollars on Chicken McNuggets. As I head to the far end of the mall, I secretly drop one of my six McNuggets in the fountain in front of Sam Goody. I play the display video games at Sears. They have Asteroids for Atari set up, and because it's a school day, I don't have to wait in line to play. Even though it's not that fun and your ship only shoots in eight different angles, I play so much that my thumb is sore, then I leave and check on the McNugget in the fountain. It's now the size of a potato, all mushy and white, just like I knew it would be. I hang around the fountain for a while, pretend to be waiting for someone, watching, but no one notices the bloated McNugget, and I walk home, imagining a bratty little girl pointing at the McNugget and screaming, or the janitor who thinks it's some sort of jellyfish, calling a scientist to examine it. It will take them weeks to figure out what it is, and there will be articles about it in the paper. Steve Fogleman will report live from the Tucson Mall even though the McNugget will have been taken to a lab at a university weeks before.

A guy once wrote in to "Ask Beth" and said he thought he was gay. He was only thirteen, and Beth wrote that boys can't really know if they're gay until they're at least fifteen, that a boy's sexuality isn't completely formed until that age. So I have three more years to do what I always do after school: page thirty-six, the Jim Palmer Jockey Underwear ad, Jim sitting on a stool in nothing but the tiniest blue underpants.

I stand at the sink with the magazine propped up on the tissue box. The fan's on and I run the water so no one can hear even if they're pressing their ear right up against the door. I can finish in under three minutes, including set up and clean up. I've timed myself.

I wash as much down the drain as I can see, then I wipe out the marble sink with toilet paper and flush the toilet paper. I run the water some more so it doesn't look like I've wiped out the sink. I sniff the sink up close. If any water drops splashed on the Jockey ad or even on the next page, I sprinkle water drops on a bunch of other pages so the Jockey page doesn't stand out. I shove the magazine back in the middle of the stack on top of the toilet, and I'm done.

Mr. Thone makes Peter and me partners for a science project where we have to germinate bean seeds on wet paper towel and keep track of the growth.

"You want to come over to my house, or do you want to do it at yours?" Peter asks me, like he doesn't care.

"Yours," I say too quickly.

"Don't call me Disco Fag at my house."

"I won't," I say. "Phil invented it."

"Bring your skateboard," he says, then we both shut up because Mr. Thone starts lecturing about plants again. Everyone pays attention in Mr. Thone's class because he failed eleven kids last year.

328

They all had to go to summer school at Amphi High School, and one kid got stabbed in the arm by a nineteen-year-old from Nogales.

I sit on the edge of the drained pool, my legs dangling over the cracked tiles. Peter pulls off 180s pretty high on the walls. He sticks his tongue out a little as he concentrates. I feel like a loser because it's my skateboard he's using, and I suck at it. I can't even go like a foot up the wall without bailing.

Just as I notice my legs are getting sunburned, Peter announces we should work on the project. As we walk toward a metal gate, he trips on a rotten cushion from a pool chair, hits the cement deck pretty hard, flat on his face. My skateboard flies back into the pool. I reach down and grab his arm to help him up, asking if he's all right, but he just looks at me like he wants to kill me and shakes my hand from his arm.

Peter stands by himself and lifts his shirt to check out the skinned part of his chest and stomach. He has a line of brown curly hair leading from his belly button into his shorts. I don't.

"Shit," he says, now looking at his bleeding elbow. "Sorry about your board." He jumps into the low end to get it for me.

It's hotter in Peter's kitchen than it is outside, and it smells like vitamins. He grabs a handful of fake cheap-brand Froot Loops called Fruit Circles from an open box on the counter and doesn't offer me any. As we walk upstairs to his room, I ask, "Did you ever learn that head thing?"

"What?" he says, crunching the cereal.

"The scalp fortune-telling thing."

"No," he says. "I mean yes." He doesn't say he'll do it on me, and I don't ask.

There are tons of clothes on Peter's bed, his dresser is missing a drawer, and his window has a crack in it that someone tried to fix with masking tape. Two porno magazines in the middle of his floor are opened to close-up pictures of wet pink and purple pussies. Peter sees me looking down at them, and he grabs one. He flips it open to a picture of a black guy getting a blow job from a chubby blonde woman who has her hands bound behind her back with electrical tape. Her eyes are rolled white like she might throw up. The black man's dick is big and veiny and his balls hang low. The woman wants out of there, I can tell. Like, maybe she was kidnapped and forced to suck his dick. She looks like my mother's friend Linda, who used to babysit my brother and me until she moved to Flagstaff to get away from her ex-husband who was a stalker. I feel myself getting hard, and I feel bad, try to think of something horrible, like rotten food or a smashed jackrabbit on the side of the road, but it doesn't work. It never works.

"You think Samuel's dick is this big?" Peter asks me.

"I don't care," I say. Samuel is one of four black kids in our whole school. "That's gross."

"We can see at camp in April," Peter says, smiling like he's excited. "We all have to take showers together."

"I know." The whole seventh grade goes to Y Camp in Oracle for three nights. Last year, when they came back, they started to call Brad Diaz a donkey because his dick was so big. Lots of girls got felt up, two got fingered. I plan on eating tons of cereal and making myself barf the night before we're supposed to go. I'll make sure my mother and brother hear me so they know it's real and I'll pretend that I'm really disappointed that I can't go. I can't take showers with other guys. I know that.

Peter shoves some clothes aside and sits on his bed, continues to flip through the magazine. "I touched Lacy's pussy," he says. "She let me. She has tons of hair."

I pretend to be interested in a map of the Grand Canyon tacked up next to Peter's window. I walk over to the map so he can't see my boner. "When are we going to start the project? Do you still even have the beans?" I ask.

"One more thing," Peter says, then he jumps up from his bed and reaches under his dresser. He pulls out a dirty baseball hat with "Thunderbird" on the front in gold thread. "You know where I got this?"

"Where?" I ask.

"From the dead lady," he says. He puts it on his head, adjusts it. "Before I told anyone about her, I grabbed it and stuffed it in my backpack."

He tries to put it on my head, but I swat it away.

"You chicken?" he asks. He picks it up from the floor and steps really close to me like he might want to fight. He looks right into my eyes. His eyes are light brown, the color of butterscotch.

"She might have had lice," I say, smiling on purpose like I'm sort of joking, even though I'm not. "Or a disease." I imagine tons of bugs pouring out of her crusty eye sockets, some of them laying eggs in the hat. My boner still won't go away.

330

"Chicken," Peter says. "Craig is chicken, Craig is a chicken. . . ." His face is so close to mine that I can feel his breath on my lips, see a few tiny hairs between his eyebrows. I smell the fruity cereal he ate, and I wish I had remembered to have a piece of gum. Our breaths mix in the tiny space between our mouths, and I can't move.

"I'm not" is the only thing I can say. My face is hot and my eyes close by themselves.

"All right," Peter finally says, and I open my eyes. "You don't have to wear it." He flings the hat across the room. "I don't know why you have to be such a baby, and I don't know why you had to close your eyes like that."

Peter puts both his hands on my head and presses on my scalp with his fingertips, tracing tiny circles. I smell the cereal again as he moves his hands down to my face, pushing my cowlick flat and stopping on my cheeks. "God," he says loudly, dropping his hands from my face. He's angry. "And don't tell Lacy or any of the other girls about the magazines."

I swallow, then say, "I won't."

Peter's on the news for a second time because the police found two more dead homeless women. Steve Fogleman interviews him again and Peter says, "I hope the police catch the person who killed them." Steve Fogleman squeezes Peter's shoulder and calls him "brave."

Lacy's wearing the dead lady's Thunderbird cap on Monday. It matches her purple Izod like she planned her outfit. Under the lights of the hallway, the hat looks even dirtier—there are white lines of salt from the dead lady's sweat. Lacy and Peter walk by me and whisper to each other and laugh.

Before pre-algebra I tell Jay that Lacy's wearing the dead lady's hat. "Peter stole it," I add when Jay doesn't say anything.

"Duh," Jay says. "They were talking about it on the bus this morning." Jay sits at his desk. "They were talking about something else, too, homo," Jay says.

My stomach falls, like I'm jumping my bike or I'm suddenly starving. "What?"

"Peter said you wanted to look at Samuel's dick at Y Camp," Jay says loudly so everyone can hear. "In the showers."

"Peter said that, not me. I swear to God."

Wanda, a girl who wore the same yellow shirt nine days in a row and has tons of white zits on her forehead, looks over. "Are you gay?" she asks me. "Just admit it." She sometimes smells like concentrated urine and someone said they saw her mother in line for government cheese downtown. "Are you?"

"Peter also said you bet Samuel's dick was really long and you were afraid to wear the dead lady's hat," Jay says.

"I didn't want to get lice or anything," I say.

The bell rings and Mr. Dunn tells us to settle down and begins to take roll.

I write Jay a note: *I didn't say that about Samuel. I swear to God. And the hat is probably police evidence.*

He doesn't even unfold it, and it falls on the floor when the bell rings for next period. I haven't heard a word Mr. Dunn has said or watched him do any problems on the board in the last forty-five minutes. I don't even care that I'll probably flunk the quiz on Friday.

Kim Fenster and some of her friends bust up to me in the hall. Kim's wearing the Thunderbird hat now, and she stands in front of me with her hands on her hips like she wants to block my way. "You're a pervert," she says. "And you're prejudice and I'm telling Samuel you said you wanted to look at his dick." She has a big wad of pink gum in her mouth, packed into her cheek.

"I didn't say anything," I tell her. "I swear to God."

"Peter said you'd probably lie about it because he said you were all embarrassed after you said it." I've never seen Kim fight anyone— girls or boys—but I bet she'd win. Her concert T-shirt today is Alice Cooper's *Madhouse Rock*. It has a picture of Alice screaming and a splattered blood background. Alice's makeup drips off his face.

"Peter said his dad was runner-up to be an astronaut, which is a total lie," I say. I notice then that Kim has hairy arms. Almost like a man. Way hairier than mine.

"You're gay and you want to see Samuel's dick," she says.

"Peter said it, not me," I say. She has hairy ape arms. I wonder why no one has ever made fun of her for them. *Ape arms, ape arms. . . .*

"In case you haven't noticed, Peter has a girlfriend," she says. Some of her friends giggle. "Duh."

I leave school, cut through the faculty parking lot. No one sees me.

*

I don't have any money, so I can't drop a McNugget in the fountain. I play the display video games at Sears again, but after a few minutes a lady whose Sears nametag says *Mrs. Wilson* asks me if I need any help, but I know she really just wants me to leave. I tell her that I don't need any help and she says, "It's only 1:20. Why aren't you in school?"

"I go to private school," I lie.

"Which one?"

"Salpointe Catholic."

"Salpointe's a high school," Mrs. Wilson says. Her glasses make her eyes look small.

"I know," I say. "I go there." I pretend to concentrate on the game more than I actually do, just so I don't have to look at her any longer. It's Space Invaders, the same patterns of missiles set after set. I could play for hours without losing a ship. I could play with my eyes closed.

"I don't believe you're in high school, and I don't believe that Salpointe has the day off."

"I'm a freshman," I say, thinking that I might start crying. I'm not even sure why. My throat bunches up, and I try to swallow it down.

"I can call security," she threatens. "You can't just hang out here all day. That's called loitering and it's illegal."

I drop the joystick and walk out, not looking back at her, the Sears Bitch. I could walk to the other end of the mall and play the display games at JCPenney's, but I don't. I hurry through, past two fat security guards, who don't even look at me. The mall is full of old ladies and men who wear windbreakers and ball caps and ugly walking shoes. They just walk around the mall all day, doing nothing. One couple wears matching purple outfits, which reminds me of the Thunderbird hat. I wonder if one of the old men I pass is the murderer. Any of them could be. I imagine that I solve the mystery, report the murderer. I'd be on the news a lot more than Peter. Steve Fogleman would interview me, call me a hero, and invite me over to his condo to hang out. We'd sit on his sofa and watch videos and eat burritos. Steve would kiss me and his mustache would tickle.

I rush out of the cool mall into a wall of heat, the white sun so bright I can't see for a minute, then I sort of jog across the parking lot toward the riverbed. It's too early to go home, so I sit on top of a knocked-over cement trash can behind Sunset Sports and read *Never Cry Wolf.*

After a minute, I notice a skinny man sitting in his truck about twenty feet away. He's chewing on a toothpick and he has his radio tuned to 13K-HIT, which is playing a stupid song by Toto that goes on forever. When I look up at him again, he nods and smiles, so I put the book in my backpack and start to walk away. Then he turns down his radio and loudly asks, "Do you like *Playboy?*"

I begin to run along the riverbed, thinking the guy was planning on abducting me. I'm not stupid. Even if he had asked if I liked *Playgirl*, I wouldn't have gone near his truck. I run faster, my mouth dry, my neck burning in the afternoon sun. Even if the guy had been handsome and not wearing his shirt and asked if I liked *Playgirl*, I wouldn't have gone near his truck. I decide the only way I would have walked over to his truck is if the guy was handsome, not wearing a shirt, offered *Playgirl*, and was someone I already knew, like if he was my mother's boyfriend, and he really liked me more than he liked my mother. Like, he was only dating my mother so he could be near me. We'd have to break it to my mother eventually, but we'd have a secret relationship for a few months. The guy would pick me up at school, and we'd go over to his giant house in the foothills, and we'd mess around. Every day. And I'd tell my mother I was on the soccer team and that's why I couldn't get home until later.

My mother keeps junk mail and new magazines in a big wicker basket by her bed. I kneel down and start flipping through the magazines, and I find one after only a minute: Jim Palmer sits on a gray cube. He wears tiny striped underpants. *The Jockey Fashion Statement is Bold*, it says. I know my mother and brother aren't home yet, but I hide the magazine under my shirt just in case they come home as I transport it to the bathroom downstairs. The magazine is cool against my stomach.

I prop the new magazine on the tissue box and unzip my shorts. I imagine I live with Jim Palmer, and he has real arcade games in his mansion that I can play for free. During baseball games I sit in the bull pen with Jim and the other Orioles. The other Orioles like me and ask me questions about what I'm learning at school. They tell me that Jim is pitching better now that he has me in his life. After Jim pitches another winning game, he takes me in his red Porsche for pizza. On the way home, he lets me drive and tells me to take it easy on the curves in the road. He insists we take a bath together every night in his giant Jacuzzi, and I show him how to press himself up against the water jet, like I sometimes do in the pool when I'm positive no one is around.

*

I'm sure Kim Fenster has arranged a fight between me and Samuel, and I almost don't go to school. The school has called my mother, though, and told her I left early yesterday and ditched three classes. She doesn't even ask me why I did it, just tells me I am grounded for three weeks—a week for each class I missed. I don't care about being grounded. Jay and Phil are dicks and there's no one else to hang out with. "You come right home after school," my mother tells me as I leave this morning, and I think, *Big whoop.*

On the bus, no one sits next to me and no one talks to me. They all know that Samuel's going to beat me up. Samuel will find me the moment I step off the bus, and he'll begin by punching me in the stomach. I'll fall onto the asphalt, and Jay and Phil will call me a fag and bark at me while Samuel kicks me in the head. I'll barely stand up, and Samuel will shove me, and I'll hit my head on the curb, and I'll die, and no one will say anything and Samuel will never even get in trouble.

I don't even see Samuel when I get to school, and when I walk into homeroom, Lacy's crying in the corner, huddled with a few other crying girls. I sit at a desk near no one and listen to find out what's going on. I hope that Peter dumped Lacy, told her he no longer liked her and that her friends were too mean to me and that I'm his best friend now. The two of us will ride BMX on the track or skateboard in the parking garages downtown every afternoon when my grounding is over. Until then, Peter will come over to my house and we'll play video games or swim and he'll tell my fortune from my palm or my head whenever I want.

Mademoiselle Rosenblatt walks into the room. She's sniffing and her eyes are red like she's been crying, too. She takes roll, reads the boring announcements, and then says, "I gather you've all heard the bad news about Kimberly Fenster. Our homeroom and Mr. Carlson's homeroom will meet in the auditorium during second period. A grief counselor from the school district will help us and answer any questions we might have."

Kim Fenster was hit by a car on Tanque Verde Road. She was riding her bike to her older sister's apartment less than a mile from her house. Before second period, I hear a few other things like they still hadn't found her arm, she had been going over there to get marijuana,

her mom was drunk so she couldn't drive her, she had been decapi-
tated by a truck's mirror. They're all probably lies. It all seems so
fake. Just yesterday, she was being a bitch to me and now she's dead,
one of her hairy ape arms possibly missing.

I think I wished her dead yesterday or this morning. I must have.
I'm always wishing people dead. I know I wished Phil dead yesterday.
I imagined him and his mom both dead, in a car accident. I've wished
Jim Palmer's real-life wife dead, I'm sure. Or I wished she never even
existed, which I think is worse.

Samuel's in Mr. Carlson's homeroom and he sits right behind me
during grief counseling. He's wearing the Thunderbird cap today.

The grief counselor is a lady with short hair, big red glasses, and
big red earrings. She wears sandals with pants. I don't really hear
what she says because I'm trying to remember if I did wish Kim
Fenster dead or not. Samuel leans over and whispers, "I'm going to
kick your ass, faggot."

I sit there, the feeling in my stomach like Samuel already did kick
my ass, and I look at the grief counselor's toenails, how they match
her dumb glasses and earrings, my heart racing, my throat tighten-
ing, until I finally turn around to face Samuel, who has the hat on
sideways now. "I didn't say that," I blurt sort of loudly, my voice
cracking. "Peter said it and everyone knows he's a liar and—"

But before I can say anything else, I feel Mademoiselle Rosenblatt's
fingernails digging into my arm. She tugs me out of my seat and pulls
me into the hall, not even letting me grab my backpack. "What is
wrong with you, Craig?" she yells. She's crying and her makeup runs
down her face like Alice Cooper on Kim Fenster's T-shirt. "What is
wrong with you?"

As she guides me to the office, through the empty halls, yelling at
me the whole way, I can only think of Jim Palmer. He has never
allowed a grand slam. He's won the Cy Young three times. If the
Orioles make it to the World Series this year and Jim pitches a winning game, he'll be the only pitcher to win World Series games in
three different decades. His perfect hair, long legs, shaggy chest. *The
Jockey Fashion Statement is Bold.*

And sitting there in the principal's office on the wooden bench,
waiting to be punished for disrupting the grief counseling, I can
barely stay still. I can't help but smile, knowing that I have Jim
Palmer for three more years, as often as I want, until I turn fifteen
and have to let him go.

Two Stories
Can Xue

—Translated from Chinese by Karen Gernant and Chen Zeping

BLUE LIGHT IN THE SKY

WHEN SUMEI WAS PLAYING a game of "catch the robber" in the yard, a piece of sharp glass cut her foot. Blood gushed out. She began crying right away and limped toward the house. Behind her, the other kids went on playing like crazy. No one noticed that she had left.

As soon as she went in the house, she stopped crying, opened the wardrobe, took a rag out of the drawer, and bandaged her foot. As the blood continued seeping out, she added another rag. Her ears were pricked up in alarm: she was afraid her father, who was in the backyard repairing a wooden tub, would come in and see her. The bleeding soon stopped. Sumei took off the two rags that were soaked in blood and bandaged her foot with a clean cloth. Then she stood up, intending to throw the two dirty cloths into the garbage can. As soon as she got up, the door opened. But it wasn't her father who came in, it was her older sister, Sulin.

"What's that?" she asked aggressively. She was quite pleased as she pointed at Sumei's foot.

"Don't tell Pa," Sumei pleaded.

"So much blood! Your foot! What a catastrophe!" Sulin was purposely shouting loudly.

In a flash, Sumei thought the whole sky was falling. She lost no time in hiding the two rags in the burlap bag behind the door. A young rat—frightened into gliding out of the burlap bag—fled in desperation. Because of her hurried, vigorous movement, her foot started oozing blood again. Sulin observed her little sister carefully for a while, then turned and went into the backyard. Sumei knew she was going to report this to Pa, and—terror-stricken—she sat down on a bamboo chair to wait. She predicted a storm would soon descend on her. But she waited and waited. Pa still hadn't made a move. So, she thought, could Pa be too busy (that morning, she'd noticed three people had come to ask him to repair their tubs) to come and discipline me? This made her feel a little better. She decided to spend the day in the woodshed. When she left, she took the two dirty rags out of the burlap bag behind the door. She limped down the steps and threw them into the garbage can. She also grabbed two handfuls of dried leaves to cover the rags.

The woodshed was more than ten meters from the house. Living inside it was Sumei's old friend, the big gray rat. As soon as she saw the nest made from bits of grass and rags, warmth surged up inside her. She knew there were a few baby rats inside. They'd been born a few days earlier and hadn't yet opened their eyes. The day before, she'd taken advantage of the time when the big gray rat was out hunting food to steal a look at the little things that were almost transparent. Sumei sat down far away from the rat's nest. From the woodshed, she could hear Sulin's voice. What on earth was she saying to Pa? Maybe they were discussing how to discipline her. And in the front yard, the kids playing "catch the robber" were shouting gleefully.

When it was almost afternoon, Sumei was so hungry she couldn't stand it anymore. She intended to slip stealthily into the house and find something to eat. When she walked into the kitchen, she saw Sulin washing dishes. Sulin was staring at her with suspicion.

"Your food is in the cupboard. Pa kept talking about you. We thought you'd had an accident!"

Sulin's voice had become really soft—even a little fawning. Sumei felt truly flattered. Sulin made quick work of bringing the food to the table. Sumei sat down, and as if in a dream began gobbling down the food. At the same time, she heard her sister talking on and on beside her.

"Sumei, Pa says you could die from tetanus. What do you think? You know Mama died from tetanus. I've never approved of your playing with those wild kids. Why didn't you ever listen? Actually, I've known for a long time that there was a lot of broken glass by the fence. Last year, I smashed a few wine bottles there. I just never imagined that you would get hurt so soon. But now you've been hurt. I'm so jealous of you. This morning, I saw that your foot was very swollen, and I ran over to Pa. He was putting a hoop around a barrel, and without looking up, he just asked me if it was the broken wine bottles that had hurt you. He also said that those wine bottles had all held poison; there'd be no way for you to escape with your life. His words upset me. As soon as it grew quiet, I remembered those patterns that you used for drawing flowers. Why not just give them to me to save? You can't use them anyhow. I know that you get along well with Little Plum. She gave you those patterns, but if you hadn't asked her for them, she would have given them to me. Right? What would you do with those things now?"

Sulin frowned. It seemed she hadn't thought this through. It also seemed she had some design in her mind. After washing her dishes, when Sumei was about to go back to the bedroom, she noticed that Sulin was still standing next to the stove and smirking. She ignored her and went back to the bedroom by herself. She and Sulin shared this bedroom: the two beds were opposite each other, a wardrobe in between. This morning, it was from a drawer in the wardrobe that Sumei had found the cloth to bandage her wound. Now she opened the wardrobe again, took out a key, opened a locked drawer, and extracted the set of patterns. The patterns were made of peach wood, a smooth red color. Altogether, there were four of them. One could draw four floral designs to embroider pillows. Little Plum had told Sumei that she had swiped them from her mother. In the last few days, her mother had looked everywhere for them. Sumei didn't know how to embroider flowers yet, but the magical patterns enchanted her. When she had nothing to do, she drew flowers in pencil on old newspapers—page after page of them. She felt this was incredibly wonderful. After holding the floral patterns for a while, she carefully put them back in the brown paper bag, then locked the drawer. Her wound was hurting a little, but it hadn't bled anymore. Sumei recalled what Sulin had said, and all at once she felt a little afraid: was it possible that she would really die? Just now, she had thought that Sulin was making a mountain out of a molehill (Sulin had never lied). And Pa—whenever she or Sulin did something wrong, he slapped them twice. This time, though, had been an exception. Was it because Pa was giving her special treatment that Sulin had said, "I'm so jealous of you"? And why in the world had Pa discarded wine bottles with poison in them in the vicinity of the house? Sumei couldn't figure it out. She didn't even bother to think it through. Her policy was always to wait for the trouble to go away. "It'll turn out all right"—that's what she always told herself. Sometimes, when something bad happened, she hid out in the woodshed and slept there. After she woke up, it didn't seem nearly so bad. But today perhaps what Sulin had said wasn't trivial. For some reason, at the time, Sumei hadn't been at all worried, but now—thinking back on Sulin's words in the bedroom—she began to feel vaguely worried. She was also afraid that Sulin would see that she was worried. She sat on the bed, took the bandage off, and looked at her foot. There wasn't anything unusual about her wound. She thought, Maybe that piece of glass wasn't from the wine bottle containing poison at all. Pa and Sulin were both too decisive about this—really oddly decisive. Sumei decided she would walk to the other end of the village. If she could walk that far, it would mean there was no problem. How could anyone who was about to die walk to the other end of the village?

By the time her father caught up with her, Sumei was almost at Little Plum's door.

"Are you asking for trouble? Go back and lie down!" her father roared ominously.

"I, I'm doing my best," Sumei said in a small, pleading voice.

"Your best! Soon we'll be watching your best drama!"

Through it all, her father's expression was stern. Not daring to look at him, Sumei glided to one side like a mouse.

"Where do you think you're going? Do you want to die? Hurry up and go back to bed and die there. If you die outside, no one will pick up your corpse!"

Chased and scolded by her father, Sumei didn't feel that her foot was lame at all. She rushed back home. As soon as she went in, she saw that Sulin was trying to open the drawer where the floral patterns were kept. She was opening the lock with a piece of wire. When she heard the door open, she chucked the wire at once and blushed.

"You can't even wait for me to die."

Sulin slammed the cupboard shut and left in a huff. Sumei knew she was going to look for Pa again. It was strange: Pa didn't even like Sulin. Of the two sisters, he liked Sumei somewhat better, but from the time she was little, Sulin had always done her best to please her father. Even if Pa was mean to her, she was never discouraged.

Sumei lay in bed, closed her eyes, and forced herself to go to sleep. She was a little worried about sleeping. After a while, she felt dazed. In her dream, she went into a forest by accident and couldn't get out. It was cold in the forest, and huge trees were growing everywhere. She sneezed a few times in a row, and suddenly, as she bent her head, she noticed that her foot had been perforated by a sharp piece of bamboo. She'd been nailed down and couldn't move. Feeling an indescribable stabbing sensation, she screamed. She woke up. Her hair was drenched with sweat, but her foot didn't hurt. What was this all about? Could it be that it was someone else who stepped on the sharp piece of bamboo in her dream? And that person was the one who would soon die? Although her foot didn't hurt, the feeling of pain she'd had in the dream was deeply embedded in her memory. The poplar tree outside the window was whispering in the wind. Sumei was afraid she'd fall into the same dream, but—without knowing why—she also really wanted to go back to that dream so that she could understand some things better. She shilly-shallied back and forth between sleeping and waking, finally waking up because of the tremendous sound Sulin made when she shattered a bowl in the kitchen.

Sumei went into the kitchen to help Sulin. Just as she was about to clean the rice out of the pan, Sulin suddenly began to be polite. Snatching the pan out of Sumei's hand, she said repeatedly, "Go and rest. Why don't you rest?" Her behavior aroused suspicion in Sumei. Sulin kept busying herself, while Sumei watched from the sidelines. She admired Sulin's skillful way of working: she could never learn how. Now, for example, Sulin was absorbed in using tongs to roll damp coal dust into little balls. She stacked them up next to the stove. It was as if her right hand was joined with the tongs into a single entity. She looked rather proud of herself.

"Sulin, I had a strange dream. I dreamed I was dying." Sumei couldn't keep from saying this.

"Shhh! Don't let Pa hear you."

"But it was just a dream," Sumei added. "Not likely, is it?" Sulin looked at her speculatively, and then buried her head in her work.

At dinner, their father didn't say a word. Only when they'd finished eating and Sulin had stood up to clear the table did he say abruptly, "Sumei mustn't go out."

"I'm OK. There's nothing wrong with me," Sumei argued, face flushed.

Father ignored her and walked away. "You're so stupid—so stupid!" Sulin said as she grabbed the bowl out of Sumei's hand. "Go off and rest!"

Lights were on in Little Plum's home. The whole family was just wolfing down their dinner. After Sumei went in, Little Plum nodded at her, indicating that she should wait, and then didn't look at her again. They were eating pumpkin porridge and corn bread. Their faces were covered with perspiration. Little Plum's two little brothers buried their faces in the large bowls. Little Plum's father and mother didn't look at Sumei either. They both looked a little angry. Sumei was standing against the wall for a long time. When the family finished eating, they all went into the other room, leaving only Little Plum to clear the table. Sumei thought, Little Plum is really

341

strange. Neither her pa nor her ma is here now. Why is she still not even glancing at me? Little Plum piled up the bowls and carried them into the kitchen. Sumei followed her, never guessing Little Plum would snatch up a cloth in the kitchen and come back to wipe off the table. And so she collided with Little Plum.

"Leave now—now! Later on, I'll come see you," Little Plum said in annoyance. She actually forcefully pushed Sumei outside.

Sumei fell down the steps of Little Plum's house. After sitting up, she inspected her foot. It was still OK. The wound was no worse. As soon as she looked up, she saw Little Plum motion to her anxiously and shout softly, "Leave now—now!" Then she shrank back into the house and didn't emerge again.

Sumei really felt it was a little dangerous now. Recalling her father's orders and his expression, she shivered. All around, it was very dark. In the dark, two people carrying lanterns were in an urgent hurry. Soon, they went past Sumei. She heard one of them say, "We need only get a move on and we'll be in time. In the past, people in our family . . ." Sumei was about to get up and go home, but Sulin had caught up with her. Out of breath, Sulin said to Sumei, "I don't dare stay home alone."

"Is Pa going to beat you?"

Sulin shook her head vigorously.

"What's going on?"

"I was at home thinking about your situation. The more I thought, the more I felt afraid. Why do you always have to go outside? Still, it's great outside. It's so dark that it seems there's no point in being afraid."

She took Sumei's hand solicitously and strolled around with her on the path. All at once, Sumei felt greatly moved. She had always thought Sulin just talked rubbish. She'd thought Sulin had stirred up their father to be against her, but at this moment, she felt puzzled. Maybe Sulin really was more sensible than she was and knew some things that she was in the dark about? Why had she taken on all the housework Sumei was supposed to do? Sumei had learned through repeated experience that Sulin was a smart person and had always had a clear head ever since she was little. Thinking this way, Sumei felt she could rely on Sulin, and she held her hand tighter. She whispered to herself, I can count on Sulin no matter what happens. She is so good, kind, and gentle. She helps me take care of everything. I should rely on her. Then Sumei suddenly found that she had been following Sulin all along. They hadn't gone far at all; they were just circling around Little Plum's home. Now no one was on the street. The wind blowing from the mountain was like a song. All the while, Sulin was silent. What on earth was she thinking about? Or wasn't she thinking of anything?

"Let's go see Pa over there."

After turning around several times, Sulin finally suggested this.

When they walked into the backyard, their father was splitting firewood in the dark. The sound was rhythmic. Sumei was very surprised: she didn't believe her father could see in the dark. But the fact was that Father was clearly working in a systematic way—just as if it were daylight.

"Pa, Pa, we're afraid!" Sulin's voice quivered.

"What are you afraid of?" Father put down his work, walked over, and spoke amiably.

Sumei couldn't get a good look at Father's face, but his tone was a relief. She thought to herself that Pa wasn't angry anymore.

"Sumei isn't afraid, is she? Sulin, you should learn from Sumei. As I split firewood here, my whole head is filled with things having to do with the two of you. Ever since your mother died, I've been fearful. Sometimes I'm so scared that I get up at midnight and split firewood. Speaking of being afraid, I'm the one who should be afraid. What do the two of you have to be afraid of?"

With that, he bent down again and resumed his work.

That night, once Sumei fell asleep, she saw the forest, and she saw herself in the forest. At first, she noticed just one scorpion. Then she noticed scorpions hiding everywhere—under the dried-up leaves, on the trunks of the trees. As soon as she found some, they disappeared and others appeared. They were everywhere.

Time after time, she screamed and woke up with a start. In fact, it was harder to take than death would be. When Sumei woke up, she saw Sulin standing motionless on the bed across from her: it was as if she were observing the night. Finally Sumei didn't feel like sleeping. She turned on the light and sat up in bed, drenched in sweat.

"Sumei, you're really brave." Sulin's voice held jealousy.

Sulin jumped down from the bed and gave Sumei a handkerchief to wipe away the sweat.

"When Pa threw away the broken glass from the wine bottles that held poison—threw the glass along the fence—I was on the sidelines. He wouldn't let me get in on the act. He's always like this. When I told you today that I was the one who threw away the broken wine bottles, that was just my vanity making mischief."

Sulin was deep in thought. Sumei suddenly thought that, under the light, Sulin's face had become a shadow. She couldn't stop herself from stretching out her hand to touch Sulin's face. But the thing she touched let out a sound like the rustling of dried leaves. Sulin moved at once and reproached her.

"What the hell are you doing? You're really insensitive. I've told you repeatedly that you should cut your fingernails, but you just don't listen. What do you think Pa is doing? Listen!"

Sumei didn't hear anything. But Sulin was terribly tense. She crept to the door, opened it, and lightly slipped outside. Sumei didn't feel like going with her. She just turned the light off and sat on the bed and worried. It wasn't just once that she thought if she woke up from a really sound sleep, then everything might change. But she was also afraid of sleeping and seeing the scorpions. Her mind was really conflicted, but finally, in a haze, she couldn't ward off sleep. She entered the forest again. This time, she shut her eyes tight and didn't see anything. When she woke up, it was already broad daylight.

Another day passed, and she found that the wound on her foot had healed. It was obvious that her father and Sulin had made a mountain out of a molehill. Although this was what she thought, she didn't feel the least bit relieved. She couldn't ever forget the dreams she'd had of the bamboo and the scorpions, dreams that were linked with the wound. Each time the wounded foot was bitten or punctured, it was exactly on the spot where the wound was. It was really strange. All right, then, go outside, look for Little Plum and other people. Maybe Little Plum had to chop grass for the pigs. Well then, she'd go with her to chop grass for the pigs. While they were doing that, Sumei could sound her out and see if Little Plum had changed her attitude toward Sumei.

After chopping grass for the pigs at home, Sumei went over to Little Plum's house.

"Little Plum! Little Plum!" she shouted as she craned her neck.

Nobody inside the house responded. After a while, though, she heard Little Plum's parents cursing—calling Sumei "a bad omen." All Sumei could do was retreat and walk back discontentedly along the path. After a while, she came to Aling's home. Aling was in the vegetable garden out front. Sumei called her several times before she slowly looked up. In alarm, she looked all around. With a gesture, she indicated that Sumei shouldn't come any closer. But just then, Aling's mother came out and walked over to Sumei. Taking hold of her shoulders, she looked at her carefully. She said, "Lambkin, lamb—" Sumei was really uncomfortable and really wanted to break away, but the woman's grip was very tight. Without listening to any protests, she forced her intimacy on Sumei.

"Sumei, your father is quite good at his craft. He must have made a lot of money—am I right? But I don't think the ability to make money is all that great and I don't want my children exposed to someone like that. I'm not so shortsighted. Let me tell you, if a person sets himself up too high and also knows things that a lot of ordinary people don't know, then he's heading for a major fall. Actually, my Aling is a lot better—quite ordinary and without any cares or worries. As the saying goes, 'content with her lot.' How's your foot?"

"My foot? It's fine." Sumei was surprised.

"Ha ha. You don't need to try to bamboozle me. This is an open secret in the whole village. Could someone like Sulin keep this quiet? It looks as though you're not happy at all about this. So I say, it's still better to be ordinary. I always wonder: what's your father up to? Aling! Aling! What the hell are you doing with the hoeing? Have you lost your mind? Run off and feed the pigs—now!"

Suddenly relaxing her grip on Sumei, she began bellowing at Aling. Aling threw the hoe down at once and began running toward the house.

Sumei wanted to leave, but the woman gripped her shoulders and wouldn't let her go.

"Your sister Sulin is much too curious. She's brought herself to an emaciated state. I don't admire her one bit. And I don't let Aling have any truck with her. But you're different. I adore you. Let me see you smile. Smile! Ah, you can't smile. You poor child. That guy has been too strict with you. I can't ask you in. After all, Aling has her own life. Everyone knows what kind of trick your father is playing. Everyone wants to know what will happen in the end. We call this 'wait and see what happens.' Understand?"

"I don't understand! I don't!" Sumei was struggling with all her might.

The woman held her shoulders even tighter and pressed her mouth against Sumei's ear.

"You don't? No wonder! Let me clue you in. Listen: you mustn't walk around aimlessly outside. And when you're home, you mustn't sleep in. Prick up your ears and spy on your father's activity.

You won't be used to doing this at first, but as time goes on, you'll get used to it."

Sumei twisted around and looked over the woman's shoulder. She saw Aling talking with Little Plum in the doorway. Both of them were excited and both were gesturing a lot. Sumei recalled the good times when she had played with them. She felt miserable. "Little Plum! Little Plum!" she shouted in despair.

Little Plum was dumbstruck, then pretended she hadn't heard and went on talking and laughing with Aling.

"You little girl, you're rotten through and through," Aling's mother said, gnashing her teeth.

All of a sudden, the woman scratched her hard on the back, hurting her so much that everything turned black and she sat down on the ground.

When she opened her eyes again, the woman had disappeared. So had Aling and Little Plum. It was as though they hadn't been here just now. It was only the pain in her back that reminded her of what had just happened. Sumei thought back on what the woman had said about her father. Although she didn't quite get it, she still knew it wasn't anything good. After going through this, she had given up the dream of finding companions. She was weak all over. Only after struggling hard did she manage to stagger to a standing position. Just now, the woman had definitely hurt her back. That was truly sinister. Weeping, Sumei walked slowly to the other end of the village. No matter what, she still felt that perverse desire: she had to walk to the other end of the village. It was as though she was struggling against her pa and Sulin. Taking breaks to rest, she walked ahead. No one else was on the street. Everything was quiet at the doorways to the homes. If she wasn't walking in the village she was so familiar with, she would have suspected she had come to a strange place. Now, even on the hill where the cattle used to graze, she didn't see one cow. At last, Sumei reached the old camphor tree at the other end of the village. Leaning against the tree trunk, she thought she'd rest a while, but the deathly stillness all around gradually terrified her. A long brown snake was swaying back and forth on the tree. Hissing at her. The frightening scene in her dream suddenly recurred in its entirety. Holding her head, she ran away crazily. She ran a long way before stopping. She sat on the ground and took off her shoe. The wound had split open again, and there was a little red swelling.

"Sumei, let's hurry on home. There isn't much time."

Looking up, she saw her father. This was really weird: was it possible that Pa had followed her?

"I can't walk any farther," she whimpered timidly.

"Come on. I'll carry you." Father bent down as he said this.

Sumei straddled her father's broad sweat-covered back. She was feeling a myriad emotions. She glued her small, thin ear to her father's body and heard clearly the sound of a man's sobbing. But her father surely wasn't crying, so where was this sound coming from? Father was rebuking Sumei and also talking of the wine bottles that had held poison. Sumei was absorbed in identifying that sound of weeping, so she couldn't care less what her father was saying.

Carrying Sumei, Father walked on and on. Sumei realized they weren't heading home; rather, they'd taken a fork in the road leading toward the river. At first, Sumei was a little scared, but the sound of weeping coming from her father's back was like a magnet drawing all of her attention. She forgot about danger and about her hatred of her family. Everything was more and more distant from her. At the back of her father's neck, she said lightly, "My foot doesn't hurt anymore."

Father began laughing. They were already in the river now. The water came up to Father's neck. Supporting herself on Father's shoulders, Sumei managed to get her face above the water. But her father gently pulled her back into the water. She heard the sound of Sulin's resentful sobbing being carried on the wind along the river. She thought to herself, Is Sulin perhaps jealous of me? She closed her eyes, and in her dream, she drank lots and lots of river water. She felt it was strange that, even with her eyes closed, she could see the blue light in the sky.

The next day, when Sumei woke up, the sun was already shining on the mosquito net.

Sulin stood motionless at the head of the bed watching her. Her face was as fresh as pumpkin blossoms opening in the morning.

"Sumei, you've completely recovered. Get up now and chop grass for the pigs. I've exhausted myself with work the last two days. I need to rest. Yesterday, Little Plum came looking for you. She wanted to take those floral patterns back. Since you were sleeping, I took the key out of your pocket, opened the drawer, and gave them to her. It never occurred to me that, after thinking about it a moment, she would turn around and give the patterns to me. God only knows what she was thinking. But to tell the truth, what good would it be for you to have them? You don't know how to embroider."

"I guess you're right." Sumei's voice was buoyant.

NIGHT IN THE MOUNTAIN VILLAGE

Our home is in Lake District, which was once a lake. Later, people stopped up the lake with dikes. All around, paddy fields stretch to the horizon. The land is fertile, and the rice and rape grow well. We should have had an affluent, peaceful life. Unfortunately, the enclosures built of earth were always giving way. Whenever this happened, our homestead was swallowed up by floodwaters in an instant. As I recall, this terrifying thing occurred every two or three years. Generally, the cresting lasted more than ten days, and Mama grew agitated. She made pancakes from morning to night, the salty sweat dripping from her forehead onto those pancakes. Finally, when all the flour had been made into pancakes, Mama put them into bamboo baskets, shouldered the load, and told my four sisters and me to each pack a suitcase and follow her out. We walked along the dangerous, high embankment. The sun beat down on our heads like a ring of fire, and the vapor from the boundless lake waters braised our heads until we were dizzy. Carrying a roll of cotton wadding, I followed Mama. Behind me were my four unkempt sisters. As I walked, I hallucinated. I felt the bank begin swaying under my feet, and so I screamed, "Help!" The people struggling on the embankment were confused for a moment, but they quickly calmed down and shouted obscenities at me. My face turned red, and tears ran down my face. When Mama saw this, she didn't stop and console me, but just pressed me to walk faster. Usually, we had to walk a whole day before getting out of the floodwaters and coming to the mountain called Seven Monkey Immortals. With the pancakes for sustenance, our whole family had to stay on the mountain for about a week. It was like this every time. When we came to the last of the pancakes, they'd gone completely bad.

Life inside the cave was unbearable. Our work each day was to go out and dig up the weeds for food and collect firewood. Several hundred people lived in this cave. As soon as it was light, we spread out over the mountain like monkeys. When we'd dug up all the edible weeds, we picked leaves. When we'd collected all the dry firewood, we cut down small trees. Every once in a while, we went to the summit to gaze out on the cresting floodwaters. In these dizzying days, I encountered some mountain people. These scary-looking people lived in a col of the mountain. Sometimes they came to the mountain to cut firewood. From their point of view, we plains people were invaders, so when they saw us, they always looked angry.

It's very difficult to describe the appearance of the mountain folk. They're a little like the savages you read about in legends. But they had unusually keen vision: it seemed they could look right through you. In general, they refused to be distracted. After expertly chopping the firewood, they tied it up beautifully with rattan into two bundles, and then sat down for a smoke. It was when they were smoking that I got up my nerve to edge closer to them. Altogether, there were six of those longhaired, long-bearded men sitting in a row on the ground.

"Hullo," I said.

As if they'd heard a signal, they turned toward me in unison. Anger quickly appeared on their faces and their mustaches quivered.

"I, I want to ask directions," I explained as I withdrew.

No one answered me. Their eyelids all drooped. It seemed they wanted to obliterate me from their minds. I heard one of the old ones say, "The waters will begin receding tonight." As I walked away, I looked back and saw that they were still sitting there smoking. Soon, I saw people from Lake District—my hometown. They said I was really gutsy. They'd seen the scene just now while they were hidden in a clump of trees. They'd all thought that I'd purposely tried to get a rise out of the mountain men, and that I was a goner for sure, because a few days ago, someone had died and been thrown into a heap of leaves, his head severed from his body. Later on, Mama came up, too. When she heard what the villagers had to say, she began beating me with a cane. I couldn't stand it, and yelled, "Mama, why not just let me die at the hands of the mountain men? Let me die at the hands of the mountain men!"

As she beat me, Mama said, "No way! No way!"

Later I saw a chance to escape.

Strolling on the mountain, I was thinking resentfully about what had just happened. I thought, violence can't get rid of my curiosity; it can just nurture it. After a few days here, I already knew where the mountain people's village was. The next day, while cutting firewood, I'd go there. From the summit where I was now standing, I saw that everything was a boundless expanse of floodwaters. I couldn't even see that long embankment we had walked along. Floating on the water were some dark specks. I didn't know if they were animals or furniture. They might also be trees or corpses. Even though Mama had spared no effort to deceive me, I still knew that we were running out of pancakes. Yesterday, when my little sister was crying for another one, Mama slapped her face. If the waters didn't recede, what other wonderful way did she have to get us through this difficulty?

This mountain was the only refuge for miles around.

It was said there was a faraway city, where people came and went, and which didn't flood, either, but to get to that place, we'd have to have a boat and we'd have to float on the water for seven days and seven nights before we'd be able to glimpse the high-rises of the city. Those buildings were as high as the mountain. For a seventeen-year-old boy to think of going there was nothing more than a daydream. I don't know why I thought that the mountain people had gone to that place; I'd seen it in their eyes.

When I went back to the cave, Mama had already lit a small fire and was simmering some beans. My eyes brightened, and my stomach began growling with hunger. My oldest little sister told me they'd gleaned the beans from the mountain people's land. They'd already finished harvesting, but they were slipshod about it, and they were also all nearsighted. And so they hadn't picked them clean, thus giving us an unexpected harvest.

"How do you know they're nearsighted?" I asked.

"Everyone says so. Otherwise, why would they live in this mountain col generation after generation? It's just because they can't see well. They really don't know of Lake District, nor do they know of the city. Everything is a blur to them. They even think that this mountain is the only place in the world!"

"You've looked into them really thoroughly," I sneered.

With beans to eat, everyone was in high spirits. All of us sat around the fire. We even ate the pods. Mama told us confidently that she'd also seen some wild vegetables near that place. As soon as it was light the next morning, we'd all go and dig them up.

It was cold in the cave at night. Our worn-out cotton wadding was placed on top of the piled-up twigs and grasses. Everyone slept together. I heard Mama sigh in the dark. Worried by the sound of her voice, I sat up.

"Are you thinking of breaking away from this family?" Mama asked me.

"I want to have a look around and find a way out. Anything wrong with that?"

My voice was filled with complaints and disgust. I knew that my sisters weren't asleep. They were all listening intently. To avoid arguments, I went outside.

The mountain wind was blowing so hard that I got goose pimples. The wind held the smell of lake water. I hadn't walked far when I ran into people from my hometown. They couldn't sleep, either, and had come out for a walk. We'd grown up in the Lake District that stretched to the horizon, and we all had very good eyesight. As long as we had even hazy moonlight, we could easily distinguish the paths. Now, for example, I saw a girl about my age standing in front of me. She was eating something. I couldn't be sure if she was a mountain person or someone from our village, so I walked up closer. When I'd almost reached her, she began tittering and turned to look at me. Actually, she was a lot older than I. Her face was pockmarked.

"How about some melon seeds?" She squeezed toward me with her hands full of them.

"No! No!" I dodged away.

Melon seeds were things that girls ate. I didn't. Now I knew she was a mountain person, but she was different from those mountain men I'd seen. She drew her hand back and snorted arrogantly.

"Coward! Your ma is too strict with you. I've been to your Lake District. That is really a barren land. In a place like that, probably no one loses any sleep."

"It's this wasteland of a mountain that's a barren land!" I flung her words back at her. "Over there, all we have to do is plant seeds and food will grow. We have plenty of food and clothing."

"Let's introduce ourselves. My name is Little Rose."

Looking at her rough, pockmarked face, I could hardly keep from laughing at this name, but I contained myself.

"My name is Long Water."

"That name is really drab. I noticed you a long time ago. You're my Prince Charming. It's a pity that you don't have a good name. Let me choose one for you. From now on, I'll call you Black Bear. How's that? I bet you'll grow up to fit that name."

"Whatever," I said. In fact, I was really pissed that she called me this. And I couldn't call her Little Rose. Privately, I called her Pocky.

Pointing to a turnoff, she said, "Let's take this path. Your mother is looking for you now."

"How do you know I wanna go with you?"

She pushed me hard from behind—pushed me onto the turnoff, and then said, "Because—because I'm the only one in your heart."

I was really pissed off now: she had actually projected her desire onto me, and even said it was my desire. Although this is what I was thinking privately, I couldn't find any reason to brush her off. It seemed as if my feet weren't my own but were being led ahead by her. As we walked into the jungle, the light dimmed. It took a strenuous effort on my part to distinguish the path. I asked Pocky how she could see the path. She said she didn't actually see it: she knew this mountain as well as she knew her own body. She went on to say that in fact we Lake District people didn't have to train our vision. We flattered ourselves in thinking we could see things; in fact, it was merely a false impression. As she talked, she walked faster, but I stumbled and fell behind. If she'd abandoned me then, I'd have been a little concerned, because lots of wild animals roamed this mountain.

We walked quite a ways on the mountainous path and kept ascending, but when we stopped on level ground, I realized that we'd already come down the mountain. This level space was the village's threshing ground. Pocky wanted me to go to her home. I asked if that would be any trouble, and she said as long as I said I was her fiancé, there'd be no trouble. She also said that it was so dark outside that there was no way I could go back: if I entered the mountain, I might run into wild boars, so I'd better just stay at her home.

"How could you turn back at this stage?" she said in an overbearing tone, her breath gushing against my face.

This was a medium-sized village. All the houses were low: if you stretched your hand out, you'd touch the eaves. The whole village was silent now. Even the dogs weren't barking. Only the pigs in their pens were snorting.

While I was still standing between the houses and looking around, a low door suddenly opened, and a hand pulled me in. Before I knew what was happening, I tumbled onto a bed.

"This is my mama. Black Bear, you mustn't make her angry," Pocky said in the dark. "Mama, what do you think of my fiancé?"

"He's too skinny," the old woman said without a trace of politeness. She was sitting to my right. "Also, where are you going to put him? There's only one bed in this house; it can't hold three people. If I had anything to say about it, he'd drown in the floodwaters, too."

Her last words scared the shit out of me. I almost started running away. I heard the old woman groping for firewood; it also seemed she'd knocked something off the windowsill. She was swearing under her breath.

"Rosy, oh Rosy. Couldn't you give me a break? How much are you going to mess up our lives?"

"Mama, how could I hold back when Prince Charming was right in front of me?"

Pocky's voice had turned into a spoiled child's voice. I couldn't help feeling jealous when I recalled my own mama. I also felt a little puzzled: Pocky actually didn't like me at all. Why did she have to talk like this to her mama? It appeared that these mountain people were all really strange; you couldn't look at them the way you looked at your fellow villagers. Just then, I heard a door creak near the bed: mother and daughter had quietly gone out and left me alone in the room. In their pen, the pigs were squealing as if being butchered. Maybe a thief had come to steal the pigs.

I sat there alone for a while, then tried to go outside and take a look. I'd just reached the hallway when mother and daughter both shouted at me to stop and asked me, "Where are you going?" They also blamed me for not doing a good job of guarding their house. "What if a thief had slipped in?" I said I'd been sitting in the dark room and nothing was visible. Even if there'd been a thief, I couldn't have done anything about it. At this, they said in unison that I "had no conscience." As they were talking, a tall man appeared behind them. He was holding a lighter. After striking it several times, it finally caught, and I saw a large mustache. He was stuffing his pipe into his mustache.

"This boy complains that he can't see anything," Pocky said to the man.

"People from over there are all like this." The man stated his conclusion as he smoked his pipe.

I wanted to engage Big Mustache in small talk, but before I'd opened my mouth, Pocky dragged me over to one side, and admonished me under no circumstances to talk nonsense. She also said that her mama had just now agreed that she could take me to get acquainted with the village.

"That man killed an old guy from Lake District." Pocky told me this only after we'd turned off the road.

"Some people say that the old guy was his father. I don't put much stock in this kind of thing. You, for example: it's impossible for you to become one of us. You grumble that our house is too dark."

"If so, why did you still say I was your fiancé?" I interrupted.

"You've been looking down on me after all!" She raised her voice sharply. "If you're so dissatisfied, you do have feet growing on your body: you can just leave! But you won't go. You're afraid there are wild boars in the forest. No. It isn't just this, either. You still intend to thoroughly check us out, so you can go back and brag. You flunky! I'll root the evil out of you."

Pocky said she'd take me to an old guy's home. He was the village head. He usually didn't sleep at night. Whenever villagers felt depressed, they sought him out. Everyone called him Uncle Yuan.

We got there in no time. Uncle Yuan's house was slightly higher than the others, the windows slightly larger, but—like the others—there was no light in the house. It was so dark that if you put your hand out you couldn't see your fingers. After I went in, I heard lots of voices: they were discussing something. When I walked over to them, they stopped talking. I felt them staring at me.

A youthful voice told us to go upstairs. Pocky said it was Uncle Yuan. He pushed me onto a very narrow staircase, and the three of us filed upstairs. The loft was very low. I had to bend to keep my head from bumping into the ceiling. Some chickens being raised in this loft let out squeals of surprise. I guessed they were shut up in a basket. Uncle Yuan pulled me down to sit on a mat. Pocky sat in another corner. My impression was that Uncle Yuan was a young guy. I didn't know why he was thought of as an old geezer.

After sitting there a while, I heard sobbing coming from downstairs. At first it was one person, and then it was a chorus. The sobbing was larded with the sound of sniveling. It seemed they wanted to unburden themselves of an untold number of sorrows. Neither Pocky nor Uncle Yuan said anything. They probably were concentrating on listening. As I went on listening, the sound of sobbing never changed. It was always so grief-stricken and hopeless, but it also lacked any explosiveness. All along, it was so oppressive. Had Uncle Yuan sent me upstairs so that the people below could cry their hearts out? It hadn't occurred to me that these mountain people were so emotional. This probably had something to do with their nearsightedness. My impression of these people was much different from the impression I'd had of the other people in the daytime.

I felt bored after sitting there for a long time, and so I started imagining Pocky's worries. I thought, this ugly girl brought me here to impress me with something novel. The reason she was being so quiet now must be that she was wondering about me, waiting for my questions. If I really did ask questions, she could show off her condescending attitude and lecture me.

Just then, a commotion downstairs interrupted my thoughts. It was as if those people were fighting with clubs. One person yelling "Save me" was about to run up to the loft. When Uncle Yuan heard this, he shouted something I didn't understand at the head of the stairs, so the guy who was halfway up the stairs went back down. I figured they'd leave then. It didn't occur to me that they'd stop fighting and once more sob in unison. This time, it was even more grief-stricken and hopeless. They were also stamping their feet, as if each one were just asking to die sooner. Their voices made the caged chickens jump constantly. My nerves were on edge. I finally asked questions, because if I went on not asking questions, I'd also start crying. I asked Uncle Yuan why the people downstairs were sobbing. He said, "Nights on the mountain are filled with intense emotions. They're summoning the souls of the dead. This is the most active time deep down in the rock formations."

"Can you people see those things?"

"That's a snap for us."

I wanted to ask more, but from her corner Pocky rebuked me unhappily, and said to Uncle Yuan, "Ignore him." Uncle Yuan was quiet for a while, and then crawled over to the chicken cage. When he turned around, he gave me two eggs and told me to crack them open and drink the insides. I did as he said. The eggs tasted great. It had been a long time since I'd eaten anything so good.

Just then, another guy charged upstairs. Uncle Yuan pushed me over and told me to ward him off. I stood there holding onto the railing tightly with both hands. In a moment, I felt that it wasn't just one person charging up the stairs but a powerful army. It was as though my legs had been broken. I involuntarily started falling down the stairs, but not all the way down: I was blocked crosswise on the stairs. Downstairs, it grew silent all of a sudden. It took a lot of effort before I could extricate myself and shout for Uncle Yuan. I shouted and shouted, but no one answered. I pricked up my ears and listened intently: I couldn't even hear the chickens clucking. Holding onto the railing, I gingerly made my way down. When I got to the room downstairs, I groped my way along the wall until I came to the benches where the keening people had just been sitting.

The front door was wide open. There was a little light outside, but you still couldn't see anything well. I didn't know if Uncle Yuan and Pocky were still upstairs or not. I guessed they had probably left from the other side of the attic. I couldn't stand this deathly silence. I wanted to smash something. I felt around, touched a kimchee vat, and threw it to the floor as hard as I could, but it didn't break. The mud floor just made a muffled sound and the salt water flowed everywhere. After throwing the kimchee vat, I was even more terrified; in desperation, I dashed outside.

I groped my way forward between the houses, sometimes touching the low eaves on both sides to keep my balance. The ground was very uneven, as though the bumpiness was manmade. All the doors were tightly closed; no one came out. Later, it seemed to me that I'd walked through almost the whole village and still hadn't run into anyone. I thought I'd go back to the village head's home, but I couldn't find it. And I didn't dare barge into these people's homes. I was afraid they'd think I was a thief. So I just stood like this on the narrow path, one hand touching the thatched rooftop to one side. I took in the night sky, as well as the monsterlike mountain below the night sky.

At this unseemly moment, I recalled Mama. If the water never receded, Mama and my four sisters would be trapped. Second Sister had gotten a stomachache from eating too many fruits and wild vegetables yesterday: she'd been in so much pain that she'd rolled around on the ground.

If the water did recede, we'd have to rebuild our house—plait the wall from thin bamboo strips, paste fresh cow dung onto it, and transport straw from far away to place on the roof. If the house had already collapsed, it would be even more trouble. I don't know why when I thought of these things it was as if I were thinking of someone else's problems: I was neither pissed off nor self-pitying. I thought these things were related only to that me of the past. I didn't know what this me of the present was all about. I was seventeen, and I'd never been to such a strange place before. The people here spoke the same language as I did, but it was almost impossible to understand them. Their innermost anguish also scared me and made me think that a disaster would soon befall the world. Still, I was inexplicably fascinated. I'd come here with the thought of finding a way out: now, though, I'd already flung the issue of a "way out" out of my mind. After listening to that keening just now, I knew that the mountain people didn't embrace any hope for the future. Just think: would any Lake District family raise chickens in the loft?

Just as I was woolgathering, a little kid tugged at my clothes. A boy.

"Black Bear, Uncle Yuan wants you to go home with me to help my grandpa take a bath." He said loud and clear, "Don't prop up our roof with your hands. The house could collapse. You're too tall for your own good."

The little kid said his name was Mother Hen. His family lived close to the highway. He walked fast, leaping along, leaving me in the dust. Whenever I shouted, "Mother Hen! Mother Hen!" he turned around and said my "stalling for time" was really annoying. We finally arrived.

Bending over, I followed him into the low house. I heard him split-ting firewood. He lit a small kerosene lamp. He said that the village head had told him he had to light a lamp as a favor to me. Holding the lamp high, he approached a bed. I saw the old guy lying on the tattered wadding. He was groaning and struggling like an injured mantis. His grandson patiently held the lamp up high. Several times, it seemed as though he wanted to sit up, but each time he fell back on the bed with a thump and then renewed the struggle. I said to Mother Hen, "Let me hold the lamp while you heat water for your grandpa's bath." Mother Hen sniffed at my idea.

"Heat the water? You moron. We all take baths in cold water."

His grandpa slumped back again and began weeping hopelessly. Without saying a word, Mother Hen held the lamp up. I was going to go over and support the old man, but Mother Hen fiercely held me fast and said I would "scare his grandpa to death." I had to retreat and wait obediently beside the bed.

"Who's here?" the old man wheezed.

"A young man. He's come to help you take a bath," his grandson answered.

"Tell him to leave. I can take a bath by myself."

Mother Hen indicated that I should go over to the door. He and I both retreated to the door, and he said softly, "Grandpa has a strong sense of self-respect. We need to be rather patient."

After struggling for a while, the old man actually moved his legs down from the bed. Holding the bedposts for support, he stood up, quivering and towering. Mother Hen joyfully cheered his grandpa, but didn't do anything. He just let the old man stand there pitifully. I couldn't go on watching. I asked Mother Hen where the basin was. He answered impatiently that it was outside the door. Then he con-tinued cheering his grandpa, shouting, "One, two, three, four . . ."

Outside the door was a well. Groping in the dark, I drew two buckets of water from the well and poured them into the basin. I shouted for Mother Hen to help me carry it into the house. He came out with poor grace, grumbling that I was useless. I couldn't even carry a basin of water. We put the basin of water in the middle of the room. Mother Hen undressed his grandpa. With arms like a marionette, the old man tried to break loose from his grandson and howled like a wolf. But when all is said and done, he was decrepit. He wasn't the least bit strong. His grandson quickly undressed him. In the faint lamplight, his body looked strange: it wasn't at all like a human body. He didn't have any muscles, and his body was creased

357

with wrinkles. His old dark skin adhered to his frame. If I hadn't heard him talk, I'd have been freaked out by now. Mother Hen swiftly hauled him into the water basin, where he sat down. He ordered me to start giving him a bath.

The water was cold, and the old man was crying sorrowfully. When I washed his neck with a washcloth, he cussed me out bitterly. He said I was too heavy-handed. It would be better if he washed himself. I noticed that he wasn't at all afraid of the cold. Maybe he'd been numb for a long time. He was terribly dirty. It was impossible to think that one basin of water could get him completely clean. I suggested to Mother Hen, who was standing there holding the lamp, that we change the water. He said that wouldn't work, because "Grandpa has a strong sense of self-respect." All I could do was help the old man stand up and hurriedly dry him off. I wanted to get him dressed, but he held me off with his arms. He said I hadn't gotten him clean. I'd just tricked him. As he was talking, he sat down in the basin again. I had to wash him again with the filthy water. This time, he seemed more or less satisfied. He didn't cuss me out again, nor did he cry. He sat in the water with his eyes closed. Because he'd been sitting in the cold water too long, he started sneezing. I urged him to stand up and let me help dry him off. He refused, saying the towel was too filthy and it would make his washed-clean body dirty.

Just then, Mother Hen said from the sidelines that his grandpa was hallucinating. I waited a long time, but the old man was still stubbornly sitting in the water. It took all my strength to prop him up. He was crying sorrowfully in a loud voice. All of a sudden, he broke loose from me with strength I didn't know he had and threw himself onto the pile of tattered wadding on the bed. His body dripping wet, he fell into the cotton wadding. I sighed with relief, and Mother Hen and I emptied the dirty water from the wooden basin. When I came back inside, I suggested that we help his grandpa get dressed, but Mother Hen said coldly, "Mind your own business."

It was as if Mother Hen had changed into another person. He didn't pay any more attention to me. He marched over and extinguished the kerosene lamp.

Once more, I couldn't see a thing. The old man was still crying on the pile of tattered wadding in the bed. As he cried, he poured out the miseries of his life: he was so old and yet he had to endure such suffering. Over and over, he said, "Why can't I die?" I was standing bent over against the door frame, my eyes fighting to stay open. I thought to myself that it must be almost daylight.

Just then, I smelled the aroma of smoke. It was Mother Hen lighting a fire in the stove. I couldn't help respecting this little boy. He was probably only about ten years old, but he was shouldering the heavy burden of caring for his sick grandpa alone. How could he bear it? He was also so composed in all his movements. Following the aroma of smoke, I felt my way to the kitchen and saw that Mother Hen was conquering the damp firewood with a thick blow tube. He sat on the floor, absorbed in the task. He was skillful at lighting the fire. When the fire was blazing, he stood up and added water to a large iron pot. He was cooking something in that pot.

"You, Black Bear, you can't do anything. When the village head handed you over to me to take charge of, I knew my work wouldn't be light."

Manipulating the cooking paddle in his hand, he talked arrogantly. I was jealous of him. Such a little child—yet he was in the dominant position. He could look down from on high and tell me what to do.

He told me to sit down on the floor with him and began probing into the details of my arrival in the village. When I mentioned Pocky, he interrupted and said her name was Rosy. He went on to say that he really wasn't interested in listening to me talk of her. I shouldn't have looked for her in the beginning. If he'd known earlier that I'd found her, he wouldn't have agreed to take me under his wing. His face looked very serious in the firelight. He even looked a little indignant. I sort of regretted mentioning Pocky.

"They don't even cook at home. At mealtime, they go to other people's homes and cheat them out of food. They also took advantage of me and took my food by force."

I apologized to him repeatedly. He wanted me to guarantee that I wouldn't pay any attention to that family anymore. If I ran into them on the street, I had to look down and pretend I hadn't seen them. As we were talking, the food in the pot finished cooking. Mother Hen ran over and bolted the door. He said that we had to eat fast; otherwise, someone would break in and steal our food. We stood beside the pot, each of us holding a large bowl and drinking this stew. There seemed to be rice bran, kidney beans, and something like taro in it. It was hot and scalded our tongues. I hadn't eaten a real meal like this for a long time.

I asked Mother Hen if his grandpa was going to eat with us. He muttered that his grandpa had a strong sense of self-respect: he didn't want other people to see what he looked like while eating. With that, he filled a bowl and took it to his grandpa's room. The fire had already gone out, and the kitchen turned dark again. It must still be the middle of the night: why were we eating breakfast? In the room over there, Mother Hen coaxed his grandpa to eat. He kept talking tenderly. It was hard to understand his attitude toward his grandpa. It seemed that I couldn't understand even one mountain child, much less the other people of the mountain.

After feeding his grandpa, Mother Hen came back to the kitchen. Then he washed the dishes. I considered helping him, but I couldn't because I couldn't see anything. I heard him sigh like an adult and say, "Grandpa—you know, he is exuviating."

"What on earth?"

"Molting. When he's in bed, he's always thinking about shedding his skin. Every morning, he tells me that he's a different person. In the evening, he sobs again and says he's going to shed a layer of skin. Listen: Rosy and her mama are beating on our door. These two bad eggs don't raise any food. They specialize in eating other people's food. My parents live on the summit. Right after I was born, they gave me to Grandpa. It was lucky they did; how else would I have been able to get such good training? Now you've come, and I have even more to do. I was born to a life of hard work."

His adult tone of voice made me chuckle. I asked why it wasn't light since it was already morning. He replied that the mountain blocked the rays of light: it wouldn't be light until afternoon. After putting the bowls away deftly, he swept the kitchen. Then he sat down next to me again and rested his head on my leg. Whispering that he was exhausted, he soon dozed off. Just then, a dark figure appeared at the kitchen door: it shouted miserably, "Ah, Mother Hen!"

It was his grandpa. The old man had actually gotten out of bed. Mother Hen was dead to the world. The old man shouted again. The sound was like a saw slicing through nerves; it made me think he was about to die. Then I heard him fall with a thump. I pushed Mother Hen hard, but he still didn't wake up. All I could do was put him on the floor and get up to help the old man.

The old man who'd collapsed at the kitchen door wasn't dead. He was naked, and his chest was rising and falling strongly. I lifted his upper body, intending to put him back to bed. He was resisting feebly. A wave of nausea came over me. Finally, I did carry him back to bed. When I covered him with the tattered wadding, he suddenly whispered to me, "I was a worker at an oil press factory in Lake District." Then he was quiet again. I thought, Perhaps he's finished molting. After settling him in, I was wiped out and decided to fall into the bed and sleep for a while. As best I could, I lay down on the edge of the bed, but the old man still detected me. He was very displeased and kept kicking me in the back. I put up with his kicks, sometimes sleeping and sometimes waking. In my dreams, I had just walked to a well when Mother Hen woke me up with his bellowing.

"This is my grandpa's bed. How can you lie in it? Ah. My grandpa will start crying again. When he cries, I won't be able to get anything done! You beggar from Lake District. I really shouldn't have let you stay!"

I explained that I wasn't a beggar. In Lake District, I had a mama and a family; we had ample food and clothing. If it wasn't for the flood, I'd never have come to this place. As I talked, I wasn't sure of what I said. After just one day, I already felt my previous life wasn't real. I was imagining a boundless flood, and I became deeply suspicious of everything under the water. Could everything still go back to the way it was? Even if it could, could I still go on like that? I didn't know why: I was growing more and more certain that Mama and my sisters would die in that cave.

Mother Hen was still lighting into me, but the door was pushed open from the outside. It wasn't Pocky who came in, but the village head, Uncle Yuan, and a young person.

"Did you have your bath? Are you clean?" Uncle Yuan shouted.

At that, Mother Hen's grandpa groaned grievously in the tattered wadding.

"The old man is worried." Uncle Yuan bowed in his direction. "What did you say? His hand is heavy . . . and he doesn't treat you with respect! Ha ha. These people from Lake District are all like this! You mustn't mind. He's also struggling with you for the bed. . . . Let him sleep in one corner. This bed is very wide! Mother Hen! Mother Hen!"

Mother Hen walked up.

"Be a good mentor to Black Bear. This poor guy can't go home anymore."

"I'll train him until he's as industrious as I am," Hen said seriously.

Uncle Yuan couldn't keep from laughing and praising Mother Hen. I quietly asked the lad with Uncle Yuan why Uncle Yuan had said I "couldn't go home." The lad taunted me, "That's because your wonderful villagers headed west yesterday. They decided very quickly to abandon their homesteads."

361

When Uncle Yuan heard the young man say this, he turned around and admonished me not to lose heart. He went on, "Men can survive anywhere in the world. Does it have to be your old home village?" Then he praised me for adapting and being a quick learner.

For the moment, I couldn't make any response to the news they'd brought. I just stood there dumbfounded. Maybe encouraged by the presence of so many people, Mother Hen's grandpa told Uncle Yuan about me: he said that just now I'd carried him as if carrying a load of firewood—carried him to the bed and thrown him down there. The rough treatment had almost broken his ribs. He was stuttering and actually wanted Uncle Yuan to help him up so that he could demonstrate what had happened. Bending down, Uncle Yuan softly and gently urged him to be patient, because "everything is difficult in the beginning." While the two of them were talking, although Mother Hen and the young person were quiet, I felt that they were both rebuking me with their stares. Their attitude made me really feel guilty.

I was like a stupid clod. I couldn't do anything right, and couldn't learn, either. I was just a heavy burden for all of them. My sixteen years of life at Lake District had been for nothing. At the same time I was feeling guilty, I also felt rather indignant: I really just wanted to get out of there, but where would I go? It was obvious that no one in this village would have a different opinion of me. I knew that already from experiences here. I didn't quite believe that Mama and the others would have left me and gone to the west. I was her eldest son—the family's main worker. Even though they might still survive if they moved far away without me, that wasn't the way she usually operated. I thought she must be waiting in the cave: even if all the others left, she'd still be there. But this would be dangerous for them. If they stayed in the cave, they might all starve to death. At this point in my thinking, I acted impulsively and slipped quietly toward the door. Mother Hen woke up in a panic, and said loudly, "Look: he's running off!"

At that, the young person shot to the door like an arrow and stopped me. He said, "So you still don't believe me. You're so mixed up. See here, this is your teapot. Before she left, your mother asked me to bring it to you. I brought a message from her, too—'If you can't go on living, you should die away from home.'"

Touching the little clay pot, I didn't understand Mother anymore at all. Did everyone who came to this demonic mountain become abnormal? If she'd had this idea of abandoning me from the

Can Xue

beginning, then why did she have to beat me that one time? Mother was neither muscular nor strapping, but she had hit me vigorously with the club.

The old man in bed said something again. He seemed to be criticizing me for being flighty. He also cried and said, "He always disappoints me. He didn't satisfy me even once." As soon as he cried, the three of them leaned over the bed and consoled and massaged him. The scene made me want to crawl into a hole. Mother's attitude made me realize that my sixteen years had truly been lived in vain. That must be so—even if I wasn't fully convinced. In this torture-like instant, I suddenly thought of Mother Hen's grandpa shedding his skin. I couldn't help saying, "I want to shed my skin, too! I want to shed my skin. . . ."

At first, they were amazed; then they began laughing in unison. Uncle Yuan stopped laughing right away, and said, "Don't dash cold water on this commendable enthusiasm." He turned around and hugged me and said affectionately, "You need to keep your temper in check. After a while, Rosy will come to take you away. She's a beautiful young girl with lofty aspirations. If you're with her, you'll make progress day by day."

After coaxing Mother Hen's grandpa into going to sleep, they surrounded me. They wanted me to take out the clay pot for them to admire. They passed it around from one to the other, but they didn't give their opinions. Even Mother Hen didn't utter a word. He just brought the pot to his ear and listened. Then Uncle Yuan asked me if I'd already made up my mind to stay in the village. When I said yes, he sighed and gave the clay pot back to me. Reaching a decision, the three of them left. Just as he was leaving, Uncle Yuan told me to wait in the house.

There was a foul smell in the house. Mother Hen's grandpa was always talking fiercely in his sleep. I felt my way to the kitchen and sat down. I put the clay pot in the cupboard and groped around in the kitchen. I discovered that there was a large pile of grasses—used for kindling—next to the stove. It was fluffy and soft. I fell onto the grasses, thinking I'd have a good sleep, but my plan quickly went by the boards. The old man began to shout himself hoarse with crying. The sound was so loud that probably everyone for several miles around could hear him. With bad grace, I felt my way back to the side of his bed. As soon as he saw me, he stopped crying. Sniffling, he asked me why I sometimes struggled with him for the bedding and sometimes left him all alone. Did I want to trick him? Then he said something obscure. Through his sobs, he repeated what he'd said. Since I couldn't hear him clearly, I took my shoes off, felt my way into the middle of the large bed, and drew close to him to listen. Then I could finally hear him. What he said was, "You have to stay with me."

Since I was lying down on the filthy bed, he seemed discontented. He angrily complained that I hogged too much of the bed, and that what he'd meant before wasn't that I should get into the bed, but just that I should keep watch over him. A person who was dying, as he was, certainly didn't want someone else in bed with him. I ignored him and lay there sleepily. Then he kicked me, propped himself up, and swatted me in the face with his withered hand. He kept stuttering, "Are you going to get down or not? Are you going to get down or not?" Neither resisting nor withdrawing, I dozed off on the bed. He was tired out from struggling and slumped back with a thump. He was still cursing. I slept a long time this time.

When I woke up, it was already light. I slowly swept my eyes over the room. I was filled with amazement at the crude, rundown nature of this place: the walls were exposed adobe—jet-black from the soot of the firewood and caved in in lots of spots. The grasses on the roof were all waterlogged. In several places, the light came through. Except for the wood-plank bed, there was no furniture in the house. Behind the door were several kinds of farm implements. The so-called bedding was simply a heap of smelly garbage—pieces of dirty tattered wadding held together by some yarn. Burrowed under this pile of garbage, Mother Hen's grandpa was still sleeping, one leg outside the covers. On that leg were several large infected sores. I jumped out of bed, because if I'd stayed there any longer, I'd have puked. As I was bending over to tie my shoelaces, Pocky came in. Only then did I remember that I hadn't locked the door before going to sleep. I asked her warily what was up. Squinting at me, she said in a contemptuous tone, "So Uncle Yuan arranged for you to stay in this sort of home."

"What's wrong with this sort of home? Don't you come here often to scrounge a meal?" I said sarcastically.

"That twerp has given me a bad name everywhere. I'll break his legs."

In a single movement, Pocky sat down on the bed and patted Mother Hen's grandpa's leg. She made quite an uproar. "Look, just look, at how thin he's become—all because that evil kid kept some of his food and starved Grandpa to this point! He's a bloody little hoodlum!"

I was puzzled: how come none of them thought this house was dirty? Pocky not only didn't think it was dirty, she even knelt on the bed and tidied the tattered wadding and bits of cloth. She stirred things up so much that soot covered everything. I coughed several times in a row. After she was finished putting things in order, she also brought a small whisk broom from the kitchen and swatted the bed with it. She said she was "whisking the soot." With that, my best option was to escape and stand outside. She didn't think anything of that thick dust. And Mother Hen's grandpa was still asleep. Thinking back on the attitude the village head and the others had toward the old man, I was certain that all the villagers respected him. Finally, Pocky finished cleaning the house. She came outside, brushing the dust off her clothes with a colorful cloth. She said she wanted to take me to see some great fun on the summit. She urged me to get a move on; otherwise, it would soon be dark. And as soon as it was dark, I—this guy from Lake District—would be blind.

She pushed me out of the small house, and as we threaded our way between the eaves, I saw some people in small groups talking about something in the alley. Their appearances all fit the stereotype of wild men. By comparison, Pocky actually was the best-looking person among the mountain people. What did Uncle Yuan look like? I couldn't remember. As soon as those people standing on the road saw us, they retreated into their houses. They didn't forget to close their doors either. Pocky lifted her head arrogantly and said to me, "These people are jealous of me." This had begun the day before. They didn't like Lake District people, but when they had heard that she'd found a young guy from Lake District to be her fiancé, they were rather jealous of the person she'd found and wished they could take his place. I didn't quite buy this. I thought she was bragging, but I didn't care. I wished she would be a little quicker about taking me to the summit. When we reached the summit, maybe I could figure out a lot of things. But she began dillydallying. She said she wanted to go back and say good-bye to her mama. She actually said "good-bye." It was really funny. I thought she wanted to go home, but she didn't go. She stood where she was, deep in thought. I couldn't help but urge her. She criticized me, "What's the big hurry?" So we just walked in fits and starts. It was a long time before we finally reached the mountaintop.

Looking down from the summit, I saw this scene: the floodwaters had already receded, but that long embankment we'd walked on was already gone. Those Lake District houses inside the embankment had also disappeared. At a glance, I saw that the flat earth had only low-lying water reflecting light. Looking to the west, I saw a large crowd of people moving like ants. I watched excitedly, but they quickly vanished into the distant mist. On the west side, everything was divided into square paddy fields, just like what one would see in a dream.

"You can't catch up with them—it's too late," Pocky said. She'd no sooner said this than the sky darkened.

Holding my hand, Pocky ran down the mountain. I couldn't see anything in the dark. I had to follow her. Her sweaty hand was disgusting. Gasping for breath, she said we had to run without stopping. The wild boars on the mountain frequently attacked people. When we were roughly at the middle of the mountain, I heard someone talking ahead of us. I thought, Could there still be some people in the cave who didn't leave? I flung off her hand and felt my way toward the place where the voices had come from. After a while, I smelled the aroma of tobacco: it was exactly the kind the Lake District people smoked. Just ahead, in a small clearing, were three people's figures. They were arguing about something. Then it seemed they reached a consensus. I just saw the one who was a little shorter raise a knife and hack ferociously at another person. Because he exerted himself so much, he fell onto the ground as well.

Then the skinny one plunged a spear into the short one's back. Not until that person was no longer moving did the skinny one pull it out and sit down for a smoke. He seemed to be waiting for someone. After smoking for a while, he looked in all directions. Pocky said to me, "This person is waiting for me to help him." This scared me so much I wanted to run away then and there. Grabbing my hand, she led me off. At the sound we made, that person spun around and chased us. Several times, I thought he'd quickly overtake us, but each time he stopped and waited for us to run a little farther. Then he continued chasing us. He also flung the spear at a large tree trunk ahead of us. I was scared out of my wits.

The person chased us straight to the entrance to the village. I heard him stop and shout, "Long Water! Long Water! You beast! You killed your mama!"

He shouted time after time. The villagers all came out. Even though I couldn't see them well, I knew they could all see me. I wished so much that Pocky would hide me, but she was strutting arrogantly on ahead of me and deliberately striking up conversations with the people, as though she wanted to exhibit my wretched appearance to all of them. The people were all talking about me: they said I'd "only fled after committing a crime." Pocky said to her neighbors that I was now her bodyguard. "I picked him up because of his brutality," she said.

After showing me off, Pocky finally led me into her small house. When we went in, her mother was groaning in bed. Then she propped herself up, and then—just like the last time—she went over to the windowsill to look for matches. This time, she found a match, but it was damp. No matter how she struck it, it didn't light. She was so angry that she threw the box of matches on the ground and stomped on it several times. Then she said, "I wanted to get a good look at this guy in the light. It seems I can't. You've brought this sort of person back, but how are we going to deal with him? He isn't a teacup that can be put on the table."

"You can just act as if he isn't here."

"Not here! Do you mean to say that he won't take up any space in this house?"

"Sure, Mama, sure. I'll make him burrow into the heap of kindling in the kitchen. Please don't piss him off. If you do, how will I have the face to look people in the eye?" Pocky was extremely agitated.

As the old woman moaned and groaned and complained, she went back to bed again. It seemed she was in pain all over. Pocky quietly told me that the older villagers were all like this. By comparison, her mother was in good health. She also said that my top priority right then was to hide in the pile of kindling in the kitchen. "Don't let Mama hear any activity—her nerves couldn't take it," she said. I asked her where the kitchen was. She said, "Right here. We have just one room. The stove is at one side." Following her, I groped my way. Sure enough, I felt my way to the stove. I thought uneasily, since I was in the same room, how could I be inaudible? In fact, there wasn't a pile of firewood next to the stove. There was just some rubble. I recalled what Mother Hen had told me: he'd said that this mother and daughter never cooked. Day after day, they cadged food from others.

"This isn't a bad spot. You can have a good sleep in the kindling. You need to think everything through. Don't complain. People can come into this village, but no one leaves afterward. You've come to our village. You can't leave. That guy who lit into you just now was very smart, because he stopped at the entrance to the village and didn't step in."

I shifted the rubble, swept out a flat spot, and sat down. Pocky seemed to have found some pity for me. She squeezed into the corner and sat down with me. Although she told others that I was her fiancé, I could see that she didn't have the slightest interest in me. It was obvious: I wasn't her type at all, but why did she want to say I was? She sat beside me, her hands hugging her knees. I thought her expression must be serious. Just then, I started feeling hungry: I was dizzy with hunger. I told her this, and she laughed and asked why I hadn't said so earlier. She got something from the stove and gave it to me. A bowl of cold rice. And a pair of chopsticks.

She whispered to me, "Take it slowly. Don't let Mama hear you." Shoveling the rice into my mouth with the chopsticks, I restrained myself with all my might to keep from making a sound. Not until I'd polished off the rice did it occur to me that Pocky had also gone without food that night. I asked her quietly, and she said that was right, she hadn't had anything to eat, because she'd given her own rice to me. But it didn't matter—she wouldn't starve. Sometimes she was actually so hungry she couldn't stand it and went to Uncle Yuan's second floor and grabbed a couple of eggs to stave off her hunger. Perhaps her mama had heard our whispers, for she began fidgeting in bed and threw something like a pillow down to the ground. We stopped talking at once, and I marveled at the old woman's sense of hearing.

After I'd been sitting on the floor for a long time, my rear end was numb and sore. I began shifting restlessly. I looked at her: she was absolutely still and sitting bolt upright. In a flash, I realized how wretched I was. Plagued by this thought, I was looking for an escape hatch. Finally, I stood up and stretched a few times. Heedless of everything, I walked to the door and quietly opened it. Immediately, a storm swept through the house: the mother was pounding the bed boards for all she was worth. She shouted, "Ah! Ah! He's going to murder me! Save me!! Uncle Yuan! Uncle Yuan!!"

Pocky jumped up and held her mother in her arms. The two of them rolled around on the bed. I was panic-stricken by the extent of the old woman's strength as she struggled mightily to break free. She actually broke the bed's headboard with her kicking. The pillow and quilt flew to the floor. As I saw the terrible trouble I'd just caused, I wanted even more to sneak away. Pocky stopped me with a stern shout. She said I shouldn't even think of making a move. After several attempts she finally brought her mother under control. The two of them lay on the bed, gasping for breath.

A long time passed before the old woman finally broke her silence. She said resentfully, "OK. Let this bad boy stay. If you weren't my daughter, I'd break your neck, just the same as I did away with that wolf cub not long ago."

Pocky got out of bed. Taking my hand, she wanted me to go with her to the pigpen to "avoid upsetting Mama."

Once outside, we turned and went up several flights of stone steps into the pigpen. The two pigs began making a hubbub with their snorts. She asked me to sit with her on a pile of straw. Outside, the moon had already come out, its silver rays flashing. Sitting here, we could unexpectedly see the entire village. I thought this place was wonderful, and I thought to myself that I wouldn't think again of leaving. She was uncomfortable, though: she was worrying about her mama. She also said the pig shit was much too stinky. She'd never thought she would be disgraced to the point that she could only stay in this sort of place.

"Before you came, Mama and I were always very close," she said haughtily.

As I sat comfortably on the straw, admiring the beauty of the mountain village, I recalled the days at Lake District and the enigma of my family. And also for the first time in a long time, I recalled my father, who had drowned in the lake. Father had drowned while fishing. An eyewitness had said the boat had definitely not capsized. It was Father's impatience: he had to wrestle with the large fish he had speared. He'd jumped into the lake and hadn't come out. Afterward, his corpse hadn't floated up, either. I also thought back on those mudholes I'd seen this afternoon from the summit: they used to be my homestead. In no time, it had ceased to exist.

But now, I didn't feel at all sentimental. I was sinking into a humongous shadow, in which life was brand-new and I was completely unable to understand. I thought I would certainly become an industrious mountain man. After several more years, I would have the same piercing, penetrating eyes that they had. And I'd also be accustomed to distinguishing everything in the dark. As I was thinking these thoughts, I also felt a spark flickering in my heart: it was the first time since I'd come to the village that I'd felt a faint sympathetic response to this homely girl beside me. I didn't know what kind of sympathy this was. I thought I'd eventually figure it out.

From Nursery Rhymes
Stéphane Mallarmé

Translated from French with a preface by John Ashbery

PREFACE

FROM ABOUT 1879 TO 1881, Stéphane Mallarmé began to compile a textbook for young students of English comprised of 141 English nursery rhymes, each meant to be followed by the poet's own prose translation and notes on the vocabulary and grammatical constructions used in the verses. These exercises had been mentioned by some of his former pupils, but the incomplete manuscript was unknown until it was discovered and published in 1964 by the Mallarmé scholar Carl Paul Barbier.

The nursery-rhyme project was only one of a number of similar schemes with which Mallarmé sought to eke out his meager salary as a teacher at the lycée Fontanes in Paris. His *English Words* was published in 1878; other books, paid for by the publisher but not printed, were *What Is English, The Beauties of English Prose and Rhyme, New English Mercantile Correspondence* (!), and *English Themes.* The last was eventually published in 1937, with a preface by Paul Valéry. Mallarmé's superiors at the lycée seemed unimpressed by his poetry, such as *L'Après-midi d'un faune.* One inspector wrote: "This professor busies himself with things other than his teaching and his pupils. . . . Those who have read the strange lucubrations emanating from the brain of M. Mallarmé should be surprised that he occupies a chair at the lycée Fontanes."

But his academic work with nursery rhymes failed to reassure them. During the winter of 1880 the inspector called again while Mallarmé was explicating his theme (Lesson No. 43) based on this rhyme: "Liar, liar, lick spit; / Your tongue shall be slit, / And all the dogs in the town / Shall have a little bit." "Since M. Mallarmé remains professor of English at the lycée Fontanes," noted the inspector, "let him learn English . . . and refrain from dictating to his students such foolishness as this: 'Liar, swallow your saliva, and the liar has more saliva than anyone, because of the numerous words he must utter to avoid speaking the truth. Although his tongue is

370

already forked like a viper's, because he often speaks evil of others, it will be further cut up into little bits and every dog in the town will get one.' One is tempted to ask if one is in the presence of a lunatic."

Today, of course, no one is concerned about Mallarmé's effectiveness as a pedagogue. What might matter to us with regard to these long-forgotten exercises is the brilliant fragments of prose poetry resulting from his sometimes straightforward, sometimes fanciful translations of the nursery rhymes. He was trying by various means to interest French boys of twelve in material that English children of five or six would have already assimilated. So his narratives can take on strange hues, as in the example above. He was also aiming to instill bourgeois morality into his charges (his living depended on it); some of the themes suffer from his arch attempts to do so.

The most successful ones seem to announce motifs that will be developed later on in his poetry, and they are as electrifying as the magic-lantern images of Golo and Geneviève de Brabant were for the young Marcel in *À la recherche du temps perdu*. Is the "book" in Lesson 32 a precursor of Mallarmé's own posthumously published *Livre?* The nursery rhyme goes: "When the book's in the press, no man can it read." The poet qualifies: "The book I was promised is still in the press.—Thus, no one could read it." Fabulous and fabulously unreadable, like the book still in the press, *Le Livre* embodies Mallarmé's explosive aesthetic ideal pushed to its furthest limit, which curiously resembles the unfettered imagination of childhood.

Note: The English texts of the nursery rhymes printed here are reproduced as they were in Mallarmé's written draft; he used various contemporary English anthologies, such as those illustrated by Kate Greenaway, Randolph Caldecott, and Walter Crane (*Baby's Bouquet*). For obvious reasons, I haven't reproduced his questions on grammar and vocabulary in the cases where they exist. I am indebted to Carl Paul Barbier's introduction to the *Recueil de "Nursery Rhymes"* (Paris, Gallimard, 1964) for information in this text.

Stéphane Mallarmé

LESSON NO. 4

Little Tom Tittmouse,
Lived in a bell-house;
The bell-house broke,
And Tom Tittmouse woke.

THEME

How deeply you sleep; a rat could gnaw your clothes and your books and not wake you. You're like young Tittmouse.—Oh? I never heard tell of him.—The one who lived in a belfry . . . —What became of him? The belfry fell down and Tom Tittmouse woke up on the grass of the village green, crying: "It must be very early, I don't hear the bell!"

LESSON NO. 5

I.

Who killed Cock Robin?
I said the Sparrow,
With my bow and arrow,
I killed Cock Robin.

Who saw him die?
I, said the Fly,
With my little eye,
And I saw him die.

THEME

Who saw Cock Robin die?—Me.—Who?—The Fly.—How?—With my little eye.—Well, then! Who killed him?—I don't know, I only saw him die, wounded by an arrow.—Then it's you, Sparrow, with your bow?—I tell the truth, answers the Sparrow, I killed your Cock Robin.

LESSON NO. 6

II.

Who caught his blood?
I, said the Fish,
With my little dish,
And I caught his blood.

Who made his shroud?
I, said the Beadle,
With my little needle,
And I made his shroud.

THEME

—But I wasn't the only one (the Sparrow continues), for here is the Fish, who took the blood of poor Cock Robin.—You—Yes, me, in my little dish.

We must make a shroud; who has a little needle? The Beadle says: "Me! Here is some gossamer on the tall grasses. I'll make the shroud."

LESSON NO. 7

III.

Who'll be the parson?
I, said the Rook,
With my little book,
And I'll be the parson.

Who'll be the clerk?
I, said the Lark,
If 'tis not in the dark,
And I'll be the clerk.

THEME

—But there's no parson? Here I am, me, the Rook, with my little book under my wing; if you wish, I'll be the parson. My clerk? It's the Lark, if it's not during the hours of darkness, for she sleeps then. Well, in broad daylight she seems much too merry to accomplish that mournful task.

LESSON NO. 8

IV.

Who'll carry him to the grave?
I, said the Kite,
If 'tis not in the night.
And I'll carry him to his grave.

Who'll carry him the link?
I, said the Linnet.
I'll fetch it in a minute,
And I'll carry him the link.

THEME

The Kite says: If it's not at night, then I'll help too (since if it was night, I couldn't see where I was flying), I'll carry Redbreast to earth, to his tomb at the foot of a tree. The torch—what torch? There isn't any.—I'll go get one, says the Linnet, and I'll bring it; and back he came in a minute, carrying a yellow cowslip.

LESSON NO. 9

V.

Who'll be the chief mourner?
I, said the Dove,
I mourn for my love,
And I'll be chief mourner.

Who'll bear the pall?
We, said the Wren,
Both the cock and the hen,
And we'll bear the pall.

THEME

—Chief mourner, draw near.—The Dove arrives. Even when I'm not mourning my friend, I weep all alone, she says.—Good, you'll be a fine chief mourner. The pall is big, made of a sycamore leaf. Two relations will bear it, male and female; who shall they be? We, say the Wrens.

Stéphane Mallarmé

LESSON. NO. 10

VI.

Who'll sing a psalm?
I, said the Thrush,
As she set in a bush,
And I'll sing a psalm.

And who'll toll the bell?
I, said the Bull,
Because I can pull:
and so, Cock Robin, farewell.

All the birds in the air
Fell to sighing and sobbing
When they heard the bell toll
For poor Cock Robin.

THEME

—The Thrush, perched in a bush, sings a psalm as the procession passes by, and the church bell is heard. Who is tolling? The Bull, for only he can pull the rope. This bell says, "And so, Cock Robin, farewell." All the birds of the fields and the woods arrive on hearing these words that only they can understand; and a thousand creatures join in, and those who don't sob are sighing.

LESSON NO. 11

I.

I saw a ship a-sailing
A-sailing on the sea;
And O! it was all laden
With pretty things for thee.

THEME

What a beautiful ship!—I don't see it,—A ship, sailing on the sea.— Mama, do you think it's laden with pretty things for me? Candies, especially? Perhaps.—I still haven't seen it. Close your eyes and listen to me singing, then you'll see it, along with everything it contains.

375

Stéphane Mallarmé

LESSON NO. 12

II.

There were comfits in the cabin
And apples in the hold;
The sails were made of silk
And the masts were made of gold!

THEME

I know of one, a pretty ship that had jam in the cabin.—Which kinds, pear, cherry, or strawberry?—All of them, but listen: there were sugar apples in the hold. As for the masts, they were just made of gold, and the sails were of silk, but that can't be eaten, you greedy little thing.

LESSON NO. 13

III.

The four and twenty sailors,
That stood between the decks;
Were four and twenty white mice,
With chains about their necks.

THEME

I like candies, but I like toys too; and more than anything, I like little live animals, and sharing my sweet treats with them.—Then I'll tell you that the sailors, lined up on deck, were white mice.—Oh! How pretty it is! How many of them were there?—Twenty-four.—If I had them they would run away.—No, for the song goes on to say they all had chains around their necks.

LESSON NO. 14

IV.

The captain was a duck,
With a packet on his back;
And when the ship began to move,
The captain said: Quack, quack.

THEME

And the captain, who was he? A duck, with a packet on his back. What was inside it? Greedy boy, this time there were sugar almonds.—Everyone obeyed him, and when he said: "Quack! Quack!" and nothing more, the ship began to move. Do you see it now, that beautiful ship?—Yes, Mother, in the land of fairy tales.

LESSON NO. 15

I.

There were three jovial Welshmen,
  As I have heard them say,
And they would go a-hunting
  Upon Saint David's day.

All the day they hunted,
  And nothing could they find,
But a ship a-sailing,
  A-sailing with the wind.

THEME

Do you see those three merry Welsh hunters with nothing better to do than celebrate Saint David's day by hunting? The saint didn't reward them, for I heard people say they hunted all day long without finding so much as a little bird; and from the seashore, all that they saw fleeing far ahead of them was the great wings of a ship sailing in the wind.

LESSON NO. 16

II.

One said it was a ship,
  The other he said, nay;
The third said it was a house,
  With the chimney blown away.

And all the night they hunted,
  And nothing could they find
But the moon a-gliding
  A-gliding with the wind.

Stéphane Mallarmé

THEME

Two of these hunters saw correctly that it was a ship, and said so immediately; but the third, who must have forgotten his glasses, insisted that it was a house, square like the sails, and without chimneys. So it was hardly surprising that a man with such poor eyesight could find nothing all night long, while the moon glided, glided in the wind.

LESSON NO. 17

III.

One said it was the moon,
The other (he) said, nay;
The third said it was a cheese
And half o't cut away.

And all the day they hunted,
And nothing could they find
But a hedgehog in a bramble bush,
And that they left behind.

THEME

—The one who mistook the moon for a cheese was a notorious glutton, accustomed to think of nothing except things concerning his meals. He thought he saw half of the cut cheese, and hoped no doubt to find it on his plate when he got home. For want of game, it would have at least been something to eat, for they could only find a poor hedgehog, behind a bush, and they left it behind.

LESSON NO. 18

IV.

The first said it was a hedgehog
The second (he) said, nay;
The third it was a pincushion,
And the pins stuck in a wrong way.

378

And all the night they hunted,
 And nothing could they find
But a hare in a turnip field,
 And that they left behind.

THEME

—What a strange idea the first one had, to say that the moon seemed to him to be a porcupine! for that animal resembles a pincushion with the needles stuck in backward, and the moon is perfectly round and distinct like a fresh white cheese. The second, the one who always says no, found something better in a turnip field—a real, live hare—but they chased it in vain all night long. The hare ran away and left them behind.

LESSON NO. 19

V.

The first said it was a hare,
 The second (he) said, nay;
The third said it was a calf,
 And the cow had run away.

And all the day they hunted,
 And nothing could they find
But an owl in a holly tree.
 And that they left behind.

One said it was an owl,
 The other he said, nay;
The third said it was an old man,
 And his beard growing gray.

THEME

—As they were running along like this, they continued to argue. The first, who, decidedly, saw things clearly, asserted that it was indeed a hare, but the second, obstinate and contradictory, merely said no. What did the third one say? You will laugh. The hare seemed so fine to him that he swore it was a calf, browsing on the turnips in the field—all alone, his mother the cow having fled at their approach. [Incomplete]

Stéphane Mallarmé

LESSON NO. 31

THE FOUR PRESENTS

I.

I had four brothers over the sea,
And they each sent a present to me.

The first sent a goose without a bone,
The second sent a cherry without a stone,
The third sent a blanket without a thread,
The fourth sent a book that no man could read.

THEME

Would you like to have four brothers living far away, beyond the seas, in beautiful lands from which they would send you presents?— I like getting gifts, but even more I like to live surrounded by my family: inasmuch as they don't have to be abroad to send you something . . . So my brothers, who live with me, gave me, at Christmas, the first . . . the second . . . the third . . . the fourth . . . (Take up in the lesson the nomenclature of the objects given)

LESSON NO. 32

II.

When the cherry is in the blossom, there is no stone,
When the goose is in the egg-shell, there is no bone,
When the wool's on the sheep's back, there is no thread,
When the book's in the press, no man can read it.[1]

THEME

—All this seems to me an enigma: for I don't know when one can say of a cherry that it has no stone inside; of a goose, no bone; that there is wool without a thread, or a book that no one of any language can read. I fear that your gifts are impossible, that they don't exist; and that you are simply saying that your four brothers gave you nothing.—Not at all. Think about it. I shall explain everything. The cherry was in bloom.—Hence, no stone.—The goose was in the egg.—No bone!—The wool was on the back of a pretty sheep. And so

---

[1]" . . . , no man it can read" (*Baby's Bouquet*)

no thread! The book I was promised is still in the press.—Thus, no one could read it.

LESSON NO. 99

Girls and boys come out to play,
The moon it shines, as bright as day;
Leave your supper, and leave your sleep,
And come to your playmates in the street;

Theme

In the evening, in the grand days of summer, when night doesn't come, the little boys and little girls go home for supper, not to sleep right away; and they dream only of going out again. The moon shines as bright as day and invites them out. No sooner has one of them returned to the street again to play and shout, than the whole joyous band of his comrades follows him, for another hour or two.

LESSON NO. 100

II.

Come with a whoop, come with a call,
Come with a good will, or come not at all;
Up the ladder and down the wall,
A halfpenny loaf will serve us all.

[copied but left untranslated by Mallarmé]

LESSON NO. 101

One foot up, the other foot down,
That is the way to London town.

Theme

When I go from my village to London, I see people traveling there in carriages, on horses, even on donkeys. The more modest ones content themselves with going on foot, with a stick that serves them for company and for support. As for me, I don't so much as pick a stem of grass at the edge of my road; my head high, gazing into the distance where the city should be, I raise one foot and lower the other, and that for twelve hours.

Caves

Robert Creeley

So much of my childhood seems
to have been spent in rooms—
at least in memory, the shades

pulled down to make it darker, the
shaft of sunlight at the window's edge.
I could hear the bees then gathering

outside in the lilacs, the birds chirping
as the sun, still high, began to drop.
It was summer, in heaven of small town,

hayfields adjacent, creak and croak
of timbers, of house, of trees, dogs,
elders talking, the lone car turning some

distant corner on Elm Street
way off across the broad lawn.
We dug caves or else found them,

down the field in the woods. We had
shacks we built after battering
at trees, to get branches, made tepee-

like enclosures, leafy, dense, and in-
substantial. Memory is the cave
one finally lives in, crawls on

hands and knees to get into.
If Mother says, don't draw
on the book pages, don't color

that small person in the picture, then
you don't unless compulsion, distraction
dictate and you're floating off

on wings of fancy, of persistent seeing
of what's been seen here too, right here,
on this abstracting page. Can I use the green,

when you're done? What's that supposed to be,
says someone. All the kids crowd closer
in what had been an empty room

where one was trying at least
to take a nap, stay quiet, to think
of nothing but oneself.

*

Back into the cave, folks,
and this time we'll get it right!

Or, uncollectively perhaps, it was
a dark and stormy night he

slipped away from the group, got
his mojo working and before

you know it had that there
bison fast on the wall of the outcrop.

I like to think they thought,
though they seemingly didn't, at least

of something, like, where did X put the bones,
what's going to happen next, did she, he, or it

really love me? Maybe that's what dogs are for,
but there's no material surviving

Robert Creeley

pointing to dogs as anyone's best friend, alas.
Still here we are no matter, still hacking away,

slaughtering what we can find to, leaving
far bigger footprints than any old mastodon.

You think it's funny? To have prospect
of being last creature on earth or at best a

company of rats and cockroaches?
You must have a good sense of humor!

Anyhow, have you noticed how everything's
retro these days? Like, something's been here before—

or at least that's the story. *I* think one picture is worth
a thousand words and I *know* one cave fits all sizes.

*

Much like a fading off airplane's
motor or the sound of the freeway

at a distance, it was all here clearly enough
and no one goes lightly into a cave,

even to hide. But to make such things
on the wall, against such obvious

limits, to work in intermittent dark,
flickering light not even held steadily,

all those insistent difficulties.
They weren't paid to, not that we know of,

and no one seems to have forced them.
There's a company there, tracks

of all kinds of people, old folks
and kids included. Were they having

384

a picnic? But so far in it's hardly
a casual occasion, flat on back with

the tools of the trade necessarily
close at hand. Try lying in the dark

on the floor of your bedroom and roll
so as you go under the bed and

ask someone to turn off the light.
Then stay there, until someone else comes.

Or paint up under on the mattress the last
thing you remember, dog's snarling visage

as it almost got you, or just what you do
think of as the minutes pass.

*

Hauling oneself through invidious
strictures of passage, the height
of the entrance, the long twisting
cramped passage, mind flickers, a lamp
lit flickers, lets image project
what it can, what it will, see there
war as wanting, see life as a river,
see trees as forest, family as
others, see a moment's respite,
hear the hidden bird's song, goes
along, goes along constricted, self-
hating, imploded, drags forward
in imagination of more, has no
time, has hatred, terror, power.
No light at the end of the tunnel.

*

The guide speaks of music, the
stalactites, stalagmites making a
possible xylophone, and some
Saturday night–like hoedown
businesses, what, every three
to four thousand years? One
looks and looks and time
is the variable, the determined
as ever river, lost on the way,
drifted on, laps and continues.
The residuum is finally silence,
internal, one's own mind constricted
to focus like any old camera
fixed in its function.

Like all good questions,
this one seems without answer,
leaves the so-called human
behind. It makes its own way
and takes what it's found
as its own and moves on.

*

It's time to go to bed
again, shut the light off,
settle down, straighten
the pillow and try to sleep.
Tomorrow's another day
and that was all thousands
and thousands of years ago,
myriad generations, even
the stones must seem changed.

The gaps in time,
the times one can't account for,
the practice it all took
even to make such images,
the meanings still unclear
though one recognizes

the subject, something has
to be missed, overlooked.

No one simply turns on a light.
Oneself becomes image.
The echo's got in front,
begins again what's over
just at the moment it was done.
No one can catch up, find
some place he's never been to
with friends he never had.

This is where it connects,
not meaning anything one
can know. This is where
one goes in and that's what's to find
beyond any thought or habit,
an arched, dark space, the rock,
and what survives of what's left.

NOTES ON CONTRIBUTORS

JOHN ASHBERY has published more than twenty collections of poetry including, most recently, *Where Shall I Wander* (Ecco/HarperCollins, 2005). His *Selected Prose* was published in 2004 by Carcanet and the University of Michigan Press. Since 1990 he has been the Charles P. Stevenson, Jr. Professor of Languages and Literature at Bard College.

"The Distillery" is an excerpt from EMILY BARTON's novel *Brookland*, which will be published by Farrar, Straus & Giroux in March 2006. Her first novel, *The Testament of Yves Gundron* (Farrar, Straus & Giroux), won the Bard Fiction Prize in 2003.

CAN XUE lives in Beijing and has published numerous short stories and novels. Her three books that have been published in English translation are *Dialogues in Paradise, Old Floating Cloud* (both by Northwestern), and *The Embroidered Shoes* (Henry Holt). She has a volume of recent fiction forthcoming from New Directions.

MARY CAPONEGRO's most recent collection of fiction is *The Complexities of Intimacy* (Coffee House). "Girls in White Dresses" is excerpted from her novel in progress, *Chinese Chocolate*, the opening passage of which appeared in *Storie XI*, Nos. 52-53, in English and Italian.

DAVID MARSHALL CHAN's first book, *Goblin Fruit: Stories* (Content Books), was a finalist for the 2004 *Los Angeles Times* Book Prize. He lives in New York City and is completing his first novel, *Memoirs of a Boy Detective.*

CHEN ZEPING, professor of Chinese linguistics at Fujian Teachers' University, has published extensively in his field.

KIM CHINQUEE's work has appeared in *NOON, Denver Quarterly*, and *Mississippi Review*, among other journals.

ROBERT CLARK is the author of four novels: *In the Deep Midwinter, Mr. White's Confession, Love Among the Ruins*, and *Lives of the Artists* (all HarperCollins). He has also written three books of nonfiction: *The Solace of Food* (Steerforth), *River of the West*, and *My Grandfather's House* (both Picador).

LUCY CORIN's novel *Everyday Psychokillers: A History for Girls* was published last year by FC$_2$. She is working on a collection of stories. "Walking Hand in Hand with Dinah" is a collage text derived from Lewis Carroll's *Alice in Wonderland.*

ROBERT CREELEY (1926–2005) was one of the great poets of the twentieth century. "Caves" came out earlier this year from Paradigm Press in a limited edition. Next spring, the University of California Press will publish *Earth*, a collection of his last poems, as well as an essay, "Whitman in Age," that he wrote last year over Christmas. *Conjunctions* published memorial tributes to Robert Creeley by nearly one hundred fellow writers, available on *Web Conjunctions* (www.conjunctions.com).

HENRY DARGER (1892–1973) was a self-taught artist who created hundreds of paintings, mostly of young girls, that were made during the more than thirty years he lived in an apartment on Chicago's North Side. After his death, the typescript of his 15,000-page novel about a bloody war between soldiers and prepubescent girls was discovered. This is believed to be the longest novel ever to have been written.

RIKKI DUCORNET is the author of seven novels, including *The Fan Maker's Inquisition* (Henry Holt)—a *Los Angeles Times* Book of the Year—and *The Jade Cabinet* (Dalkey Archive), finalist for the National Book Critics' Circle Award. She received the Lannan Literary Award for Fiction in 2004.

JULIA ELLIOTT's fiction has appeared in *Puerto Del Sol, Mississippi Review, 3rd Bed, Black Warrior Review*, and other journals. She lives in Columbia, South Carolina.

ELAINE EQUI has written many books including *The Cloud of Knowable Things* (Coffee House). *Ripple Effect: New & Selected Poems* is forthcoming in 2007. She teaches in the graduate program at The New School and City College of New York.

BRIAN EVENSON is the author of a half dozen books of fiction, most recently *The Wavering Knife* (FC₂). He is the director of the Program in Literary Arts at Brown University.

JOSHUA FURST's story collection, *Short People*, was published by Knopf. He is currently at work on his second book, a novel entitled *The Sabotage Café*.

ARIE A. GALLES was born in Tashkent, Uzbekistan. Director of the Creative Arts Program at Soka University of America, his paintings have been exhibited nationally and he has worked collaboratively with Jerome Rothenberg.

SCOTT GEIGER's fiction has appeared in *Lady Churchill's Rosebud Wristlet*. The two stories in this issue are part of *The Rise of the Addison Balloon*, a collection in progress.

KAREN GERNANT and Chen Zeping's translations have appeared in earlier issues of *Conjunctions*, as well as in *Manoa, Black Warrior Review*, and *turnrow*.

PETER GIZZI's books include *Some Values of Landscape and Weather* (Wesleyan), *Artificial Heart* (Burning Deck), and *Periplum and Other Poems, 1987–1992* (Salt).

FANNY HOWE has written many books of fiction and poetry including, most recently, *Economics* (Flood Editions), *On the Ground* (Graywolf), *Selected Poems*, and *Gone* (both University of California). She lives in New England.

SHELLEY JACKSON is the author of *The Melancholy of Anatomy* (Anchor), *Patchwork Girl* (Eastgate), and many multimedia works. She has written and illustrated several children's books and is currently publishing a story in tattoos, one word at a time, on the skin of volunteers. Her novel *Half Life* will be published by HarperCollins in 2006.

ILONA KARMEL (1925–2000) published two novels during her lifetime: *Stephania* and *An Estate of Memory* (both Houghton Mifflin), now literary classics.

PAUL LA FARGE is the author of *The Artist of the Missing* and *Haussmann, or the Distinction* (both Farrar, Straus & Giroux), as well as the translator of a work by Paul Poissel, *The Facts of Winter* (McSweeney's). "Adventure" is an excerpt from his novel in progress, *Luminous Airplanes*. He won the 2005 Bard Fiction Prize.

BEN LERNER's first book is *The Lichtenberg Figures*, published by Copper Canyon, which will also publish his second book, *Angle of Yaw*, in 2007. He co-edits *No: A Journal of the Arts*.

STÉPHANE MALLARMÉ (1842–1898) is perhaps the most extreme example of the nineteenth-century French poets whose work anticipated modernism. Influenced initially by the Parnassian poets (in his *Herodiade*), then by symbolism (*L'Après-midi d'un faune*), he is perhaps best known for his last long poem, *Un Coup de des jamais n'abolira le hazard.*

MALINDA MARKHAM's first book of poetry, *Ninety-five Nights of Listening*, won a Bakeless Award and was published by Houghton Mifflin. Her translations of Japanese poetry have recently appeared in *Factional, How(2)*, and the *Denver Quarterly*. She works as a financial translator in Tokyo.

S. G. MILLER's work has appeared in *Massachusetts Review, Alaska Quarterly*, and *Prairie Schooner*. She has recently completed her first novel.

MICAELA MORRISSETTE lives in Brooklyn. This is her first appearance in print.

HOWARD NORMAN's books include *The Bird Artist, The Haunting of L.*, and *The Museum Guard* (all Farrar, Straus & Giroux). His most recent book is the memoir *In Fond Remembrance of Me* (North Point Press).

DANIELLE PAFUNDA's first book is *Pretty Young Thing* (Soft Skull Press). Her manuscript *My Zorba* was a recent finalist for the Juniper Prize for Poetry. Her work has been published in *Best American Poetry 2004, American Letters & Commentary, Chicago Review*, and *LIT.* She is co-editor of the online journal *La Petite Zine.*

MARK POIRIER is the author of two collections of short fiction, *Naked Pueblo* and *Unsung Heroes of American Industry*, and two novels, *Goats* and *Modern Ranch Living* (all Miramax). He lives in New York City.

MELISSA PRITCHARD has published six books of fiction, most recently *Disappearing Ingenue* and *Late Bloomer* (both Doubleday/Anchor). Her work has appeared in *The Paris Review, Pushcart Prize Stories,* and *The O. Henry Awards,* among other publications. She teaches creative writing at Arizona State University.

DONALD REVELL's most recent collection is *Pennyweight Windows: New & Selected Poems* (Alice James). His selected prose, *Invisible Green,* has been recently published by Omnidawn.

ELIZABETH ROBINSON's two new collections—*Apostrophe* (Apogee Press) and *Under the Silky Roof* (Burning Deck)—are forthcoming. She is also co-editor of *26 Magazine,* Ether Dome Chapbook series, and Instance Press.

KAREN RUSSELL's first book, a collection of short stories, is forthcoming from Knopf.

DAVID SHIELDS is the author of eight books of fiction and nonfiction, including *Remote* (originally published by Knopf, recently reissued in paperback by University of Wisconsin), winner of the PEN/Revson Award, and *Black Planet* (originally published by Crown, reissued in paperback by Three Rivers), a finalist for the National Book Critics Circle Award. He is currently a Guggenheim Fellow.

GILBERT SORRENTINO's latest book is *Lunar Follies* (Coffee House).

DIANE WILLIAMS's most recent collection of short fiction is *Romancer Erector* (Dalkey Archive). She is the founding editor of *NOON.*

GAHAN WILSON's cartoons appear regularly in *Playboy* and *The New Yorker,* among other periodicals. His newest books are *The Best of Gahan Wilson* (Underwood Press), which features much of his color work, and *Gahan Wilson's Monster Collection,* from Barnes & Noble Books.

LOIS-ANN YAMANAKA is the author, most recently, of the novel *Father of the Four Passages* (Farrar, Straus & Giroux) as well as a children's novel, *The Heart's Language* (Hyperion Books for Children). Her work has been adapted in two short prize-winning films, *Silent Years* and *Fishbowl.* Her fifth novel, *Behold the Many,* will be published in February 2006. "The Big Betty Stories" is from the forthcoming *Dead Dogs R.I.P.*

YAN LIANKE grew up in the remote town of Tianhu, Henan province, China. While in the army, he graduated from Henan University and the Arts Academy of the People's Liberation Army. Author of eight novels, more than forty novellas, and more than sixty short stories, Yan has received numerous literary awards.

Black Clock

blackclock.org

Published by CalArts in association with the MFA Writing Program

photo © Augusta Wood, 2005, *untitled (underwater #24)*, detail

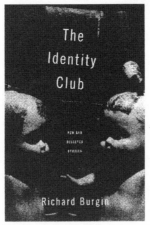

You, Me, and the Insects by Barbara Henning
ISBN 0-9720662-6-8 $14.95

This is not a pretentious New Age memoir but an ageless picaresque and imaginative voyage. A major accomplishment for this extremely salient, charged writer.
—Anne Waldman

spuytenduyvil

SPUYTENDUYVIL.NET
AND BOOKSENSE.COM

Gowanus Canal, Hans Knudsen by Tod Thilleman
ISBN 1-933132-00-0 $14.00

Tod Thilleman has written not so much a novel as an investigation, a *bildungsroman* whose hero has no magic mountain to ascend or descend, but who yet desires that the intellectual and spiritual contexts for a life might still exist. —Martin Nakell

Mobility Lounge by David Lincoln
ISBN 0-9720662-5-X $13.00

Mobility Lounge is at heart a global love story, a virtual tale of intersecting strangers who tumble into connection despite themselves.
—Catherine Bush

NOON

NOON

A LITERARY ANNUAL

1369 MADISON AVENUE   PMB 298
NEW YORK   NEW YORK   10128-0711

EDITION PRICE $9 DOMESTIC $14 FOREIGN

Kate Wilhelm's Storyteller

is an affectionate history of the Clarion Workshop (an intensive 6-week program for novice writers—known as "boot camp for writers"). Wilhelm explains why participants feared red pencils*; what she learned; and how she and Damon Knight passed a love of writing onto generations of writers.

Storyteller includes a section of writing exercises and advice.

(*See page 121 for the origins of "The Red Line of Death.")

Writing Lessons & More from 27 Years of the Clarion Writers' Workshop

TPO · $16
1-931520-16-X

Award-winning author **Maureen F. McHugh** wryly and delicately examines the impacts of social and technological shifts on all of us in her luminous and long-awaited debut collection, **Mothers & Other Monsters.**
"Enchanting, funny and fierce by turns—a wonderful collection!"
—Mary Doria Russell, *A Thread of Grace*

A Book Sense Notable Book

$24
1-931520-13-5

Kelly Link's second collection, **Magic for Beginners**, is filled with engaging and funny riffs on rabbits, haunted convenience stores, husbands & wives, zombies, apocalyptic poker parties, witches, superheroes, and cannons. Includes three new stories, as well as stories from *Conjunctions, The Dark,* and *The Faery Reel.* "Stone Animals" was selected for inclusion in *The Best American Short Stories 2005.*

Illustrated by Shelley Jackson

$24
1-931520-15-1

Naomi Mitchison's **Travel Light** is a wonderful story that will transport you into Halla's world where a basilisk might be met in the desert, heroes are taken to Valhalla by Valkyries, and a fortune might be made with a word to the right horse. This short, fabulous book transports the reader from a cave in the forest to a dragon's lair to the wonders of early Constantinople. It's dense and light, joyful and sad: amazing.

Peapod Classics No.2

TPB · $12
1-931520-14-3

DELILLO FIEDLER GASS PYNCHON
University of Delaware Press
Collections on Contemporary Masters

UNDERWORDS
Perspectives on Don DeLillo's *Underworld*

Edited by Joseph Dewey, Steven G. Kellman, and Irving Malin

Essays by Jackson R. Bryer, David Cowart, Kathleen Fitzpatrick, Joanne Gass, Paul Gleason, Donald J. Greiner, Robert McMinn, Thomas Myers, Ira Nadel, Carl Ostrowski, Timothy L. Parrish, Marc Singer, and David Yetter

$39.50

INTO *THE TUNNEL*
Readings of Gass's Novel

Edited by Steven G. Kellman and Irving Malin

Essays by Rebecca Goldstein, Donald J. Greiner, Brooke Horvath, Marcus Klein, Jerome Klinkowitz, Paul Maliszewski, James McCourt, Arthur Saltzman, Susan Stewart, and Heide Ziegler

$35.00

LESLIE FIEDLER AND AMERICAN CULTURE

Edited by Steven G. Kellman and Irving Malin

Essays by John Barth, Robert Boyers, James M. Cox, Joseph Dewey, R.H.W. Dillard, Geoffrey Green, Irving Feldman, Leslie Fiedler, Susan Gubar, Jay L. Halio, Brooke Horvath, David Ketterer, R.W.B. Lewis, Sanford Pinsker, Harold Schechter, Daniel Schwarz, David R. Slavitt, Daniel Walden, and Mark Royden Winchell

$36.50

PYNCHON AND *MASON & DIXON*

Edited by Brooke Horvath and Irving Malin

Essays by Jeff Baker, Joseph Dewey, Bernard Duyfhuizen, David Foreman, Donald J. Greiner, Brian McHale, Clifford S. Mead, Arthur Saltzman, Thomas H. Schaub, David Seed, and Victor Strandberg

$39.50

ORDER FROM ASSOCIATED UNIVERSITY PRESSES
2010 Eastpark Blvd., Cranbury, New Jersey 08512
PH 609-655-4770   FAX 609-655-8366   E-mail AUP440@ aol.com

Fiction Collective Two   Publishers of Experimental Fiction

What Begins with Bird
by Noy Holland

This book is both an investigation of
family relationships and a sophisticated
study of language and rhythm. Holland
creates an exhilarating tension between
the satisfactions of meaning and the
attenuated beauty of lyric, making her
fiction felt as deeply as it is understood.

What Begins with Bird
Noy Holland
1-57366-125-2
$15.95

"Holland's scrupulousness and respect
for the language keep this text alive and kicking.
What Begins with Bird is a book to be read slowly
and thoughtfully, shared, passed along."
— John Edgar Wideman

"*What Begins with Bird*
is a remarkable achievement."
— William Gass

www.fc2.org

NEW DIRECTIONS

Fall 2005 • Winter 2006

ELIAS CANETTI
PARTY IN THE BLITZ. The English Years. Tr. Hofmann. Afterword, J. Adler. A new volume of the Nobel Laureate's autobiography. $22.95 cloth

MIRCEA CĂRTĂRESCU
NOSTALGIA. Tr. w/afterword, Semilian. Intro. Andrei Codrescu. English debut novel of one of Romania's foremost writers. $19.95 pbk. orig.

JENNY ERPENBECK
THE OLD CHILD & OTHER STORIES. Tr. Bernofsky. Work by Germany's most original young writer. *PEN Trans. Fund Award* $14.95 pbk. orig.

LAWRENCE FERLINGHETTI
AMERICUS, Book I. Ferlinghetti's born-in-the-U.S.A. epic. "From the heartland of true heart comes this eloquent poem" —Creeley. $14.95 pbk.

FORREST GANDER
EYE AGAINST EYE. New powerful poems about the ways we see each other and the world, with ten photos by Sally Mann. $14.95 pbk. orig.

JOHN GARDNER
OCTOBER LIGHT. Intro. Tom Bissell. Reissue of Gardner's masterful novel of complex sibling rivalry. *Winner of the NBCC Award.* $14.95 pbk.

JOHN HAWKES
SECOND SKIN. *New* Preface Jeffrey Eugenides. Novel about Skipper, an an ex-navy officer. "An extraordinary writer" —Saul Bellow. $14.95 pbk.

GUSTAW HERLING
THE NOONDAY CEMETERY AND OTHER STORIES. Tr. Johnston. **One of the Ten Best Fiction Books of '03** —*LA Times Bk. Rev.* $14.95 pbk. Feb.

DENISE LEVERTOV
MAKING PEACE. Intro. Rosenthal. Anti-war poems by "a poet of fervid political conviction" (Mel Gussow, *NYT*). *An ND Bibelot.* $9.00 pbk. Feb.

JAVIER MARÍAS
WRITTEN LIVES. Tr. Jull Costa. A gallery of 20 great world authors including Nabokov, Arthur Conan Doyle, and Brontë. $22.95 cl. Feb.

TERU MIYAMOTO
KINSHU: Autumn Brocade. Tr. Thomas. Japanese epistolary novel about a couple ten years after their divorce. Simple and beautiful. $22.95 cloth

PABLO NERUDA
SPAIN IN OUR HEARTS: *España en el corazón.* Tr. Walsh. Epic Spanish Civil War hymn against fascism. *An ND Bibelot. Bilingual.* $8.00 pbk

RENÉ PHILOCTÈTE
MASSACRE RIVER. Tr. Coverdale. Preface, Danticat & Trouillot. Surreal novel about the actual 1937 slaughter of Haitians. $22.95 cloth

FREDERIC TUTEN
THE ADVENTURES OF MAO ON THE LONG MARCH. Preface, John Updike. The revolutionary 1971 comic novel. *An ND Classic.* $11.95 pbk

ELIOT WEINBERGER
WHAT HAPPENED HERE: Bush Chronicles. Essays. "Immensely satisfying and intensely enraging" —*Times* (London). $13.95 pbk. orig.

 Please send for free complete catalog.
NEW DIRECTIONS, 80 8th Avenue, NYC 10011
www.ndpublishing.com

Master of Fine Arts

Summer 2006 June 5 – July 28

Current Faculty include: Peggy Ahwesh, Maryanne Amacher, Polly Apfelbaum, David Behrman, Caroline Bergvall, Anselm Berrigan, Bob Bielecki, Alexander Birchler, Nayland Blake, Roddy Bogawa, Nancy Bowen, Michael Brenson, Marco Breuer, Sammy Cucher, Nancy Davenport, Taylor Davis, Margaret De Wys, Linh Dinh, Cecilia Dougherty, Mark Durant, Barbara Ess, Rochelle Feinstein, Kenji Fujita, Leah Gilliam, Chuck Hagen, Rachel Harrison, Teresa Hubbard, Brenda Hutchinson, Arthur Jafa, Suzanne Joelson, Michael Joo, Jutta Koether, Paul LaFarge, Ann Lauterbach, Les LeVeque, George Lewis, Jeanne Liotta, Ken Lum, Miya Masaoka, Rodney McMillian, Eileen Myles, Hal Niedzviecki, Pauline Oliveros, Karyn Olivier, Larry Polansky, Seth Price, Yvonne Rainer, Christian Rattemeyer, Blake Rayne, Dario Robleto, Marina Rosenfeld, James Rouvelle, Keith Sanborn, Joe Santarromana, Leslie Scalapino, Nancy Shaver, Amy Sillman, Laetitia Sonami, David Levi Strauss, Erika Suderburg, Richard Teitelbaum, Cheyney Thompson, Edwin Torres, Penelope Umbrico, Oliver Wasow, Stephen Westfall, Arthur Gibbons, director.

Our unusual approach has changed the nature of fine arts graduate education:

- One-on-one student/faculty conferences are the primary means of instruction.

- Students meet with faculty from all disciplines.

- Three years of eight-week summer sessions and independent winter work fulfill the requirements for the MFA degree.

Film/Video

Music/Sound

Painting

Photography

Sculpture

Writing

Milton Avery Graduate School of the Arts
Bard College
Annandale-on-Hudson, New York 12504

Bard College

845-758-7481 ● email: mfa@bard.edu ● web: www.bard.edu/mfa

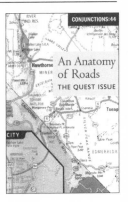